DK MARIE

Author Note

This story is a contemporary romance where love and hope prevails, but some topics might be troubling to some readers, such as emotional manipulation and coercion, family betrayal and infidelity, and financial extortion. Also on the page are power imbalances in relationships. Readers who may be sensitive to these topics, please take note.

To my fellow romantics who live for the swoon, breathe stories like air, and understand that books help us discover not just what love is—but the kind we want and deserve.

Contents

ChapterOne

Rosalia

I run my hand along the spine of the limited-edition romance novel. Tonight's book club is going to be so excited to see these. Setting it atop the others at my checkout counter, I accidentally bump a stack of monthly statements tucked beneath a framed photo. Both clatter to the floor. From the glass frame now resting at my feet, Dad and I smile up at me from the opening day of my bookstore. His proud grin beneath the "Novel Idea" sign he'd carved himself is as wide as mine.

The old brass bell we'd hung over the door to my store clangs. I set the dropped items on a shelf behind the counter and look toward the entrance. The world goes quiet like I've just opened a new book, and my pulse races like it wants to get to the good parts. This always happens when I see Sebastian Blackstone.

"Are you here for book club?" I joke, tapping the illustrated cover of a couple embracing.

His sporadic visits began days after my grand opening almost a year ago, and are always a treat. And not only because his looks rival my book-boyfriends, but because he's interesting. Each time, he leaves with something unexpected I've recommended. Last month's selection is tonight's romance book club pick.

I stifle a laugh at the image of him in his custom three-piece suit and shiny Oxfords sitting in a folding plastic chair, sipping coffee from one of my chipped mugs. The man runs the largest bourbon distillery in Kentucky, and his family owns most of the state, including the building I'm leasing. Men like him frequent exclusive clubs for the privileged few, not indie book clubs.

"I did enjoy the small-town romance you suggested," he says, his full lips pulling into a smile, revealing a dangerous dimple. "But I haven't read much fiction lately."

No way! He actually *read* the romance novel I recommended. I thought he was being polite buying it. Heat rushes to my cheeks. I'm way too pleased. But who can blame me? He's Kentucky royalty and movie star handsome, and took the time to read one of my book suggestions. And a romance novel.

"I—" My hand collides with a small stack of books on the counter, toppling them. Kneeling, I gather the scattered novels.

We reach for the same book, and our fingers touch. A current races up my arm. I glance up and catch him staring. Those eyes, the color of expensive bourbon, hold mine with an intensity that makes me forget how to breathe.

"Ms. Rosalia!" shouts a child, startling me. I nearly fall on my butt. Sebastian hands me the book with a smile before turning to the young boy.

Jake, one of the kids I tutor, barrels into me and wraps his arms around me. "I just finished that shark book. Do you have more? Do you like sharks, mister?" he asks Sebastian.

"This is Mr. Blackstone—"

"Are we back to that, Ms. Manchester?" asks Sebastian, his right brow quirks. Why is it so sexy?

"Sebastian," I correct, then ruffle Jake's hair. "This little guy is an amazing reader who loves adventure stories."

The seven-year-old steps forward, holding out a hand. I look at his mom and see her proud smile. "I'm Jake. I love to read because of Ms. Rosalia. She makes it fun."

A flush of warmth fills me at the little guy's praise. They remind me of why I pour so much of myself into my fledgling bookstore and its community outreach, even in months when the budget is tight. "He's in my reading program," I explain.

Sebastian nods, then crouches slightly and shakes the small boy's hand. The movement highlights his jawline, defined and sharp in profile. "What kind of adventures do you like to read about?" he asks.

"Sharks and dinosaurs and space!" Jake beams.

"A man of excellent taste," Sebastian says with a nod that makes the little guy stand taller.

"Those are good subjects. Let's see if I have some." I lead them to the special shelf of donated books I reserve for my reading program students. As he carefully browses the titles, I glance at Sebastian, who's hunched down, talking about books with Jake. And his mom is watching Sebastian with open appreciation. I can't blame her.

I also can't help cataloging the scene. The way Jake lights up when an adult takes his interests seriously, and how his mom relaxes seeing her son so engaged. It's the kind of genuine connection I love reading about, where people surprise each other by caring about the small things. These are the moments that make the best stories, the ones where everyone discovers something unexpected about themselves.

A few minutes later, their arms are laden with books from the donation section, and Jake and his mother say their goodbyes. After they leave, I turn to Sebastian. "Sorry about that. Where were we?"

His eyes meet mine, and I swear there's a flicker of something deeper than mere politeness, maybe a hint of admiration, perhaps even attraction, shines in them. The man is unfairly gorgeous, with a presence that fills the entire bookstore. And yet, there's a gentleness I don't expect from someone so powerful.

"I believe you were about to recommend some books to me," he says.

Book recommendations are my jam, and I rub my hands together, turning and walking backward toward the fiction section. Keeping my gaze on Sebastian, I say, "Are you in the mood for horror? There's an amazing one I just read from a local author. There's a haunted house, which I know is overdone, but not that way she does it," I gush, then close my mouth.

I'm about to start babbling. He always makes me nervous and excited, turning me into someone who knocks things over and can't stop talking

"It still surprises me—your love for romance and horror," he says, amusement dancing across his features.

Picking up the haunted house book from the nearby shelf, I hand it to him. "I've read somewhere that there's a thin line between love and hate. Pain and pleasure."

As soon as the words leave my mouth, a wave of heat washes over me, turning into a full-body blush. I sound like a flirt. Or a weirdo.

I need to shut up around this too-handsome and intriguing man.

He chuckles. "That's true. But today, I'm looking for a travel book for Thailand. Oh, and a fun beach read."

A gentle flutter stirs in my chest, awakening a dormant wanderlust. One day I'm going to travel, and more than just inside an amazing story.

"Sounds like you have an adventure in your future," I say, walking us to the travel shelf. One day, when the store is more established and the business loan isn't eating so much of my income, I'll travel too.

"I wish. I'm getting them for my nomad sister, Lillianna. She's currently in Australia for another few weeks. After that, she's heading to Thailand. She's not big on touristy 'hot spots,' but if you have a book about unique travel, she'll love it."

Bending to the bottom shelf, I grab a travel guide that comes highly recommended by a sweet retired couple who frequent my bookstore and adore the author's worldly perspectives. I hand him the book. "Having siblings must be wonderful. I've always wanted them," I sigh. Some people are so lucky.

"It depends on the sibling." He laughs, but it holds a slight edge.

I get the sense there's tension, but family businesses are complicated. And since I hate when people nose in my business, I don't ask him to elaborate. Instead, I study his profile while he's busy reading the back of the book. His thick, slightly wavy black hair is styled to perfection, and my fingers itch to mess it up, to see what it would look like rumpled from sleep—or something more interesting.

Settle down, woman. I need to stop lusting after the poor man who just wants to get a few books for his sister. Putting on my professional hat, I ask, "Are there any books you'll be getting for yourself today?"

His face relaxes, and his other dimple makes an appearance. Double whoa. "Don't think poorly of me," he says. "With the Derby only a little over seven weeks away, there's no time for fun fiction."

"How could I think less of you? Even super busy, you came here to get books for your sister. You're a good brother," I tell him as we leave behind the shelves for the checkout counter.

"Or maybe I'm using it as an excuse to see you." He gives me another heart-stopping grin.

A tingle of excitement dances along my skin. "A-are you?"

"Possibly."

His unexpected flirting makes me daring. "Then even better. For me," I reply. Heat rushes to my cheeks, but I hold his gaze, secretly thrilled by my audacity. I've never been this forward with anyone, let alone someone who looks like him.

And Sebastian Blackstone is definitely something to look at. His eyes seem to darken, and he leans slightly closer. "You know, I've been thinking. Instead of my monthly drop-ins, maybe we could actually sit down and talk books properly sometime. There's a new coffee place on Main that I've been meaning to try. I'll be back in the city on Monday and Tuesday. Are you free on either of those days?"

My heart cartwheels in my chest. Is Sebastian Blackstone really asking me on a date? Monday is usually perfect since the store is closed, but I promised Grandma Rose I'd help with her garden project. Not that I'll be telling my gossip-loving grandma about this. She'd have it plastered all over social media.

"Yes," I blurt before I can overthink it. "I'm free on Tuesday after six when my store closes." I'm writing myself into a plot I can't control.

His smile widens. "Great. I'll swing by around six?"

"Maybe...I close at five," I manage, my voice surprisingly steady despite the butterflies in my stomach.

"Perfect, looking forward to it," he says, and there's something in his tone that makes me believe he means it.

I press my palm against my racing heart. Sebastian Blackstone asked me out. Me, the bookworm drowning in business loans while he commands an empire.

The monthly statements peek out from under the counter, the morning accounting I've been avoiding. Dad always said dreams were worth chasing, but he never mentioned how terrifying it would be when they start chasing you back.

Sebastian pauses at the counter, his fingers drumming lightly against the wood as he glances around the store. "You know," he says, "I've always wondered, what made you choose this particular location? Whiskey Row isn't the most obvious spot for a bookstore, but it works so well."

I follow his gaze, seeing my little sanctuary through his eyes: the mismatched furniture I've collected and refinished, the hand-painted signs that took me three tries to get right, and the cozy reading nook I created in the corner with cushions I found at a thrift store and recovered myself. I'm proud of what I've built from nothing, even as my attention snags on every imperfection. From the slight wobble in the display table to the way the paint doesn't quite match on the trim I touched up last month. What if he sees all the places where I've cut corners, where my dreams are held together with determination and discount supplies?

"It chose me," I admit, self-conscious about how the modest space compares to what he must be used to. "When I came across the 'For Lease' sign online and then saw it in person, it felt right."

The way he's really listening shows he's genuinely curious about my little world. Nodding, he glances around the store again, making no move toward the door. He surprises me with how much he seems to actually care.

Spending my teenage years as the scholarship kid at the private school where my mom taught English and History, I've seen how the wealthy operate up close. The whispers, the exclusion, the constant reminder that I didn't belong in their world. Even knowing real-life romances between different worlds like ours rarely end with a happily ever after, I'm still willing to see where this story goes.

Chapter Two

Rosalia

The bell on Novel Idea's door rings out again, followed by a burst of cheerful chatter and laughter that shatters our crystal-delicate moment. I tear my gaze from his. Half of the Wednesday afternoon romance book club pours through the door. Any other time, I'd be delighted to see them. They're practically family, but right now, the timing is...inconvenient.

Anna, the group's unofficial leader, glances at Sebastian's retreating form, then back at me. She raises an eyebrow and the corner of her mouth quirks. I can practically hear her thoughts. Last time Sebastian visited at the same time as the book club, she shared her theory: "He's here for the bookstore owner, honey, not the books." I'd laughed it off, the idea too ridiculous to entertain.

Looks like I'm better reading books than people.

Anna sidles up to the counter immediately. "Was sexy Sebastian here to check out your...books?"

I fidget with the button of my worn, well-loved cardigan. "He's just a regular customer."

"Mmhmm," she hums. "A regular customer who looks at you like you're his favorite novel."

"Your table is ready in the back. I put on fresh pots of decaf and regular coffee." I say, hoping to change the subject.

Part of me wants to gush with excitement, but Sebastian probably isn't interested in me and only wants to talk with another book lover. I mean, seriously, we are from different worlds. I grew up around the super wealthy and know how most of them think. They talk about "pulling yourself up by your bootstraps" without realizing some of us couldn't afford boots to begin with.

"Did you get the muffins from Paige's Pastries?" someone calls out.

"Of course." The coffee and goodies are a nice bonus. My friend, Paige, makes the most delicious treats at her popular bakery a few doors down.

My cell chirps from a hidden pocket of my skirt. Blackstone Business flashes across the screen. I glance out the large window at the front of my store as if I'd see Sebastian, but only nameless tourists and locals stroll by.

"I have to get this," I tell Anna, swiping my thumb to answer.

"Good afternoon, Ms. Manchester," replies a man who is all business. "I'm Daniel Poncelet, an attorney representing Blackstone Bourbon Holdings. I'm calling about your current lease agreement with our client. Do you have a few moments to discuss this?"

"Okay..." The lease for the bookstore and my apartment doesn't renew until mid-May, and it's only the second week in March. Why would they be calling with almost two months remaining? My payments have always been on time.

"Blackstone Bourbon Holdings has decided not to renew your lease," the lawyer tells me in a business monotone.

The room tilts from the shock, and I nearly drop the phone. "I don't understand. Buying it is impossible. I was told I could rent indefinitely."

After a pause that lasts an eternity, he says, "I'm sorry, but things change. The termination papers will be sent to you via email by the end of the day."

"When signing the lease I was told I could rent indefinitely." I know I'm repeating myself, but I don't care. Novel Idea is supposed to celebrate its second anniversary in May. And if I lose this place, it won't only crush all my plans and dreams. Dad's face flashes in my thoughts, the way he'd smiled when signing as guarantor for my loan, putting his house on the line so I could chase my dream. My stomach twists with guilt.

"Like I said, things change," drones the lawyer.

"Tell that to the kids in my programs," I snap. Jamal, the shy boy who'd blossomed into a confident reader thanks to the after-school tutoring sessions, waves from my mind's eye. He's replaced by Molly, the teenage girl who'd found solace in poetry during her mother's illness.

"Ms. Manchester," the lawyer says, his voice softening almost imperceptibly. "I understand your frustration, but my clients are well within their legal rights. There's nothing in your lease contract saying you can rent indefinitely."

No, I'd trusted the Blackstones to keep their word. That had been my first mistake—trusting the wealthy. They didn't care whose dreams they destroyed in their pursuit of buying another yacht, private jet, or whatever the heck rich people bought.

"If you have any questions about Blackstone Bourbon Holdings' position on this matter, you can reach me at the number on my email signature. Good day, Ms. Manchester."

The call ends with a click that echoes through me. I'm frozen behind the counter, the cheerful chatter of the book club becomes distant and muffled, as if I'm underwater.

Blackstone Bourbon Holdings.

Sebastian Blackstone. He'd been here not thirty minutes ago, full of smiles and coffee date invitations. Now he's somewhere across town, probably signing my eviction papers. My cheeks burn with embarrassment and anger.

"Rosalia? Are you okay, honey?" Anna rests a hand on my shoulder, jerking me from my daze.

I plaster on a smile that feels brittle enough to crack my face. "A business call. Everything's fine."

But nothing is fine. My dream, everything I've worked so hard for, is slipping through my fingers with a simple phone call.

Sebastian's words from a few months ago echo in my head. I'd confessed my fears to him about running an independent bookstore in the age of e-books and online giants. He'd reassured me. "You've created more than just a place to shop and get books; you've built a community," he'd said, his expression earnest. "That's not something that can be easily replicated or replaced."

And like a fool, I'd swooned over the sexy, kind billionaire, believing he understood me. That he might actually see me as more than just his tenant, but reality comes crashing down. To him, I'm a line item on a spreadsheet. Sebastian's never had to choose between paying rent or owning a car.

The coffee date invitation takes on a new, sinister meaning. Was he planning to soften me up? Make the blow of losing my store easier to take?

I move through the rest of the afternoon on autopilot, somehow managing to host the book club while my mind churns with possibilities, none of them good. The women and men notice my distraction but attribute it to Sebastian's visit, teasing me good-naturedly about my crush.

If only they knew my crush was crushing my soul.

After they leave, I flip the gorgeous hand-carved sign my dad made from OPEN to CLOSED, resting my forehead against the cool glass and letting a few tears fall. Dad had remortgaged his home to help me get a loan I needed for the upfront costs of turning this former tasting room into a bookstore. How in the hell will I be able to keep paying on my current one *and* get another for a new location?

Dragging my tired feet to the checkout counter, I pull out my laptop and type "tenant rights Kentucky small business" into the search bar. Maybe there's something, anything, that could help me. But as I scroll through legal jargon and complicated statutes, my stomach sinks further. Without money for a lawyer to interpret all this, I'm at a serious disadvantage.

I sigh, looking out onto Whiskey Row. The historic buildings that once housed bourbon empires mock me. All the trendy bars and restaurants are packed with people spending money without a second thought.

The Blackstone name is everywhere. A distillery tour bus with their logo passes by. The sleek office building at the end of the street is theirs. A few blocks away, the historic courthouse bore a plaque thanking the Blackstone family for funding its restoration.

I should have gotten Sebastian's number when he'd asked me out. I'd call him and…and, what? What would I say if he were standing in front of me right now? What good would confronting him do? In his world, business is just business. Nothing personal.

Except it is personal to me. This store isn't just my livelihood, it's my dream. The apartment above isn't just a place to sleep. After living under Mom's roof for years and then my ex's, where I couldn't even hang a picture without his permission, having my own sanctuary means everything.

And now the Blackstones are about to rip it all away from me.

Novel Idea isn't just a bookstore. It's where kids like Jake discover the magic of reading, where the lonely can find community, and where stories bring people together. It's that and so much more.

But I can't afford to pay off the current loan for this building and get another for a new space. The romance novels I'd so carefully arranged earlier catch my eye; their illustrated covers promise happy endings and fairy tale romances. I almost laugh at the bitter irony. Here I was, buying into the fantasy that someone like Sebastian Blackstone could be interested in someone like me.

Reality check: I'm not the heroine of a romantic novel. I'm another small business owner about to be crushed under the wheel of progress and profit margins.

My computer buzzes with a notification, and I turn from the window to the screen. Instagram. A post from a Kentucky social account I follow. Sebastian and his brother stare back at me from a photo taken at a charity gala. They're both in tuxedos with champagne flutes in hand and perfect smiles for the camera. The caption reads:

> "Are the Blackstone brothers mending their rift to support the Children's Hospital Foundation?" #GivingBack #BlackstoneFamily

The differences between them are striking. Thorne stands with the confident swagger of old money, his smile practiced and sharp, like a man accustomed to getting exactly what he wants. I'd heard the rumors about the elder Blackstone. The reckless deals, the high-stakes gambles that somehow always paid off. The tabloids called him "The Bourbon Gambler" for a reason. Unlike his more measured brother, Thorne seemed to thrive on risk, making him both feared and respected in Kentucky business circles.

And then there's Sebastian, whose eyes still manage to look kind even in this posed shot. Where Thorne dominates space, Sebastian inhabits it with quiet authority. The articles I'd read describe him as the steady hand of Blackstone Bourbon, the master distiller whose innovations had breathed new life into the family brand while respecting its heritage. The bourbon world revered him for his palate and vision; the business world, for his integrity.

On my screen, they raise glasses worth more than my daily sales, "giving back" through charity. Meanwhile, I'm about to lose everything, including the free literacy program I run that actually changes lives. The cruel irony would be almost laughable if it weren't crushing me.

The coffee date looms in my mind. He'll walk through that door, all charm and dimples, expecting to take me for coffee while his company prepares to wipe everything I've worked for. A part of me wants to throw his hot drink in his perfect face. How pathetic am I: the bookstore owner attracted to the villain of her own story.

Come Tuesday, I'll have to decide whether this story ends with the heroine's fiery confrontation, her humiliating surrender, or her dignified silence. But tonight, I let myself mourn the ending I never saw coming.

ChapterThree

Sebastian

The early sun glints off the polished Bentley as we roll to a stop, the shadow stretching across the weathered cobblestone driveway of Blackstone Distillery. My driver, Tom, parks in front of the office. The elegant structure of dark red brick, black trim, and large, imposing windows is more of a home to me than any of my actual houses.

I end a call at the same time my car door opens. Tom stands beside it. He's a short white man, nearly as broad as he is tall, who looks more like a bouncer than a driver, but he moves quickly.

Grabbing my sister's book I bought yesterday from the seat, I step from the car and stretch my legs, stifling a yawn. "Today will be long. I'll call this afternoon with my end time," I tell him. Derby season's obligations always dominate my spring schedule, starting with sponsor meetings and culminating in the Blackstone Bourbon Classic party that is still two months away.

"Okay. Have a good one, Mr. Blackstone."

"You too," I reply.

My polished black Oxfords strike the weathered stones of the path with steady, unhurried steps. At the entrance of the main building, the metal door handle feels smooth against my palm, cool enough to briefly ground me. I love what I do. There's an almost meditative precision in detecting the subtle differences between barrels, selecting the ideal blend of vanilla and oak, caramel and spice, that will define our signature bourbons for generations. I don't even mind the meetings and power plays in the boardrooms. But with the rifts in our family and everyone watching, waiting for a Blackstone to break, work doesn't provide me the peace it once did.

So it's also another morning, another performance.

The muted clacking of computer keyboards and the low hum of conversation fill the air, underscored by the soft, distant ringing of phones. The head receptionist nods when I enter and rises from his seat behind a solid, wide desk. "Good morning, Mr. Blackstone."

"Morning, Sam," I reply. "Please call Hanna and have her pull the Tobar account. And make sure the Derby Festival sponsorship materials are ready for my review by this afternoon." The Kentucky Derby Festival's Thunder Over Louisville was coming up in five weeks, officially kicking off the two-week countdown to Derby Day. We must have everything in order.

"Right away, sir." Sam hands me a sheet of paper, the phone already at his ear.

I wave a thanks, heading to a meeting at the far end of the building. Entering the windowed hallway, my steps slow to a stop, as I squint at the bright sunlight. To the west, lush green lawns stretch into the distance, scattered with rickhouses. They sprawl across the lawn like sentinels—stark, unyielding.

My gaze fixes on one particular rickhouse, and memories leak through its wooden walls like aged spirits, sharp and burning. I'm pulled back to that summer when my father had all three of us Blackstone kids leading tours. It had been both terrible and marvelous. We'd had to deliver the same spiel four to five times a day for three months straight. That part was torture, but in between the tours, we were free to do as we pleased. And we made the most of it, flirting with visitors and employees, playing pranks on each other, and essentially raising hell.

I shake my head, recalling a specific time toward the end of that summer in that very rickhouse. All the tours had ended for the day and Lillianna, Thorne, and I had opened a barrel and gotten shitfaced. Sometime that night, we decided a game of hide-and-seek was the best idea in the world. Lillianna was supposed to seek us but fell into a boozy sleep. I found her in a shadowed corner, against a barrel, out cold.

Later, Thorne and I returned to the scene of the crime and took a bottle's worth of bourbon from that barrel, then convinced a label maker to print a special one for us. We presented it to Lillianna that Christmas: Lush-Lillianna's Boozy Bourbon.

My heart pinches. Does she still have the bottle? After that summer, things began to erode between the three of us. Competition and greed overtook camaraderie and closeness between Thorne and me. Lillianna fought constantly with our father and was rarely home.

Fast footsteps draw me back from the glass and the memory. Hanna, my PA, rounds the corner at a near run, then skids to a stop. "Oh! Mr. Blackstone, sorry," she says. "Although I was looking for you."

Her face is chalky, and she's clutching her tablet against her chest. "What's wrong?" I ask.

She glances over her shoulder as if afraid someone might overhear. "It's your brother. He... he took the files from me. And when I tried to explain that you need them for today's meeting, he..." she trails off, biting her lip.

"What did he do, Hanna?" I ask, my gut sinking into a pool of slime.

Hanna shifts her weight from foot to foot. "He said that if I ever questioned his authority again, He'll fire me and make sure no one ever hires me. He said he could ruin my career with one phone call."

"That asshole." My insides still. It's the opposite of calm or peace but the quiet of a circuit about to blow. His threat isn't merely about her job but another calculated move in our endless chess game of corporate warfare.

"I–I'm sorry, Mr. Blackstone. I didn't mean to cause any trouble. I'm only telling you now because he took the Tobar file you need for the meeting."

"You did the right thing. I'll deal with Thorne. And don't worry about your job. You're not going anywhere."

She gives me a grateful smile, but the fear in her eyes remains. "Thank you, Mr. Blackstone. I appreciate that."

I nod. "Right now, I need you to go to the conference room, offer them drinks, and let them know I'll be a few minutes late."

"Right away, Mr. Blackstone." Hanna walks away, and I change directions to Thorne's office.

My irritation hardens with each step. It's bad enough that he's interfering with my work, but threatening my employees is unacceptable.

Outside Thorne's door, I square my shoulders and straighten my tie, making sure my expression is schooled. I'll give him nothing, not even my anger.

I enter without knocking and demand, "Why did you take the Tobar paperwork from Hanna?"

My brother takes a leisurely sip of his espresso. Its strong, bitter aroma is laced with the unmistakable undercurrent of bourbon. The only sound between us is the clink of his small cup as he places it on the saucer. His blue eyes, as cold as our father's, take their sweet time meeting mine. "I wanted to see how much they're paying for our old barrels because I'm talking to a coffee conglomerate in the

Midwest who's interested in them." His voice drips with the exact condescension that our father uses when dismantling someone's argument. I know every nuance of this performance, from the casual sip of espresso to the calculated pause and the way he measures each word, like a chemist mixing a volatile compound.

He motions for me to sit. I ignore the gesture, preferring to loom. "What the hell does a coffee chain want with our barrels?"

"They want to store their beans in them, then charge top-dollar for 'Blackstone bourbon coffee.'"

I lean on the wall next to Thorne's prized Picasso, a grotesque carnival of clashing colors and mutilated forms. He acquired it at auction last year, outbidding three museum directors just because he could.

"Give me their number," I tell him. "I'll have Hanna call them to get more information and forward everything to the right department."

"I emailed her all the details just before you stormed into my office," Thorne replies.

"Next time, keep me updated, so I don't have to waste my time coming here. And don't ever threaten one of my employees again." I glance at my Rolex. "I have to get to a meeting."

"*I* should be in that meeting. *I* should be the master distiller," Thorne grinds out, some of his cool detachment slipping.

"Well, you're not. And we've been in our positions for years. When are you going to get over it?" I straighten my tie, a gesture that feels more like armor than adjustment.

And I honestly don't understand why he wants my job or title. Thorne is good at what he does. He has a flair for acquiring valuable properties and turning even the most mundane business ventures into profitable investments that command attention.

"When I'm running the family business, as I should be as the oldest son. That's when I'll get over it."

"That's not today. So besides threatening my employees and handling coffee clients, is there anything else I should know?" I ask, making it clear I'm not impressed with his meddling.

Thorne has always been a gambler at heart. When he'd turned twenty-one, he'd wagered his entire inheritance advance on a single horse at the derby. Three years ago, he'd risked millions on a failing distillery outside Loretto that everyone said was beyond saving. Where I see hazards, he sees possibilities; where I calculate consequences, he rolls the dice. His willingness to bet big when the odds seem impossible is probably what makes him brilliant as Director of Acquisitions and what makes him terrifying as an enemy.

His eyes light up, and the bitterness that had been etching lines around his mouth moments ago suddenly vanishes. "Actually, yes," he declares, his voice brimming with the same fervor I get when crafting a new bourbon blend. "I've been working on something big."

I no longer like or even love my brother, but I admire his drive for the deal. He is fantastic as Director of Acquisitions. And, I can't fathom why Thorne is so resentful of our father's decision to name me master distiller. Dad is a bastard, but there is no denying he possesses a keen eye for recognizing people's unique abilities and placing them in positions where they excel within Blackstone Bourbon.

"Then tell me," I say.

"The Willows are *finally* putting their hotel up for sale. I want to grab it. The location couldn't be more ideal. It's on the iconic Whiskey Row and situated perfectly between the two major convention centers. The potential is endless. It could create a unique space for a tasting room or a trendy restaurant. Hell, I may even keep it as a little boutique hotel. Its vintage charm and our modern vision would make it a destination in its own right."

The idea of acquiring The Willows is a good one. I can envision the potential transformation he paints.

"Sounds promising," I nod. "Any obstacles?"

"Just one small thing," Thorne says with a dismissive wave. "We're not renewing the lease for that little bookstore next door. We need that space for my vision with The Willows."

"Novel Idea? The bookstore?" The words slip out before I can stop them.

Thorne's eyes narrow, his attention laser-focused on me. "You know the place?" he asks, his voice deceptively casual.

Shit. I shift, keeping my expression neutral. "You know I like to read. I've been there a few times. She and I talk about books."

He studies my face with the same intensity reserved for acquisition targets, and I hope like hell my mask is in place. Thorne has always possessed an uncanny ability to read people, to spot the smallest flicker of interest or hesitation, and use it to his advantage.

"Just books, huh?" he snatches up his phone, his fingers swiping across the screen. A moment later, he straightens in his seat, a smirk playing at the corners of his mouth. He turns the cell towards me. The screen displays a photo of Rosalia beaming next to her one-of-a-kind book counter. He taps on the screen again, his eyes scanning like he's reading. "Well, well, well. It seems Ms. Manchester is not only pretty but also single." His voice drips with insinuation. "I bet you like more than her books, little brother."

"Don't be crass. Rosalia is a smart business person, and her shop is good for the community." I hold his gaze, refusing to look away.

Something calculating flickers in his eyes. It's so far from the person he was that summer in the rickhouse, miles away from the guy who helped me craft Lillianna's special bottle of bourbon. "Rosalia, huh?"

Fuck. Thorne had always possessed an uncanny talent for locating vulnerabilities, for spotting the tell that would win him the hand. And he sees mine. Rosalia. The slight softening in my voice when I said her name was all it took. One momentary slip, and he was already calculating how to use it.

He continues to study me, tapping his fingers against his desk. Then a slow, predatory smile spreads across his face. "Well, this is interesting," he says, setting his phone down with deliberate care.

My coffee curdles in my stomach. Despite years of perfecting my poker face, I know Thorne can sense weakness. Our father taught us both how to hunt for it.

Thorne leans forward, his eyes gleaming like a wolf that's caught a scent. "You know, Sebastian, I think our Whiskey Row property just became much more... personal."

Chapter Four

"Leave Rosalia alone," I tell my brother.

The command hangs between us, sharp as a broken bourbon glass. I stand rigid before Thorne's mahogany desk, while he lounges in his executive chair. We're two strangers who once shared rickhouse secrets and midnight bourbon raids. Now we share nothing but a last name and an ocean of resentment.

"You're interested in her," he says softly. Thorne has always been able to read my tells, even when we were kids playing poker with bottle caps.

"I'm not," I lie. The less my brother knows about my personal life, the better.

"Then why do you care that we're evicting her?"

"I merely appreciate what she's doing for the community," I tell him. "Novel Idea is more than a business."

"Always a fucking bleeding heart for the underdog," my brother mutters.

"Leave her alone," I repeat.

Thorne leans forward, elbows on the desk. "You *are* interested in her. Are you fucking her?"

"Fuck off," I say coolly. Each word is like ice despite the furnace building inside me.

"Stop grinding your teeth before you break one," he sighs. "I'm asking as your older brother, not HR. No need to get your boxers in a twist."

"Don't give me that 'brother' bullshit," I sneer. "We share a last name. That's where the connection ends."

Thorne's smirk falters, and for a moment, his eyes betray a deep, aching hurt. But I've seen that look before. It's a mirage that no longer touches me.

"Fair enough," he replies. His vulnerability vanishes, replaced with his usual glacial demeanor. "I don't give a rat's ass who you're screwing, as long as it doesn't screw with Blackstone's profits. And passing up the Willow's place will."

I press my teeth together so tightly that my jaw clicks. That's what sucks about family, they know exactly which buttons to push. But mine has also given me plenty of opportunity to learn how to transform hot anger into something lethal and controlled, to freeze out those who shouldn't matter—like a brother who betrays.

"She's just... an acquaintance," I say evenly. And it's true. I don't have friends. They're a luxury I can't afford, a weakness I refuse to indulge in. "Anyway, her shop doesn't mess with the company's profits. And she has great mentor programs, book clubs for kids and adults, and a lot of other stuff important to the community. Louisville needs more books, not bourbon."

My brother snorts, folding his arms. "That's not the best tagline for the face of Blackstone Bourbon."

I shrug. "I'm talking to a family member, not the press."

"Ah, so now I'm family." Thorne narrows his eyes and stares at me as if trying to figure me out. "If we didn't work at the same distillery, would you ever talk to me?"

"No. And don't pretend you care."

"I do," he sighs, his gaze drifting to the floor for a moment before meeting my eyes again. "When will you forgive and forget?"

My body locks as tension ripples through my muscles. "I have a right to my anger," I snarl, my words sharp and biting. "You crossed a line. Do you really expect me just to forgive and forget what you did?"

Thorne's gaze darts to the side, and he shifts in his seat. His mouth opens, but only silence escapes, as if his words have disappeared into the hostile air between us. Then his expression hardens into a defensive scowl. "Stop blaming me."

"Who should I blame? Myself? Because I trusted you to be alone in a room with my wife," I sneer, "during a damn family Christmas party?"

It's been two years and the memory still hits like the first inhale of cask-strength bourbon, burning all the way down. Dad always said the Blackstone men carry their pain like they carry their whiskey—neat, strong, and hidden behind a practiced smile. But some betrayals cut too deep to mask.

"She never should have been yours." Thorn's eyes flash with resentment. "But you think everything of mine is yours to take. Dad handed you the master distiller position, even though I'm his eldest son. And if that wasn't enough, you had to go and steal Tiffany from me too. You couldn't let me have even one fucking thing, could you?"

I hold my brother's gaze, my anger distilling into something colder. "Father made his choice based on what he thought was best for the company. And I didn't steal Tiffany. She picked me."

He shoots up from his chair, sending it clattering to the floor. He leans across the table and the sharp smell of bourbon and coffee on his breath assaults me. Spittle lands on the desk between us as his voice rises. "Tiffany was mine first!" he bellows, veins standing out on his neck. "You had no right to come between us and you know it."

A bitter laugh escapes me. "You think you own any woman who crosses your path, regardless of whether she actually wants you or not." The chasm between us opened when Dad named me head of Blackstone Bourbon, then widened the night I met Tiffany.

"She'd come to the party with me," he snarls.

I inhale deeply and exhale through my nose. "And I've told you countless times that she never mentioned you that night. I didn't know you had a thing for her. I didn't know until I brought her home a month later."

Thorne's face reddens and he jabs a finger at my chest. "Bullshit. I told you about her before the party."

"Not her name. Only that she was blonde with—" I straighten and hold up a hand. I'm done with this pointless argument. "Believe what you want, but you're still the asshole in this story. You did what you did when I was *married* to Tiffany." I slam my mouth shut and silently count to ten. Then count back down.

"Like I've said a million damn times, that wasn't my fault. Tiffany pursued me. She's the one who didn't care about her marriage vows or your feelings." His words come out rehearsed, like he's repeated this explanation so many times he's worn the edges smooth. But they still cut me.

I stand to face him on equal footing. "And you? You just... what? Closed your eyes?" I'm not blind to the fact that it takes two, but he's my fucking brother. And all he's given me are excuses.

"Yes, damn it. I'd been drinking. Pissed at you. She came on to me. Fuck, it was a mistake. One I'd take back if I could—"

I hold up my hands. "But you can't."

"And you'll never forgive me, will you?" he asks.

"How can I?" I shout, then snap my mouth shut. I keep it closed until I can talk without yelling, I say, "How can I when you won't even admit you were in the wrong?"

Thorne frowns. "And what, Tiffany is blameless? Women are ruthless. They'll do whatever it takes to get what they want, no matter who they hurt along the way. It's their nature. They use their bodies, their wiles, to manipulate and control men. And we're helpless to resist." He points at me. "Your bookworm, she's cut from the same cloth. I'll bet you anything that she'd throw her grandmother under the bus if it meant getting ahead."

Years of board meetings with temperamental investors have taught me to stay stone-faced when others lose control. But this is different. He's my blood, my childhood co-conspirator who helped me steal sips from the aging barrels after hours. The same hands that pulled me from the frozen creek as kids now clench into fists.

"She's not mine." I cross my arms over my chest. "And no, she wouldn't."

My brother snorts. "You really think she's special, don't you?" His chair squeaks as he rights it, sitting down.

I do the same. "She is. Kind. Caring."

He rolls his eyes. "You don't need to make her into a saint just because you want to fuck her."

"That right there," I snap, jabbing my finger at him, "is exactly why you'll never understand someone like her. Or why she'd never look twice at a man like you. Not everyone sees people as disposable. Some of us still have a soul." I lean in slightly, my gaze never leaving his. "Now, I'm late for a meeting. Let Rosalia renew her lease. Look at properties on Main Street. That area is just as popular as Whiskey Row. I've heard a building near the Louisville Slugger Museum is for sale."

He shakes his head. "No. Whiskey Row is better."

"I'm the master distiller, and last I checked, that title means I get the final say."

Thorne's jaw ticks, and the knuckles of his clasped hands turn white. His eyes hold mine, calculating, measuring. "Not in everything. As Director of Acquisitions, I make these decisions." his smile is razor-sharp. "But I'm willing to make a wager. Something with real consequences."

"No." I turn toward the door.

"If you care even a little bit about your bookworm, you'll want to at least hear me out."

Against my better judgment, I pause. "I'll give you one minute."

"If you can convince her to date you." The fuck-face wiggles his brows. "Like you want to, and you invite her to the Blackstone Derby party."

My hand falls from the door knob and I face him. "I don't get it. What's the wager?"

"I'll approach Rose tomorrow and offer her a deal. I'll renew her lease if she agrees to date you and take that business portfolio from you at the party." He points at my red leather folder. "If she refuses the deal entirely, or if she accepts it but then changes her mind and chooses her integrity and feelings for you over saving her store, you win." He chuckles darkly. "But let's be honest, when has anyone ever chosen principles over survival?"

I don't bother correcting Rosalia's name. The less he remembers about her, the better. "What makes you think she'll even agree to date me, let alone go along with your scheme?"

"She might tell us both to go to hell and refuse the whole arrangement. But given her financial situation, I doubt she'll have that luxury." His eyes narrow slightly, reading my expression like a poker player watching for tells. "Here, let me sweeten the winnings for you. If I lose, I'll leave Kentucky permanently. Transfer to Tennessee or Illinois. Shit, I'll go to our newest distillery in Quebec. And I'll sign over my share in the company to you."

I freeze, fighting to maintain a neutral expression. Relief and peace fill me at the mere thought of his absence. Thorne might have destroyed my marriage and shattered my trust, but bourbon and business continue, and I've had to endure his presence at work every single damn day. The constant reminder of his betrayal is a festering wound that refuses to heal.

Then I remember Rosalia. It's nearly two months from March until the Blackstone Bourbon Classic party. Dating her isn't the issue. It's the lying, the manipulation, the hidden agenda hanging over every interaction. The thought makes me sick.

I shake my head. "No."

"No? What about your Rose losing her bookstore?" he taunts.

"I'll help her find another location."

"If you don't agree, I'll make sure she never opens another bookstore in Kentucky. I'll blacklist her with every bank and property owner from Louisville to Lexington."

My blood runs cold. "You can't do that."

"Can't I? Who do you think the property managers listen to? Who has connections with every major bank in Kentucky? Hell, throughout the U.S?" The threat emerges as a hushed promise. "I can ruin her, Sebastian. Not just evict her—destroy her. She'll never recover."

My hands curl into fists. "This is blackmail, Thorne. You're using an innocent woman as collateral damage in your power play."

My brother's smile doesn't falter. "I prefer to think of it as creative negotiation, but you can call it what you want. Business leverage. Incentive structure."

"There's nothing creative about it," I snap. "Are you really willing to destroy an innocent woman's livelihood over our feud? Commit actual criminal extortion?"

"Don't be so dramatic." He waves his hand dismissively. "In bourbon and business, we all use the leverage we have. Dad taught us that, didn't he?"

"Dad never taught us to be criminals," I growl, but it's more from frustration than indignation. Our father had his own moral blind spots when it came to getting what he wanted.

Thorne shrugs. "If your precious principles are too expensive for you, then refuse the bet. I'll continue with the eviction process and follow through on everything else I promised," he says in a silky whisper. "But if you accept and she proves me wrong about her character, I'll not only leave Kentucky, but I'll sign over ownership of the building to her. She'll never have to worry about eviction again."

"And if I lose?" The words scrape my throat.

"You step down as master distiller. The position is mine, as it should have been all along. And you sell me your controlling shares at half their value."

"That's absurd," I scoff.

"Is it?"

I stare at my brother, seeing the malice behind his smile. "Yes. You're threatening to demolish everything she's built. All because you're pissed Dad named me head of Blackstone Bourbon."

Thorne doesn't answer, just continues to stare at me. I'm trapped. If I agree to this twisted wager, any genuine connection I might have built with Rosalia will be poisoned from the start. I'll be courting her under false pretenses, manipulating her to win a bet. And even if she passes his test, even if she chooses loyalty to me over saving her store, how could I ever tell her that our relationship began as a bargaining chip? The thought of her warm brown eyes turning cold with betrayal makes my chest tighten.

"What's to stop me from telling her everything the moment we're alone?" I challenge.

His smile turns predatory. "The agreement will state that if you tell her or hint at our arrangement in any way, you forfeit immediately. Meaning, I'll win. And, Bastian, I'll know."

"How? Planning to spy on us?"

"I don't need to. You're my little brother who's painfully transparent when you feel guilty." He leans forward. "Besides, part of you wants to know if she's different. If you can really trust your judgment when it comes to women."

His words hit like a sucker punch, targeting my deepest insecurity: that I'm blind when it comes to reading people I care about. Tiffany isn't the first to leave me bleeding after I handed over my trust.

"This way, you get certainty," Thorne continues, his voice almost gentle, like the sociopath actually cares. "If she passes, you'll know for sure she's different. If she fails..." He shrugs. "Better to know now than later."

The worst part is, some wounded part of me finds his logic appealing. But then I picture Rosalia, trapped by this arrangement, believing she has to betray me to save her store.

"You know," Thorne says, swirling the last of his bourbon espresso, "this is just the latest in our long line of competitions, isn't it? From the science fair in seventh grade to the bidding war for the Wilkerson estate whiskey collection."

"This isn't a competition. This is you ruining an innocent woman over our personal vendetta."

"It's about character. Like when Dad would test us." His eyes darken. "Remember when he'd leave cash on the counter to see if we'd take it? Or how he'd ask one of us to cover for his affairs to see if we'd lie to Mom?"

The memory of those "tests" burns like cheap moonshine. "Don't compare this to that."

"Why not? We learned something valuable, didn't we? That people will always disappoint you, given the right incentive." His voice hardens. "You think your bookworm is different? That she's somehow above basic human nature?"

"And this 'test' is as faulty as one of Dad's. You're asking her to betray me before she even knows me. Of course, she'd agree now. Why wouldn't she? She'd be saving her bookstore by betraying a stranger."

"But she'll know you by the derby party," Thorne counters.

"And by then it will be too late. She'll know me better, might even care about me, but she'll still be bound by an agreement she made when I meant nothing to her. She'll have wasted months that could have been spent finding another location."

"I'm not a complete monster," he says, leaning back. "The deal will have an out clause. I'll tell her she's free to find another building for her bookstore from now until the party. I'll even provide names of bankers and lawyers who handle real estate and business ventures. If she finds another place, showing she's willing to take the harder path rather than fucking you over, I won't hold her to our agreement." He smirks. "Hell, I'm such a nice guy that if she passes our test, I'll make up some excuse for renewing her lease. You two can keep dating, build your life together, whatever. She'll never know it started as a wager. And you'll know she's worth trusting."

"Why are you really doing this?" I frown, unable to piece it together. "Either way this plays out, you won't get her bookstore for the Willow Hotel purchase and expansion."

"Because this is so much better. Why settle for her little corner when I can have the whole damn company?" He settles back in his chair like a chess master who's announced checkmate.

Shit. I shouldn't agree. It's wrong, but damn, he's backed me into the perfect corner. I can let him destroy an innocent woman for certain, or take a gamble that might save her *and* finally get him out of my life.

My brother sits forward, steepling his fingers. "If you think about it, I'm doing you a favor."

"If you truly wanted to do me a favor, then just leave. That solves my issue and Rosalia's. And it's quicker than this asinine bet."

Thorne throws his head back with a laugh that echoes through his corner office. "Oh, Bastian. That's what I love about you, always the optimist. But let's be honest here. When this is all over, I'll have proven what we both already know: everyone has their price, even your precious bookworm. And once she betrays you, I'll finally take my rightful place in the family business." He spreads his hands across the mahogany desk, as if already claiming territory. "Dad may have given you the crown, but I'm the one who was born to wear it. So enjoy your last few months as the golden boy of Blackstone. Those controlling shares you're so proud of? Consider them mine at half price. After all, it's only fair that family gets a discount."

I draw a slow breath, weighing my options. This is manipulation, plain and simple. Another of my brother's games where he's already arranged all the pieces. I tap my fingers against my thigh, a quiet metronome counting the cost of each choice. Whose future do I risk, hers or mine? The decision shouldn't be this difficult, yet I'm paralyzed.

"Okay, walk away." He shrugs. "I'll start making calls this afternoon. By the end of the week, your precious bookworm will be facing financial ruin."

I hold up a hand. I can't let him destroy her. "Wait."

His face lights up with triumph.

"Fine," I grit out. "But we put it in writing. Every detail."

"A handshake isn't good enough between brothers?" he mocks.

"No. We'll have a formal contract drafted by independent counsel, with explicit terms for both scenarios. Daniel will contact you shortly."

Thorne drums his fingers on the desk. "We'll need an ironclad NDA as part of the package. Complete confidentiality. If you breathe a word of this to anyone, including your bookworm, you forfeit immediately."

"You mean you want to protect yourself from anyone finding out about your blackmail and extortion," I shoot back.

His smile falters slightly before turning cold and calculating. "Call it what you want. The NDA is non-negotiable. After all, we're just two businessmen making a gentleman's wager. No need for outside interference."

"I want it stipulated that if she passes your test, you not only leave Kentucky but sign over legal ownership of her building to her directly, not to me. And it needs to be ironclad with no loopholes, no 'creative interpretations' like when you reneged on the Marshall property."

His jaw tightens. "Fine. And when she fails, I want similar ironclad terms for your surrender of your position here and the shares."

He extends his hand. "Deal."

We shake, it lingers on my palm like a stain I can't wash off. I've signed away a small piece of my soul. Then it hits me with the force of a sledgehammer, knocking me off-kilter. Thorne's a mirror image of our father, doing whatever it takes to win. And like our dad, he'll manipulate and destroy anyone in his way.

"I'll have my papers drawn up today," Thorne says, reaching for his phone. "I look forward to running this company, little brother."

I turn to leave, disgust churning in my gut like poisoned bourbon. This is a mistake that will haunt us both.

"Oh, and Sebastian?" he calls after me. "Every man has his weakness. And I think you are about to know yours. Intimately."

I walk to the door without looking back, the weight of what I've agreed to is suffocating me like an anchor dragging me to hell. I've put Rosalia in the crosshairs of my brother's twisted game. But what choice did he leave me? None. I'm left to save her by destroying any chance we might have had.

Chapter Five

Rosalia

Sunlight streams through the front window of Novel Idea as I unlock it. The rays illuminate the "Road to Derby" poster I'd hung to attract racing enthusiasts. There are eight weeks until the big day, and already tourists are trickling into Louisville, their numbers set to swell as May approaches.

When I hung the sign I was full of excitement. Now, it feels like a countdown to the death of all my dreams.

I stare down the mostly empty street, melancholy holding me tight. A shiny black car with tinted windows crawls past, probably looking for Paige's bakery. Besides her place and my bookstore, Whiskey Row's other businesses don't open until around noon.

Leaving the door open to let in the spring breeze, I turn from the street and head inside. The familiar scent of paper greets me. The old hardwood floors creak beneath my feet as I make my way to the checkout counter. The quiet, sleepy sounds mingle with the occasional creak of the old building settling. I scan the stuffed shelves lined with rows upon rows of books. A heavy sigh escapes from me, and the urge to cry returns. No surprise, it's been hanging out with me since the phone call from the lawyer, Daniel, two days ago.

The non-renewal notice still sits open in a tab on my laptop, the corporate letterhead mocking me every time I catch sight of it. Sixty days. That's all I have left in this space I've poured my heart into. Sixty days to somehow find a new location, gather enough money for security deposits, cover renovation costs, plan for the inevitable lost revenue during the move, and somehow keep paying off my original loan.

Dad's worried voice plays on repeat in my mind. "Rosie, honey, are you sure you can handle this?" I'd been ridiculously confident when I called him with my grand plan three short years ago. So sure that moving to Louisville and opening a bookstore was exactly what I needed. I'd convinced him I could do this, and he'd believed in me enough to put his house on the line for my loan. Now I can't even look at his number in my phone without feeling like I might throw up. How do I tell him that in two months, I might cost him everything?

Last night I stayed up until three in the morning running numbers, calculating and recalculating, hoping I'd find some magical formula that would make every- thing work. First month's rent, last month's rent, security deposit, moving com- pany, new shelving, signage, permits—the total kept climbing to an impossible sum. My store brings in steady money, but not nearly enough for this kind of financial hit. Not while I'm still paying off the original loan for the bookstore and helping Dad with his remortgaged home payments.

Pushing my worry aside, I leave the checkout counter for a much-needed caffeine boost. At the beverage cubby, I start a pot of coffee. The rich aroma fills the air. I close my eyes and lean against the counter, savoring the moment of calm before a busy day.

I look up at the sound of footsteps on the threshold. "Good morning," I say automatically.

A man who looks a little familiar strides toward me, wearing a suit that practically gleams at the seams. Even my untrained eye can tell that nothing on him is off the rack. His light brown hair is neatly styled and looks as expensive as his suit. He is incredibly good-looking and moves with a calculated grace, but his handsomeness is marred by clinical detachment in his gaze.

"Good Morning." He extends a hand, his cufflinks glinting. His voice is smooth, as if accustomed to commanding attention. "I'm Thorne Blackstone."

The name hits me like a blow. Blackstone.

Sebastian's brother. I should've recognized him from the papers and social media. His eyes and hair are lighter, but there's no mistaking that perfect jawline, full lips, and Greek nose.

I start to reach for his hand, then pause. The calculating assessment in those cold blue eyes makes my skin prickle with warning that goes deeper than just his last name. His eyebrow arches slightly at my hesitation, and his smile sharpens. I force myself to complete the handshake, but his grip is like a trap closing.

"A Blackstone in my bookstore. What did I do to deserve the honor?" I ask dryly.

He chuckles. "Do I sense sarcasm?"

"I'll admit, I tend to like people better when they aren't tossing me out onto the street."

"I take it you received the lease non-renewal notice." Concern cloaks his words, but there's a predatory gleam in his eyes, like a cat toying with a cornered mouse.

"My sixty days aren't up yet." Keeping the tinge of desperation from my voice is impossible. I run my fingers down the plastic buttons of my powder blue rayon blouse, acutely aware of how it's faded from too many washes. Between the scuffed flats and worn heels, this outfit is like a physical manifestation of my dismal bank account.

He holds up his hands. "I'm not here to lock the doors early. In fact, the opposite. I have a proposition."

I rub my eyebrow. "That sounds ominous." Whatever deal he's about to offer, I'm certain it won't come cheap. To make matters worse, I suspect he knows exactly how few cards I have left to play.

"More like a gift horse. Perfect for Kentucky, right?"

"Depends on the gift." I move behind the check-out counter. For reasons I can't name, I need a barrier between us.

"How about a new lease? Five years, locked in rate."

I step back. "Why would you offer that when your company sent me an eviction notice two days ago?"

"Let's just say I have my reasons." His smile is practiced, hollow.

"And those reasons are?" I press, not willing to take the bait so easily.

"Does it matter?" He shrugs one expensive shoulder. "You need a place for your books, I can provide one."

"That's not an answer," I press.

"Why," he shoots back. "You should focus on what matters. Saving your store."

His evasiveness bothers me, but desperation makes me swallow the rest of my questions. "You'd put it in writing that I get to stay?"

"Learned a lesson about getting things in writing, did you?"

Embarrassment curls in my stomach. "Yes."

"I'll have my lawyer draft the contract today."

"Will your lawyer be the same one who told me to get out?"

He holds up an index finger and ticks it back and forth like a pendulum. "The Blackstone empire, not me personally, honey. But I do have the power to stop it."

I cross my arms against the tightness forming in my chest. His non-answers are making this worse, but I can't let it go, and ask, "And why are you personally getting involved with my mess?"

Thorne pauses, as if carefully choosing his words. "Sebastian has been making some... questionable decisions lately. Decisions that affect not only my family's legacy but also the families who work for us."

My stomach drops. "Sebastian? What does Sebastian have to do with me or my bookstore?"

"His judgment is compromised. He's pouring money into feel-good projects while our core business suffers. If he continues, we'll have to cut jobs—lots of them."

I recall the Louisville Business Journal article I'd skimmed last week about Blackstone's board questioning new investment directions. At the time, I'd thought it was typical corporate politics, but maybe there was more to it.

"If I can demonstrate his reckless nature to our board, they'll reconsider some of my changes." Thorne's voice turns confidential. "That's where you come in."

The polished way he delivers this makes me wary, but major layoffs at Blackstone would hurt more than Bardstown. The whole region depends on that company.

"What exactly do you want me to do?" I ask.

"I need you to date him," Thorne says bluntly.

My eyebrows shoot up. "Excuse me?" Did he know that Sebastian asked me out right before the phone call that's ruining my life?

"Just a few dates. Enough to get him to invite you to the annual Blackstone Bourbon Classic."

"What's that?"

"It's our company's derby party."

"And then what? I ask innocently if he's mentally fit to run the company?"

His lips twist into a tight smile. "You'll need to take the folder he'll bring to the party."

A horn honks outside, followed by an angry shout. I flinch, but Thorne doesn't even blink. His focus is unwavering as if the world outside these walls is irrelevant to whatever game he's playing.

"Take? You mean steal?" I ask, appalled.

His voice stays level, matter-of-fact. "Not steal. Retrieve. Sebastian's planning to bankrupt us with his pet projects, and the board needs to see his written plans. He'll bring a red leather portfolio to the party, stamped with our logo. You can't miss it. The folder's stuffed with his 'visionary' ideas that will destroy our family business."

I inhale, and the earthy scent of books mixes with Thorne's expensive cologne. The combination turns my stomach. It's the scent of my failure.

Thorne's deal could save me.

I can't do it. My head shakes back and forth. "No."

He stills. "Why?"

"Because all of this makes me feel gross. Dating a man to get him kicked out of his family's company?" Anger bubbles inside me. The more I think about the offer, the sicker it makes me. "Seriously, what the hell is wrong with you?"

My heart flips at the fury that flashes over his features. Then it's gone as quickly as a lightning strike, and his easy smile returns. "Welcome to corporate America, honey," he says with a shrug. "Sometimes you have to make tough decisions for the greater good of the company."

"Well, it's not for my good. How do you think he'll feel about me when he finds out my part in your scheme?"

Thorne runs his tongue along his front teeth. "How do I put this delicately? He'll be furious about the board situation, but you as an individual, you're unimportant to him."

I choke out a surprised laugh. "That's delicate?"

He shrugs again.

I recall my easy conversations with Sebastian, his flirting the last time he'd been in the store. I'm not buying what Thorne is selling. "I wouldn't say we're friends, but Sebastian doesn't treat me like I'm inconsequential."

"That's probably because he wants to fuck you. My brother has a way of making women feel special. But once he has them... the charm fades. Just ask his ex-wife."

The words hit harder than I expect. Is that really how Sebastian sees me? "E-excuse me," I stammer.

"Don't slap the messenger, honey. I'm just telling you how he is. He loves the chase. Not the prize. And—"

"I'm not your honey," I bite out. "And If you're about to make some analogy about how I'm a crappy prize, you can see yourself out of my store." My unexpected boldness sends shockwaves from my chest to my stomach.

"You mean my building? The one you get to keep for another two months—unless you help me." Thorne's gaze sweeps the empty store with theatrical slowness. "Though honestly, opening a bookstore on Whiskey Row? A street famous for bourbon, not books?" He practically sneers the word. "Maybe you're better suited to being an employee than an owner."

"I opened five minutes ago," I sputter. "I'm doing great. I cater to locals, tourists, readers, and the bourbon industry. My place is the calm oasis before my customers head out to the distilleries and bad decisions."

"Bad decisions, huh?" He grins, and a dimple appears on his left cheek, but the sight doesn't make my heart flip as it does around Sebastian.

I don't return his smile. "Is this what rich people do for entertainment? Manipulate people's livelihoods for corporate games?"

"This isn't a game," he says, his voice suddenly hard. "I'm trying to protect my family's legacy."

I can't tell if he's worried about the distillery or if he's angry because I'm not falling in line. What's real and what's an act?

"Why me for this scheme? There must be dozens of women who'd be eager to date a Blackstone."

"Because you're the easiest—"

"Excuse me!"

"Settle down, honey. Rumor is, he's interested in you." He slides his hands into the pockets of his tailored slacks. "If you smile pretty and stroke his...ego, I'm sure he'll invite you to the Blackstone Bourbon Classic. While there, take the portfolio." He snaps his fingers. "The next day, I'll have my lawyers draft a five-year lease of this building for you."

The burst of cheerful chatter announces the arrival of several customers who step through my open door. Their laughter bounces off the bookshelves, filling the space with an infectious energy that contrasts with my unsettled state. I greet them with a forced smile, unable to fully register their faces.

Thorne lowers his voice. "I need your answer by tomorrow."

"This is insane," I whisper back. "I might not mean anything to him, but he *will* be angry. Who wouldn't be? And even if you remove him from his position within the distillery, he's still a Blackstone. He could do worse than just kick me out of this building. His money and connections have the power to crush me completely. He might blacklist me with vendors, ruin my reputation in town, make sure I can't keep my doors open."

Thorne waves off my concern. "Sebastian has bigger fish to fry than some bookstore owner who played along with his brother's game. Trust me, I know how he thinks. He'll be angry at me, not you, which is nothing new." His eyes harden. "I, on the other hand, don't share my brother's restraint. Something to consider before you turn down my generous offer."

Thorne's barely veiled threat scares the hell out of me, but what am I giving up of myself if I agree? If I refuse, there is a very good chance I won't be able to reopen the store or my programs. And it feels like I'm erasing my favorite book. First, the colorful descriptions are removed, followed by the supporting characters, until all that remains is a thin plot that barely resembles the story I'd imagined for myself.

But at least I will be able to look at myself in the mirror each morning. Sure, my integrity won't pay the bills, but it's the only thing they can't take from me.

"Thanks, but no thanks," I tell him.

His head jerks back. "Why not? Don't you care about your business?"

Fury surges through me. "You don't deserve an answer to that question when you're treating my livelihood like a bargaining chip. But, yes, this place is every-thing to me."

"Apparently not, if you're willing to let it go without a fight." He counters, straightening his expensive cufflinks.

"This isn't a fight. It's a transaction where I'm supposed to sell my integrity along with the books. I'd rather lose the store than become that kind of person."

"Integrity," Thorne scoffs. "Is that what losers call their fear of taking risks? Let me tell you something about the real world—principles don't pay bills. They just make failure feel noble."

"I have other options." They are slim but better than this crap.

"Do you really?" His gaze tracks over me, from my coupon-clipped haircut to the frayed cuffs of my blouse. At this moment, I'm acutely aware of every patch and stitch holding my world together. His eyes narrow. "I had my people look into your finances, Rosalia. I know you still haven't paid off your original loan. That your father remortgaged his home for your startup costs. Do you have the money to move? The cost of new rent, security deposits, renovations, and lost revenue. I know you'll never secure another loan with your credit history."

A cold wave washes over me, starting at my scalp and rushing downward. How dare he invade my privacy? "You had no right," I hiss.

"I have every right to know who I'm doing business with," he counters, clearly unfazed by my outrage. "And from what I've seen, you're not exactly in a position to turn down my offer."

"My store is doing just fine," I retort, lifting my chin. I've built a loyal customer base, and my sales are steady. I'd have been fine if your company had stuck to its agreement."

"What agreement? I've read the contract. There's no mention of letting you rent indefinitely."

The earlier cold turns to heat that creeps up my neck and floods my cheeks. I'd been so excited about finding the perfect spot on Whiskey Row that I'd signed the rental agreement without a lawyer. The Blackstone's leasing agent had assured me that as long as I was a good tenant, renewals would be automatic. I'd believed her and never thought to get it in writing.

"It was a verbal agreement," I say, the words sounding pathetic even to my ears.

Thorne's eyebrow arches slightly as he grins. It's a look of pure condescension, as if I've confirmed every assumption he's made about my intelligence. "Regardless, you don't have enough to cover a move and your debts. Not in the time frame you need. Face it. Without my help, you'll lose everything you've worked so hard for. Your father will lose his house."

I rub my clammy palms on my shirt. He might be right. My financial position is precarious, and his offer could be my only chance to save my store. But, again, the cost is too high.

"No." I fight back the tears that threaten to spill. "I don't need your pity or your condescension. I'll find a way to save Novel Idea without your help."

Thorne drums his fingers on the counter, glancing around the store as if bored. "Fine, call around, see if you can find another place without my help. If it doesn't work, give me a call." He reaches into his suit jacket and pulls out a card from a small gold case. "Hell, I'm feeling generous. I'll let you look all the way up until the Derby party, and if you find something, then back out of our deal. Leave one of the most popular streets in Louisville. No hard feelings."

He strolls toward the exit. Before passing through the door, he reaches up, hitting the antique bell. Its cheerful jingle now sounds more like a warning bell. The desolate tone pierces me.

His broad form moves down the street and from my view. I turn the thick cardstock over in my hands, running my thumb over the embossed lettering. His bold signature mocks me.

Is he actually giving me an out? It sounds too good to be true. Thorne Blackstone doesn't strike me as the type to make genuine concessions. More likely, he's confident I'll fail, which isn't great for my confidence. Not that it matters. I have to try.

I lean back and hold the card over the garbage. That's where it belongs. But I can't seem to let it fall.

Chapter Six

Rosalia

I look around Novel Idea, taking in the quirky shelves and lovingly stacked books. These walls hold so many stories—stories that might soon fade into silence, along with my dream of expanding the reading and working here until I'm old and gray.

A long, weary sigh escapes from me. Setting my cell on the beautiful counter made with love and books, I run my hand over the smooth wood top. Each grain is a testament to the hours my dad spent sanding and varnishing it. We built the rest together. When I left Michigan and moved here, our weekends were spent at thrift stores and digging through free bins for old books to build this counter.

I'd told him about the lease issue, but downplayed how serious it was. He'd offered to help again, but I couldn't let him. Dad's heart might be bigger than Kentucky, but his house is already on the line for my first loan. There is no way I'd ask or take more.

At least I had the sense not to tell him about Thorne's offer. It was not an option. Instead, I pretended to have options to keep my father from worrying and doing something drastic.

Quitting isn't on the table. At thirty-two years old, I shouldn't still need to ask my parents for money. And Dad has already done more than enough. I could ask Mom for a modest loan to get a small shop somewhere off the beaten path that will be a lot cheaper than this place. But the thought of asking her made my stomach churn. I knew exactly what would happen. She'd swoop in, take over, and manage every aspect of my life again.

My inbox is full of unanswered emails to banks, and my call log shows a dozen outgoing calls with no returns. It's been two days since Thorne's visit, and I've reached out to every financial institution within fifty miles, but so far, I've received nothing but silence. Surely one of them would see the potential in my bookstore and get back to me?

Tapping my phone against the counter, I watch dust motes drift through the afternoon light. The peaceful scene mocks me. Time to stop stalling.

I dial Mom's number. "Is everything okay, sweetie?" she answers, her voice tinged with perennial worry.

She is kind and caring, but her love is a suffocating embrace. Normally, I respond to her catastrophe-ready greetings with sarcasm and jokes, but today the words catch in my throat, heavy with unspoken fears. "No, things aren't good."

"What happened? Let me help." There's a sharp intake of breath on the other end of the line, the telltale pause that her anxiety is growing.

A knot forms in my stomach. She's probably mentally packing her bags to rescue me because that's who she is, a first responder to my every crisis. But at thirty-two, I should be handling this alone, not feeding her anxiety.

Yet, I'm only two years into my business venture and I'm begging for help. But asking for a small loan is better than returning to Michigan a complete failure, so broke I'd have to move back in with my mom. It's so easy to picture myself hunched on the fold-out couch in Mom's basement, surrounded by cardboard boxes and childhood memorabilia, while she calls down the stairs each morning to ask what I want for breakfast.

"Rosalia? Are you still there?"

I swallow the lump of desperation lodged in my throat. "Sorry, Mom. It's the bookstore..." I give her the edited version—lease troubles, financial strain—and hint that I might need help.

"Let me see what I can do, honey. But I'm not sure there's much. We haven't talked in a while, so you don't know this..." She sighs, and I hear what's unsaid: I'm all alone and my daughter rarely calls.

"Mom, we talked last week."

She hums, then continues as if I hadn't spoken. "I've decided to leave the school. I told them on Monday. The last few years haven't been great, and, with no need for free tuition, I figured it's time for a change. I've applied to places closer to your grandmother."

"That's exciting," I tell her, meaning it. She needs a change.

"I thought you'd be upset."

"Why?" I ask, though I already know the answer. Mom thinks I loved that school.

The Hayek sisters and our volleyball team were amazing, but the rest of my classmates could suck it. I straighten a stack of books on the counter, the familiar movement grounding me.

"I'm happy if you're happy," I say. "Where have you applied to?"

"All the public schools in Ann Arbor. Two have called me for an interview."

I love the joyous lilt in my mother's voice. "I bet grandma is thrilled. I'm so happy for you."

"Thanks, honey, and she is, but I feel awful. I'm not sure any bank would give me a mortgage loan, knowing I'll soon be temporarily unemployed."

The familiar edge of financial worry in her voice takes me back. Some things never change. Money was always tight in our household, every dollar stretched thin. Even now, the phrase stings the same way it did when I was the charity case kid at Michigan's most exclusive private school. While my classmates casually discussed their European vacations, I'd felt the burden of every dollar my parents struggled to provide. The stark economic divide had been a constant, painful reminder that I didn't belong.

"That's okay. And I hope you get the job. A2 is such a great school system." I say cheerfully, not wanting her to hear the old hurt. She'd worked so hard and had been so proud to have me in that school, never knowing about the jerks who made fun of my second-hand uniforms.

"You know..." There is a world of suffocating hope in her pause. "They have a posting for a librarian at one of the high schools too. You should apply for it."

"I live here." I inhale deeply, letting the familiar scent of old paper and binding glue fill my lungs with a sense of reassurance.

"Come home. I'll take care of you."

A tightness squeezes my chest. "Kentucky is my home now."

"Your dad can't take care of you like I can."

"I'm thirty-two, Mom," I tell her, unable to hide the subtle undertone of exasperation. Inhaling deeply, the air fills my nostrils with the musty fragrance of fresh pages. "Don't you think it's time I take care of myself?"

"Nonsense. We've always taken care of each other. Even before your dad and I divorced."

That wasn't true. She, not I, had managed and handled everything in our lives. That needs to end.

The bell on the door chimes and I glance in that direction. The knot in my chest loosens at the sight of Paige, her arrival a welcome interruption to my spiraling thoughts. Her blonde pixie cut is a little flat from the long morning and afternoon hours in her bakery's kitchen. In contrast, the smile on her generous mouth is as vibrant as the rest of her.

My lips form their first genuine smile since before Thorne's visit. "Mom, I have a customer."

"Okay, sweetie. Call me later. Let's talk more about you coming home."

I make a non-committal sound before hanging up. Paige places a wrapped sandwich between us, and I shake my head. Moving around the counter and hugging my friend, I pull back and wag a finger. "Like I've told you a million times, you don't need to feed me."

Though there's no denying my mouth is watering. I might have eaten a few hours ago, but Paige's food is paradise for the taste buds.

"And, like I've said, I enjoy feeding people. It's my job," Paige replies.

And she's very good at it. Customers from all over Kentucky flock to her bakery that's just three doors down from my store. She leans on the counter while I unwrap the sandwich. "When does your next book club arrive?" she asks.

"Cozy Mysteries will be here in an hour." I look around at the empty table, the expensive reading chairs—all the pieces of my dream that might soon need new homes. An ache spreads through my chest. "What's wrong?" Paige asks.

"It's been a rollercoaster of a day."

"Do you love or hate the ride?"

My stomach turns. "I despise them."

Paige looks at her watch. "I've got an hour until I need to get back to prep for tomorrow's baking, and you, surprisingly, don't have any customers. Spill. What happened?"

I hesitate, but next to the Hayek sisters, Paige is my closest friend. I tell her about her lease issue and then Thorne's deal. By the time I finish, her eyes are as big as serving plates. "No joke?" she asks.

Nodding, I pull Thorne's card from a drawer and hand it to her. "No kidding."

"Wow. I've heard about those two, but damn..." She flips the card over. "So Sebastian shows up, invites you to coffee, then his lawyer—"

"A Blackstone lawyer," I correct.

She rolls her eyes. "Isn't he a Blackstone? And he asks you out right after the lawyer calls... The timing is suspicious, don't you think? It could be a red herring to make you think he's not involved with the eviction."

"Maybe, but even if that's true, it goes against who I am to do something that could harm him or his career. Plus, I can't see what Sebastian would get out of all this."

She shrugs. " I heard they compete over everything, from work to women. The rumor is that Sebastian's marriage ended because of some rivalry between him and his brother."

I absorb this information, letting the weight of it settle alongside everything else. Marriage destroyed by family rivalry makes me wonder about Thorne's offer. But dwelling on their mess won't save my store.

"I've thought about getting a second job," I admit. "But who would run the store while I'm gone? And would I make enough money fast enough to secure a new lease somewhere else? This feels like a waking nightmare. But then I imagine the looks on the kids' faces when they come for story time and find the doors locked, and I realize the real nightmare would be letting them down. Everyone who comes through these doors isn't just a customer, they're my community. My family. How can I walk away from that?"

Paige taps Thorne's card on the table. "You should do it."

I frown. "Do what?"

"Accept Thorne's deal to keep leasing this place."

My mouth falls open. "Huh?"

The bell on the door rings, drawing my attention from our conversation. A woman in her early forties approaches, her gaze bouncing from me to Paige. "Hi, um, are you the owner of this place? Ms. Manchester?"

"I am. Please, call me Rosalia."

The woman nods. Her gaze skitters to Paige, then to her feet. "I'll just..." Paige gestures toward the shelves and drifts away, giving us privacy.

Once she wanders away, the woman says, "We haven't met because my boyfriend usually brings our daughter. I wanted to thank you for the incredible reading group you've created for kids. Lily used to struggle with reading, but since starting with you, she loves it. Especially since you let her read comic books."

My heart swells. "That's wonderful to hear. I'm so glad Lily is enjoying the graphic novels and coming here."

The woman glances at Paige, who seems engrossed in a book she plucked from a nearby shelf. Lowering her voice, the woman continues, "I want to encourage my daughter's love for reading, and I think the best way to do that is by modeling it myself. Do you have anything similar for adults?"

A pang of regret spreads through me. "I do have one, but I'm afraid there's a waiting list at the moment. I'm actively seeking more volunteers and funding to expand the program and accommodate more participants."

The woman's shoulders sag a bit, but she nods. "I see. Well, if anything changes, please keep me in mind."

I long for a magic wand that could conjure the resources to help every person who walks through my doors. Lily's mother leaves, and Paige makes her way back to the counter. "It breaks my heart to turn people away," I tell her. "I wish I had the means to expand our programs and eliminate the waiting list so no one would ever have to leave here without the support they need."

"And that's why you should agree to Thorne's deal. You'll be able to keep the store and this location." She picks up the discarded card and taps it on the counter. "Consider your deal with Thorne a backup plan. He said you can keep looking for another place. There are also grants and Small Business Development Center assistance. Or maybe a partnership with a complementary business. Or hell, crowdfunding. Meanwhile, you've already told Sebastian that you'll go out on a date with him, so go and enjoy yourself. You might have a horrible time—"

"Doubtful. I always enjoy his company when he comes here."

"Yes, but this will be outside of your book bubble. He might be a dud. Arrogant like his brother. Or he's a terrible boss and they might actually be better off with

Thorne in charge." She raises her hands as if weighing all the options. "There are so many factors, and he didn't say it's all or nothing. Accept, but keep looking."

I stopped pacing. "You make this all sound so simple."

Paige squeezes my hand, her eyes full of understanding. "I know it's not simple. I can't give great advice on love, because I suck at it," she laughs. "But business, that I understand. The first few years of my bakery were touch-and-go. And I did what I had to in order to make my dreams happen."

"That sounds like a story."

She shrugs. "For another day. Today is yours. Our community needs your programs. And honestly, some of this is me being selfish. I don't want you to move to another location. Or, if you have to, not outside of Louisville."

I want to argue, but Paige has a point. This isn't only about my dream anymore. Dad's house is tied up in my loan, kids are learning to love reading here, and adults are getting the literacy help they need and want. I can't let my pride hurt all them.

The once-absurd notion kindles a defiant flame in my heart. To take Thorne's deal might tarnish my soul, but losing my bookstore would break it. My heart races as I come to a decision. Lifting my chin, I meet my friend's gaze. "I'm going to do it," I say, the words taste of victory and defeat.

Paige nods. "Good. Give that hottie hell."

A ghost of a smile pulls at the corner of my mouth. "Are we talking about Sebastian or Thorne?"

"Either. They are both sexy as sin."

A weak smile tugs at my lips as I take in my sanctuary—a sanctuary for many others as well. This place is worth fighting for, worth compromising for.

"Yes, I'll accept Thorne's offer. But it's not the end. I'll find another way, a better way. Whatever it takes, whatever the cost, I will save Novel Idea."

The promise lodges itself between my ribs, not quite hope, not quite desperation, but something wilder and more dangerous. I drop Thorne's card on the countertop. Its glossy surface catches the light. I've always prided myself on my integrity, on playing fair even when others don't. Now I'm stepping into murky waters, and part of me wonders if I'll recognize the person who emerges on the other side.

Chapter Seven

Sebastian

I stare at Novel Idea from my Bentley. The book-shaped sign above the door swings lazily in the Monday evening breeze. A quick glance at my watch confirms it's nearly closing time. The once-charming facade now mocks me. "I'll let myself out, but stay near," I tell Tom. "I'm not sure if this will take an hour or five minutes."

He nods, but I don't leave. Instead, I open the middle console and remove a glass bottle of water. Unscrewing the cap, I take a huge swallow. Pretending I'm happy to see Rosalia is going to be difficult. When I'd first asked her out, it had been because of a simple attraction. Now, thanks to Thorne, nothing is simple.

The bet has poisoned what could have been. She and I are playing the same game, only for different stakes.

How am I supposed to pretend for the next six weeks? Six long weeks of forced smiles and hidden agendas until the derby party. Six weeks to either win her heart or lose my place at the head of Blackstone Distillery to my brother. I'm an idiot to risk all I've worked for. God knows what Thorne could do to the company if he were to take over.

My phone rings on the seat. I glance at the caller ID and my mood drops further. The ringing cuts off, going to voicemail. I wish I could ignore the memory of our last conversation as easily as this call. Yesterday, I made the mistake of answering.

"What do you want?" I'd snapped.

"Good afternoon to you too, brother," he drawls.

"Again, what do you want?"

"The bet's on."

The sentence lands like a punch to the gut. Rosalia seemed different, but she is just another person willing to use me for her gain. "It's been days. I assumed I'd refused."

"She took her time getting back with me," Thorne admits.

Anger flares in my chest. "You, asshole, did you pressure her?"

"No, jackass. I left her my card in case she changed her mind. The pretty little book mouse called me this morning asking for her cheese."

The implications of the bet slam into me. And not just for Rosalia. "The distillery is more than a business," I tell him. "It's our family legacy, and I've poured my heart into making it better. I won't let you dismantle everything I've built or treat our employees like nothing more than numbers on a spreadsheet." And he would undo all the progress and prioritize profits over the well-being of the employees. Why hadn't I considered my employees? Yes, Rosalia's bookstore is important, but so are the jobs of those who work for me. Thorne can't win.

My brother snorts. "You should have thought about that before agreeing to the bet."

"This bet, it's a mistake. For the distillery and Rosalia."

"Get over yourself." His voice takes on that patronizing smoothness he's honed through countless negotiations. We're giving her the opportunity to keep her little store, which she wouldn't have without us."

"It's because of us that she's in this situation."

"Regardless," he says with an air of indifference. "She agreed, and I'm halfway to winning. Start packing."

"Fuck you, Thorne."

His condescending laughter filters through the phone. "Enjoy your dates with Rosalia." He hangs up, leaving me alone with my disgust and worry.

She has no idea about the real game being played. Rosalia thinks she's choosing between her integrity and her livelihood, but she's actually just a pawn.

"Sir?" Tom asks.

He's staring at me, probably wondering why I'm sitting like a statue, not getting out of the car. I rub a hand roughly down my face. The guilt and anger have been driving me to distraction ever since I learned Rosalia had accepted my brother's deal. I can't decide if I'm disgusted with myself or disappointed in her.

"Lost in my head. I'm going," I tell him, opening my door.

Getting out of the car, I straighten my suit jacket. I push open the door to Novel Idea. The bell overhead chimes softly, but it might as well be a fork scraping on glass.

The bookstore is nearly empty now, the day winding to a close. As if pulled by a magnet, my gaze lands on Rosalia at the counter. Her hair is slightly disheveled from a long day's work, a strand falling across her cheek as she chats with an elderly woman. A tangle of emotions tightens around me: desire, longing, anger, and shame.

"Same time next week for the book club, Mrs. Abernathy?" Rosalia asks, smiling as she hands over a receipt.

"Wouldn't miss it, dear," the woman replies, patting Rosalia's hand. "You take care now."

Mrs. Abernathy shuffles toward the exit, passing a table filled with kids around twelve or thirteen years old packing up their bookbags. I overhear them discussing an upcoming science fair. A boy drops a book with a robot on the cover in front of a girl. The picture pulls me even farther into the past, to a conversation I'd had with my father when I was around the same age as those kids. I'd come home from school excited about a new friend I'd made in science class.

"Dad, I invited Lennox over to work on our robotics project together tomorrow," I'd told him excitedly.

"What's the boy's last name?" he'd asked.

"Hayes."

Dad pushed the paper he'd been looking at aside, giving me his full attention. "His Pa works at the distillery."

My bony shoulders had hunched in a shrug. "So?" I hadn't understood why that mattered or why my father's expression was so stern.

He pointed to the chair across from his massive desk. "Sit down. It's time we had a talk."

I'd obeyed, even though I'd had the urge to run and cover my ears.

"You need to be careful about who you let into your life." He pinned me with his cold and authoritative stare. "People will always want something from you, whether it's money, status, or connections. They'll pretend to be your friend, but in the end, they're using you for their gain."

"Lennox isn't like that," I'd protested. "He's a good guy."

My father's laugh was a harsh, humorless sound. "That's what they all say. But trust me, son, everyone has an angle. The sooner you learn that, the better off you'll be. In this world, you can only rely on yourself and maybe your family. Everyone else is just looking for a way to exploit you."

I'd ignored the advice, thrilled to find a kindred spirit, someone who'd shared my love of science. We'd spent countless hours together, talking about our dreams and aspirations. But as time went on, Lennox began to ask more and more questions about my family, my vacations, and the perks of being a Blackstone.

At first, I'd been flattered by his interest, eager to share my world with my friend. But as time passed and we entered high school, Lennox started asking for favors—small ones at first, to borrow money he never paid back, or an invitation to exclusive Blackstone events and parties. I was happy to oblige, believing that's what friends do for each other.

It wasn't until I overheard Lennox talking to another classmate that the truth sucker-punched me. Lennox was bragging about how he'd befriended the "Blackstone jerk" for the perks.

I shake my head, pulling myself from the painful memory. Rosalia is arranging bookmarks while chatting with a blonde woman. The soft lighting catches in her hair, giving it an amber glow. Despite everything, my pulse quickens.

Anger surfaces, although I'm not sure if it's aimed at her or Thorne. I'd been looking forward to this coffee date, but his phone call and her agreement tarnish it. The betrayal stings.

Guilt follows quickly. Am I any better? I'd agreed to the bet first, treating her livelihood like a poker chip. I press my fist against the knot in my chest.

She's wiping down the counter and laughing at something the blonde woman said. I think her name is Paige, and she owns the bakery a few doors down. And is Rosalia's closest friend. She turns in my direction. Her eyes widen, and she pales before glancing away, no doubt remembering our coffee plans made days ago before this bet complicated everything. Did she think I wouldn't show? She doesn't know about my brother's asinine bet, so maybe it's the guilt of agreeing to her deal with him.

Rosalia straightens her shoulders and gives me a smile that doesn't reach her eyes. "Hi, Sebastian. I'll be ready for our coffee date as soon as I close up."

There's something in her tone I can't quite place. Resignation? Determination? Whatever game we're playing, she's decided to face it head-on.

So will I. "No rush," I reply, aiming for casual but landing somewhere near stiff.

Paige slides off her stool. "Text me when you get home." She gathers her purse from behind the counter and gives me another once-over as she passes.

Rosalia turns to the group of kids at the table. "I'm sorry, but the shop's closing in ten minutes. Do you need help finding anything before you go?"

A girl with thick glasses looks up. "We're good, Ms. Rosalia. Thank you for letting us work on our science fair planning here."

"Anytime. Your project is on renewable energy, right?" Rosalia asks.

A boy nods enthusiastically, shoving a book into his already stuffed backpack. "We're going to build a working solar panel!"

"Sounds impressive," Rosalia smiles.

"Thank you," chant several voices on their way to the exit.

The easy way she connects with the teenagers doesn't feel calculated. But then again, Tiffany had been good with kids too, when it served her purposes. I want to believe this is different, but wanting something doesn't make it true.

I stand awkwardly by a new releases display, pretending to examine a hardcover while she moves through her closing ritual. She counts the register, powers down the computer, and adjusts displays that don't need adjusting.

"It'll just be a few more minutes," she says, not quite meeting my eyes as she flips through a ledger, making final notations.

"Take your time," I reply, studying her methodical movements. Is she dragging this out to avoid being alone with me? Or just being thorough?

Finally, she locks the cash drawer, grabs her purse from beneath the counter, and approaches the door. She flips the sign to "CLOSED" and turns the deadbolt with a decisive click.

"Ready for coffee?" she asks, still not quite looking at me directly.

Time to place our bets and play our games.

ChapterEight

Sebastian

The silence between us stretches like a taut wire as we walk to the coffee shop. I'm certain Thorne manipulated the situation at least a little to get Rosalia to accept his twisted deal. My rational mind understands this, but my bruised ego doesn't care about logic or my brother's machinations. Despite everything, I'm still hurt that she agreed to use me as her pawn, and in turn making her mine.

Sure, we weren't close, but we got along well. And I'm not imagining the attraction between us. Yet, she has no problem using me to save on interest for a bank loan. It feels like another confirmation that my people skills end precisely where the boardroom door begins—another personal misread to add to my impressive collection.

Steam fogs the coffeehouse windows as we approach, reflecting my own clouded thoughts. I hold the door for Rosalia, and the rich aroma of roasted coffee beans and freshly baked pastries wafts out. The cozy chatter inside creates a lively backdrop, a jarring counterpoint to the cold silence between us.

After she enters, two women exit while I'm still holding the door. One of them glances at me and then stops. I don't recognize her. But she clearly knows who I am. She elbows her friend and mouths, "Blackstone." They wheel around and go back inside.

I let out a low groan as the weight of unwanted attention settles upon me like a suffocating blanket. That damn "Most Eligible Bachelor" article that ran a month after my divorce still haunts me. Giving the woman my back, I ask Rosalia, "What do you want to drink?"

"I'll get my coffee," she tells me.

"How about I get it, and you find us a table?" I suggest.

"But—" She hesitates, then gives me a small smile. "That's sweet of you, thanks."

There's the performance Thorne's paying for. At least she's good at it.

A flash goes off, and we turn in that direction. The woman who recognized me is sliding her phone into a coat pocket, looking resolutely in the opposite direction.

"Was she taking a photo of you?" Rosalia glances at the amateur paparazzi, then back at me. She bites her lip. Her tongue darts out, wetting the indentations. I can't help but track the movement.

Forcing myself to look away, I say, "Probably. Let's sit where she is not sitting." I point to an empty table on the other side of the coffeehouse. "Want to grab that one?"

Rosalia nods and tells me her drink order before making her way to our spot. I take in her straight spine. Then glance to her ass, pausing way too long there. Giving myself a mental push, I turn to the counter and give the barista our order.

After a brief wait, our drinks are ready, and I navigate around packed tabletops and cords snaking from outlets to laptops. Rosalia has removed her red cardigan. The matching tank top is lacy and fitted, reminding me of lingerie. I picture her in matching panties, sprawled on my dark green sheets like a Christmas gift.

I squeeze my eyes shut briefly, confronting the maddening truth that my attraction to her persists despite everything. If anything, seeing her fight for her business makes her more appealing. That's just fucking fantastic. I'm supposed to be protecting myself, not finding more reasons to admire her.

"Here." I plunk her chocolate dessert masquerading as a coffee on the table, then sit with my arms crossed.

She accepts the drink but doesn't meet my eyes, her fingers fidgeting with the handle. "You could have gotten these to go."

I glance toward the photographer, but she's gone. "Um, why?"

Rosalia waves a hand at me. "You seem unhappy. Annoyed."

More like conflicted. Part of me understands why she'd agreed to my brother's deal, but another part still feels the sting of being used. Either way, I can't let these feelings complicate things further.

Alienating her won't help either of us. I need her to choose me over Thorne's deal.

"My apologies," I say. "It has been a rough day."

"What happened?" Rosalia asks. She blows on her mocha latte and takes a careful sip, her lips parting slightly as the liquid meets her mouth.

I'm captivated by the simple act, and a warmth that has nothing to do with coffee spreads through me. To dispel it, I take a much too big drink and let the burn cool my heat for her. I *need* to remember that she accepted Thorne's terms a few days after he offered, which tells me she didn't even try to negotiate or find another way. The sting of betrayal sharpens, cutting through my conflicted feelings. If she's willing to use me, maybe it's time I stopped playing the gentleman.

I'll try a move from my dad's book: fear. Make her second-guess stealing from me. It's shitty, but in the end she'll keep her store and I'll get rid of my brother.

What I need is a story. Something that will make her think twice about crossing me without being too obvious about it. I glance outside and see a pear-shaped, balding man shuffling past the window, thick glasses sliding down his nose, mumbling to himself as he adjusts his crooked tie.

He disappears from view, and an idea pops into my head. I arrange my face into a stern expression. "I found out this morning that my receptionist was stealing office supplies. I had to fire him. And press charges."

She draws back. "For stealing paperclips?"

"Pens and notepads, too," I add as if that makes the action reasonable.

Rosalia holds my gaze like she's trying to read between the lines. "I see," she says slowly, sipping her latte.

I swear a small smile is hiding behind her cup. She knows I'm full of shit. I blow on my coffee to hide mine.

She sets her mug down and asks, "R-red s-staplers as well?" Her impression of Milton from *Office Space* is spot on, and genuine laughter escapes me.

"I let him keep the Swingline. I didn't want him to burn down the distillery."

"Smart." She sucks in her lips, but laughter breaks free. The sound is beautiful, like sweet tea on a hot day.

I should be calculating my next move, but all I want is to hear that sound again. So much for intimidation.

"Did your sister like the books you picked out for her?" She asks, settling back in her chair, seeming more relaxed.

"Yes. They arrived the day before she left for Thailand. She loved your beach read recommendation. She's trying to get me to read it."

"You should. It's a fantastic story."

"I'd love to, but it's too easy to lose track of time when I'm thoroughly engaged. And this time of the year is incredibly busy at the distillery."

I can't help it. My gaze takes in her lacy tank top, travels to her neck, to her cupid's bow lips, and then rests on her eyes, which are focused on my mouth.

Our knees accidentally brush under the table, and I catch Rosalia's quick intake of breath. A thrill zings through me. Maybe she isn't immune to me either.

I grin and that breaks the spell. She leans back as if needing space and focuses on her mug. After a beat, she pivots. "I have big hopes for Novel Idea," she says slowly as if choosing her words carefully. "I don't want it to be just a one-off thing. I want it to be the start of something bigger, something that can make a real difference."

My stomach drops and I struggle to read between the lines. I'm unsure if there's hidden significance in what she's saying. Is she revealing why she's agreed to help Thorne, or is this merely small talk?

"One store can touch a community, but imagine what a network of them could do," Rosalia continues, her eyes taking on a distant, dreamy quality. "Spreading the joy of reading, providing access to books in underserved areas, creating a chain reaction of literacy and empowerment... that's the dream."

She shakes her head, a soft laugh escaping her lips. "I know it sounds a bit grand and idealistic. But I can't help but think about the potential, you know?"

Her vision unexpectedly moves me. Rosalia's aspirations are a refreshing change in a society driven by profit. "The world could use more people who think big and want to make a positive impact," I say, but as the words leave my mouth, the bitter taste of suspicion coats my tongue. Is she this altruistic, or has she crafted this persona to manipulate me? I study her face, searching for any hint of deception behind those earnest eyes.

"Thanks. It's a long way off, but it's something to work toward." She shrugs. "For now, I'm just focused on making Novel Idea the best it can be."

I take another sip of my coffee, trying to quell the conflict inside me, but the tug-of-war between distrust and my growing respect for the woman before me only intensifies. She seems genuine, her passion shining through with every word. But I've been burned before. I've seen how easily people wear masks to get what they want. And the fact remains: she's agreed to help Thorne. Maybe everything she said is true, and she's simply paving her path by using me.

I can't afford to lower my guard, to be influenced by a pretty face and a captivating story. So much is at stake, from my business to my reputation and my future, along with nearly everyone who works for me.

She switches topics back to Lillianna, asking about her time in Thailand. The conversation is a safer topic, and we chat easily until our mugs are both empty. I check my watch and am surprised that nearly an hour has passed. I have to stop by the Louisville office before returning to Bardstown, but I'm reluctant to leave. I'm an idiot.

"I need to head out, but are you free this Saturday evening?" I ask, annoyed that I'm invested in her answer.

She stands, reaching for her cardigan and covering her gorgeous body. "My store's open until six."

"Would you like to go out to dinner after?"

"Sure," she says, her smile not quite reaching her eyes this time. Her fingers fidget with her purse strap, and she glances away as if nervous. Or maybe having second thoughts about Thorne's deal?

A man can hope.

As we walked to the exit, I ask, "Anywhere you'd like to go?"

Her lashes flutter as if surprised I asked her opinion. "I've wanted to try Fantastic Fusion but haven't had a chance, " she says.

As we leave the coffee shop our shoulders brush. Neither of us is quick to pull away or create space. "I'll make a seven-thirty reservation. Is that time good for you?"

She nods.

"If you give me your address, I'll pick you up at seven-fifteen," I say.

Rosalia shakes her head and her hair brushes my arm. I catch traces of vanilla and flowers. The two are an intoxicating mix of innocence and desire. Why does she have to smell amazing too?

"Sebastian?" She stares at me like this isn't the first time she's said my name.

"Sorry, what?"

She nods and leans in, presumably thinking I hadn't heard her over the traffic. I search for imperfections. There is a small scar above her left eye. A tiny speck of latte sits on her upper lip. But both make her more adorable. "I said, it isn't the kind of place that needs reservations. It's casual. And I'll meet you there."

My gaze locks with hers and, for a moment, I see a flicker, a hint of the same longing and uncertainty that churns in me. But then she blinks, and it's gone, replaced with that polite smile that doesn't reach her eyes.

"See you Saturday," she says, her voice carefully neutral.

"Perfect," I mutter. What would be perfect is pressing my lips against hers.

No. That is a terrible idea. Thorne's bet told me all I needed to know about Rosalia. I might be attracted to her, and still don't want her to lose her bookstore, but I have to win this twisted wager.

Tom must have spotted us leaving the coffeehouse because my Bentley glides to the curb next to Novel Idea. Offering Rosalia a stiff nod, I say, "See you Saturday." Getting into the vehicle, I refuse to look at her as the car slides into traffic.

I have four days until our date—four days to get my head in the game. This is my brother's game, his test. But as the city lights blur past the window, I can't shake the feeling that none of us understand what we're really playing.

Chapter Nine

Rosalia

I spin in a slow circle in front of the full-length mirror in my shoebox bedroom, sighing. I must say, I do look cute in my powder-pink linen-blend slacks and a sleeveless blouse adorned with tiny grey sparrows. It is my favorite spring outfit. Too bad the circumstances aren't different. If Thorne wasn't holding my store hostage, I might actually be excited about my evening with Sebastian instead of second-guessing everything.

He had been odd, almost angry when he'd asked me to have coffee with him, but then we fell into our usual easy banter. Still, something is different. Is there a chance he knows about my deal with his brother? If so, why hasn't he said anything?

Checking the time tears me from my contemplations. I have to get moving, or I'll be late. After putting on my tennis shoes, I toss my gray ballet flats in a plastic bag. Then, I throw it and a sweater into my oversized purse. The days have been warm, but the nights still have a bite. Not that I'll be out after dark. Dinner shouldn't take more than an hour and a half.

I step onto the metal landing of my apartment's stairs and lock my door. Reaching the bottom, I go to the delivery door of Novel Idea. My trusty bike is locked to a pipe protruding from the brick wall. Owning a car isn't in my budget, and given the much milder weather here than in Michigan, the sacrifice isn't huge.

As I maneuver my pretty purple bike down the alley, a familiar voice calls my name. Paige is sitting three doors down on a crate outside the back door of her bakery.

I wave, walking over with my bike and asking, "How's the new, huge order going for that wedding?"

"It's going to make my bottom line look pretty, but the Groom-zilla can't decide on a flavor. They were here today to taste the sample cakes. The bride loved all of them. The groom wasn't," Paige makes air quotes, "'blown away.' He's searching for that 'wow factor.' I just wish he'd stop talking in clichés and pick a damn flavor."

Stopping next to Paige, I balance the bike's frame against my body. "That sounds frustrating."

"Yeah, this part, with customers who are hard to please, is tough, but in the end, when it all comes together, and they're happy, it makes everything sweet as sugar." She stands and nods her chin toward my bike. "Where are you heading off to? You're usually cuddling on your couch with your book-boyfriend at this hour."

"I'm meeting Sebastian for dinner." My hand hovers over the bike's bell, and I give it a lackluster flick. The little ding it makes is as pitiful as my mood.

"Wow." Paige laughs. "Your enthusiasm is off the charts. Sorry, but you're not getting much pity from me. You're having dinner with the hot billionaire."

I shrug. "That I really like, but can't actually like because of his brother's damn deal. Plus, he has to know his company isn't renewing my lease, right?"

"Maybe. The Blackstone empire is massive." Paige grins. "But just in case, get the most expensive thing on the menu."

"No way." I shake my head with enough vigor that my hair swings. "I'll pay for my food. I don't want his money."

"Please don't shoot the messenger, but you're halfway to accepting Thorne's bribe to keep your store. That's kind of taking Blackstone money."

The truth of my friend's words sting, but I can't deny the reality of my situation. "Then I don't need to be a bigger asshole and have him spending money on me as well."

"But what if it's like you suspect and Sebastian's playing some angle?"

"Then at least we'd both be playing the same game. I want to save my store and outreach programs—nothing more, nothing less." I sigh, then mutter, "Although a big part of me hopes we're right. That he does know and is playing some angle."

"Why?"

"I'd feel less gross about accepting the deal. What if I can't find another store or can't get another loan for the startup cost of a new location?" I stare at the spokes of my front tire, defeat seeping into me. "I've called damn near every bank in Kentucky, even the shady ones. Half don't bother to call me back and those that do are only to tell me no."

Paige's brows push together. "That's odd."

"Yeah, a paranoid part of me wonders if that is Thorne's doing, but more than likely it's because I took out a big loan for the startup cost of Novel Idea and still owe a lot." A gust of wind pushes against my back, and a paper bag skitters down the alley, its crinkled form dancing a lonely ballet across the uneven pavement. I shiver, feeling as empty and discarded as the piece of litter. "I contacted Legal Aid. They turned me down."

"Shit. How come?"

"I didn't meet the income requirements. But I've made an appointment with the Small Business Administration." I straighten my shoulders and infuse my voice with positivity, hoping it'll manifest the results I need. "The soonest they could fit me in is two weeks from now."

"Have you looked into grants?"

"I've started. A few are promising."

"Okay. Keep reading and researching, but also enjoy your time with the billionaire. Let him buy you expensive food and drinks. Get some top-shelf wine and let me know if it actually is better than my cheap box stuff." I snort. Paige squeezes my hand. "Just remember, don't fall for him. Don't trust him."

"I'm the one who shouldn't be trusted."

Paige shakes her head. "Don't think that way. Remember, your livelihood and the programs you've set up wouldn't be hanging in the balance if the Blackstones had kept their word.

That's true. "And for what? So Thorne can prove a point, win some power play? Rich people are warped."

"Not all of them. My uncle and his wife are loaded and one of the kindest couples you'll ever meet," she says.

"Wowwww. One couple."

She knocks my shoulders gently, laughing. "I'm sure there's more. They just don't hang out with me."

"That proves my point," I say. "They're an exclusive club that doesn't let people like us in."

Paige lifts a brow. "You're in."

"No. I'm a toy to amuse at least one of them. I really don't think Sebastian knows any part of this."

Paige taps the handlebars of my bike. "He couldn't bother to pick you up? Hell, even if he's busy, I'm sure he has a driver or three.

"He had offered, but I refused." I point to my apartment above the bookstore. "And I'd rather he didn't know where I live."

"Blackstone owns the building; don't you think he knows?"

"He asked for my address so he could pick me up for this date," I point out. Though it could be manipulation, a small part of me whispers that maybe he doesn't know about my lease issues—that he actually likes me. I'm not sure which is worse.

"Do you want to borrow my car?" Paige asks. "You could drop me off at home on the way to the restaurant."

A tightness grips my throat. "You are the best, kindest friend in the whole world. And thanks, but I'll pass. The exercise and fresh air will do me good. They'll help me think of questions to ask him. I'm going to figure out what's really going on. Maybe I can tell if he knows anything, or if this is real to him."

"Have you considered that he asked you out because you're hot, and all this is a coincidence?"

I snort and roll my eyes. "Yes, hot, successful billionaires are lining up to date the plain bookworm."

"You aren't plain."

"You have to say that. You're my friend." I hop on my bike and wave bye before she can argue.

Twenty minutes later, I'm pedaling along one of those quaint streets with flower baskets hanging from lampposts and art galleries tucked between restaurants. The blue and gray sign of Fantastic Fusion is only a few shops down.

Good, I'll be a few minutes early. A deafening horn blares behind me, the sound ricocheting off the surrounding buildings. My heart leaps into my throat. I glance over my shoulder. My pulse explodes. A massive, gleaming SUV is barreling toward me, its engine roaring like an enraged beast.

Before I can swerve out of the way, the SUV swings around me, so close that the heat of the metal grazes my skin. Then its back bumper clips my front tire. The impact jolts me, wrenching my handlebars from my grip. My stomach drops, followed by my body. This is going to hurt.

Gravel bites into my arm. My ribs slam down. The sharp scent of hot pavement fills my nose as my bag bursts, spilling everything. A lipstick tube bounces off my knee. Quarters dance and ping around me before rolling into silence.

My chest heaves, and my heart pounds against my ribs like a caged mouse desperate for escape. Slowly, I push into a sitting position, wincing. I glance at my arm. There's road rash but, thankfully, neither my shirt nor slacks are torn. Talk about lucky.

The SUV squeals to a stop in an open spot near the bike rack, its tires scraping against the curb. The driver's door opens, and a tall, lanky man emerges, his linen slacks and polo shirt rustling in the breeze.

He cast a dismissive glance at me, his lips curling into a sneer. "The road's for cars, not bikes," he drawls.

My blood boils. I push myself from the ground on trembling legs. "I was in the designated bike path, you ignorant jerk," I shout.

He flips me off, heading for the restaurant where I'm supposed to meet Sebastian. The rude driver reaches for the door, but Sebastian pushes through. He looks like a violent storm ready to destroy everything in his path.

ChapterTen

Sebastian

My pulse pounds and my hands curl into fists. I stare down the lanky man who almost ran over Rosalia. "What the fuck is wrong with you?" I don't shout, but my quiet fury reverberates through me, hitting him like a fist. He pales.

The guy swallows, his oversized Adam's apple bobbing in his thin throat. "Mr. Blackstone. You know her? I'm sorry."

Oh, now she's important. This guy's an asshole. I lean into his personal space. "Don't tell me. Tell her."

He turns in Rosalia's general direction and snivels, "I'm sorry, miss."

She nods, picking up a gray shoe from the sidewalk. After the jerk scurries inside the restaurant, my attention snaps back to her. She looks relatively unharmed but shaken, collecting her belongings and sitting on a nearby bench. I sit beside her. "Are you hurt?"

"I'm fine," she says, but her hands shake as she changes from her tennis shoes to the flats. The need to do something roars in me. I kneel beside her, gently holding her shoe steady. She slips her foot in and her eyes meet mine briefly.

There's no Hollywood moment, no time stopping, but the opposite. Everything accelerates: my thoughts, my heartbeat, the city noise around us. I take in the asymmetry of her pupils in the sunlight, a distinctive feature I want to catalog alongside all the other things that make her beautiful. She looks away first, not with embarrassment but with wariness.

My mood is different from ten minutes ago when I was sitting at the table, lost in thought. I'd been holding onto reasons to keep my distance from her. All week I'd been cultivating them like thorny barriers, and they'd kept me company until Rosalia came pedaling up on a damn bike.

What adult still rode a bicycle? Sure, in the gym, with a trainer, but not on the street where dickheads could run her over and make me forget I'm not supposed to feel anything for her.

"Ready?" I stand, offering my hand.

She takes it and a spark of electricity passes between us when her soft fingers intertwine with mine, sending a wave of warmth up my arm. Her wide gaze flashes to mine. A faint blush colors her cheeks. Then she lets go of me and steps toward the restaurant.

I follow, reminding myself why I'm here. Not for a pleasant evening, but to win Thorne's bet. I need to charm her into choosing me over my brother's deal, without letting her charm *me* into forgetting what she's really here for. It's a fine line to walk.

Holding open the door for her, I glance around the restaurant. It's the typical Kentucky décor of plush leather booths and walls painted in earthy tones of greens and creams. I steer us past a section of old bourbon barrels converted into standing tables to the dining area. All the while ignoring the people watching us. A few whisper discreetly, others not so much.

Rosalia side-eyes a nearby group who is staring at us. "How do you stand it?"

I lean in and breathe through my mouth so her inviting scent doesn't distract me. "They'll soon forget we're here. Once the novelty wears off," I tell her quietly.

"But why is the two of us going to dinner gossip worthy?" She's walking ahead of me, and I take in her tense shoulders. The way she's holding herself like she's bracing for another impact. "Is it my spectacular arrival when my bike fought—and lost—to an SUV?" she jokes, but her laugh comes out shaky.

I search for the careless SUV asshole but can't spot him. Reaching our table, I pull out her chair. "Are you sure you're okay?"

"The scare was worse than the hit." Sitting, she arranges her silverware and then fiddles with the menu. "Sorry if my embarrassing spill caused you unwanted attention."

The urge to reach for and comfort her is strong, but my brain screams to keep my distance. The tug-of-war is a damn nuisance.

I won't touch her, but I can't resist alleviating some of her discomfort. "Don't worry about it. It's usually like this when I go out."

Her lips twitch. "Jerk drivers follow in your wake? You could have warned me. I'd have worn body armor."

I grin at her quick wit. "Unfortunately, asshole drivers are everywhere. I meant the attention in public."

"Ah, like your lady fans at the coffeehouse."

I scratch the back of my neck. The attention is embarrassing as hell. "Yes, like that. And it has gotten worse since my divorce." Why, I can't understand. I'm a businessman for shits-sake, not some movie star.

"That was a year ago, right?"

"Almost two." I shift my attention to the menu and hopefully away from the topic of Tiffany. "What looks good to you?" I ask.

"Were you heartbroken?"

My gaze shoots to hers. Damn, that's direct. And nothing I want to talk about. "Um. That's complicated. She and I…" I'd craved a family and home, believing Tiffany was both. But neither is meant for me. "I'd rather not discuss my ex."

Her cheeks flush pink and she looks at her menu. "Oh, um, I'm so sorry. That was way too personal." A cute, nervous giggle escapes between her pretty lips. "I can't believe I asked that. And we haven't even had an appetizer."

I smile. "We should order one or two. What would you like?"

"I'll get the soup."

"As an appetizer?"

"No. My meal."

My brows furrow. "That's it?"

"That's it," she repeats. Our waiter arrives and she smiles at him. "Separate checks, please." The words come out fast and she looks down at her napkin.

Hell, no. I shake my head. "Together, please. We'll take a bottle each of your house white and red."

After he leaves to fill our drink order, Rosalia shifts in her seat. "I really should pay for my meal." She hesitates, then adds more quietly, "It's important to me."

She seems genuinely uncomfortable taking my money. A flicker of hope sparks in my chest. Maybe she won't go through with it.

"But I invited you to dinner, so it's my treat," I reply.

"Your company is payment enough," she says, but her smile is strained, like she's forcing the politeness. I suspect she'd rather dine with the man who'd almost run her over than me.

"I've already asked to put the checks together," I counter.

"I'll Venmo or Apple Pay you."

I nod, pretending I'm giving in. "If you wish. But, if I'm getting myself an appetizer or two, will you share them with me?"

She tilts her head, tucking in a corner of her mouth. The expression is cute. "Okay," she concedes.

The waiter returns with the two wine bottles, opens and pours a glass of each, then waits. I ask Rosalia, "Red or white?"

"I was going to have water…"

"You don't drink?" I probably should have asked before ordering.

"I do, but had planned on skipping tonight."

"I won't push, but if I drink both the whispers around us will get louder. My PA, Hanna, told me one of the most recent rumors is that I don't go out because I'm passed out drunk by six every night. Which is odd, given that I usually work until well after dark." I tap my chin. "Maybe that's why the other current rumor is more popular."

There's a playful light in her eyes. "What's the other?"

"I'll tell you if you help me dispel rumors." I point to the two bottles.

She shakes her head, laughing, and tells the waiter, "I'll have white."

I nod, and after tasting the wine and giving our approval, I order every appetizer. After the waiter leaves, Rosalia tips her chin, the corners of her mouth tipping up. "All of them?"

I shrug, "I can't pick. You'll help, right?"

Her smile breaks free and knocks me in the chest. "I shouldn't." She pushes her wine glass toward me. "And I should give this back to you. Let the gossips call you a glutton *and* a drunk."

I laugh, idly wondering when I stopped seeing this dinner as a chore. I'm no longer pretending to enjoy myself. "Please don't," I groan. "There's already plenty of fuel for the gossip fire."

"Because you're a hermit," she teases.

"I'm not a hermit." I pause to reconsider, then tilt my head from side to side. "Well, maybe a little."

Shit, I've smiled more tonight than I have all year. I need to remember why I'm here. This is about winning the bet, not actually enjoying myself.

"Why don't you go out more?"

Why would I? My work is satisfying and doesn't let me down like family, friends, and love. I don't bother to share my morose outlook. "The distillery keeps me busy."

"I get it. I'm not running a world-famous distillery," she muses. "But my little bookstore and its programs take a lot from me. And what little bit of free time I have, I prefer to spend it relaxing alone with a book or with a close friend."

"Not a partier, huh?" I ask. It is refreshing to meet someone like me who needs solitary time to recharge.

"As you might have guessed from my overly personal questions, small talk isn't my strong suit," she says with a shy smile. Then it widens. "Which reminds me, you said there were two popular rumors, what's the other?"

I laugh again. "That my ex left me when she discovered me in bed. With a man."

Her lips twitch. "So, which would be the bigger scandal, that you're killing your liver with wine instead of liquor, or that you prefer men?"

"Definitely the first. This is bourbon country after all." I lean in closer over our small intimate table for two. The scent of vanilla and wildflowers draws me in, and I lose my train of thought.

"And you're the owner of the largest bourbon distillery. Fine," she sighs, taking my hand. Her simple touch zings through me. "Good thing I saved your reputation by drinking with you."

My gaze is fixed on our hands. Mine is larger and has a deeper hue, contrasting with her paler one. After a few beats, she lets go.

"Anyway, I love chatting with my bookstore visitors and friends, but I prefer them over groups of acquaintances and such. And my absolute favorites are my fictional adventurers I meet in books," she says.

"I one hundred percent understand." A big part of my job requires socializing, and while I do it, the task is draining. I'd rather be at home, out with my horses, or reading a book. What other interests might we share? I quickly push the question away. Getting sidetracked and forgetting her deal with Thorne isn't smart, no matter how engaging she might be. "Did you grow up in Louisville?" I ask, returning to mundane questions.

"No, I'm from Michigan. Though I spent most of my childhood summers here. My dad's family lives outside of Lexington."

"The Great Lakes are beautiful. At least Superior and Michigan are; I haven't seen the others," I say, refilling her wine glass. I tell myself my interest in her personal life is just polite dinner conversation, and not because I find her alluring and want to know more about her.

"You've been?" she asks.

I nod. "I travel to Chicago often for work. Early morning runs along Lake Michigan are my favorite part of visiting. Well, that and the pizza."

"When were you at Lake Superior?" she asks.

"A while back, between my sophomore and junior years of high school, Thorne decided to get his pilot's license, so we flew to Marquette for a weekend at the end of summer." The reminder of the good times cut through me like a jagged blade, leaving behind a wound that refuses to heal. I sip on my drink, letting it wash away the bitter taste of unresolved pain. "We rented motorcycles and rode them to Pictured Rocks. Have you been there?"

Pushing away her wine, she shakes her head, "No. I'm from the Detroit area. The farthest up north I've made it is Traverse City."

Her eyes have turned distant and her shoulders are suddenly rigid. Shit, she's withdrawing. Was it the mention of Thorne, the reminder of her deal with him? Am I seeing the first cracks in her certainty? A small ember of hope warms my chest. Maybe she's reconsidering.

Afraid pushing the topic might backfire, I switch subjects. "Where do you see yourself in five years?"

She outlines her plans for expanding the bookstore and creating a larger community outreach program—here and, possibly, in Michigan. I love the way her eyes sparkle with ambition. "I started a reading mentor program pairing adults with children, but that's only the beginning," she explains. "I want books to transform lives, to reach people who've never had regular access to literature before."

Her hands animate her words, drawing invisible shapes in the air between us. A flush colors her cheeks as she speaks, and I can't help but lean closer, drawn in by the genuine passion in her voice. Her passion for her literacy programs seems genuine, but I've been fooled by passionate speeches before. Still, the way her eyes light up when she talks about the kids is hard to fake.

She pauses to take a sip of wine, and I notice a small dimple appear and disappear at the corner of her mouth. It's another detail to add to my growing collection.

I find myself asking question after question until our food arrives, gradually relaxing as we talk. Every time Rosalia laughs, her expression lights up with genuine amusement. It's a dangerous pull that grabs me. I can almost see more evenings like this, learning the map of her expressions, discovering what else we might share. But I rein in the thought before it can fully form. It's too soon, too complicated by Thorne's interference and the web of secrets between us. Still, the glimpse of possibility lingers, unwanted but undeniable.

A brief and comfortable silence falls between us and, despite my better judgment, I find myself studying her, cataloging more details. My gaze traces the graceful line of her collarbone visible above her neckline, the way the restaurant's soft lighting casts shadows that accentuate her features. Looking away before she notices, I remind myself why we're here. I can't help resenting Thorne for his interference. His poisonous meddling killed any chance for something real to grow between us.

I draw a deep breath and focus on the nearly empty plate before me, pushing away thoughts of what-ifs and maybes. The waiter takes our empty dishes at the same time Rosalia's phone dings from its resting spot on the table. She glances at it. Her fingers curl momentarily before she loosens her grip and tucks the device away.

"Everything okay?" I ask, though the way she won't meet my eyes gives me the answer.

"Yes. I was checking the time." She finally looks at me, but the openness from moments ago is replaced with something more guarded. "I enjoyed dinner." Her tone is formal, distant.

We're suddenly strangers again. Our brief camaraderie has evaporated like the angel's share from my aging whiskey barrels, gone without a trace, claimed by whatever was on that phone.

"It wasn't what I expected," I admit. The truth, at least partially.

Her eyes find mine in the dim lighting, searching. "What did you expect, Sebastian?"

I could lie, deflect, or try to charm my way past the question. Instead, I say, "I'm still figuring that out."

She nods, then says quietly, "I should probably get going soon. Early day at the bookstore tomorrow. And riding home in the dark will take a little longer."

I should ask for the bill. For a few hours, I'd almost forgotten the web of bets and lies between us. But the reminder doesn't stop me from asking, "Any interest in dessert?"

Her gaze darts toward the sweets display before she shakes her head. "I shouldn't..."

"I've heard you haven't lived until you've tried their chocolate bourbon bread pudding."

Delight flickers across her face. "I never say no to chocolate."

I should have known. She'd ordered the sweetest drink on the menu at the coffeehouse. I wave over the waiter.

Tonight I met the woman who lights up when talking about kids discovering books, who gets flustered over separate checks, and rides a bike through downtown traffic. But my brother's offer is still there, settling in my chest like the char at the bottom of a barrel—dark and impossible to ignore.

The question gnawing at me is whether she'll choose the easy money or find another way.

And whether I'm fool enough to hope it matters.

ChapterEleven

Rosalia

I swirl my nearly empty glass and study the ruby liquid, pretending to read the dessert menu. Our dinner conversation had flowed as smoothly as the wine Sebastian ordered, except now my attention keeps drifting to my phone, turned face down. The screen is no longer visible, but the email notification from the Blackstone lawyer is in my mind's eye. The subject line is "Regarding Your Lease Termination." Guilt and desperation eat at my full stomach, souring our shared wonderful meal.

Given our sudden tension, I'm surprised that Sebastian didn't ask for the bill. Instead, he ordered us an amazing dessert sampler. "Try the chocolate one." He points to a decadent-looking truffle cake at the edge of the plate.

And while I might be upset, chocolate is not something I'm going to pass up. I take a small bite, and the rich ganache momentarily pushes away my worries. "Oh my god," I murmur, forgetting my situation. "That's incredible."

"I looked up this place. The pastry chef was trained in Paris," he says, his smile returning. "I thought you might like it."

He remembers my sweet tooth from our coffee date. My heart does a little skip. I take another sip of wine, letting it relax the knot between my shoulders and push away thoughts of Thorne, leases, and the precarious position of my bookstore.

"I'm sorry," I say, not entirely sure what I'm apologizing for—my distraction, the secrets between us, or the fact that I'm enjoying his company far more than I should. "Which one are you going to try?"

"All of them." He grins and his playfulness dissolves the rest of my tension.

"Whew," I laugh. "I was hoping you'd say that so I could too."

"I still can't believe you love hiking and horseback riding," I muse, then pause, trying the carrot cake.

"Why?" he asks.

I can't picture him, the high-profile billionaire, doing something as simple as walking in nature for relaxation and fun. I giggle at my mental image. "Do you hike and ride in a three-piece suit?"

He laughs, straightening his already straight tie. "Of course. How else would one hike?" he jokes, exuding charm and irresistible allure.

He's handsome, but under the formal business tycoon is a cute man, which is dangerous. I like this side of him way too much.

He holds up the nearly empty bottle of white wine. "Would you like more?"

"No. No. I've had more than enough." I've had at least three glasses. The crisp wine had gone down way too smoothly. My bike ride home is going to be interesting. Glancing outside, my heart sinks at the last bit of light bleeding from the sky. Have we been chatting for over two hours? "I should have water. My return trip will take a little longer because of the dark."

Sebastian raises his hand and seconds later the waiter is next to our table. After giving his credit card, he says, "Let me give you a ride home."

I'm tempted, and convince myself that all the wine is why I'm at ease with him. "What about my bike?"

"I'll come back and get it after dropping you off."

I almost agree, but hold back. Mainly because of how much I want to spend more time with him. Keeping him at arm's length is a must, at least until I find a new store location without Thorne's help.

"Thanks, but I'll manage. The night ride will be lovely." Unless I break my neck navigating in the dark while a little drunk. That thought has my heart racing like a frightened rabbit.

Sebastian's sexy mouth presses into a thin line like he wants to argue. Instead he nods. "I'll walk you to your bike."

He stands and offers me his arm and I slide mine through his. My body tingles where we touch. He is solid, and his cologne is amazing, primal, and sophisticated. Stepping outside, he halts so abruptly that I stumble.

His grip tightens, and I steady myself. "What's wrong?" I ask.

He points and my good mood deflates like the front tire of my bike. Hell, even a few spokes are dangling from the slightly bent rim. Great, another bill.

What if the nearest bike repair shop isn't close to my apartment? Or the cost of repairs is too much. Tears burn my eyes and I wobble slightly when I walk to the rack to inspect the damage. I need my bike.

"Let me give you a ride home," Sebastian says.

"My bike..." It's hard to speak through the sudden thickness in my throat. "Sorry, I'm being ridiculous. The wine's affecting my emotions." There is no way I can share with a billionaire whose driver is idling at the curb in a freaking Bentley that my bicycle is my only transportation.

"I'll come back and get it after dropping you off." He slips his hands into his slacks and searches my eyes. "Do you want me to wait here while my driver drops you off?"

I raise my brows. "Um, why?"

"You seem hesitant to accept a ride. If it's because you're uncomfortable being alone in the car with me, I don't mind waiting here."

That's thoughtful. The urge to hug him is nearly impossible to resist. "No, I'm not," I tell him honestly.

I'm not afraid of him. My only fear is how he makes me feel.

Opening the door to the backseat, he motions for me to get inside. The supple cream seat hugs me and is cool against my bare arms. Sebastian's car smells like him—masculine and expensive.

He comes around and gets in on the other side. "Could you give Tom your home address?" he asks, motioning to the driver.

"It's the bookstore."

A single brow ticks, and he tilts his head. "Really?"

I nod, studying his surprised reaction. It seems genuine. He really doesn't know I live above the bookstore, which means he probably doesn't know about the lease situation either. Relief floods through me, followed immediately by a sharp twist of guilt.

If he truly is clueless about his brother's plans, then he has no idea Thorne is using me as a pawn against him. Another terrible thought creeps in: What if Sebastian actually deserves to lead Blackstone Bourbon, and I'm helping Thorne destroy someone who's done nothing wrong?

"I didn't realize there was an apartment in the store," he says, unaware of my internal breakdown. "I thought...well, it doesn't matter what I thought." He frowns, staring at his large hands resting on his knees.

Is he embarrassed for me? Or is this a reality check on how differently we live? Although something about his posture screams guilt. I shake my head. No, that can't be right. It's wishful thinking.

I cross my arms and accidentally bump a serious-looking control panel in the center console. The back of the driver's seat hums and shifts, revealing a laptop mounted to a polished wooden tray that matches the pristine interior. Sebastian presses a button and it returns to its hiding place. He hits another and the chrome rectangle between us in the middle of the back seat rises, revealing a built-in cooler. A cooler! He hands me water then twists a knob. A wide leather armrest slides over the NASA-looking control panel as if it had never been there.

Thank sweet baby Jesus, it's gone. I might accidentally hit another button and reveal the secret space where he hides all his little yellow Minions. I cover my mouth, but a giggle escapes.

"This is Gru's car," I wheeze. I'm a buzzed idiot. A man like Sebastian won't know the cartoon *Despicable Me*.

He snorts. "The impression I'm making is terrible. First, I remind you of Bill—"

"Who's Bill?" I ask, confused.

"The boss from Office Space." Sebastian holds an imaginary coffee cup and mimics Bill's famous line, "Yeah...that'd be great, um-kay."

"I can't believe you remember his name." I laugh. Oh my, he likes old comedies *and* is funny. The combination is my Achilles' heel.

I'm in trouble.

He chuckles. "Between him and Gru, it appears I'm the villain in your story."

My smile wilts a little. No, that's me—dating him under false pretenses. Why couldn't he be an arrogant billionaire? Lord knows there's enough of them.

"Are you okay?" he asks.

"Fine." I remind myself it's Sebastian Blackstone's company that has put Novel Idea at risk. Managing to bury some of my guilt, I tap my index finger against my lips. "Hmm, if you had a black and gray scarf, you could pass for a leaner, younger version of Gru."

His deep, melodious laughter fills the space between us, warming me in areas he absolutely should not. The car pulls in front of my store and a hollowness fills my chest. I don't want to be alone with my self-reproach.

Plus, now what? Do I kiss him goodbye? Offer my hand to shake? Wave?

"I'd love to see you again. Can I call you this week?" he asks as his driver opens my door.

"I'd like that." Using the last of my fading liquid courage, I lean forward, intending to kiss his cheek. But he turns at the same time and my lips land on the firm corner of his mouth, igniting a burst of fireworks through me. Heat rushes from the unexpected contact, and I'm certain a blush is racing up my cheeks. Without daring to meet his gaze, I scramble from the car, closing the door with a soft click.

Standing in the narrow alley, the tall buildings loom on either side. The sleek vehicle idles at the curb, its engine purring softly. I turn to the exterior staircase that leads to my apartment. The cool night air is a stark contrast to the warmth that had enveloped me moments ago.

As I approach the stairs, I glance over my shoulder, my gaze meeting Sebastian's through the car window. He nods, a silent acknowledgment I take to mean that he'll give me space but will wait until I'm safely inside before leaving. The simple gesture sends a flutter through my chest.

Grasping the cool handrail, I make my way to my apartment, the metal steps clanging softly beneath my ballet flats. Halfway up, I pause, turning to look at the alley below. The car's headlights cast a soft glow, illuminating the pavement and the base of the stairs.

I rummage through my bag, my fingers brushing against various objects—a pen, a tube of lipstick, a crumpled paper, the elusive keys playing a game of hide-and-seek amid the clutter. My hand bumps against something unexpected, and I pull out a small box I don't remember placing there. Holding it, I continue my search for my keys.

Finally locating them, I unlock my door and step inside, flipping on the lights. I drop my keys on the counter with a clatter that echoes in the quiet space. Only then do I examine the mysterious box. Opening it, I find a single chocolate truffle, identical to the one from dessert, wrapped in elegant paper with a note: "For your sweet tooth. —S"

Sebastian must have slipped it into my bag when I wasn't looking. The gift is thoughtful in a way that's both wonderful and terrible. I run my thumb over the elegant paper. The wine buzz fades, replaced by the uncomfortable clarity of what I'm really doing with him.

I place the chocolate on my nightstand, a sweet reminder of a night I shouldn't have enjoyed nearly as much as I did. There's something disarming about his attentiveness, not calculated but genuine, which only makes it worse.

Part of me wants to believe he's exactly as he seems: thoughtful, funny, surprisingly normal despite his wealth. That part savors the lingering taste of chocolate and wine, the memory of almost-kisses and shared laughter.

But the other half hopes it's all an act. If he's playing me too, then my deception stings less. If he's the corporate mess Thorne painted, then I'm not betraying someone good; I'm doing what's necessary to save my store.

I change for bed, glancing at the chocolate one more time. The truth is painfully simple: the more real the connection, the more I become the villain in this story.

Chapter Twelve

Rosalia

The sheets twist around my legs as I shift positions again, replaying every moment of tonight's dinner with Sebastian. And I swear I can smell the decadent chocolate wafting from the nightstand. The scent seems stronger now in the quiet of the night, becoming an invisible thread pulling at my memories.

I reach for the truffle, picking it up and running it under my nose. It's dark chocolate with hints of something deeper, more complex—like the man who gave it to me.

I place it back, unsure whether to savor it or throw it away. I lie back down and close my eyes. I will sleep to come, but it's elusive.

Pulling the comforter over my body, I snuggle into the soft embrace of my bed, hoping it might wrap me away from the day's tension. And from a desire I can't afford to feel.

But when I close my eyes, I'm back in his car. The leather seats cool beneath me, the space intimate and charged. Sebastian has asked if he can call me, and I've leaned in to kiss his cheek, but this time, when my lips accidentally brush the corner of his mouth, neither of us pulls away.

The distant sound of a siren wails somewhere in the city, rising and falling before fading, much like my resolve to stop thinking about him. I should force my thoughts away from where I know this is headed, but screw it, I'm in.

In this version, there's no impending doom hanging over my shop. There's only him, me, and the electricity crackling between us.

Guilt about my deal with Thorne threatens to surface, but I push it down. Tomorrow, I can hate myself. Tonight, I want Sebastian.

His hand comes up to cup my face, holding me there for a heartbeat. "That wasn't quite right," he murmurs, brushing his lips over mine.

"Your driver," I whisper.

"Not a problem." Sebastian's gaze never leaves mine as he pushes a button, and the privacy divider glides up, sealing us in our own world of shadows and anticipation.

His lips curve into that crooked smile that makes my knees weak. "Now, where were we?"

He pulls me closer, his mouth claiming mine in the darkness. The kiss is deep and hungry from the first touch. There's no hesitation this time. In my fantasy, he takes what he wants. And what he wants is me. His hands move from my face into my hair, angling my head to deepen the kiss.

"Sebastian," I gasp when we break apart, both breathing hard.

My hand drifts down my stomach, drawn by the heat pooling between my thighs. I slide my fingers into my panties

In my mind, Sebastian's hands are everywhere, exploring with confident precision. The luxury of the car cocoons us with its tinted windows, soft leather, and the faint hum of the engine, providing a veil of privacy in the middle of the city.

My back arches as I sink deeper into the mattress. My body trembles as pleasure builds with each stroke of my fingers.

The fantasy shifts, transforming into his bedroom or a luxury hotel suite. He backs me against a wall, one hand braced beside my head, the other tracing the curve of my waist. His touch is reverent yet possessive, as if he's mapping territory he intends to claim thoroughly.

"I've wanted to do this since the moment you smiled at me over that stack of romance novels." His lips hovering a breath above mine. "Do you have any idea what you do to me, Rosalia?"

My breath catches as my fingers find their target, circling with increasing pressure. Heat radiates outward from my center like ripples in a pond, each circle of sensation more consuming than the last.

The smooth texture of his expensive shirt slides beneath my fingers as I unbutton it, revealing warm skin underneath. His cologne intensifies with the heat of his body, oak and spice, making my head swim.

He looks at me with those penetrating eyes, darker now with desire. "I need to see all of you," he breathes, his thumb brushing across my lower lip.

My hips rise involuntarily from the mattress as I sink deeper into both physical pleasure and fantasy. My entire body is flushed and trembling. The sheets slide across my sensitive skin, adding another layer to the mounting tension.

In my fantasy, he undresses me slowly, each newly revealed inch of skin explored with fingers and lips. There's no rush; time doesn't matter, only pleasure. He lavishes attention on my collarbone, the curve of my breast, the sensitive skin of my inner thigh.

"You're exquisite. Even more beautiful than I imagined." His fingers trace patterns of need across my skin. "I want to memorize every sound you make. Every sigh, every moan."

My movements become more urgent, chasing the release that hovers just out of reach. In the fantasy, Sebastian is everywhere. His hands, his mouth, his words of praise wrap around me like the darkness that fills the bedroom.

"Sebastian," I whisper his name aloud, the sound barely audible in the quiet room. The fantasy is so vivid I can almost feel the warmth of his breath against my neck, the slight roughness of his stubble against my tender skin.

My hips rock as sensations cascade through me like falling dominoes, each triggering another more intense than the last. My mouth parts in silent pleas as Sebastian's imagined touch becomes more real than the sheets beneath me.

When he finally moves inside me, the fullness, the perfect friction, is everything I've craved and more. "So good," I moan.

"Look at me," he commands.

The hunger in his gaze pushes me over the edge. Wave after wave of pleasure crashes through me, leaving me trembling and gasping his name. My free hand clutches at the bedsheets as my body bows off the mattress.

As the aftershocks gradually subside, I lie still, eyes pressed tight, prolonging the fantasy for a few more precious seconds. Sebastian would gently kiss my forehead, my temple, my cheeks, bringing me back to earth. He'd pull me against him, my head on his chest, and I'd listen to his heartbeat slow to normal.

But then reality seeps back in, cold and unwelcome. My tiny bedroom is suddenly too large, too empty. I readjust my pajamas that had become twisted. The soft fabric is a poor substitute for the imagined touch of Sebastian's hands. I hug a pillow to my chest, trying to fill the emptiness that's crept in now that the escape of pleasure has faded.

My phone chimes from the nightstand and I jolt. The sound is jarring in my too-quiet bedroom. I reach for it, heart leaping when I see Sebastian's name on the screen.

> **Thank you for dinner tonight. I haven't enjoyed myself that much in a long time.**

I'm frozen, my fingers hovering over the keypad. What am I supposed to say? That despite your company, or at the very least your brother, is threatening to destroy everything I've worked for, I just brought myself to climax imagining your hands on my body? That I'm furious and heartbroken and still, somehow, desperately attracted to you?

After several minutes of deliberation, I type simply:

I had a nice time too.

Safe. Non-committal.

A car door slams outside my building, the sound sharp in the night air. The faint hum of my refrigerator pulses like a metronome, counting the seconds as I lie here alone with my thoughts.

I set my phone back on the nightstand and curl deeper under the covers, pulling my knees to my chest. The warmth of my fantasy has completely dissipated now, leaving only cold reality in its wake. Tomorrow, I'll need to be practical and start making more contingency plans for my store and my life.

But tonight, in the quiet darkness of my bedroom, I allow myself one more moment of weakness and imagine a world where Sebastian Blackstone is an ordinary man who I met at my bookstore or the library. A man whose touch I crave, whose smile I've memorized, whose presence makes my heart race for all the right reasons instead of all the wrong ones.

Screw it. I reach out and take the chocolate truffle from my nightstand. I place it on my tongue, letting the dark, bitter exterior melt until it reveals the sweet center hidden inside. The complex flavors bloom across my palate—rich, forbidden, complicated, just like Sebastian. I swallow, wondering if giving in to this small temptation means I'll eventually surrender to them all.

ChapterThirteen

Rosalia

"I am the Lorax who speaks for the trees, which you seem to be chopping as fast as you please!" I read in the gruff and wise voice that makes the children on the reading rug giggle.

The warm, golden glow of the afternoon sun filters through my store's front windows, casting a cozy atmosphere over story time. Parents line the edges of the reading rug, some scrolling on phones, others watching their children with indulgent smiles. A few snap photos of the scene.

Moments like this make the long hours, the financial stress, and the constant worry about how I'll keep the doors open worthwhile. That all melts away when I read to a room full of adorable, eager faces filled with wonder as they're transported into the story.

Well, most of them. Benny is more interested in picking his nose, and Alice is focused on tapping the toes of her sparkly red shoes together. Not that I can blame her; the little girl's Mary Janes are super cute.

The jingle of the store's bell pulls my gaze from the story to the entrance. Thorne enters my store like he owns it. My insides twist, followed by a surge of adrenaline because, well, he does.

What could he possibly want? The little book slips in my now clammy hands, and I grapple to catch the slick cover. My fingers press into the cardboard pages, but I manage to continue to read, bracing myself for whatever unpleasantness is to come. From our two short interactions, I'm certain Thorne is the type to revel in making others feel small and insignificant.

I finish the story, and when the parents begin chatting amongst themselves, I leave the reading circle and find Thorne flipping through a business magazine. He sets it on the rack and faces me. "That was precious. Were you practicing your domestic dream of becoming a mom?"

"I'm sorry, Mr. Blackstone, I didn't realize you were an expert on my innermost desires. Please, tell me more about myself," I say with a polite smile that seethes underneath.

I'm proud of my ability to connect with children. It's a strength, not something to be belittled. But I resent being reduced to a stereotype.

"Let me guess, you're not like other girls. You're special." His voice drips with insincerity. "You don't want to marry a rich man so he can buy you your dream of a white picket fence and two point five kids? Uh-huh, sure."

My hands ball into fists at my sides. My fingernails dig into my palms as I struggle to maintain composure. "Did you not get enough hugs and stories as a kid? Is that why you're so bitter?" I touch my lips. They tingle with my unkind words. "That was rude. I'm sorry."

Thorne's sharp and unexpected laugh breaks as if startled by its sound. "I didn't think you had bark, let alone a bite."

His eyes, a moment ago cool and detached, now sparkle with an unsettling curiosity. I imagine a mouse finding herself under the steady gaze of a cat feels the same.

"Is there a reason you stopped by?" Desperate to shift the topic and his focus from me, I blurt, "Have you heard from Sebastian?"

He's been on my mind constantly since our date. Part of me keeps hoping he'll somehow find out what his brother is doing and put it right. Pathetic, maybe, but I'm desperate.

Thorne's eyes narrow. "We've talked a little at work. Why?"

My heart sinks. "No reason." The faint glimmer of hope I'd been clinging to extinguishes.

"Anyway, I'm here to check on your progress," he says, checking his watch as if time itself is a commodity he controls. "It's the last week of March. May will be here before you know it, along with the Blackstone Derby party." His eyes narrow. "Will you be handing over the keys? Or do you have my brother under your thumb?"

I hate the way he talks about Sebastian, but I bite my tongue. I need to find another location before I can tell him what I really think. That is difficult to do when not a single bank will return my call. At least I've made an appointment with the Small Business Administration, and I've found some possible grants.

"We went out to dinner last Saturday." Even with all this stress, the memory makes me smile, recalling his playful teasing and quick responses. "I'm going to his place this weekend."

"His place, huh? Looks like you're about to earn your store..." His gaze slithers along my body, pausing in all the places that make me uncomfortable. How is this snake related to Sebastian?

My mouth falls open. "I—we're going horseback riding. You told me—you said." My heart thuds so hard it might break free from my rib cage. "Nothing else."

He holds up a hand. "My brother is merciless, not a cretin. He won't do anything you don't want to do. Of course, that's not to say he won't manipulate you into wanting to sleep with him. Especially if he suspects you're helping me." He comes closer, licking his bottom lip. "But if you're worried or aren't interested in fucking him, we could drop this game now. Go out with me instead." His gaze falls to my chest. "We'll work out a different deal."

A sour tang fills my mouth. Does he honestly think everyone is for sale? My shoulders stiffen, and I draw back. "No, thanks."

The warmth drains from his gaze, leaving a chill that seeps into my bones. "Sebastian isn't better than me," Thorne growls.

Whoa. Someone has brother issues. "I never said he was. I'm not dating him for fun." My mouth twists around the words, sour as unripe fruit. "Thanks to you, it's a business transaction. To save my bookstore. That. Is. All." But that is a half-truth.

This conversation needs to end. Thorne's slimy deal might keep Novel Idea open, but I don't like him. He has the charm of a snake oil salesman. "Is there anything else I can help you with? I need to get back to my customers."

"Actually, I might be able to help *you*. Again."

"I'm in this mess because of you Blackstones," I retort.

"You're the one who didn't bother to get important terms and conditions of your lease in writing," he scoffs.

His words twist like a knife in my gut. I can't argue with him, and the truth burns like cheap bourbon. I should have been smarter in my business. So much for proving myself. I wanted to show everyone I could adult, but instead, I'm drowning in my failures.

"Do you want my help?" he asks, his eyebrow arching in a perfect, calculated curve.

I swallow hard, my pride crumbling under the weight of my desperation. "Yes," I whisper.

"Sebastian is a vain man who is proud of all he's amassed. When you're at his place, compliment his wealth. He's especially fond of his horses and house.

He loves to show them off. I'm sure that's why he invited you over. Be sure to compliment him. He'll eat it up like caviar."

My stomach roils, bile rising in my throat. The thought of fawning over Sebastian's obscene wealth, of stroking his ego to get what I need makes me feel dirty.

Thorne's hand rests on top of mine. "I'm looking out for you. I want to make sure you protect your heart and your business." His words are smooth as silk, but I can sense the venom lurking beneath the surface.

Or maybe I'm projecting because I *am* charmed by Sebastian. And even though Thorne's motives are murky as the Ohio River, I have had to consider the suggestion.

I nod. "I'll think about it, but right now, I have a local author coming in shortly for a book signing. I need to get her table ready."

His face twists into a mask of contempt, his perfect features momentarily distorted by the ugliness of his true nature. He obviously doesn't like being dismissed. I should take care around such a powerful and ruthless man, but I am too raw with worry and guilt.

"Follow my advice and think carefully about whose side you're on," he warns before turning and leaving.

The bell chimes as he leaves, but his presence lingers, his words echoing. I lean against the counter, my fingers gripping the edge until my knuckles strain against my skin. I focus on the familiar scent of books and the soft murmur of conversations, but my mind keeps drifting to my upcoming date with Sebastian.

Thorne's advice plays on a loop in my head, each repetition making my stomach tighten. Sebastian had seemed so charming, so down-to-earth at the restaurant—heck, during all his past visits to my store. He's nothing like the egotistical billionaire his brother paints.

I walk to a table stacked with books. Sitting on top of the pile is a high school reading list. I'd been the poor kid at my prestigious school, surrounded by classmates who judged worth by designer labels and trust funds. Had that been Sebastian as a teenager? Will the opulent trappings of his estate bring out a different side of him, one that craves validation and admiration above all else?

Having to stroke Sebastian's ego and pretend to be impressed by his wealth is gross. The very idea tastes bitter as if I'd bitten into something rotten. It goes against everything I believe in and everything I stand for.

How did I end up here?

The idea of fawning over Sebastian's wealth, playing some shallow role I'd despised in high school, makes my skin crawl. It's made worse because I'm already selling pieces of myself to Thorne.

A customer approaches me with a question about a fantasy novel. I answer automatically. I answer automatically, slipping into my familiar role as the cheerful, helpful bookseller.

When she leaves, I practice a different tone under my breath. "Your house is stunning," I whisper, then cringe at my words. I grab a cloth and scrub at an invisible stain on the counter as if the act could somehow erase my compromised integrity.

Chapter Fourteen

Rosalia

I press my forehead against the cool glass of the Bentley's window, tracing the lines of the vibrant green hills that roll through pastures like waves. The view pulls me into childhood nostalgia of summer days at my grandparents' house, riding horses and exploring the forest half a mile down their gravel road.

A ringing from my purse pulls me into the present. Checking the caller ID, I grunt in surprise. Had thinking of my dad's parents summoned him? My thumb hovers over the "Decline" button as I debate the wisdom of avoiding his questions versus the guilt of lying to him. Keeping quiet about going to Sebastian's house is the best option. Mentioning it would only open the door to questions better left unanswered.

Sighing, I press "Accept," bracing myself for the conversation. "Hi, Dad."

"Rosalia, what in the world is going on?" he demands. "Why is your grandma showing me pictures on social media of you with Sebastian Blackstone?"

I tighten my grip on the phone and stare at the black fencing along the road. I want to confide in him, but I need to deflect his worry more. "It's nothing."

There's a muffled conversation between my dad and someone. Then I hear Grandma Rose declare, "My granddaughter is in the social paper."

Unlike her son, she sounds delighted. And it solves the mystery of how my dad, who is nearly allergic to the internet, found out about my dates with Sebastian. Grandma loves her socials, especially when it comes to gossip about Kentucky's elite—almost as much as baking and gardening.

"It's nothing, Dad," I repeat, not sure what else to say.

"Are you sure? Is that slimy asshole blackmailing you?"

My jaw drops at his intense reaction and his quick jump to such a conclusion. "Why would you say that? Sebastian and I are friends. That's all." The words are heavy, like stones in my mouth. Friends don't use each other.

"You told me the building you're leasing is owned by Blackstone. The lease they won't renew. And now you're being seen around town with him."

"Isn't it great?" Grandma Rose thrills in the background.

"No, Mom. It isn't great." I swear I can hear my dad grinding his teeth.

I glance at the front seat where Tom's driving, grateful there's plenty of space between us, and that I didn't put my phone on speaker. "Dad, I promise it's not what you think. He's been coming to the store since it opened. We talk about books. I don't think he even knows about the lease issue."

"How could he not know? He's a Blackstone."

"He runs the distillery, not the real estate." I bite my lip, unsure of the truth of my words.

Dad grumbles a reply I miss, then says, "Anyway, about your place. I can get a third mortgage on my house and land—"

"No. Absolutely not." My breath hitches, and tears fill my eyes. "I have an appointment with the Small Business Administration. They promise to help." I nearly choke on the lie. They had said no such thing.

"Calling the SBA was smart. You're a fantastic businesswoman, Rosalia."

I close my eyes; the praise is a heavy weight pressing on my chest. A good businesswoman wouldn't have relied on a verbal promise or agreed to steal to save her store.

"But a friendship with a Blackstone is still a bad idea. They're untouchable in this town," he warns. "I've seen too many people crushed under their heels."

I open my mouth to ask him about his animosity toward the Blackstones, but Tom stops at a red light and twists toward me. I quickly mute my phone.

"Ms. Manchester, we're about fifteen minutes out." Tom meets my gaze in the rearview mirror. "Mr. Blackstone wanted me to check if you'd like to stop for lunch."

"Please, call me Rosalia. And no, thank you. I ate right before you arrived."

Dad's tinny voice comes through the phone, "Rosalia, are you there?"

"No worries," I assure Tom. He nods and turns toward the road. I unmute the phone. "Sorry, I accidentally hit mute," I say, adding another lie to my growing pile. Desperate for a subject change, I ask, "The Great Balloon Race is coming up next month. Want to go with me?"

"It's on a Saturday. What about your store?"

"I'll open after. After hearing all your stories, I need to go at least once."

"It's a date," he says, a smile in his voice. "Speaking of derby stories, did I tell you about sneaking into the races when I was fifteen?"

Dad recounts his youthful antics, and laughter bubbles from my chest, easing the tension that has settled in my body. The warmth of his happiness spreads through me like a comforting balm, momentarily overshadowing my worries.

My giggles subside as the Bentley pulls next to an elegant guardhouse of a gated community. A woman steps from the booth and waves to Tom. Then the ornate gate slowly opens, the metal glinting in the afternoon sunlight.

The neighborhood is the epitome of opulence. As we drive, the homes grow larger, each surrounded by perfectly manicured acres and pristine black fences.

"Dad, I have to go."

"Oh, you have plans on your early day?"

Of course, Dad would remember that the bookstore is only open until two on Sundays. My guilt returns, oozing through my heart like thick, black tar. "Yes, with Paige," I lie, reasoning that this deception is for my dad's peace of mind.

"Alright. Love you, honey," he says warmly.

"Love you too." I hang up, my frown reflected on the phone's screen.

Tom drives for another five minutes, heading to the very back of the subdivision. We approach a mansion with more acres than I can count, complete with an imposing gate. Seriously, does Sebastian's home have a gate inside a gated community? And what man needs that much house? Or that many horses? There are at least thirty grazing in the countless pastures.

My stomach flips as I consider what Thorne told me earlier in the week. Maybe he was right. The thought of stroking an already-inflated ego makes me queasy.

The wrought-iron gates part for us, revealing a world so far removed from mine that it might as well be a different planet. I swear the house grows larger with every passing second. Marble columns rise three stories high. Every window gleams like it was polished this morning.

I sit in the car for a long moment, staring at the front door. Everything I taught myself about integrity feels very far away right now.

Opening the door, I step out. My boot heels sink into the perfectly manicured lawn. Unease wraps around me. There's no backing out now.

Chapter Fifteen

Sebastian

Closing the back door, I take the terrace steps two at a time, hating how much I'm looking forward to seeing Rosalia. I walk past the granite pool that Tiffany insisted on having but never swam in during our brief marriage. The damn thing is a monument to poor judgment.

The late March sun still manages to peek through the gathering storm clouds as I pull my phone from my back pocket. I text Tom while walking to the barn, asking him to have Rosalia meet me there, knowing I'm walking straight into whatever trap we've set for each other.

Before I put my phone away, it rings. Thorne. My brother's timing is impeccable when it comes to stirring up trouble. I hit "Ignore." Seconds later, a text buzzes. Can't he take a hint?

I visited your bookworm earlier this week. She tells me you two are meeting at your place.

Why are you visiting her?

Just because this is my brother's game doesn't mean he won't cheat to win.

She and I made a deal. It'd be odd if I didn't stop by.

Though unwelcome, the reality check is needed. I enjoyed my dinner date with Rosalia too much. I have to keep reminding myself this isn't real.

Your point?

You might want to see if our Tennessee distillery needs a master distiller.

Piss off. I'll be keeping my job.

My steps slow on the damp grass as I resist the urge to throw my phone.

She's more devious than I thought. I suspect she is going to play us both.

Don't ask. Don't ask. But doubt creeps in like poison, and I hate myself for it. This is exactly what happened with Tiffany and others in my past. It started with small questions, tiny inconsistencies, until I couldn't tell what was real anymore. Am I seeing patterns that aren't there, or ignoring what's clearly there?

How?

Why deal with me when her new billionaire boyfriend can buy her a bookstore?

The tightness in my chest eases, and I continue walking. Rosalia had pushed back at me paying for her meal, so I highly doubt she'll ask me to buy her a building. And here I thought my brother would be more subtle in his attempts to sow discord.

I reach the barn and shove my phone in my pocket. Stepping inside, I nod at John, my stablehand, who's getting Goliath and Cinnamon ready. I walk along the stalls, checking on my other horses. The light scent of silage, wood, and earthy manure never fail to soothe me.

A flash of auburn fur streaks into the barn, skidding to a stop next to me. "I'd wondered where you'd run off, Twain." I stroke the silky and, thankfully, dry coat. "And I'm glad it wasn't into the pond."

The Irish Setter's tail wags so hard that his whole back end swings like a pendulum. He stills, and his head cocks toward the open door at the opposite end of the barn. His long ears perk up, and then he takes off after a sound only he can hear.

"Mr. Blackstone," calls John, "Goliath is ready. How would you like me to saddle Cinnamon?"

"If those are the names of the horses we will be riding, I hope Cinnamon is mine," comes a velvet-smooth voice who has visited too many of my recent late-night fantasies.

Rosalia stands at the open exterior doors. Her gaze bounces around the barn, lips parting slightly as she takes in the horses, then the polished leather tack hanging on the walls. But then her posture straightens, her face smooths into something more guarded. "Your place is lovely," she says, sounding oddly formal.

"Thank you," I reply, moving closer. "But not nearly as beautiful as the company." The flirtation falls easily from my lips, too easily. I'm supposed to be charming her, but this feels less like strategy and more like instinct.

"Smooth." She smiles, but the tension lingers in her eyes. She clears her throat, looking past my shoulder to the pastures where horses graze in clusters, then takes in the row of stalls. "You must have what, twenty horses out there? Thirty?" The awe in her words makes my skin crawl. "That's... that's quite the collection. Quite the investment."

Why is she focused on the numbers? Is she calculating their value, or merely curious why a single man has so many horses?

"Most of them are rescues or retirees that needed a home," I say, watching her reaction carefully. "Only a handful are actually rideable."

Her eyes soften, and she moves toward the stall nearest the pasture doors. "Rescues? What happened to them?"

The genuine concern that replaces her initial amazement catches me off guard. This isn't the reaction of someone tallying up assets. "Various things. Neglect, abuse, some are just old and their owners couldn't care for them anymore," I tell her.

The afternoon sun lights her from behind, hugging her curves and heating my blood. I drink in every detail, from her fitted T-shirt to her sexy-as-sin worn jeans and equally loved cowboy boots.

Oh shit. I forgot to ask if she rode Western or English. I call to my stable hand. "John, do we have All-around saddles?"

"Damn. Don't worry about it," Rosalia cuts in. "It's my fault. I should have asked, knowing you all ride English here. But these are the only riding boots I have, since Western has always been my preference."

Behind me, nails click rapidly on the cement, and before my dog can give his usual overexcited greeting, I say, "Twain, sit."

The Irish Setter halts next to me, but his tail twitches in obvious glee.

Rosalia laughs. "You said that with such command, I almost sat too." She bends slightly and scratches behind Twain's ears. He promptly flops onto his side and then rolls onto his back. She rubs his belly and giggles when he kicks a leg in bliss. My smile grows watching them.

Straightening, her gaze moves to me. She studies me from head to toe, taking in my gray polo shirt, dark navy riding pants, and well-worn paddock boots.

"What?" I ask.

She shrugs. "You look different out of your three-piece suit. "

Heat prickles up my neck and I rub the back of it. "Is that a good or bad?"

"As if you don't know you look good in everything," she huffs, giving Twain a final pat and standing. "And it isn't that clothes matter, but what's underneath that counts."

No matter what my outside looks like, beneath it lies a Blackstone heart, through and through—cold and cunning. But to keep things light, I quirk a brow and tuck my thumbs in my belt loop. "Are you saying you want to see me naked?" I tease.

Her face flames. "I was referring to your personality."

"Uh-huh, sure." Her pretty pink cheeks are adorable.

"New topic," she begs, her lips twitching and a half-smile escaping. "Please."

I grin. "As you wish, Buttercup."

"Quoting a book. A man after my heart."

"I was referring to the movie version of **The Princess Bride**," I joke. "And unlike you, my movie comparisons are much kinder. I get Bill and Gru. You get Princess Buttercup."

"Gru is cool. And he has the Minions."

John returns with an All-Around saddle. "I'll get this on Cinnamon."

"I'm sorry for the trouble, and thank you, John." Rosalia shuffles her feet. "Do you need help?"

He smiles, shaking his head. "I've got it, ma'am."

"I feel weird just standing here watching him get my horse ready," she whispers to me.

Her self-sufficiency is so different from my ex-wife's. It's a nice change. "Since it's his job, he and I would feel weirder watching you. Come here." I lead her to the feed room and grab a bucket of carrots. "Let's give these to the other horses while we wait."

We walk over to Cosmo's stall. "So, you spent your summers here, were they with horses? Or was that in Michigan? You seem to know your way around them."

She nods, taking a carrot. "Both, but more so here."

"You didn't mention it when I invited you horseback riding…"

"You asked by text."

She doesn't sound upset, but just to make sure, I ask, "Was that rude? Should I have called?"

"No. I'm just a lazy texter and didn't feel like typing out my backstory."

I chuckle, moving closer. "Said the bookstore owner."

She grins. "I like to read, not write."

"Fair enough. Will you tell me about it now?"

She scratches Cosmo's withers. "My grandfather was a horse farm manager. So is my dad."

"That explains your natural way with them." I watch her gentle touch on my normally skittish horse. "Cosmo here came from a neglectful situation and usually only interacts with me."

"Poor guy," she says softly. Leaning against the stall, she looks around. "My dad would love this place. He's always had a soft spot for horses that need help."

"Is that what brought your family to Kentucky, his work?"

"No, a divorce. After my parents split, my dad moved back here to be closer to family. I followed a year later."

"Are you and your father close?"

"Yes," she replies.

An unexpected longing tugs at me. After college, I'd spent a lot of time with my father, preparing to take over the family business, but even so, we're virtually strangers. "What about your mom?" I ask.

She turns, resting her elbows on the bottom half of the stall doors. "Are your parents together? Do you like them? Do they both work for Blackstone Bourbon? What's your blood type?"

I laugh. "Is that your polite way of telling me to stop asking so many questions?"

"Not at all." She crosses her feet at the ankles. "But only if you're willing to share too."

I nod. "My parents are still together, but not happily. My father's mostly retired from the distillery and business, which is a relief. We don't see eye to eye on much. And my mother's basically a full-time socialite." I grin. "And my blood's AB negative. Any other questions?"

"Hmm." She taps her chin. "Do you have more siblings than the two?"

"My dad has a teenage son with a former mistress. I've never met either." Shit, once the cork's loosened, I spill secrets.

"Well, hell," she mutters. "I'm, um, an only child. I think they wanted more but couldn't have them. Because of that, I have enough mothering for five kids. Both of my parents are extremely kind people, but I suppose they're not right for each other. They divorced right after I graduated from high school." We stare at each other, and the weight of honesty is heavy between us. Humor flickers in her eyes. "I don't know my blood type."

I laugh. "Our next date should be the Red Cross."

"Only if they're giving out double chocolate chip cookies that day."

"I'll call ahead."

John tells us Cinnamon and Goliath are ready. Thanking him, I lead Rosalia to the horses. I unclip Cinnamon and pat her saddle. Rosalia places her boot in the stirrup, grabs the saddle horn, and swings up in one smooth motion. She settles in with a natural confidence. The way she adjusts her seat, completely at ease, is the opposite of every other woman I've dated who treated horses like expensive props.

I mount Goliath, focusing on my stirrups instead of how good she looks. This is dangerous territory, appreciating her authenticity while knowing she's here for less than authentic reasons.

Gathering my reins, I point west. "We are going to the state park trails that butt against my property."

She follows me out of the barn and then comes up beside me. Twisting in her saddle, she scans my land. "Your place is beautiful. Peaceful."

"Thank you." I look around. Tiffany had liked the house. My love is for the grounds. And today, nature is putting on a show. The grass nearly glows from last night's rain shower. The color is a stark contrast against the black fencing. The mature trees lining the west fence are a mix of green, with a few late bloomers sporting flowers.

It only takes a couple of minutes to reach the gate between my place and state land. A stable hand waits at the gate. She locks it after we pass through. Since I've ridden the trails many times, I let Rosalia take the lead to have the freedom to explore.

We ride until our stomachs rumble with hunger, and the afternoon sun fights with the heavy clouds rolling in. And even then, I'd rather risk the storm than return. The simple afternoon is damn near perfect.

She points out a hawk circling above, and her smile is genuine, her laugh unguarded. Derby and the party loom a little over a month away. I wish time would slow. Even with all the lies between us, I'm in no hurry for this game to end.

We cross back onto my property under a darkening sky. As we approach the barn, Rosalia's relaxed chatter begins to fade. Her posture straightens, becoming anxious and stiff. Her gaze, which had been meeting mine freely all afternoon, now darts between my house, the barn, and anywhere but at me. It's as if crossing the boundary line has reminded her of something, or perhaps of who I am.

She fidgets with the reins, urging Cinnamon to canter and then walk, seemingly unaware of what she's doing. The same nervous energy that had consumed her when she first arrived appears to have returned.

The quiet grows tense. "What's wrong?"

She draws a deep breath. "Your place is beautiful. Really... impressive." There's a forced quality to her voice that wasn't there minutes ago.

"Thanks, but you already said that. Twice." I eye her. What's behind this nervous repetition?

"I know, I just—" She stops, then starts again with that same wooden tone. "The way you've built your fortune is remarkable. The business, this estate... it shows how brilliant you are with money and investments."

Thorne's text flashes in my mind: **Why deal with paying off loans when her new billionaire boyfriend can buy her a bookstore?**

The pleasant warmth of the afternoon curdles in my gut. Here it comes. The real reason she's here. My brother might be right, and everyone wants something in the end. And really, I should have seen it coming, she has a damn deal with my brother to manipulate and use me.

"Rosalia." My voice comes out harder and I don't care. "I can't give you the building you're leasing."

Her head snaps toward me, the color draining from her face. For a split second, shock renders her features vulnerable. Then her eyes harden to flint.

"I wasn't asking." The transformation is immediate. Gone is the nervous woman of seconds ago, replaced by cold fury. Her eyes narrow to slits. "So you do know about your company not honoring the agreement to renew my lease. Good to know."

She presses her heels into Cinnamon's sides, urging the mare forward. Not just a trot but a gallop, putting distance between us with every second.

"Rosalia, wait! That's not—" I urge Goliath into motion, but she's already disappearing down the path to the barn, the sound of hoofbeats fading under the first drops of rain.

Chapter Sixteen

Rosalia

Sebastian calls my name again. He knows that his company screwed me over on my lease. What else does he know?

I'm tempted to ignore him and have Cinnamon sprint to the barn. But the move is juvenile and pointless. I'll have to talk to him once we're off the horses or while I wait for Tom to arrive with the car to take me home. At times like these, I wish I had my own vehicle. Sighing, I tug gently on the mare's reins.

The clop of hooves slows as Goliath and Sebastian pull up level with Cinnamon and me. I narrow my eyes at him and hiss, "You knew about your company going back on its word with my lease, and you don't even care." I search his face for any hint of guilt or remorse, but his expression remains inscrutable.

"I...," he begins, then looks away. "It's complicated."

My anger flares, hot and huge. Complicated. My fists clench around the reins, nails biting into my palms. "Try to explain," I say in a hoarse whisper.

He runs a hand over his face, his shoulders slumping. "I didn't know about the lease issue until a few days ago. And the truth is, I don't have control over the properties the company leases out. That's my brother's domain. If I get involved, it'll be messy. Very messy."

My stomach drops at the mention of Thorne, a cold sweat prickling along my hairline. Sebastian had basically called me a gold digger, but he isn't far off. It doesn't matter that I was attracted to him before I made my bargain with his brother—now I'm here because of what Thorne promised me.

We ride in strained silence. The rhythm of hoofbeats melds with rustling bluegrass beneath an ambitious March sky. Our horses move in practiced tandem, close enough to share the same dappled shadows, yet worlds apart.

I study his profile, noting the tension in his shoulders, the way he carries himself like someone bearing a burden too personal to name. During his visits to my store, he's always alone. I googled him after our coffee date, and it revealed a man surrounded by empty space. In photographs from galas and charity events, he stands isolated in crowded rooms, his smile never reaching his eyes. Since his divorce, no companion graces his side. No friend's shoulder brushing against his, no lover's hand in his.

"Do you ever get lonely?" The question slips out.

He glances at me, surprise flickering in his eyes. "What do you mean?"

"Out here. Away from the city." I add, knowing that the true question is too probing.

"I'm not alone. I have my staff, my horses..."

"But no friends? Family?" So much for not prying.

His gaze slides away, focusing on some point in the distance. "I have acquaintances. Business associates. That's enough."

I frown, sensing a deeper story beneath his terse words. Is this who he really is, or just his way of staying safe?

Before I can probe further, the rain turns insistent, and he says, "We should return before the storm arrives." Together, we spur our horses into a canter

We reach the barn seconds before a crack of thunder booms from the dark sky. I'm greeted with the musty scent of hay, leather, and safety.

I dismount, my legs slightly stiff from the ride. Sebastian's stable hand waits with an expectant nod. "Thank you, John," I say, handing him the reins.

He leads Cinnamon toward the tack room. I stand awkwardly for a moment, watching as he efficiently removes the saddle and bridle, hanging them on their designated hooks with practiced precision. The thunder crashes again outside, but Cinnamon barely flinches under his confident touch. I linger, feeling out of place in Sebastian's world, where even the care of my mount is handled by others.

I move to the nearest stall, seeking comfort in the familiar act of petting the American Quarter Horse. Sebastian follows close behind. He leans against the stall door, his shoulder nearly brushing mine.

"Rosalia, about earlier..." His voice is low and earnest. "I am sorry for assuming the worst. It's just, in my world, people always seem to have ulterior motives."

His words sting because they're too close to the truth. Given my arrangement with his brother, I have no right to stay angry about Sebastian's assumptions. I should put distance between us, but instead I'm drawn to the vulnerability in his voice. Despite the lies, the deal with Thorne, the mess with my lease, this pull between us is stronger than my guilt.

"It's fine," I tell him, stepping closer.

The crunch of footsteps has us jumping apart like two teenagers about to be caught by adults. A guy enters the barn. "Bastian, are you in here?" he calls, his gaze sweeping the space before landing on us. His eyebrows shoot up. "Sorry, I thought you were alone."

The man is around our age, with hair a shade lighter than Sebastian's, and he wears the same expensive look. He carries a leather folder and has an air of confidence that suggests he is used to being in charge.

Sebastian's shoulders stiffen and a frown tugs at his lips. "Daniel. I wasn't expecting you."

"Clearly." His gaze darts between us. "I hope I'm not interrupting."

Sebastian doesn't confirm or deny, and an awkward silence descends. He shakes his head. "I really need to change the code on the gate."

Daniel grins, revealing white teeth with a slightly crooked canine. "You can't keep me out. And you'd miss me."

Sebastian snorts. "Rosalia, this is Daniel, an old friend from college. Daniel, this is Rosalia, my..." He hesitates, as if searching for the right word.

I offer my hand. "Nice to meet you."

Shifting the leather folder, he shakes my hand, "I'm Daniel Poncelet."

His last name smacks me like a physical blow. "You're the lawyer."

His brows furrow and his gaze jumps between Sebastian and me. "I am a lawyer."

"Who works for Blackstone. Who works for you." I say, glaring at Sebastian. He found out about my building issue a few days ago, my ass. What else is he lying about?

"I thought you said you didn't have control over the leasing side of things." I point at Daniel. "But if he's your friend and the lawyer in charge..."

Sebastian glances away momentarily. His expression turns guarded. "Like I said earlier, it's complicated."

Daniel clears his throat. "I should let you two talk privately. Sebastian, I'll head inside." He offers me an apologetic smile before ducking out of the barn.

In the tense silence that follows, I study Sebastian's face. It seems he isn't a hapless, innocent bystander who knows nothing of my mess brought on by his company. But does it matter? I'm the one who's made the devil's bargain with Thorne, sacrificing my integrity to save my store and literacy programs.

I need to get out of here and clear my head. "I should go," I murmur, moving toward the door.

"Let me drive you home instead of Tom," Sebastian offers.

"You know how to drive?" My joke is feeble, but he snorts. "Stay and visit with your friend. The Blackstone lawyer," I can't help but tack on.

The rain has turned into a drizzle, and I'll get wet, but I need to get away. It's time to leave and be alone with my thoughts. However, I don't make it far before he catches up with me. "I'll tell Tom to pick you up here so you don't get wet." He pulls out his cell and makes the call.

After hanging up, he waits with me. The silence is oppressive.

He breaks it. "Daniel is a friend from college. That's why he's here. Blackstone has a lot of lawyers, and they don't all report to me."

It's on the tip of my tongue to demand to know if Daniel does, but again, I'm not innocent, so why demand Sebastian's truths? Instead, I ask, "He's a close friend?"

The Bentley pulls to the barn's imposing carriage doors and Tom starts to get out, but Sebastian holds up a hand and opens the car door for me. "I don't have close friends."

"Why not?"

"They are a liability."

Wow. I'm not sure if his answer makes me feel better or worse. He might not know about the bet, but that was the answer of either a heartless or very lonely man.

Which is Sebastian Blackstone?

Chapter Seventeen

Sebastian

I tilt my face toward the heavy rain clouds blanketing the sky. They match my mood. My gaze shifts from the darkening sky to Rosalia, and I catch the shadows of the storm playing across her face. The hard lines of her anger have softened, but her eyes are distant and troubled.

Silence stretches between us. I'm afraid to break it with the questions hovering on the tip of my tongue, so I swallow them back with the fear of what the answers might drag into the light.

If she learns about the bet, she'll hate me. Given that she's here only because of Thorne's deal should bother me, but all I feel is guilt for putting her in this situation.

I take her hand. "Are we okay?"

Her lips curve into a small smile that doesn't reach her eyes. She nods and turns to get into the car. I watch her leave, unease keeping me rooted until the Bentley becomes a tiny dot in my long, tree-lined driveway. I shake myself and head toward the house.

As the soles of my riding boots hit the bottom step of the front porch, Alex, my housekeeper, opens the door. Twain rushes out, circling me with his tail wagging joyfully. Scratching behind his ears, I find comfort in his simple devotion. He doesn't want anything from me, doesn't judge, doesn't have an agenda. I can't remember the last time I had that with a person.

Twain and I take a right at the marble foyer with the double staircase, his nails clicking as we walk through the sitting room with its dark oak floors, past the large bay window. A familiar pang of loneliness fills me. The vast rooms and hallways are like ghosts haunting the expansive space. I rarely use most of the house, confining myself to my bedroom, study, and the barns. The thought of moving has crossed my mind, but it'd be too hard on the horses. Plus, the security and privacy the estate provides are invaluable. I've never had anyone take my photo when I'm out on my walks with Twain or riding my horses.

I turn left and step into the library, although the name is a misnomer. This room is for guests. My real reading material is strewn on my nightstand and in the sitting room of my master bedroom. Besides a few collector books, the library's shelves are lined with rare bottles of Blackstone Bourbon.

Daniel sits in a black leather chair next to the ornate and empty fireplace. his other leg crossed over his knee, clad in perfectly pressed linen slacks

He sits casually, one leg crossed over the other, his perfectly pressed linen slacks sharp against the dark leather. A Glencairn glass rests in his hand, and seeing me, he holds it up in a salute.

Twain trots past me to his bed beside the built-in liquor cabinet. I follow him and lean down to pet him before straightening up and pouring my favorite single-barrel. The rich, caramel aroma wafts from the glass, inviting me to take a sip. "Great for Blackstone. A long evening for me."

It's the curse of all master distillers to stay until closing at all major events. I don't mind talking craft. In fact, I love it. But being rich and single makes me more popular than my bourbon. Especially later in the evening when drinks have lowered inhibitions.

I sit on the other side of the fireplace, opposite Daniel. The supple leather creaks slightly as I settle into the chair. We clink glasses.

"Was that Rosalia Manchester?" he asks.

I lower my drink and nod.

Daniel taps the portfolio on the side table. "When I called her to terminate the lease, I had never felt so much like the villain."

I open the folder and scan the familiar terms that have haunted my sleep while Rosalia goes about her life completely unaware that her heart is being wagered like poker chips. "We're all villains in this story," I sigh.

Daniel's brow furrows. "Even her?"

I nod. "Though she didn't have much of a choice."

"Sebastian." He doesn't say more until I'm looking right at him, then finishes, "She didn't have any choice."

Annoyance flares in my chest. "She'd agreed to Thorne's deal. And you showing up here claiming to be my friend definitely helped my brother. She probably assumes I'm in on it."

"You are."

"Because I was forced to be," I say between clenched teeth.

"Just like her."

Fuck. I want to argue, but can't. He's right. She's not manipulative, she's desperate. And I'm the asshole who put her in this position. I grip my glass tighter. "Thorne backed her into a corner, and I… I let him use her as a pawn in our game."

Daniel nods. "You should have told her about your brother's extortion."

"If I'd done that, he would've followed through. This seemed easier."

"Is it?"

"Not at all." I like her too much, and that complicates everything. I stare into my bourbon, the amber liquid catching what little light filters through the windows.

Daniel shifts forward in his chair, the leather creaking. "Hey, what's this 'claiming to be your friend?' I am your friend. Or we used to be friends. Until Thorne decided to fuck with your head and you shut everyone out."

"People I care about have a funny way of either turning on me or using me." I meet his gaze directly. "And now that you work for Blackstone, we need clear boundaries. You're my attorney, not my confidant."

"Spoken like a true Blackstone." He taps the leather folder again. "This is the contract for his bet. I figured you'd want a physical copy."

"I do. Thanks." I take it and hold up the file. "You did read the part about him leaving Kentucky when I win?"

"*If* you win."

A soft patter of raindrops against the library windows grows louder. I look outside. My dark mood matches the landscape. "I'll win. There's no other option. Thorne can't lead Blackstone. He doesn't care about crafting bourbon or our employees, only profit."

"But you care about people?"

I stiffen, my blood pressure rising. "Are you saying I don't treat my employees well?"

"Oh, no, you do. I'm referring to Rosalia. You're using her as a pawn in your rivalry with your brother."

"I'm in this bet for her," I nearly shout.

"Don't pretend to be a martyr. You also did it because you want Thorne gone."

That's the other shitty thing about letting people get close to me. They know when I'm full of shit. Yes, protecting Rosalia is important to me, but I can't lie. The day my brother walks away for good will be the first day I wake up without yesterday's anger

I admit none of this, and instead dig into my false self-righteousness. "Rosalia made a deal with Thorne to play me."

"So?" Daniel shrugs.

I want to punch him. "What the fuck do you mean, 'so'?"

"Unless I'm mistaken, none of this was her idea. Thorne pulled Rosalia into this game. And she has the most to lose." His calm and composed tone grates on my nerves.

"She can move to another location. There are other great spots besides Whiskey Row," I growl.

The words feel like betrayal even as I say them. Part of me understands that she's fighting for her business, and starting at a new place isn't ideal. Hell, if someone threatened Blackstone Bourbon, I would do whatever it took to crush them. But understanding doesn't quiet the old familiar whisper: what if this is who she really is?

"How do you do it?"

I narrow my eyes. "Do what?"

"Talk around that solid gold and diamond-encrusted spoon that's been in your mouth since birth."

I stand, chair scraping against the floor. "I don't need to listen to this shit."

Daniel makes a sit-down gesture with his hands. I'm tempted to flip him off and walk from the room, but he'd only follow. I settle my features into the carefully neutral mask I've perfected over the years. "Fine, fine. Please, spell out for me the ways I'm an asshole."

He smirks. "Glad we're now on the same page. Not everyone can get a loan or have family help them financially." I open my mouth to argue, but he points his finger at me and keeps talking. "I'm in no way saying you haven't worked your ass off to get where you are, but during your climb to head of Blackstone and master distiller, you've never had to take a semester off because of bills. You've never had to shackle yourself with student loans that you'll be paying off until you're ninety."

Daniel's custom suit and handmade shoes hide his upbringing in one of the poorest Appalachian counties. "Hell, even with you hiring me right out of college, those first couple of years were rough. I'd come dangerously close to having my car repo'ed. And the apartment I'd rented with three other guys was…" he shudders.

The mention of a car reminds me of Rosalia being knocked from her bike during our dinner date. Does she not have a car because of the cost? Was that also why she'd ordered a cup of soup during dinner? Was that all she could afford?

I stare at the golden amber of my two hundred dollar bottle of bourbon in the lead-crystal glass. Christ, today she'd told me her dad is a barn manager. His job is essential to Kentucky life but doesn't pay shit.

Shame crawls up my spine like ivy on old brick. I've prided myself on hard work and dedication, but I can't ignore my advantages. It's difficult to maintain my sense of righteousness when I meet Daniel's steady gaze.

Leaning my head against the leather wingback, I glare at the ceiling and mutter, "Guess I am an asshole."

"Yup, but underneath all the privilege and entitlement is a good guy." I hear the grin in Daniel's voice, but given all he's said, I'm not so sure.

We drink in silence, though I barely taste the smooth liquor as a sinking sensation cements in my stomach.

"How are your dates with Rosalia going?" Daniel asks.

A mix of heaven and hell. "That's a complicated question. Even more so since talking to you."

"I'm a lawyer. I like complicated." He rolls his wrist in a go-on motion.

"They've been great," I admit.

Daniel snorts. "That's not very complicated."

"At least when I thought she was manipulating me, I could be pissed about enjoying her company. Now I just feel like garbage about it. Thanks."

"That's what you get for not listening to your lawyer," he tosses back.

He'd warned me not to sign the contract for the bet, that it'd blow up in my face. The derby party is over a month away, and I already sense the inevitable fallout brewing.

I set my drink on the side table and shift forward in my armchair. "How can I—"

Daniel holds up a hand. "No."

"You don't know what I was going to say," I huff.

"How can I get out of the bet? That's what you were going to ask, right?" he says with a self-satisfied smile.

"Smug asshole," I mutter.

Daniel laughs. "Your brother specified in the contract that if you back out, he automatically wins." He points to the leather folder I've taken. "Reread the contract. You'll see that stipulation in the second paragraph. I'm sure Thorne was certain sooner or later you'd want out. Most people realize it's shitty to play with other's lives."

"Fuck." I grip the back of my neck, pressing the skin together until it hurts. "What am I supposed to do?"

"So prickly," Daniel says, not seeming the least bit bothered by my attitude. "It doesn't seem like dating her is a hardship. And you are a good man. She'll see that—"

"A good man wouldn't have agreed to Thorne's stupid, fucking bet."

"He's your brother. He knows how to push your buttons."

"Let her get to know you. The real you. That's how you'll win the bet. Then Thorne will be gone, and *you* can renew her lease. Hell, give her the damn building if that eases your guilt. Just not before the bet ends because if you do either, you automatically lose."

"I'll try." I drag my hand from my neck into the back of my hair and pull. Rosalia does seem to like me, at least sometimes, but enough to give up her bookstore?

"You need to do more than try. If you lose, Thorne will have total control of Blackstone Bourbon's largest distillery."

I open the file and stare at the contract. The weight of my actions is nearly physical. I'd let my pride and competitive nature cloud my judgment, and so many people could end up paying the price. Agreeing to the bet was a damn disaster.

But self-reproach will have to wait. Right now, I have to concentrate on fixing my mess.

"I'll win," I say, tucking my uncertainty under my determination. "I'll do my best to show Rosalia the real me, but..." I pause, rubbing my jaw, searching for the right words. I stand, pacing the room and stop in front of the window. The rain trickles down the glass. Each drop follows its inevitable course, just as I had followed mine without question.

"But what if the real me isn't enough?" The worry escapes before I can stop it.

Daniel raises an eyebrow. "What do you mean?"

I turn to face him, leaning against the windowsill. "The real me is the guy who agreed to this bet in the first place. The real me keeps people at arm's length. The real me is..." I gesture vaguely at the vast, empty house around us. "This. Alone."

"Sebastian—"

"I saw her face today, Daniel. When she was leaving. I put her in this impossible situation because I can't stand my brother." My voice drops. "She's being forced to choose between her dream and her integrity, and it's my fault as much as my brothers."

Daniel sets his glass down. "You can still make this right."

"Can I?" I look at the contract resting on the end table. "The more I get to know her, the more I see what I've done. She doesn't deserve any of this." I let out a hollow laugh. "And the irony is, the more I see that, the less I deserve her."

"So what are you going to do?"

"Win the bet. Get Thorne out of our lives. And then..." I trail off, staring back out at the rain. "And then try to make amends, knowing she may never forgive me if she learns the truth."

"And if she doesn't forgive you?"

I don't answer. I don't have to. We both know that some messes can't be neatly cleaned up, no matter how much money or privilege you have. And this one might cost me the first genuine connection I've felt in years.

ChapterEighteen

Rosalia

I greet two women entering Novel Idea. They ask for the romance book club schedule, and after discussing the month's pick, they wander off to browse the shelves. The conversation reminds me of what arrived in the mail yesterday.

Turning to Paige, who's sitting on another tall stool behind the check-out counter, I lean down and grab two novels from underneath. "Remember a few months back when I mentioned that I was thinking of reaching out to authors whose books are selected for the book clubs?"

She nods, and I run my fingertips over the top glossy dust jacket of the signed book. The weight of it in my hands feels substantial, a tangible reminder of the author's generosity and the community I've built within these walls.

"They've all been very kind and appreciative that their books are featured in my clubs. A few have even sent me swag that I've shared at the meetings. This month's author sent two signed copies." I hand the top hardcover to Paige.

She slides off the tall chair and jumps up and down a few times, nearly shouting, "Oh my God! Will you do a giveaway? Please, say friends and family can take part in it. "

April's romance author is Paige's all-time favorite. I point to the books she's holding. "You don't need to. That one's for you."

"For me?" Paige squeaks, holding it tight to her chest. "Are you sure?"

"Of course. You're my closest friend and the one who introduced me to her books." Her books are sweet and sexy, and the characters linger long after the story ends.

Paige opens the title page and gasps. "It's made out to me. You shouldn't have. What you should have done was auction the book. Use the money to buy this building. I love this author, but I love you more. You have to stay on this street. In Kentucky."

Tears sting the backs of my eyes. "I want to stay too. And your idea's great, but one book can't save my store."

Paige's eyes light up, and she slaps her hand on the book cover. "Hey, that's an idea! Why don't you reach out to more authors and see if they'll donate signed copies for an auction? You could raise money to save the store."

I chew on my bottom lip, considering. It is tempting. My mind races, picturing signed books and special editions from dozens, if not more, authors lined up. A flutter of hope rises in my chest. Then reality crashes in.

"The idea has merit," I sigh. "But organizing a proper auction would take months, not weeks. I'd need to contact dozens of authors, coordinate shipments, market the event, set up an online bidding platform, and all this while trying to find a new building. I couldn't ask authors to donate to save a store I can't save.

Heck, I couldn't even tell them when and where the new bookstore would be." My voice trails off as hopelessness sets in.

Paige's enthusiasm doesn't waver. "You could start small! Just the authors you've already connected with."

"I've thought about that," I admit. "But what if I put all that work in and still don't raise enough? Or worse, what if I can't pull it off before the deadline? These authors have been so generous already, and if I promise an auction to help save my store and then fail anyway." I shake my head. "I'd never be able to face them if I open in a new location someday. Those bridges would be burned."

I run my fingers across the other signed book. "And the timing is impossible. Derby weekend is a little over a month away. The weight of it all presses down on me. "There just isn't enough time."

Paige sets the book on the counter and hugs me so tight that the breath whooshes from me. "You'll figure out something." She holds me tight until her phone sings Rihanna's "Birthday Cake." Reading the message, she punches the air. "Yes! Groomzilla finally picked a cake flavor. Two, actually."

"Oh? What did they choose?"

"A champagne and strawberry cake and chocolate bourbon cupcakes with salted caramel buttercream." As Paige rhapsodizes the virtues of buttercream, my mind wanders to the night Sebastian and I shared dessert at the restaurant. The rich flavor of chocolate cake on my tongue, the warmth of his smile across the table, the easy laughter that had flowed between us. The truffle he'd snuck into my bag. A pang of longing pierces my chest. If only things could always be that simple, that sweet.

"Earth to Rose." Paige snaps her fingers, cutting through the haze of my thoughts.

"Sorry, what did you say?' I ask.

"Nothing important, just that I should have started with the bourbon cake. This is Kentucky."

I nod. "Although I'm tempted to get married just to taste the champagne cake."

She laughs, returning to her seat. "How about I make you one? Way less hassle. Oh, speaking of commitment. How's it going with Mr. Bourbon?"

"Good, I guess. On our last date we had a small argument." I tell her how my flattering tactic with Sebastian had backfired, and that he knows about my leasing troubles.

"And he never mentioned a word during your other dates? That's suspicious."

A now familiar sour tang of dread and confusion settles in my stomach. I'm not sure what to make of Sebastian's silence about my store troubles. "His apology was sincere, and it's easy to forget he's a Blackstone when he's sweet and thoughtful," I tell her. "Wait here."

I walk to the storage room and return with his present. "He also stopped by and dropped off this." I set the electronic bike bell between us.

My thumb runs over its sleek surface. It's such a small thing, but the thoughtfulness behind it makes my heart stumble over itself.

Paige hits the bell's button and a train horn bellows from it. We, along with every customer, jump. She hunches her shoulders and apologizes to the startled group.

"Well, that'll definitely keep you safe," she says with a grin.

Safe. If only my heart felt the same way around him. This is getting complicated. I need to focus on what Thorne asked me to do, not get distracted by how much I like Sebastian. But damn, he makes it hard to keep my guard up.

"He said it was to help keep me safe on my bike," I say, unable to hide the soft smile that comes unbidden.

Paige tilts her head. "Huh, that is sweet."

"Yeah, and the more I think about the date, the more my gut tells me Thorne is playing us," I confess. Despite feeling foolish for sharing my suspicions, I trust Paige not to dismiss them without at least listening.

"How?"

"The only reason I mentioned the store issue to Sebastian was on Thorne's prompting. And something is off about him."

"Who? Sebastian or Thorne?"

"Thorne. He's a walking contradiction. He acts like he's concerned for Blackstone Bourbon and how Sebastian runs it, but there's this hunger to take down his brother that radiates off him like overpowering cologne. But then in the same breath, he's hitting on me, like his real goal might be to mess with Sebastian."

Paige frowns. "He hit on you?"

"Yeah, he offered," I make finger quotes. "To work out a different deal."

"Pig," Paige sneers.

I nod in agreement. "He is, but is he manipulating me, or am I casting him as the villain because I like Sebastian?"

A teenager sets two graphic novels on the check-out counter, halting our conversation. It takes a conscious effort to plaster on a smile and go through the motions of ringing up his purchases. My hands move automatically, but internally I'm grappling with the impossible tangle of emotions.

After he leaves with his purchases, Paige picks our conversation back up. "So, do you like Sebastian? Or do you like Sebastian?"

Her question strikes me like a splash of cold water. Do I like Sebastian? My mind flashes to the sensation of his hand on the small of my back as we left the restaurant, the glint in his eye when he teases me. My face flushes. "Both," I admit.

Paige rubs her hands together. "Oh, the plot thickens."

I laugh. "You are such a dork."

"That's a fact." She slaps the counter, grinning.

The bell over the door chimes. I glance up and freeze mid-motion. Sebastian.

He hasn't noticed me yet, still shaking raindrops from his coat as he steps inside. For three seconds, I have the luxury of watching him unobserved. The careful way he closes the door behind him. The slight smile as he takes in a display of new releases I arranged yesterday.

Then he turns my way. Our eyes lock, and my pulse quickens, cheeks warm, and a smile forms unbidden. He mirrors it with his own, weaving between the stacks toward the counter.

The weight of my deception sits heavy in my gut. Sebastian's looking at me with those trusting eyes, and I'm harboring secrets that could destroy whatever this is between us.

I paste on a cheerful expression, but the question burns: Will I come clean before it's too late, or will my desperate gamble cost me the one thing I'm beginning to want as much as my bookstore?

Chapter Nineteen

Rosalia

I don't like the way my heart expands at the sight of Sebastian. We aren't a real couple; everything between us is built on deceit and dirty deals. Yet, I have to grip the counter to keep from coming around and hugging him when he reaches me.

He sets a tray of take-out drinks in front of us, and I blink, taking in the vibrant hues of three cups filled with smoothies. One is deep purple for mixed berries. Another is a soft green. The last is bright orange. "I stopped at that new smoothie bar around the block. These are the top recommendations." He places the deep purple in front of me and hands the green kale and banana to Paige.

Scanning the flavors, Paige asks, "How'd you know I'd be here?"

"Rosalia mentioned you usually stop by after your bakery closes."

That heart-expanding feeling intensifies. Why does he have to listen to me when I talk?

He takes a sip of his and looks at me. "Do you have plans Saturday night?"

"No. Why?"

"Want to do me a huge favor?" he asks.

"Ah, were these smoothies a bribe?" I tease, intrigued. What could little ol' me do for a powerful Blackstone?

His head tilts slightly, and his grin widens, popping a dimple. "Maybe."

"What is it?"

"Attend Bits and Barrels with me."

"What's that?"

"A gala. Which is like prom for adults," Paige whispers.

"I know what it is." I bump my friend with my hip, hiding my sudden distress.

The thought of attending makes me nauseous. I can already hear the whispers and sideways glances from Sebastian's wealthy peers. They'll wonder what he's doing with someone like me, a small-time bookstore owner who'll stick out like a paperback novel in a rare manuscript collection. And if they ever learned about my deal with Thorne, they'd brand me a gold-digger, a manipulative opportunist. The scandal would not only embarrass Sebastian but could also turn the community against me, jeopardizing the business and programs I've worked so hard to build.

"The party officially kicks off the derby season," Sebastian says, oblivious to my distress. "And my mother is hosting the fundraising dinner."

I smile and hope it looks genuine. "That's right. All the fun is about to begin and I finally get to take part in it."

A child runs from the kids' section, followed by a harried man. The toddler chucks the book he's holding with all his might, letting out an exuberant squeal of delight. The guy apologizes, picks up the board book and the kid, and retreats into the rows of shelves.

"You've never been to any of the derby stuff? Didn't you come here all the time as a kid?" Paige asks.

"Yeah, but we were here in the summer, months after derby. And last year, I was too busy settling in and opening the store to go to any of them. This year, Dad and I are going to the Balloon Races. And I definitely won't miss the parade. And the fireworks. Oh! And the bed races." I clap my hands, then tell my inner child to settle down. "Sorry. I've heard my dad talk about these different goings-on, and this is the first time I'll get to take part.

"Oh, my brother, Noah—the one I told you about, who lives in Ohio, he's visiting. We plan on going to the Balloon Race," Paige says. "You should come with us."

"Okay." I take a sip of my smoothie. The cool, tangy sweetness of the berries is amazing. "Are you attending?" I ask Sebastian.

"No. I'm not a fan," he replies, looking at his drink.

"Who's not a fan of pretty, colorful balloons?"

"They're fine, but if I go, I'll be expected to ride the Blackstone Bourbon balloon." He shudders. "I have no interest in getting inside something that is kept in the sky with a flame and highly flammable nylon."

I nod. "Can't argue that logic."

"When my sister's here, she goes *in* the balloon. It's her favorite." He smiles, and the love I see there makes him even more handsome.

"Let me guess," Paige says, "Your favorite event was last week's Bourbonville."

"That was a lucrative day for Blackstone, but no, my favorite is Thunder Over Louisville." He steps around the counter, and the faint scent of his cologne, a blend of sandalwood and citrus, fills my senses as he leans closer. "About the fundraiser..."

From my high school years at a wealthy private school, I know what's expected at these events. I tally the cost and my gut twists. Even a cheap dress is impossible on my budget, let alone the other necessities like hair, makeup, and nails.

"I'm not really a gala girl," I say, fidgeting with the straw of my smoothie.

A flicker of disappointment crosses Sebastian's face and his grin falters. "If you don't want to go, I understand," he says softly, his tone tinged with resignation.

My heart clenches at the sight of his crestfallen expression. "It's not that I don't want to go with you. It's just that I don't have anything suitable to wear. The last time I wore a gown was at my senior prom. And that outdated dress is in Michigan." And it is probably way too basic for any event Mr. Billionaire attends.

"Not a problem. I'll get you one," Sebastian replies.

"What?" I scoff. "You'll get me a gown so that I'll go."

"Yup. Whatever you need." He rubs the back of his neck. "Listen, you'll be doing me a huge favor. These events are torture, whether I go with someone or alone, but I'm certain if you're there, the night will be tolerable."

"Wow, tolerable," I laugh. "Aren't you a charmer?"

"Fine. Fine. I can do better." He clears his throat. His brown eyes sparkle with warm humor, drawing me in like a moth to a flame. "The night will be magical if you attend, lovely Rosalia. A fairy tale come true. Better than Christmas when I was a kid. How's that?"

Paige clutches her heart. "That's good."

I agree. I am one hundred percent charmed but pretend to be unaffected. "Much better. But it sounds like you'd rather skip it. Why don't you?"

"That was the original plan. I was supposed to be out of town, but things had to be rescheduled. Now I'm expected to go. If I don't, my mom will guilt me until the next one. No thanks."

"I don't know..."

My gaze moves to Paige, who mouths, "Do it."

"How about I book a spa day for you and Paige on Saturday? There's a place my sister loves that has it all—hair, makeup, nails, and massages. I'll have Hanna, my PA, arrange everything for the day of the event. My treat for helping me out."

"I—"

"She'll do it," Paige says. "Just tell us where and when."

"Paige!" I sputter through my laughter. Looking at Sebastian, I ask, "When is it?"

"Saturday."

"This Saturday? Today's Wednesday. My store is open every day until the gala. And while I don't mind closing early—I can stay open a little later on Sunday—how will I find a dress or book a hair appointment in such a short time?"

"Do these questions mean you'll go?" My lingering ambivalence vanishes at the happiness in his voice.

"Yes, but there's no way I'll find a gown in two days. Plus, my store's open both days until most dress shops close."

"I'll take care of that. Hanna will schedule a Saturday morning appointment at the dress boutique where most women buy their gowns. Let me know your favorite colors; they'll set them aside for you to try on. The same goes for hair and makeup. Hanna will book a spa for anything you and Paige want done. " He pulls out his phone. "I'll call—" His cell rings, and a slight frown touches his perfect lips. "I have to answer this and get to a meeting, but I'll call Hanna in between."

He nods goodbye while answering the call. I watch him leave, rocking on my heels. Why had I agreed to go? Galas aren't for women like me. And why is my pulse sprinting because I get to spend an entire evening with Sebastian?

I turn to Paige. "What just happened?"

"You're going to the ball, Cinderella."

I bite my lip, my gaze dropping to the counter. "Because of my damn deal with Thorne I should be looking at my time with Sebastian as a business arrangement, but I can't. It feels like so much more. What if I'm making a mistake by going with him? What if I end up hurting him?"

Paige shakes her head, her expression softening. "Rose, it's okay to have feelings for him. If you find another way to save your bookstore, he'll never have to know about your deal with his brother. And, maybe for now, don't be afraid to embrace the magic of the moment. Worry about tomorrow, tomorrow. You deserve to feel like Cinderella for one night."

I nod, but I don't agree. I can't help but wonder if the fairy tale will disappear when the clock strikes midnight, leaving me with nothing but a broken heart.

And if I hurt Sebastian, that's exactly what I deserve.

Chapter Twenty

Rosalia

Sebastian's driver, Tom, hits the hazard button on the Bentley, then comes around to the sidewalk and opens the car's door. Paige exits, and I follow. Tom retrieves my gown from the front passenger seat, and I open my arms like I'm going to hug it. I should tamp down my enthusiasm, but I love my gorgeous red dress.

Tom shakes his head. "I'll carry it inside, ma'am."

"What about the car?" I glance at the congested road. There hadn't been a spot, so he parked in front of the elegant salon, blocking a lane of traffic.

"I'll only be a minute." He grins. "And it's not like anyone will ticket a Blackstone vehicle."

Paige leans close. "What do you think that feels like, wielding that kind of power?"

"Probably powerful. And it explains the Blackstone brothers' arrogance."

"True," Paige says, stepping through the spa's automatic door. "But after today, it's difficult to dislike a particular Blackstone."

That's the truth. After agreeing to help Thorne, I'd kind of hoped spending time with Sebastian would reveal the coldness and pretentiousness I'd read so much about online and in the gossip papers. No such luck.

Inside the salon is like another world. The outside noise evaporates when the doors close. The only sounds are the gentle, trickling water from a nearby fountain and soft, ambient music. "This top-tier treatment is something else," I mutter.

When we arrived at the dress shop, a salesperson was waiting for us. She took us into a dressing room as big as my entire apartment. Waiting for me were gowns in red, black, and sage lined up on a rack, along with an assortment of refreshments and snacks.

I glance at the garment bag Tom is handing to the man at the spa's front desk. My pulse shudders and then races. The crimson dress is exquisite, but what if the bold color and style are too much for an elegant gala?

Tom tells me he needs to pick up Sebastian's tux and deliver it to his office. He instructs me to call or text when I'm finished at the spa.

"You're delivering his tux to the distillery?" I ask.

"He's working until the party."

A sharp pang of disappointment pinches me. I'd hoped we'd arrive together, but it's ridiculous to crave those extra moments alone with Sebastian. I shouldn't need him to calm my nerves before the event.

Shoving down my ridiculous sense of letdown, I thank Tom. Then Paige and I are whisked deeper into the spa. An employee with brown skin and eyes so light they look gold tells me that Sebastian informed them to give us whatever treatments we wish.

"I'll just get started on hair and makeup," I say.

Paige holds up an index finger to the spa attendant, turning to me. "We have a lot of time. Get a facial or massage."

"There's no sense because I'll be tense as soon as I head to the gala."

Paige squeezes my hand. "Don't let those rich assholes make you small. You're worth more than every million they have in the bank."

"You're ridiculous, but I love you for it." I pull Paige into a hug. "Alright," I say when we separate, "facials first? Then you can get a massage while they're doing my hair and makeup?"

She agrees, and it turns out that the spa's luxury facial includes a scalp, neck, and shoulder massage. The extras cost me prepping time, but with the masseur's magic fingers and hands, I couldn't care less.

"We need to schedule these monthly. No, weekly," Paige says from the table next to mine.

The skilled therapist smooths warm, velvety massage oil over my skin, working out the knots in my shoulders, each touch sending waves of relaxation through my body. "That's a wonderful dream," I agree. But I don't think these will ever be in my budget. And let me say right now, I'm regretting my life choices that led me to a place where I can't afford them. I should've used my business degree to work for a Forbes Global company so I could do this daily."

"We could combine forces. One building, but both our businesses." Paige jokes. "We can call it Baked Books."

I laugh. "That sounds like an accounting firm for crooks."

After a moment of relaxed silence, Paige asks, "How are things going with your bookstore? Anything promising?"

"I have an appointment with the SBA next Monday," I reply. "I hope they'll offer some guidance and help. Just in case, I'm also applying for grants." My stomach twists. "It's only three weeks until derby, and I need to have my financing options figured out before then." My internal clock is ticking like a bomb. Every day that passes pulls me closer to an impossible choice."

"You got this. I feel it in my bones."

Paige's certainty is contagious. "You're a fantastic baker, but you'd have made a hell of a Life Coach," I tell her.

A warm towel is placed on my neck. "There's no rush," my masseuse says in his calm, quiet cadence. "I'll wait outside while you both get ready. Afterwards, I'll walk with you to hair and makeup."

"What are you going to get done next?" I ask Paige. "I've heard a body scrub is amazing."

"Nah, I want to come with you. See the transformation," she says, sitting up.

I do the same. "Are you sure?"

Paige nods and a weight lifts from me. I touch her shoulder. "Thanks. I'd love your help. I have no idea what to do with hair or makeup."

We are taken to a private room that has one of those electric massage chairs. That lessens my guilt about Paige passing up primo self-care. As soon as we settle in, the pretty spa attendant from earlier returns along with an older white woman with glossy black hair. She introduces herself as Sade, telling us she is the stylist. She looks more like a yoga or triathlon instructor.

I soon learn that Sade is kind, patient, and very good at her job. She takes the time to explain evening makeup and what would look best with my coloring. She also gives easy tips for everyday wear. And though I'm not used to such bold makeup, the final result is amazing.

The same is happening with my hair. The three of us decided on a crown braid. Sade is nearly finished with the style, and I'm already in love with it.

"You are such a pretty palette to work on," Sade says through a mouth of bobby pins, placing another in my hair. "I thought you looked great after makeup. You are flat-out stunning with this up-do. The epitome of elegance."

"I just want to fit in. Not make a fool of myself." The gentle tugging of the brush through my hair is oddly soothing, each stroke transforming my locks into a work of art. It lessens the nervous energy tingling through me. Kind of. I shake out my hands, accidentally bumping Sade and knocking a thin comb to the floor. "Sorry," I say.

"Honey, you'll fit right in." Sade picks up the comb and lightly taps my ear with it. "And they're just people, trust me. I've been making them look beautiful for years, and the stories I overhear would make your hair curl."

"Want to share?" I hold onto the sides of my chair to keep from fidgeting. "And preferably one that showcases the fact that they don't have perfectly polished, totally figured out lives."

I'd told Paige of my fears of standing out like a hillbilly at a ball. She's probably tired of my whining. Since Tom drove us to Glamorous Gowns, she's had to listen to my litany of worries.

"I could tell you one about the man you're going to this gala with..."

"Sebastian?" I ask, my stomach dropping.

Sade nods.

"How did you know who I'm going with?"

"Please, honey, everyone knows. You're going to Kentucky's fanciest event with the state's most eligible bachelor." She looks at me in the mirror and grins. "And Gus, the receptionist working today, received a call from Mr. Blackstone requesting a carte blanche afternoon for a mysterious woman. Trust me, everyone here is talking about it."

A cold wave washes over me. Not at the loose-lipped Gus, but because of what Sade might tell me about Sebastian. What if I learn he has a harem of women or a sex dungeon? Okay, maybe I should worry less about his sexual tastes and instead about the ruthless nature Thorne and gossip have hinted at.

Sade keeps her gaze locked on mine, a little worry showing in her eyes. "You're not going to spread this around or tell people it came from me, right? That family keeps their secrets locked down tighter than their bourbon recipe and yeast strain—"

"Yeast strain?"

"Live here or date him long enough, and you'll learn the importance. But what's important now is that I have your word not to gossip about what I'm telling you."

"Got it. Don't gossip about the gossip."

Sade snorts, playfully tugging at the braid she's creating. "Exactly. Now, I've never worked for Sebastian's family. They are the type that have the salon come to them, not the other way around. However, a regular of mine is a close mutual friend of theirs. She's one of those clients who sees her beautician as her secret keeper—or at least, the keeper of others' secrets."

"Anyway, let's start with Daddy Blackstone. He's a brilliant businessman, and judging by how their distillery has been booming since Sebastian took over, his son is too. But let's hope he didn't inherit his father's womanizing ways. His wife, Sebastian's mother, is stunning, yet the man can't keep his dick in his pants. He has at least one child from a mistress, possibly two, but that one's harder to pin down because the woman and child live farther south. New Orleans, I believe." Sade pauses, tilting her head. After placing a few more pins, she continues, "From what I hear, his sister is a vagabond who wants little to do with her family, except she's perfectly fine with mommy and daddy sending her money so she can travel the world."

I'm tempted to defend Lillianna, but all I know about Sebastian's sister is what he's shared. Still, I didn't get the impression she's the frivolous mooch Sade is painting her to be.

"Then there's Thorne. He's an even bigger bastard than his father." Sade's lip curls. "That shit he did with Tiffany was wrong. Sure, the woman's a bitch, and Sebastian could do so much better, but his own brother..." She shakes her head.

"What happened?" I ask quietly, not sure if I really want to know.

Paige obviously doesn't have the same hesitation. She is literally on the edge of her massage chair.

"Almost everything." Sade huffs. "Sebastian walked in on them one thrust away from having sex."

A wave of sympathy crashes into me, followed by a surge of anger. How could Thorne be so callous and selfish? And how could I even consider aligning myself with him? My resolve to protect my bookstore wavers, overshadowed by a growing impulse to shield Sebastian from further pain.

"No shit. Daaamn," Paige gasps. "And Sebastian is the master distiller. The top man. I bet he makes his slimy brother pay every day. I would."

I knew there was tension between them, but this goes beyond mere sibling conflict. The mere thought of the folder I'm supposed to steal burns like a guilty flame. Thorne claims it contains information that could damage Sebastian's position, but help their family's company. What if it's all a lie? What if this is just another way to twist the knife?

The tightening in my throat intensifies, making it difficult to breathe. But if I don't help Thorne, I lose everything. My store, the reading programs, and probably my father's house.

Maybe.

The revelation about Thorne and Tiffany burns in my chest. "How could he? His own brother." Disgust coats my words, though I know I'm being a hypocrite. "He's going to be at the gala tonight. How am I supposed to make it through the evening without throwing my drink at him?"

But even as I judge Thorne, I know I have to find another way than stealing from Sebastian. The SBA meeting, the grants—they have to work.

"Aw, look at you, getting all protective over your man," Paige says.

"He's not my man." However, the more time I spend with him, the more I wish for the opposite.

Sade's brows rise. "He's not?"

Oops. "I meant we've just started dating. We aren't official or anything." I shift in my seat. "I have to admit, it's nice to learn the rich are as messed up as the rest of us mortals."

"Yup." Sade sprays my hair with a product that smells of lavender. "The only difference is they have the money to hide their mistakes."

Paige pats my hand. "And honey, you *aren't* going to fit in with the group. You're going to outshine them all." She looks behind me at Sade. "You should see her dress."

My heart skips and trips, falling to my belly. "I should have gotten the black one." I planned to play it safe. Get a sophisticated gown, maybe even subdued. Instead, I went with a crimson number with a plunging neckline.

"I am so glad you didn't. It was lovely, but this one…" Paige fans herself.

"And combined with your hair and makeup." Sade stands back, then makes the chef's kiss gesture, handing me a mirror.

I reach out and touch the cool, smooth surface of the mirror. The woman in the reflection is a vision. I lean closer, marveling at the way my brown eyes pop thanks to the expertly applied makeup. My skin glows, and the contours of my face are highlighted to perfection. And my hair is an intricate updo that makes me feel like royalty; each curl, twist, and braid is a work of art.

I turn to Sade, my pulse fluttering. "You've transformed me. I barely recognize myself."

Sade grins. "Oh, honey, I just enhanced what was already there. Mr. Blackstone won't be able to take his eyes off you tonight."

Butterflies dance in my stomach, imagining his intense gaze sweeping over me, his hands itching to touch me. My phone chimes with a text, and my heart flips. Sebastian's name flashes on the screen.

> **Counting down the minutes until I can see you. Save me a dance?**

His words ignite a full-body flutter of excitement. I can almost picture the charming grin as he types out the message.

My fingers hover over the screen. Am I ready to dive into flirtation? To let myself be swept away by the handsome and enigmatic Sebastian Blackstone?

After a moment's hesitation, I type, surprising myself with my boldness.

> **Prepare to be dazzled. I may even save you more than one dance if you play your cards right.**

I hit send and a thrill rushes through my veins. This is a side I rarely let out to play—the confident, flirtatious woman who knows her worth. It is exhilarating and terrifying.

Yet beneath the excitement, a nagging voice reminds me of my deal with Thorne. I shouldn't develop feelings for Sebastian, knowing that I might ultimately have to betray him.

I push that thought away, determined to enjoy this moment of lighthearted connection. Tonight, I will allow myself to be dazzled by the magic of the gala and the charm of Sebastian Blackstone. Tomorrow, I'll worry about the consequences.

After I return my cell to my purse, Sade wishes me a fabulous night. I attempt to tip her, but she informs me that Sebastian included it in the final bill. His thoughtfulness continually surprises me.

"Are you ready to put on your dress? Ready to spend the evening with Mr. Blackstone Bourbon?" Paige asks. "I can't wait to see it all together."

I nod, stepping behind the privacy screen. Slipping into the gown, I can't shake the feeling that I'm stepping into a role I'm not prepared to play.

Zipping up the dress, I take one final look.

I'm walking into a minefield. And I don't mean just tonight, but with this whole Sebastian thing. Everything could explode in my face. I can only hope that when the dust settles, I'll still recognize the woman staring back at me in the mirror.

Chapter Twenty-One

Rosalia

By some miracle, I'm ready when Tom arrives at the entrance of the spa to take me to the gala. Although there had been a moment of pure panic when I couldn't find the garnet earrings my father had given me the previous Christmas. I'd put them in my purse before heading out in the morning, figuring I'd need their comfort. But the little velvet bag they were supposed to be in was empty. After dumping out my purse, I found them hiding in the crumb-filled corner.

Sebastian had arranged for Paige to get home safely in a separate car. After a quick goodbye hug and promise to call tomorrow, I step from the dim, lavender-scented cocoon of the spa into the bright evening air. The contrast momentarily blinds me, and I shield my eyes, scanning the street for our ride.

I'm about to ask Tom where he parked when I see the sleek car a little way up the street. Then I notice a guy standing next to it. A firework goes off in my chest. Sebastian is leaning against the side of it in a black tux that fits him like a dream. The cut showcases his broad shoulders, trim waist, and long legs. The fabric catches the slanting evening light, and the rich material absorbs and reflects it like liquid shadow. The man is a walking fantasy.

A smile splits my face. We're going to arrive together.

I practically skip to him until we're a few feet apart, and then I slow, my steps faltering. He's standing still as a stone. I run a hand to the waist of the dress. The smattering of gems and beads press into my palm. Is the gown too much for a refined gala? Too red? The plunge neckline too revealing?

Sebastian shakes his head and comes toward me. "You are beautiful." The worship in his voice makes me a little light-headed. He brushes his lips along my cheek. The barely-there kiss heats my desire and his words cool my anxieties. He steps back, his gaze drinking me in. "Seriously, you look ethereal."

"You too." His tuxedo fits as if it were custom-made, which it undoubtedly was. I adore the fact that, like he does with regular business suits, he's wearing a vest. This one is a few shades lighter than his black slacks and jacket, matching his bowtie and pocket handkerchief. "Do you have a tailor on speed dial, or is there a secret lair of tuxedo elves at your beck and call?" I tease.

"No, not elves." Sebastian laughs, then winks. "Have you already forgotten about my Minions? I have a whole army of them toiling away in the depths of the distillery. But instead of helping me steal the moon, they make bourbon smoother than silk. But don't tell anyone, it's a closely guarded family secret."

I laugh. The sound escapes before I can stop it. Being with him is so effortless, so wonderful. For a heartbeat, I let myself forget the complications, the reasons I have to hold back.

He hands me a bouquet of beautiful flowers. They are a mix of vivid shades of red roses, calla lilies so dark they're almost black, and a few tiny white blooms I can't name. Their perfume rises, complex and intoxicating, sweet with undertones of spice that remind me of him.

"These are gorgeous. Red is my favorite color."

His gaze travels over my dress. "It's now mine too."

"That's as smooth as your bourbon," I joke, smiling into the flowers.

"Not smooth, only the truth. You are exquisite, Rosalia. A goddess made flesh." His voice is low and rough, making me shiver.

He offers his arm, and I slide mine through his, my palm settling against the warm fabric of his sleeve. The material of his suit is as soft as cashmere. Heck, it probably *is* cashmere. But what has my pulse jumping is his warmth and scent—a dark and heady spice I want to lick from his neck.

On our other dates, we'd barely touched or even sat close. Tonight would be different. Forget the torture of trying not to look like a fool at the gala; the true test will be spending all evening on Sebastian's arm.

We walk a few steps to the car, idling at the curb. Sebastian opens the door for me, and after he goes around to the other side, he gets in. The Bentley's leather seats cradle me in luxury, still warm from the day's sun.

Sitting here pulls me into the memory of my very vivid and dirty fantasy I had the night after our first dinner date. And okay, fine, it wasn't my only one.

"Do you have a glass divider between the driver and the backseat?" I blurt, then my cheeks burn hot. No. I did not ask that aloud.

Sebastian pauses, eyebrows lifting slightly before a small smile tugs at one corner of his mouth. "No. I don't think this car comes with the option." His eyes glitter with mischief, his half-smile curling wider. "Why are you asking?"

I duck my head, suddenly fascinated with arranging the flowers in my lap. "Curious is all." Needing any new subject, I ask, "How far is the venue?"

"A little over an hour. It's at the distillery in Bardstown." He sucks in his bottom lip, and the enticing visual has all my attention until I notice his hesitation before he adds, "My mother has invited practically everyone who matters in Kentucky bourbon circles. Family tradition."

"Will there be many people you know there?" I ask, aiming for casualness, but the undercurrent of anxiety seeps out.

Sebastian's smile turns wry. "Everyone I know will be there. Small industry, big egos. My family has a way of drawing crowds." He pauses, as if choosing his words carefully. "Including some people I'd rather not see. But having you there changes everything."

My pulse trips over itself. "So...at your distillery?"

His brows furrow. "I didn't tell you?"

"You only said your mom had organized that event." Being surrounded by his family at their distillery is terrifying.

"Oh, when she heads them, they're usually at our place because we have a building that hosts events like weddings and galas that's well away from the day-to-day operations." He smiles. "Sometimes I forget you're not a local and wouldn't know this."

I've spent enough summers in Kentucky that the state is my half-home. However, I'm not from the same Kentucky as him. "It's fine. No worries."

"Are you sure?" He runs the pad of his thumb along the corner of my frowning lips. His touch has me forgetting all about my worries, replacing them with a sudden urge to draw his finger into my mouth to see his reaction.

He withdraws slowly as if he's thinking the same thoughts. When he rests his hand on his knee, I cover it with mine. He flips his wrist and entwines our fingers. The simple contact sends electricity racing up my arm, settling somewhere deep in my chest. My heartbeat stutters, then races to catch up, each pulse sending heat through my veins.

We fall into a silence that is charged yet peaceful. The quiet stretches, comfortable and electric, until the Bentley merges onto the freeway with a gentle surge of acceleration. I ask about his week, and the conversation flows effortlessly into talk of the upcoming derby events. When he invites me to watch the air show and fireworks with him the next weekend, I hold my breath for a few beats before accepting. I tell myself my racing heart is anticipation for finally witnessing the famous spectacle and not because I'll be spending an entire day with Sebastian. By the time the car is winding down the road to the distillery, my earlier worries have dissolved like morning mist, swept away by the wave of unexpected joy I've found in his presence.

We slide between the open iron gates that display Blackstone Bourbon in brass lettering with the silhouette of their bottle behind the script. We drive past dark red brick buildings, both small and large, their windows glowing amber in the fading light. Copper stills gleam through some windows, polished to a mirror shine. The surrounding hills roll into the distance, dotted with aging warehouses. The air itself seems different here—richer somehow, carrying the sweet, woody scent of bourbon that's been soaking into the soil for generations. The property is stunning, a perfect blend of industrial utility and Southern grandeur, yet I can't concentrate. All of my insecurities have returned to suffocate me.

I smooth my hands over my dress, trying to quell my nerves. "This isn't my world. I don't want to embarrass you tonight," I admit. "I know these events are important for your business and your reputation."

"You could never embarrass me, my Red Rose." His voice wraps around the endearment like velvet, landing low in my stomach. I have to press my thighs together, shocked at how three simple words can affect me so viscerally. He cups my cheek like I am his delicate, perfect flower. "I need you to hear this. Are you listening?"

I nod, still internally swooning over the term of endearment.

"I know this might feel overwhelming, but when you agreed to come with me, I actually began to look forward to it. Our worlds don't have to align perfectly. What matters is how we are together. And when we're together, it's like I can finally breathe."

I lean into his touch, savoring the warmth. "I feel it too. You make me forget about everything else—all the stress, all the pressure I'm under. When we're together, I'm drawn to you in a way I can't rationalize. It's physical, but it's more than that." The confession feels like stepping onto thin ice and the absolute truth.

"But there are things about my life right now, complications I haven't told you about." The words stick like honey laced with poison. Every smile, every touch, every connection with Sebastian makes Thorne's leverage over me a noose that tightens.

"We all have complications," he says softly. "But I love watching your face break into laughter, how you pull it from me when I least expect it." He shifts in his seat, angling his body more fully toward mine, his eyes never leaving my face. "The way you lean forward, talking about storytelling, noticing things others miss. You listen as if each syllable holds weight. You remind me there's more to life than balance sheets and bourbon."

His words resonate somewhere beneath my ribs, but then twist painfully. He may see what others glance past, but he's blind to Thorne's bargain. We might be able to move past our very different backgrounds, but my complications aren't just complexities—they're betrayals taking shape. My arrangement with his brother contaminates whatever might grow between us.

"You know," I say, carefully stepping around the truth, my fingers nervously smoothing a non-existent wrinkle from my dress, "for someone born into such wealth, you move through the world with unusual awareness of others."

He laughs. "Daniel might disagree."

I smile. "Well, I see a man who rescues injured horses that vets had written off, and somehow had my bike fixed and delivered to my doorstep after the accident without making it seem like charity. You pay attention to things most people in your position wouldn't bother with."

He studies my face for a moment, a smile breaking across his features. "And you've turned your bookstore into something magical. You listen to people, really listen. Whether it's a reluctant teenager or kids who light up when they see you, you make everyone feel seen."

"That's nothing," I argue, but who am I kidding? I love his words.

His thumb brushes along my cheek, the touch light but deliberate. "Most people who meet me see dollar signs or a stepping stone. But you, you challenge me, question me, make me defend my opinions. When you listen, I know you're actually hearing me, not just waiting for your turn to speak." His voice softens. "Do you have any idea how rare that is? How refreshing?"

The intensity in his eyes makes my breath catch. For a suspended moment, I forget about Thorne, about deadlines, about everything except the way Sebastian is looking at me as if I'm something precious he's discovered unexpectedly.

I turn my face into his palm, nuzzling his skin. I want to memorize every detail of this moment, from his scent to his warmth, and the surprising rough calluses on his fingers. A perfect, fleeting snapshot of what could be, if only...

Almost of its own accord, my body sways forward. My lips graze his cheek, a ghost of a kiss. The contact ignites a fire in my blood, and a yearning so intense it steals my breath. I should pull away and put some distance between us. But I can't move, can't bear to shatter this fragile, charged moment.

Sebastian turns his head. His mouth is a hairsbreadth from mine, so close I can taste his exhale. The air crackles with tension, electric and palpable. My lips tingle in anticipation, and my body hums with a want so fierce it borders on pain.

I meet his gaze. The raw need, the hunger, the desperation sears my soul. "Rosalia..." His voice is rough and strained. "Could I..."

A sharp knock on the window shatters us apart. A camera lens is outside the window like a hungry Cyclops. When had the car stopped moving? "Who's your date, Mr. Blackstone?" asks a reporter.

Sebastian ignores the chaos outside and tells me, "Wait. I'll come around and open your door."

He exits and my mind spins. We almost kissed. And I want it like my next breath. But I shouldn't. Not until I find a way to save my story without Thorne's "help."

My pulse quickens as I brace for the night ahead. I can't get swept up in this fantasy, no matter how tempting it may be. Yet with every touch, every smile, and every whispered word, my resolve crumbles. How long can I keep pushing him away when all I want is to pull him closer?

Chapter Twenty-Two

Rosalia

The moment I enter the gala on Sebastian's arm, the weight of curious gazes lands on me. The air hums with a mix of excitement and judgment. Whispers follow us across the marble floor, each click of my heels against the stone announcing my presence to people who silently question my right to be here.

The opulent room and high-society chatter remind me of the ever-present sense of being an outsider in such lavish surroundings. I'm still that girl with the wrong shoes and the wrong accent, trying desperately to blend into surroundings that seem designed to expose every way in which I don't belong.

I press my free hand into the torso of my dress, wishing I'd chosen something less loud. The red doesn't feel elegant but garish under the glittering lights of the chandeliers. I glance at the other women, all sleek and sophisticated in muted tones. What had I been thinking? My grip tightens on Sebastian's arm as nervous energy courses through my body.

"Hey," he says softly, turning to face me. "You okay?"

I smile, but it probably lands more like a grimace. "I don't belong here."

He reaches out and tucks a strand of hair behind my ear. "You belong with me," he says firmly. "And I belong with you."

His words settle over me like a warm blanket, easing my nerves. They can't be true, not with my lies standing between us, but I'll pretend. And, like in high school, I won't let those who look down on me see me sweat.

I bite my bottom lip to keep my chin from trembling and nod. Hand in hand, we step further into the room, into the glitter and the glamour.

We mingle, and I find myself relaxing. Sebastian's hand stays anchored at my side, providing comforting stability amidst the buzzing conversations where one person after another vies for his attention. When admirers approach, women and a few men attempt to flirt with him. He politely introduces me while pulling me close in a gesture that makes his interest clear.

An elegant older woman with black hair swept into a classic twist announces dinner will be served and asks everyone to find their table. I'm certain I've never met the lady, but she looks familiar.

In my three-inch red stilettos, I reach Sebastian's ear and whisper, "Who's the lady on stage?"

"My mother," Sebastian says, offering his arm.

Ah, no wonder. I rest a hand on his forearm. "You have her mouth and eyes."

He nods and then moves us toward the front of the room. I'm no longer shackled by the weight of small talk and nerves, and my gaze wanders. The interplay of the chandeliers' light on the pine plank ceiling and the warm hues of the setting sun through the large windows is stunning. I'm overwhelmed by the gala's rustic elegance.

Stopping at a table next to the stage, Sebastian pulls out a chair for me. His body brushes against mine, and the fleeting contact ignites an electric tension along my skin. Warmth radiates from him, and I catch another hint of his masculine scent that makes my pulse quicken.

I sink into the chair, hyper-aware of his proximity. He takes a seat, and his knee brushes against mine under the table. A brush of warm wool against bare skin that sends electricity shooting up my thigh. He doesn't pull away. Neither do I.

The heat of his leg seeps through the thin fabric, and my breath catches. I imagine those long fingers mapping the curve of my spine, those muscled thighs wrapped around mine. My nipples tighten against my dress, and I quickly adjust my posture, crossing my arms casually over my chest while reaching for my water glass. I press my legs together to contain the ache building between them.

Needing a distraction from my desire, I look around the table at those already seated. My heat dies instantly when my gaze snags on cold, assessing blue eyes. Thorne sits across from us, staring back at me.

My displeasure must show because his eyebrows flicker and then furrow. I quickly smooth my features as Sebastian introduces me to everyone at our table. First is his father, Louis. His hair is full gray but thick as his son's. He is the one who gave Sebastian his proud, straight nose and strong jawline. On his other side is a man and a woman around his father's age, whose last name I recognize. They own a chain of very popular ice cream parlors.

Sebastian doesn't introduce Thorne or his date. After what I learned today, I can't blame him. Working alongside someone who stabbed you in the back has got to be torture.

The sick irony makes my heart hurt. I'm sitting here sympathizing with Sebastian's pain while knowing I might do the same. What kind of person does that make me—feeling sorry for him while planning to hand over files to his backstabbing brother so he can force Sebastian out of the family company. He started the damage, but I might be the one to finish it.

Thorne's jaw flexes, and he looks at me. Uh-oh. "Hello, Ms. Manchester. I hope you are well." He rests an arm around the chair of the beautiful auburn-haired woman next to him. "I'd like you to meet my date, Gina."

"It's a pleasure to meet you," I tell the other woman. After learning what he'd done to Sebastian, I can't share pleasantries with him, but there's no reason to be rude to his date.

Thankfully, the small talk is cut short as an army of waiters descends on us with silver trays of food. The chair next to Louis remains empty. Sebastian leans toward me, his suit jacket brushing my bare shoulder, his heat warming me even more. "Don't wait for my mother. She rarely sits down at parties, even when she's not running them."

Seeing his family in one room, I wonder about the one missing. "Is your sister still in Thailand?" I ask.

"Yes. She'll be there for another month."

Louis swirls his drink. "Ms. Manchester, my son mentioned you're renting one of our buildings."

My stomach clenches. Which son? There is something in Louis's tone, a casual curiosity that feels like a trap. I look at Sebastian, but he's talking with the woman next to him.

"Yes, Mr. Blackstone. I have a bookstore on Whiskey Row."

He nods. "How's that going?"

"I'm committed to my business," I say carefully. "I'm willing to do whatever it takes to make it work."

Louis raises an eyebrow. "Whatever it takes? That's an interesting choice of words."

My heart skips, then hammers. Does he know something? Has Thorne told him about their deal? The thought has my palms sweating.

I struggle to keep my expression neutral, but if Louis knows about my agreement with his son, would he tell Sebastian? The thought of betrayal blooming in his eyes has nausea clawing up my throat. He'd never forgive me. I'd become another person who used and lied to him. It wouldn't matter that I'm looking for alternatives. The fact that I'd even considered betraying him would be enough.

Taking a deep breath and hoping my voice doesn't shake, I say, "I'm fortunate, the community is supportive, and I've worked hard to build a loyal customer base, but my business is new... and things come up."

Louis leans in his chair, gaze never leaving my face. "Fortune favors the bold, isn't that what they say? I wonder, Ms. Manchester, just how bold you'll be."

My breath catches. I hear the insinuation. He knows something, and he is toying with me.

I look at Sebastian again, desperate for an escape. But he's laughing at something the older woman has said, oblivious to my distress. Thorne's mouth curves into a smirk, full of cruel amusement when our eyes meet.

I'm on my own. And I'm drowning.

"I hope it works out for you." Louis leans back with obvious satisfaction, like he's relishing in my discomfort. He's as awful as Sade described.

"What works out?" Sebastian asks.

"Her little bookstore."

"Dad," Sebastian growls.

"Son," Louis replies, and a sardonic chuckle follows. "I only mean that the first store is always precarious."

"That is the truth," agrees the man next to him. "Opening that initial business takes a daunting leap of faith that is fraught with uncertainty and potential pitfalls."

Louis shifts in his seat, his brow rising. It's a mirror expression of Sebastian when he's amused. "Did you start a new venture? Your ice cream parlors have been a Kentucky staple since your granddaddy opened during Prohibition."

The man's smile is crooked and charming. "Good thing too, since it allowed *your* granddaddy to hide his moonshine in the empty ice cream containers." He turns to me. "I was speaking of my daughter. She opened a shoe store about five years ago, specializing in handmade riding and style boots. She struggled at first, but now her business is booming. She just opened her fourth store last month."

The pride on his face makes me smile, yet beneath the surface, the tendrils of jealousy stir. The luxury of a safety net is a privilege I've never known.

When the server arrives with our entrées, I notice the sprigs of cilantro decorating the rim of Sebastian's plate. Before he can react, I reach over with my fork and remove the offending herb, transferring it to my plate.

He catches my eye, and a look of surprise and warmth fills them. "You remembered," he murmurs.

I shrug lightly. "You'd scraped it off your steak at Fantastic Fusion." The memory of him pushing aside the herb with obvious distaste was a casual moment I'd filed away without realizing.

"It tastes like dish soap." His smile reaches his eyes, crinkling the corners in a way that sends a current of recognition through me. In this room full of people vying for his attention, he looks at me like I'm the only one who truly sees him.

The rest of dinner passes more pleasantly with Louis turning his attention to the ice cream parlor owners. Sebastian occasionally catches my eye across the rim of his bourbon glass, and those brief moments of connection anchor me.

As the servers clear our dinner plates, Sebastian's mom steps to the microphone, gently tapping it. A hush falls over the room as heads swivel toward the stage, conversations trailing off into expectant silence. She gives a short speech, and one by one, the major donors take their turns at the podium, talking over the crowd's murmurs. Then Sebastian is called to speak.

His tall frame commands attention on the stage, shoulders broad under his perfectly tailored suit. The spotlight catches in his dark hair as he speaks passionately about the racing horses, his hazel eyes flashing with intensity. He's magnetic like this—not merely handsome, but alive with conviction, drawing everyone's gaze.

When his speech draws to a close, everyone erupts in applause, the energy palpable. His mom joins him on the stage, announcing that dessert will be served shortly, followed by drinks in the main room and dancing in the ballroom.

Sebastian returns to our table, and admirers immediately surround him. He acknowledges them politely but keeps his focus on me as we're served our dessert.

Everyone at our table receives elegant crystal dishes of panna cotta with berry compote. Everyone except me. The server places a different plate before me: a perfect slice of chocolate Sacher torte.

"There seems to be a mistake," I begin, looking up at the server.

"No mistake, ma'am," he replies with a discreet smile, nodding his chin toward Sebastian.

I turn to find him watching my reaction with barely contained pleasure. Looking between him and my dessert, a warmth spreads through me that he'd noted such a small detail.

"You did this?" I ask.

A hint of vulnerability flickers across his features, mingling with the quiet pride in his eyes. "I might have made a special request."

"You remembered from that conversation we had about desserts? When I told you about my grandmother making this for my birthdays?"

He dismisses the gesture with a tilt of his head, but the thoughtfulness behind it resonates louder than any grand declaration. "Try it," he encourages, leaning forward slightly. "See if it measures up."

Louis and Thorne exchange curious glances at my unique dessert, but I'm too touched by the gesture to care about their scrutiny.

I take the first bite. The rich chocolate and subtle sweetness of apricot transport me back to my grandmother's kitchen. I close my eyes for a moment, savoring both the flavor and the thoughtfulness behind it.

"So good," I moan. "It's almost as good as hers." I offer him a taste from my fork, our eyes lock, and something shifts between us. This small moment feels more intimate than an embrace.

Around us, guests rise from their tables as dessert ends. The gentle notes of a string quartet drift from the ballroom, drawing guests toward the sound.

Sebastian leans closer, his voice low and meant only for me. "I believe I was promised a dance."

The way he says it, somewhere between a question and a statement, sends a pleasant shiver down my spine. "I believe you were," I reply, setting my napkin beside my now-empty dessert plate.

He stands and offers his hand. I place mine in his, and the warmth of his fingers is a promise. A few attempt to pull him away to talk business, but like earlier, he is polite but firm, telling them he's promised me a dance. The gazes of strangers press into me, and the flash of the cameras follow us, but I ignore them all, falling under the spell of my date.

When we reach the dancefloor, the song transitions to something slower. His hand slides from my waist to the small of my back, fingers splaying against the fabric of my dress. Each point of contact sends a wave of heat through me. We sway to the music, and I'm lost in the dark hazel depths of his eyes as he draws me closer with gentle insistence.

My breath catches. The space between us, once proper and formal, has disappeared. His cologne and something uniquely him envelops me, making my head swim with every inhale.

"I'm really glad you're here with me tonight," he whispers, his lips so close to my ear that his breath caresses my skin. The sensation sends a cascade of goosebumps down my neck, across my shoulders, and along my arms.

"Me too," I manage to reply, my voice giving away my desire. My fingers curl against the nape of his neck, brushing against the soft hair there.

The music swells and he pulls me closer until our bodies are flush. My nerves come alive, mapping every exquisite point where we meet. The solid plane of his chest against mine, the strong thigh occasionally pressing between my legs as we move, the heat of his palm burning through the thin material of my dress. I feel his heartbeat—or is it mine?—racing beneath the layers of clothing.

His rhythm falters for just a moment when my fingers trace small circles at the base of his skull. His pupils dilate, and his grip on my waist tightens ever so slightly. The corner of his mouth lifts in a smile meant only for me.

We're barely dancing now, just swaying in place. The rest of the room fades until there is only Sebastian and me. My nipples tighten against my dress, and

I arch toward him, seeking more contact. His hand slides lower on my back, decidedly possessive.

"Sebastian," I breathe his name like a prayer, an invitation.

He draws closer, our breaths mingling. The hunger I see on his face matches the ache building between my legs. His gaze drops to my lips, and I lean in, drawn by an invisible force I neither can nor want to resist.

"Honey, there you are," says a woman.

We turn, and I recognize his mother. Up close, she is even more glamorous, with the same dark hair and light brown eyes as Sebastian. Her slender frame appears delicate at first glance, but the determined set of her jaw reveals an inner strength that belies her fragile appearance.

"I wondered if you'd make time to say hi to your son," Sebastian teases. "You know, the one you bullied into coming here. Mother, this is Rosalia." He slides an arm around my waist and says, "Rosalia, this is my mother, Catherine."

Catherine's attention is fixed on where his hand rests on my hip, her eyes narrowing almost imperceptibly. The intimate and relaxed way he touches me should be thrilling, but his mother's disapproval drains all the pleasure from it.

She nods at me. "Pleasure." Then, resting a delicate hand on Sebastian's shoulder, she says, "For someone who didn't want to be here, you seem to be enjoying yourself." Her perfect peach lips press into a thin line as if she's sipped bargain-bin bourbon.

Why wouldn't she want her son to have a nice time? I look at Sebastian. His smile has vanished, replaced with a slight frown.

"Is there a problem?" he asks in a flat tone.

"Of course not." She pats his arm in a placating gesture, but she glances at me with barely concealed bewilderment, as if puzzled why I'm with her son. Then she lowers her voice. "People are gossiping. They want to know who your date is, and if your rather *risqué* dancing is—"

"We're dancing close, not grinding on the damn dance floor." Sebastian's arm tightens around my waist, drawing me closer to his side as if physically shielding me from his mother's judgment.

She leans in. "Some say it's because Tiffany's here."

His head jerks up, scanning the room. "Why the hell is she here?" he hisses.

My stomach twists. Damn, first is brother. Then his cruel father and disapproving mom. Now his freaking ex-wife. Hell, maybe my gaslighting ex-boyfriend will make an appearance at the gala next?

"The Birchsky family bought a table and brought her as their guest," Catherine says. "I'm sure for the entertainment factor." Her attention settles on a middle-aged couple across the room. "This gala will be the last one they attend."

Her words sound like a promise. I now see that her fragile appearance is definitely an illusion.

"And I will not be their entertainment," Sebastian says. He turns to me. "Do you want to leave?"

I glance at him. He doesn't look devastated, just annoyed. But his mother has gone pale, her shoulders slumped as if the weight of his potential departure is crushing her.

Against my better judgment, I say, "The music is great. Let's stay a little longer?"

The ice in Catherine's demeanor melts slightly, and a hint of a smile touches her lips. "I'm sorry, I missed your last name, Rosalia, was it? Please forgive my poor manners."

"Manchester," I reply.

Catherine's brow furrows, but before she can inquire further, Sebastian says, "If you don't mind, Mother, we're going to step outside for some fresh air. I'd like to show Rosalia the rose garden."

With a brief nod, she acquiesces. Relief ripples through my body as Sebastian guides me away from the probing questions and toward the promise of a moment alone together.

Leaving the ballroom, I tell him I need to visit the washroom. He steers me in that direction. Once inside, I run my fingertips under the cold water before rubbing them on my temples. The door behind me opens and a tall woman enters.

She is a vision of perfection in a sleek, black gown that clings to her every curve as if it were an extension of her. She glides to the sink beside me. The back of her dress comes into view, and wow. The daring plunge descends to the base of her spine, the expanse from shoulder to shoulder is adorned with glistening stones that drape like an exquisite necklace against her smooth skin.

The woman looks me over. "That's a bold choice," she sniffs. "I'm not sure I could pull off that color, but you wear it with such...confidence."

There is that word again, "bold." And, like when Louis said it, it doesn't feel like a compliment.

"Um, thanks," I mutter.

Pulling a lipstick from her clutch, the woman says, "You're the Rosalia everyone's talking about. Sebastian's temporary rebound."

What the hell? "Who are you?"

"Tiffany Blackstone."

Chapter Twenty-Three

Rosalia

I stare at the woman next to me. Tiffany Blackstone. Sebastian's ex-wife. She has the glossy beauty, that untouchable quality of someone who's never doubted her place in the world.

Her gaze sweeps over me from head to toe. "Enjoy your little fairy tale while it lasts," Tiffany purrs with a smirk. "Because when the clock strikes midnight, you'll be back where you belong."

"Excuse me," is all I can manage.

"You may have caught *my* Sebastian's eye for now," Tiffany's focus drops to my designer heels that her ex-husband bought. "But we both know that shoe doesn't really fit. Sooner or later, he'll realize it."

I straighten my shoulders. Anyone who treated a partner's love as though it were worth less than fool's gold won't make me cower. "From what I understand, you're hardly in a position to judge anyone else's character. I might not be rich, but you're the one who doesn't have any class."

Tiffany's flinch is almost imperceptible, and a flicker of something like shame crosses her face. She opens her mouth as if to retort, then closes it. "Perhaps I deserved that," she concedes, her voice tight. "But it doesn't change the facts. You're out of your depth. You're also temporary."

She obviously doesn't like that her ex is dating, but why? She cheated on him with his brother, no less. The marriage couldn't have been that important to her.

"What is your deal with me?" I challenge.

"You're in my way," she declares.

"Excuse me."

"Thorne was a mistake. I want my husband back." Her voice catches slightly on the word "husband," and for a fleeting moment, a wistful look crosses her face. "I never should have let him go," she confesses softly, almost to herself. Then, as if she remembers where she is and who she's talking to, her expression hardens again. "And we would reconcile if he'd take my calls. Agree to meet with me."

I have to admire the woman's confidence. She stands here, speaking about Sebastian like he's a possession she misplaced rather than a person she hurt. Something about her tone, so certain and entitled, makes me take a small step back.

I'm silent for a long moment, considering my words carefully. Then, I say, "I'm not going to pretend to understand what happened between you two. That's your history, your story. But I do know this: Sebastian is an amazing man. He's kind, generous and so deeply good. And he deserves to be with someone who sees that, who appreciates him for who he is."

My heart squeezes. Given the deal I've made with Thorne, I don't deserve him either.

Tiffany stares at me, seemingly at a loss for words, but quickly finds them. "You are out of your league. A man like Sebastian will never fall for a woman like you."

She pulls on the handle to leave, but freezes. Sebastian is standing right outside. His gaze lands on Tiffany and turns sub-zero. She steps to him and the door swings shut behind her.

I should exit as well. Instead, I rest my palms on the cool tile of the sink. My shoulders sag as I inhale deeply. Tiffany's words ring in the empty bathroom, echoing my deepest insecurities. I am out of my league. I'm fooling myself into thinking that, even if I find a way to save my store without Thorne, I'll ever belong in Sebastian's world.

Exhaling a sigh, I straighten and leave the restroom. Tiffany is gone, but not Sebastian. He moves toward me, and I see the worry in his eyes.

"Are you okay?" he asks.

"I'm fine."

He looks from me to his ex-wife's retreating back. "Did she say something to you?"

I laugh, but the sound is weak. "She wants you back."

His face hardens. "No. She wants what comes with being the wife of a Blackstone."

"There is so much more to you than your family name, Sebastian." In fact, everything in me wishes he weren't a Blackstone, just an uncomplicated man who visited my bookstore.

"Maybe, but that's the piece of me everyone wants." His gaze searches me, like he's hoping I'm different. And I wish I were, but Thorne and his damn deal...

I look away, unable to meet his eyes while carrying this secret.

Steering the conversation away from that dangerous territory, I say, "She was also being catty and hinted that my dress color is gauche."

"Bullshit. I think her envy is showing."

"The color isn't too loud?" I hate the insecurity in my voice, but the gala is far out of my comfort zone.

He steps close, his breath hot against my ear. "Are you kidding me? You're going to be the death of me in that dress. I can't take my eyes off you, and I don't think I'm the only one. Every man here wishes he were me tonight."

Someone bumps me from behind and I stumble into Sebastian. He catches me around the waist. The person apologizes, but I barely register it. All my focus is on Sebastian's touch, which burns me, sending heat between my legs.

There's no denying I like his hands on me. Leaning into him, I inhale. He smells like comfort and sensual dreams. I step away before doing something embarrassing, like kissing or climbing him.

He glances past me, then backs away. "For someone who's not a," he made air quotes, "'gala girl,' you are navigating this evening like an expert."

"Thank you." His compliment releases some of the tension in my limbs. "My mom was an English teacher at the top private school in Michigan. A perk of her job was that I attended for free. I know how to act, but that's all it is—acting. And the performance makes me anxious, afraid people will see through it." Just as his ex-wife had so easily done.

"You do belong."

I press my lips together. No, I don't.

He takes my hand. "Come on. Let's take a breather from this party and go outside. This time of year, the rose garden is in full bloom."

That sounds perfect, and I allow him to lead me outside. Once there, we walk to a waist-high iron fence. The sun set hours ago, but the gas lamps strategically placed throughout the garden give the place a wonderfully haunted romance vibe.

"Beautiful," I murmur.

"I agree." He's looking at me. My pulse quickens and I can't turn away.

All the evening aggravations and hurts disappear, and all I see is him. A breeze blows a strand of my hair loose from my braid. He tucks it back in place and then runs his fingertips along my jaw. When he reaches my lips, I shiver.

"Do you want to go back in?" he asks.

I shake my head, stepping closer to him. The only place I want to be is here, with him, looking into those bourbon eyes that promise to give me what I've desired since that almost kiss in the car—his touch, his lips on mine.

He leans closer, his minty breath fanning against my tingling lips. "What do you want, Rosalia?" he murmurs, his hand sliding up my bare back, his touch leaving trails of goosebumps in its wake.

"You."

His lips part on an exhale. Then his warm, large palm rests on my waist. He brushes his lips over mine as if testing the truth of my claim. We're crossing a line we'll probably regret, but I need his mouth on mine.

I press into the gentle kiss, and with a groan, he's all in. The hand on my hip wraps around me, pulling me against his hard body. I open for him and he doesn't hesitate. His kiss is a mix of teasing and temptation, giving me just enough to hunger for more while offering me all I want.

"Oh, pardon us," comes a man's voice I somewhat recognize.

Heat floods my cheeks as I jolt from Sebastian. I press my lips together, still tingling from his kiss, my stomach dropping as I take in Daniel staring wide-eyed at us.

"Rosalia? Rosalia Manchester, is that you?" asks the woman standing next to Daniel. My gut tightens. Who now? I'd love to see a friendly face.

Wait. I know that face!

No way. Anna from the romance book club is standing with Daniel. She looks different from her usual laid-back bookstore self. In a sleek gown and perfect makeup, she blends in seamlessly with the gala crowd.

"What are the odds? Of all the fancy galas in Louisville, we end up at the same one," I say, still processing the bizarre coincidence of seeing my bookstore friend here.

The universe seems determined to remind me tonight of all the lives entwined with mine. First Sebastian's family, then Tiffany forcing me to confront my insecurities, now Anna appearing like a sign from my real world. It's as if every corner of this gala holds someone with a stake in my decisions.

"I could say the same about you!" Anna counters. "When did you start attending fancy galas? *And* with Mr. Blackstone?"

My heart skips a beat. Anna's eyes hold a million questions I'm not ready to answer. Thinking fast, I deflect. "I didn't know you were dating anyone."

"It's recent." Anna squeezes Daniel's hand.

He smiles at her, but his gaze returns to Sebastian's arm around my waist and his mouth presses in a tight line. Is there concern in his eyes? And for whom?

The butterflies in my chest crash into my stomach. Could Daniel's disapproval have something to do with my deal to help Thorne? Daniel was probably the lawyer who had drawn up the contract I'd demanded. The one that states if I take Sebastian's red leather folder, my lease would be renewed. And that I could back out at any time.

He clears his throat. "Sebastian, why don't we go grab drinks for everyone?"

I glance at Sebastian, but he's looking at Daniel with a slight frown. His arm tightens around my waist, and then he releases me. "Sure," he says finally. "Rosalia, what would you like?"

"Surprise me," I reply, proud at my steady tone.

He nods, turning to Anna. "And for you?"

"A Kentucky Mule, if you don't mind," she says, her gaze still on me.

The men walk away, and I can't shake the feeling that Daniel made the suggestion to get Sebastian alone. Is he going to warn him about getting too close to me?

"Is everything okay?" Anna asks.

I force a smile. "Yeah, everything's fine. I'm just... a little overwhelmed by all of this." Pointing to a nearby wrought iron table, I ask, "My feet ache. Do you mind if we sit?"

"Works for me." She perches in the nearest chair and pats the one next to her. "Sit and tell all about Sebastian Blackstone. What's he like? Is he intimidating and enticing? Broody and mysterious? I told you he was interested in you. When did you start dating? How did he ask you out?"

I hold up my hand, laughing. "That's a lot of questions."

"Feel free to answer one or all of them."

I settle on the easiest. "He asked me out about two weeks ago. This is our third date."

Anna lets out a low squeal. "Woman, you're a living, breathing romance book." She opens her palms like she's reading a book. "The hot billionaire walks into a local bookstore and falls for the quiet and sexy owner."

He is a hot billionaire who kisses like the men in my favorite romances, but there won't be a happily ever after. Not unless I find a way to save Novel Idea without Thorne.

"We won't last." My heart lurches.

Anna frowns. "Why? Is the gossip true? He's hot to look at but cold to touch?"

I press my fingers to my lips. "No. Not. At. All. We're too different to have anything lasting."

"Oooh, different worlds. That's my favorite trope." Anna taps her fingertips together. "I see the story; you and Sebastian help each other see a new and fun way to live and love."

I shake my head. "Romance readers are amazing. They see the best in people."

"Nah, more like we're the worst cynics. That's why we need romance books, to remind us that happily ever afters do exist." She squeezes my hand. "And I most definitely wouldn't write off anyone who kissed me like he did you, or looks at me as he does you."

I wave this away, the denial automatic, even as my heart skips. "You saw us together for all of five minutes."

"That's all I needed." Anna fans herself. "Woman, he's into you."

Is there actually something real between us, or is it attraction mixed with all my lies? But if I go through with my agreement with Thorne, it won't matter; Sebastian will never forgive me.

"I like him too," I admit. My pulse quickens. The admission complicates everything.

However, there is a solution. I could forget about the deal with his brother and leave Whiskey Row. I'll do my best to secure a new place and save my programs. Then I can date Sebastian without my deception hanging over us. This will allow me to truly see where things go and discover if he's as kind as he seems. And if he turns out to be like the other men in his family who take whatever they want, I'd still have my self-respect.

If SBA and grants don't pan out, I could find a job as a librarian in Kentucky or in Michigan. I love Novel Idea, but at least I'd still be surrounded by books and have my integrity.

Yes, I'll tell Thorne to forget about the deal. I'll call him tomorrow. The decision frees me, and the invisible knot around me loosens.

And to make the possibility of this chapter in my life ending more real, I say, "Another reason he and I might not work out is because there's a chance I'll be returning to Michigan."

Anna blinks rapidly. "Why?"

"Complications with my bookstore."

"I don't understand. Your place is always packed. Do you not like being a shop owner?"

Tears sting the backs of my eyes, nodding. "I love it, but..." I can't tell her all the lease issues or the deal I've made.

"And you are loved. Your place is more than a shop to buy books. It's a second home for many of us. We've found amazing stories because of your recommendations, friends because of your clubs and events, and a place to belong because of you. Novel Idea is a gem. Priceless to many of us."

I press a hand to my overflowing heart. She's speaking of my true dream for my store. Yes, I'd envisioned a cute and cozy local shop in an old building with character, but even more than the window dressings, is how my place offers other book lovers a second home.

"No one in my family reads, and not many of my friends do either," Anna continues. "When I saw the flyer for the romance book club, I was over-the-moon excited. Finally, I'd have people to discuss my favorite authors and stories with.

I'm sure Jim and Kurt feel the same, considering an even smaller number of men read romance. Plus, finding a group of people who applaud them for reading is a blessing." Anna winks. "In fact, the single ladies in the group are very interested in getting to know them better and learning what they've gleaned from the stories they've read."

I laugh. "Smart women."

"Then there's Tammy..."

Anna's serious tone has my smile falling. Tammy is one of my favorite customers, another found family friend, and a cold weight settles in my chest. "She was my first book club member. Before all the other clubs I've started, there was only the romance one. That was mainly because they're my favorite to read, but also because too many bookstores overlook the genre. During that first meeting, she was the only one who showed up. We had a blast discussing the story. And she hasn't missed a single one."

"No surprise. Novel Idea has been a shelter for her during a very bad storm in her life." Anna looks toward the dark garden. "At book club, she and I have become close. Tammy told me how much your store means to her, and I don't think she'd mind me sharing her story with you. Six months before Novel Idea opened, her twin brother OD'd. He'd become addicted to an opioid after a car accident. Her parents shut down, her friends didn't know how to act around her, and she didn't know how to be around them. She'd originally gone to your store looking for a book on grief. She found one, but you'd also recommend the romance for the first book club. She read both, finding hope and healing in one and escape in the other. She also found a place that helps curb the ache and loneliness. And I'm sure she isn't the only person. We bookworms always feel at peace surrounded by books, but your cozy shop takes that comfort to a whole new level. I thought you should know."

"Thank you for telling me." A tear rolls down my cheek and I quickly wipe it away. I can't give up on my store. Not if it means so much to others. "I feel terrible."

Anna grabs her purse from the table. Opening it, she removes a small tissue packet and hands one to me. "Shit. My intent wasn't to upset you. I wanted you to know your place means a lot to many people." She offers a crooked grin. "And for my own selfish reasons. I don't want you or your store to leave me."

I dab my eyes. "I'll do my best to keep the doors open."

"If you need anything, please let me know. I'm a digital marketing specialist, and I'd happily help."

"Anna, you're amazing. Thank you." I squeeze her hand, but my stomach drops like I've missed a step in the dark.

She beams at me. "Good. Because we need you to stay."

My throat closes. Minutes ago, I decided to call Thorne tomorrow, end the deal, choose Sebastian, and my integrity. But Tammy's grief, Anna's joy, all those people who've found sanctuary in my store... How can I rip that away from them?

"Where are those drinks. I need my liquid courage to manage the rest of the night," I joke weakly.

Anna laughs. "This event is a lot. But also fun. Especially when you get to watch your friend fall for a gorgeous billionaire."

"Anna..."

"I'm just saying the way he looks at you, that's not casual interest, Rosalia. That's a man who's already halfway gone."

My pulse stutters. Every time I think I've found my path, something shifts beneath my feet. Save the store, betray Sebastian. Choose him, abandon everyone else. I'm standing at a crossroads where every direction leads to someone getting hurt.

Chapter Twenty-Four

Sebastian

My footsteps echo as I follow Daniel down the corridor, my fingers clawing through my hair, nails biting into my scalp. I don't care if I look unhinged; it matches my roiling insides.

I touch my lips. The taste of Rosalia's kiss lingers. My pulse quickens, recalling how her body melted against mine, how perfectly she fit in my arms. The memory alone makes my skin flush hot beneath my collar. But as the initial euphoria fades, reality crashes in. She's working with Thorne. My brother. The man whose very existence threatens everything I've sacrificed years to build.

We reach the polished bar in the main ballroom. Daniel leans against the agarwood surface, his usual easy grin gone. I know him too well. He's about to lecture me on the incredible kiss that captivated me, and now is suffocating me with guilt.

Yet after we order our drinks, he returns to staring at me. Annoyed, I roll my hand in an out-with-it gesture. "Say what you want to say."

"Your bookstore bet seems to be going well. Does what I saw mean you're taking my advice and trusting her?"

I scowl, tapping an agitated rhythm on the polished bar. I avoid Daniel's gaze, focusing instead on the bartender mixing our drinks. "Trust her? Not a chance. I might understand why she's doing what she's doing, but that doesn't mean I'm going to hand over my heart."

Daniel's brows raise. "And yet..."

I snort. "That wasn't my heart doing the thinking..." That isn't the whole truth. Yeah, I was turned on, but what I feel around her is more than lust. I press my thumb against the condensation on the bar top, drawing jagged patterns that mirror the chaos she's creating in me. "I can't help myself, dammit. When I'm near her, it's like gravity."

I run my thumb over my lower lip, the phantom press of her mouth still lingers against mine. Even now, well away from her, my body responds to the mere thought of her. She seems real. Genuine. But what if she's acting?

"What if she's not?" Daniel counters.

The way she responded to my kiss didn't feel fake. I shake my head and mutter, "I need to figure it out before I lose myself completely."

Daniel's staring again. "What?" I nearly growl.

"I've never seen you like this with anyone. Not with any girls you dated in college or even Tiffany. You're scared," he says, his tone matter-of-fact. "And not just of losing the company."

I scoff. "Let me remind you again, psychoanalysis isn't in your job description, counselor."

"Stop deflecting." Daniel leans in, forcing me to meet his gaze. "Every time someone gets close, you find a reason why it won't work."

"You don't know what you're talking about," I mutter, but the words are hollow.

"Don't I? You'd rather believe Rosalia is acting than consider the possibility that she might actually care about you. Because if she does, and you let yourself care back, you might have to face that you're not as unbreakable as you pretend to be."

I open my mouth to argue, then close it. The uncomfortable truth of his words settles in my gut like a stone. With a slight shake of his head, Daniel says, "You've backed yourself into a tough spot with her and this bet."

"No shit." I square my shoulders as if bracing for a fight. Which I am. I can't afford to show weakness, not now, not with so much at stake.

"But what if she doesn't go through with it?" Daniel asks.

"What if she does?" I counter.

"Then it sucks. I honestly can't blame her, but if I were in your shoes, things would be over."

"Besides all this, there's more at stake than my damn ego." I knock my fist on the bar top. "At this distillery alone, I have at least two thousand people working for me. Many for decades, but my brother would let them go if it'd save the company a short-term nickel.

"Okay, so fine, you're in this mess. A big one. What do you plan to do to get out of it? Do you plan to make her fall for you so she doesn't help Thorne, then dump her because you don't trust her?"

"Fuck, I don't know what to do," I hiss. "I want her, but can't trust her."

Maybe that's the answer. I could have her, be with her, but keep my heart out of it. We give in to our desires, but nothing more. At least until I'm sure I can trust her. Could I do that? I already like her way too much.

What scares me isn't that I like her despite her lies, it's the possibility that I could fall. With Rosalia, I catch glimpses of the man I could be if I weren't so damn guarded. She makes me want things I'd convinced myself I didn't need.

"The truth is," I say, lowering my voice, "letting someone in again feels like handing them a loaded gun and hoping they don't pull the trigger."

"Just because there were some people who were supposed to have your back and didn't, doesn't mean everyone's out to make you bleed," Daniel tells me.

I'm not so obtuse as to miss that he is also referring to himself. But Thorne is my damn brother. Tiffany was my wife. Neither of them showed me an ounce of loyalty. How can I trust a friend who works for me?

I hear how paranoid I sound, but I can't stop. It's like a sickness, this need to find the angle, the hidden motive. And as if reading my mind, Daniel says, "If I left Blackstone, if you didn't sign my paychecks, would that change things? I could put my two weeks in now."

"Yeah, it'd make a difference. I'd be pissed." I mean it. Daniel is our best lawyer. And I do trust him with Blackstone Bourbon. However, the offer to leave does mean something. Maybe Daniel is a real friend. "And I get your point."

"Cool. Does that mean I can finally give you the friendship bracelet I made us?" Daniel quips, his eyes crinkling at the corners.

"Only if it's made from gold thread," I counter with a smirk, folding my arms across my chest.

Daniel chuckles. "Elitist asshole." The bartender sets three of our drinks on the bar, telling us she needs another minute to make the last cocktail. "Did you have to order Rosalia a Vieux Carre?" he asks.

I shrug. "She wanted to be surprised. And at least I didn't get her a Commonwealth."

"Shit, we'll be waiting until dawn." Daniel takes a sip of his drink and leans closer. "What I'm about to say is as your friend, not as a Blackstone's lawyer, got it?"

Ignoring my drink, I focus on Daniel. "Okay..."

"Loan her the money. Then she won't need Thorne. Sure, she'll have to move, but so what? There are other great locations besides Whiskey Row. Then she could be with you for you."

My gaze moves over the crowded room, ignoring the details and people, considering the suggestion. The idea holds appeal but has two major flaws. "No, if my brother found out I'd cheated—"

"And you don't think he's stacking the deck?"

"I'm certain he would, but I can't see how." I push away from the bar, pace a few steps, then return. Thorne has visited Rosalia at her bookstore, and I'm certain he orchestrated that fight between us during our horseback ride. "Even if he is cheating, I can't do what you're suggesting. If I give her a store, I'd never know if she's with me out of obligation."

Daniel tilts his head back and forth as he takes a sip of his drink. "Yeah, I can see that."

The bartender returns, sliding Rosalia's drink across the bar. I shove a fifty in the tip jar. "Come on, we'd better get back."

With drinks in hand, we weave our way through the crowded ballroom, dodging dancing couples and chattering guests. As we near the French doors leading to the rose garden, I catch a glimpse of Anna and Rosalia talking. I freeze mid-step, watching her from afar.

Rosalia laughs at something Anna says, her head tilted back, exposing the elegant curve of her neck. The sight hits me like a physical blow. My breath catches in my throat. I have to force myself to breathe normally, to keep my expression neutral even as my heart hammers against my ribcage. She's captivating, radiant in the moonlight against the backdrop of roses, somehow outshining even the night's splendor.

"You going to stare all night or actually give her that drink?" Daniel murmurs beside me.

I shoot him a glare, but start moving again. "Remember what we discussed. Not a word."

"Your secret's safe," he says with a wry grin that tells me he's enjoying my discomfort far too much.

Taking a steadying breath, I step out into the garden, the cool night air a balm to my heated skin. Rosalia turns at our approach, and when her eyes meet mine, the smile that curves her lips makes my chest tighten with a dangerous mix of desire and doubt.

One thing becomes crystal clear as I hand her the drink, our fingers brushing for a fraction longer than necessary: I'm playing with fire. And despite everything I've built, everything I stand to lose, I'm not sure I want to stop the burn.

Chapter Twenty-Five

Sebastian

After a hectic week with barely any contact, I finally have Rosalia all to myself, starting with a late lunch at the iconic Galt House hotel. Thunder Over Louisville has arrived, marking the official kickoff of the derby festivals. After that, the countdown to Derby Day will seem to accelerate, along with Thorne's deadline. But right now, walking beside her through the Galt House lobby, I'm determined to focus only on her.

Rosalia's steps slow. I match her pace. The light click of her boot heels against the marble is a counterpoint to my heavier footfalls. Her gaze is fixed on the hotel, while mine is on her, drinking in her beauty and recalling our kiss that night at the gala.

"Listen," she whispers. "It's like a symphony of memories, the same sounds I remember from when I was here once as a kid."

"And now we get to add our own voices to the mix," I say, guiding her toward the elevators that'll take us to the restaurant.

We arrive as a group is exiting. I step aside to let Rosalia enter first, then press the button for the twenty-fifth floor. As we rise, the elevator continues to fill at each stop until we're packed shoulder to shoulder like the crowds along the river.

The murmur of my name comes from somewhere behind me, followed by the quiet rustle of someone shifting, and I feel eyes turning in our direction. A woman near the back whispers something to her companion, and the familiar tension of recognition fills the small space.

Rosalia's shoulders draw up, and she shifts closer to the elevator wall. I move closer to her, positioning myself between her and the curious stares. In the confined space, I catch the subtle scent of her perfume. It commands my attention more than the probing stares around us.

"You smell wonderful," I murmur close to her ear, so only she can hear. "Like vanilla and jasmine, with a hint of something uniquely you."

She ducks her head, a pretty blush coloring her cheeks as she glances up at me with a soft smile. "Thank you," she says, equally quiet and warm.

The elevator hums steadily upward, and she tilts her head back slightly, as if trying to sense the height. Which I'm perfectly content *not* to think about.

"I wish we could have ridden in the glass elevator," she muses.

I don't—not at all. "That's the east tower. The restaurant is in the west," I explain.

"Oh well," she sighs. "I'm sure it's not nearly as exciting as it was when I was eleven."

My palms turn clammy at the thought, but for a chance to see Rosalia's radiant smile, I'd endure anything. "Don't worry, you'll get your chance tonight." My voice comes out slightly strained.

She tilts her head. "Tonight?"

"I booked a suite for the fireworks." I swallow hard, focusing on her reaction rather than the impending elevator ride.

She bites her bottom lip, then releases it. "You book us a room…"

I thought this would make her happy. Replaying the last few sentences in my mind, I wince internally. "I'm staying here tonight. Since I have a morning meeting here, there's no sense driving back to Bardstown," I quickly clarify. "My plan was for us to watch the fireworks from the balcony in my suite, away from the crowds. Then I'll take you home. But if you'd rather not, I can book a table at the conservatory instead. The view is also good from there."

"No, your plan sounds lovely." The elevator doors open, and I wait for her to step out, then guide her toward the restaurant, placing my hand on the small of her back.

The hostess greets us with a professional smile. "Welcome, Mr. Blackstone and Ms. Manchester. Your window table by the Second Street Bridge is ready. Follow me."

I admire the way the warm afternoon light dances across the embroidered flowers on Rosalia's skirt. "Your outfit is lovely," I lean in to tell her.

She glances down, a smile tugging at her lips. "Thank you. I fell in love with the embroidery the moment I saw it. It reminds me of the wildflowers that grow in my grandmother's garden."

I pull out her chair, my fingers brushing against the delicate fabric of her skirt as she sits down. "Well, you look beautiful," I say, taking a seat across from her. After placing our drink order, I ask, "Is this the grandmother who makes the amazing chocolate Sacher torte?"

Rosalia's eyes brighten. "Yes!"

"Does she live here, in Louisville?"

"No, she has a gorgeous little cottage in Versailles. Horse country through and through."

"Near Woodford Reserve?" I raise an eyebrow.

She nods. "That's where I spent nearly every summer. Without a car, I don't get to visit often, but love when I do."

"What kinds of wildflowers does she grow?" I rest my chin on my palm, drawn into this chapter of her story.

"Everything imaginable," she says, her hands animating her words. "Black-eyed Susans, purple coneflowers, wild bergamot... but her pride is her patch of Kentucky lady's slippers. They're notoriously difficult to grow, but somehow she had the magic touch."

"It seems she has it in the garden and the kitchen. Is she also the one who fostered your sweet tooth?"

"Indeed," she laughs. "I've mentioned her torte, but Grandma Rose's bourbon bread pudding recipe would make you weep. I've tried for years to replicate it, but so far, no luck."

I tilt my head. "Are you named after her?"

She nods. "But with a twist, so it wasn't exactly the same."

"Just like you. One of a kind."

"Aren't you a charmer," she says, patting my hand.

"I have my moments." The waiter sets down our drinks and leaves to give us a moment to look over the menus. I smile at Rosalia. "Your grandma sounds like an interesting woman. I'd love to meet her one day." I'm surprised that I mean it.

"You say that now..." she laughs softly. "Her other hobby is reading Kentucky gossip on social media."

I groan, taking a sip of my bourbon. "Does she hate me?"

"The opposite. She's thrilled. My dad, on the other hand..." I want to ask about her father, but Rosalia continues, "My grandma also taught me to never trust a man who doesn't dance at weddings or pet stray dogs."

I suspect she's changing the subject, and I roll with it. "You already know I can dance," I say, referring to the night at the gala.

Her eyes darken, and her gaze drops briefly to my mouth. Is she also thinking about her body pressed against mine, the heat between us?

"And you've met Twain," I continue. "He was a stray. A matted mess that showed up at my house about a week after my wife left." I lean in closer, grinning. "Don't tell her… but I like him more."

Rosalia laughs, squeezing my hand. "Your secret's safe with me."

The waiter arrives with our appetizers, and I reluctantly let go of her hand.

"How did you manage to get a reservation here, of all places, and today?" she asks.

"Since the…" I squint, trying to recall the exact date. "Since the Galt House opened here on the waterfront in the seventies, Blackstone Bourbon has had standing reservations during the months of April and May because of derby business. Like my business breakfast tomorrow morning at seven."

"That's an early meeting. We don't have to stay up late to watch the fireworks."

"I want to. I'm looking forward to it."

Her eyes light up, and she gives my hand a small squeeze. "Me too."

My fingers curl around hers. "Do you still plan on taking next Friday off?"

She nods. "Yup. Friday and Saturday. I figure, why not, since I'm keeping the store open for a full day on Sunday and opening on Monday for the Fest-a-Ville. I'll have Kentucky chefs in store with their books, along with local musicians playing acoustic music to match the festival's vibe. Since the festival is so close to Novel Idea, it can't hurt." She pauses. "Sorry, I'm excited for it, so I'm babbling. Why did you ask about Friday?"

I'm drawn to her animated expressions, the way she speaks with her whole self. While my world has become spreadsheets and production targets, she reminds me there's still color outside the distillery walls. Something about her pulls me back to the present moment in a way I haven't experienced in years.

"I was asking because I wanted to know if you'd be interested in going hiking at the Red River Gorge."

"Yes! The Natural Bridge has been on my bucket list since I moved here," she tells me.

I am well aware, which is why I'd suggested it. Her casual mention of the Natural Bridge weeks ago had stuck with me, and the excitement that dances across her face now makes clearing my Friday afternoon schedule worth it, despite the chaos of derby season.

"How will you find time for a full-day hike during peak bourbon season?" she asks. "I'd think every minute of your calendar would be claimed."

Rosalia is right. I've never cleared a full day during derby season before, and I know why. Yes, I love spending time with her, but it's also because each moment with her is one where I don't have to confront what's coming. The hike and tonight's fireworks are beautiful distractions from the constant reminder of the Blackstone Bourbon Classic and the choice we'll have to make.

"Sometimes you have to prioritize what matters," I say instead, not quite ready to admit the truth to either of us.

I've been avoiding the Blackstone party. I reach for the drink menu, needing a moment to gather my thoughts. The inevitable can only be postponed for so long.

My time with her is moving too fast, our day of reckoning racing toward us. But I can't ignore it. The ice in my bourbon clinks softly. I run a finger along the rim, meeting her gaze. "Speaking of the derby, my distillery has a party at The Mansion. Would you attend as my date?"

She opens her mouth but a sudden roar fills the air, drowning out all conversation. Three military jets streak across the sky outside the massive windows, their engines screaming overhead.

Rosalia flinches, her hands gripping the edge of the table as the china rattles and the windows shudder. The deafening sound vibrates through my bones. As quickly as they arrive, the jets disappear, leaving a heavy silence in their wake.

She continues to stare out the window, her expression unreadable. I recognize the distraction for what it is—she's as reluctant to discuss the derby party as I was to bring it up. My heart hammers in my chest, the weight of my invitation lingering between us like an approaching storm we both can see but neither wants to acknowledge.

"Rosalia?" I prompt around the clinking of silverware as the other diners resume their meals.

She turns back to me. "I'd love to attend your party," she replies, but her tone lacks enthusiasm.

My stomach clenches, the reality of our situation crashing down on me. I force a grin, ignoring the sense of impending doom. "Great. I'm so glad you'll be able to go," I lie.

The countdown to Derby Day—to the moment when everything changes—ticks louder. These moments with her feel stolen, borrowed time slipping through my fingers like bourbon through a sieve.

"What are you thinking about?" she asks.

"Time," I answer honestly. "How there never seems to be enough of it."

Her eyebrow arches, a question forming in the small furrow between her brows. "For work?"

"For everything that matters." I swirl the bourbon in my glass. "You know, in distilling, timing is crucial. Rush the process, and you ruin everything. But wait too long, and you miss the perfect moment when everything comes together."

I am caught between wanting to open myself completely to her and the instinct to retreat behind my carefully constructed facade. The derby party looms like a finish line to a race I'm not sure I'm prepared to run.

"To perfect timing." I raise my glass to hers, deciding to savor what we have now, even as the clock continues its relentless countdown.

Chapter Twenty-Six

Rosalia

I shiver from the brisk April winds while nodding my thanks to the doorman at the Galt House. Sebastian and I spent hours this afternoon walking the crowded Ohio River, the atmosphere reminding me of summer festivals along Detroit's riverfront, though today's company is far more captivating than any from my past. And the air show and people-watching helped shake the foreboding that had settled over me after that derby party invitation.

A giddy rush spreads through me when we reach the glass elevator. "I'm almost as excited to ride in this as I was as a kid." I'm only half joking.

"Then I'm glad my suite is on the top floor." He presses the button, pulls out his phone, and types on it with his back to the rising panorama of the Ohio River.

"You're missing the view."

"I've seen it before." He keeps his gaze trained on his phone. The casual dismissal stings a little. The luxury surrounding him is nothing new, nothing special—the best hotels, cars, and restaurants are simply his baseline. How does this man whose life is so different from mine feel so right?

The mechanical voice informs us that we've arrived, and seconds later, the doors open. Sebastian inserts the electronic key into the door, then steps aside, gesturing for me to enter first.

Wow. His hotel room is larger and better furnished than my apartment, featuring a modern, open-floor plan with a spacious living room and kitchen. To the left are two closed doors, which I assume lead to a bathroom and a bedroom. In front of me is the best part: floor-to-ceiling windows that provide a view of the Louisville skyline.

I rush to the balcony and the setting sun. Opening the sliding door, I take in a four-person bistro table next to the iron railing, and a long couch with comfy looking cushions sits against the window to the suite.

Turning to Sebastian, who's still standing inside by the sliding door, I point to the couch. "Want to sit here?"

"Definitely." He sounds relieved. I guess cold iron chairs don't appeal to him either.

I face the darkening sky. A cold breeze ripples my skirt and I shiver. "I'll find some blankets," Sebastian offers from behind me.

Spotting a door at the balcony's far end, I nod with my chin. "I'll check in there."

A knock comes from inside the room. "That's probably our food and drinks," Sebastian tells me.

My stomach rumbles in approval. "When did you do that?" I ask.

"I set it up before we went out this afternoon."

I'm touched by his foresight, the way he's planned for our comfort without making a fuss about it.

I backtrack, hugging him. "You're such a thoughtful man." Even through our clothes, his solid warmth and the subtle scent of his cologne make my head spin.

He kisses my temple quickly before retreating into the suite. The brief contact of his lips against my skin leaves a lingering warmth that spreads across my face. I press my fingertips to my lips, shaking off the sudden flare-up of longing.

I find two fleece blankets in a closet on the balcony and drape them over the couch as a waitress enters with a rolling table, Sebastian right behind her.

"Good evening," the woman says. "My name is Jenny, and I'll be your concierge for the evening." The formal service is foreign to me, and I don't know how to reply. I settle for an awkward smile and turn my attention to the vast collection of plates, each one concealed beneath a shining silver dome. "Are other people joining us?" I half-joke. My heart dips. What if he had invited others? I want him all to myself.

"Just us." He turns to Jenny and taps the low metal table in front of the couch. "Would you set them up here instead of the bistro?"

"Certainly." She picks up the two cocktails. "Is your drink the Old Fashioned or Paloma, Mr. Blackstone?"

Sebastian shudders. "Definitely the Old Fashioned." His face scrunches up at the mere mention of the fruit, and it's endearing how this powerful man can be so dramatically disgusted by a simple fruit and herb.

I laugh while wanting to hug him. I'd ordered a Cilantro Paloma during one of our dates. Sebastian had looked aghast and had told me that grapefruit should be outlawed. Yet, he'd ordered me one this evening because he knows I love them.

After setting our table, Jenny stands by the balcony door. Sebastian tells her she can take a seat inside. If we need anything, we'll call for her.

We sit on the couch. The cushions are chilly even through my skirt, and I pull the blanket over my shoulders. Taking a sip of my drink, I grin over the glass. "Is our concierge and my drink your subtle way of saying no kissing tonight?" I tease, surprised at my unexpected boldness.

A spark of amusement lights his eyes. "I didn't want you to be uncomfortable in my hotel room. I thought having another woman here would put you at ease." His gaze falls to my lips. "As for your drink, your honeyed kisses are enough to override the gross taste of grapefruit."

My heart stutters at the intensity of his stare. It makes me feel exposed and exhilarated, like standing at the edge of a precipice knowing I'm about to fall but wanting to jump anyway.

I laugh and a gigantic boom swallows up the sound. For half a second, I'm certain my heart has exploded from this incredible man's sweetness. Then, the dark sky is aglow with the first firework of the night. "Look at that," I breathe.

In my peripheral, Sebastian nods. "They hold a little bit of childhood magic. That's probably why they're my favorite of the festivals. They bring back that sense of wonder."

I shift closer. "You're so warm." And so much better than the blanket. He smells like heaven, though his scent makes me want to sin. Our thighs press together, and even that innocent contact sends sparks dancing across my skin.

"Are you cold?"

"Only a little." Another firework lights up the sky, painting Sebastian's face in blues and silvers. I look away from the display and into his eyes. "Thank you for this incredible day."

"I should be thanking you," he replies. All the derby stuff has become work to me. With you, I'm reminded it's also fun and pleasure."

The word pleasure hangs between us, charged with meaning. I swear the temperature rises despite the cool evening air. An invisible force pulls me toward him with gentle insistence. The inches between us seem to shrink, and I lean forward. His eyes drop to my lips, and he shifts closer, his hand finding my knee. My skin prickles with awareness, as if the air itself has become heavier with intention.

"Would either of you like another drink?" Jenny asks, as if materializing on the balcony.

I jump slightly, suddenly aware of how close we're sitting. Sebastian blinks as if waking from a dream. He turns toward our concierge. "Yes. Two hot toddies, please."

"Right away, Mr. Blackstone." A few seconds later, the door clicks shut.

"Is that poor woman going to have to walk all the way to the bar on the lower level?"

Sebastian's lips twitch. Another firework showers him in green and white, the colors playing across his features, highlighting the sharp line of his jaw, the fullness of his lips that I can't stop thinking about. "Well, she can take the elevator. And you could use something warm. Plus, as a bonus, there won't be grapefruit."

I try to hold in my smile and fail. With deliberate slowness, I pluck his drink from his hand and take a sip, then swirl the drink around in my mouth, letting the smoky vanilla and caramel notes coat my tongue, the burn warming my throat and perhaps offering an extra shot of liquid courage. I hold his gaze over the rim of the glass, watching his eyes darken as they fix on my lips, my throat, tracking the movement as I swallow. "Grapefruit's gone."

"Is that an invitation?" His voice has dropped to a rasp that I feel more than hear. His gaze drags over me, hot and heavy, igniting a slow burn under my skin.

"Yes." A flash of hesitation plays across his face. Then his expression shifts from restraint to hunger, and his lips are on mine.

The kiss is deeper, more urgent than our earlier ones, as if he's finally allowing himself to take what he wants. I shift my legs so they're resting over one of his thighs, allowing me to scoot closer to him. His arm wrap around my waist, bringing me sidesaddle into his lap. The blanket falls from my shoulders. The cool air hits my heated skin, making me shiver. Or maybe it's the way his fingers dig into my hip, possessive and needy all at once. I moan into his mouth, squirming against the heat blooming between my legs.

"Rosalia, if you keep moving like that, I'm going to lose my fucking mind." The curse word in his usually controlled voice sends a thrill through me. I want to push him further, see him come completely undone.

"Good," I murmur against his lips. I shift my weight, a deliberate movement that makes his breath catch. The sound he makes – half surprise, half pleasure – is more intoxicating than any drink. His kisses are insistent yet unhurried, with perfect pressure and exploration. "More, Sebastian. Touch me." I'm pleading in a way I'd normally be embarrassed by, but I'm beyond caring.

A primal growl rumbles in his chest that makes heat pool low in my belly. He slides a palm up to my torso, taking my shirt with him.

"Mr. Blackstone," calls the concierge from inside the hotel room. "I have your drinks, sir. Would you like them brought out to you or left inside?"

The sound of Jenny's voice crashes through the moment like ice water. I hide my head in Sebastian's neck. "That's a very tactful way of saying I have to deliver your drinks, but it's not in my job description to see you or your girlfriend naked," I whisper, nearly choking on the last part of my sentence.

Girlfriend! Had I just called myself his girlfriend?

He merely chuckles and asks, "Should she bring them out here?"

My face is as hot as a sunburn. "I'd rather not have to make eye contact."

"The kitchen table is fine, Jenny."

We remain frozen in awkward proximity, neither touching nor moving away. The connection between us has been disrupted but not broken—like a livewire temporarily grounded. Keeping my position tucked into his neck, I whisper, even as my pulse hammers. "And I'm comfortable alone with you..."

Fortunately, he understands what I'm saying and tells Jenny to come back in about half an hour after the fireworks. "We should be finished with food and drinks by then," he says.

I'm tempted to tell her to come back tomorrow morning, but hold in the reckless words.

"Very good, sir," Jenny replies.

I glance through the window behind us. The door to the hotel room swings shut. We are alone again.

But the moment has shifted. The frenetic urgency of before has ebbed, leaving something more tentative in its wake—as if we're aware of lines being crossed, boundaries falling away.

He kisses my cheek. "I'll get the drinks." He lifts me off his lap.

I almost tell him all the heat I need is him, but a break is smart. So, instead, I thank him and look toward the stunning, forgotten fireworks.

My pulse is still racing, but my breathing slowly returns to normal. I watch the colors exploding against the dark canvas of the night sky, trying to collect myself. What just happened between us? What was I about to let happen before I figured out what to do about Thorne's deal?

He returns with our drinks. I cradle the warm glass in my hands and breathe in the scent of cloves, tucking my legs to the side and snuggling against him. This time, the contact feels less charged. The respite has given us a chance to regain some composure.

He encircles me with his arm and kisses the top of my head. "Traffic's going to be terrible after the fireworks. Instead of Tom driving you, I'll walk you home."

Again, it's on the tip of my tongue to tell him I should just stay the night. I roll my tongue to keep the words inside. When I'm sure they'll stay, I say, "You don't have to. My place is basically around the block."

He shakes his head. "I'd rather you didn't walk alone."

I shrug. "Why? I do it all the time."

"You do?" he looks appalled.

I suck my lips between my teeth to hold in my smile. "I don't have a car, and my store usually closes around nine. When else am I supposed to grocery shop?"

"You could have them delivered."

"No. *You* can have groceries delivered. My budget doesn't include the added costs. And running my errands isn't a big deal. I have my bike and mace."

"Rosalia, I can't stop you from going out late at night when we're not together, but when we are, I'll escort you." He squeezes me against him. "Please. If you leave alone, it'll be torture. I won't sleep. The whole time I'll be thinking of every worst case scenario."

The protective edge in his voice sends a flutter through me. The way his arm tightens around me speaks of possession and caring beyond casual interest.

"Okay. I'd love for you to walk me home." I kiss the corner of his mouth quickly.

But what starts as an innocent gesture ignites something between us again. As I pull away, his eyes darken, that same hunger from before returning in an instant.

"Thank you."

The words are ordinary, but his voice has dropped to that lower register that makes my skin tingle. The temperature between us shifts again, heating rapidly like a summer storm building. "Sebastian," I breathe.

A particularly spectacular burst of fireworks illuminates his face, casting shadows that accentuate the sharp planes of his cheekbones and the intensity of his gaze. In that flash of light, I see his control slipping, taking mine with it.

"Rosalia?" he replies.

"Will you kiss me?" I whisper.

He nods, brushing my lips lightly with his, and then pressing his mouth against mine. The pressure is perfect. He tilts his head and deepens the kiss. I open for him, moaning when his tongue swipes against mine.

My desire explodes brighter than the fireworks. I straddle him, wishing the couch were deeper, allowing us a closer connection. A fleeting thought whispers that I should slow down, but the sensation of his body pressing into mine scatters any restraint before it can take hold.

I kiss along his jaw to his ear, nipping and pulling before moving to his neck. The fireworks boom above us in quick succession. The grand finale is beginning, but I'm lost in something else entirely.

Lost in the way his breath catches when I find that sensitive spot beneath his collarbone, the warmth of his hands as they trace patterns on my back. The world outside fades to background noise as we create our own celebration, more magnificent than any display lighting up the night sky.

"I shouldn't want you this much," he murmurs against my skin, the confession rough with honesty. "Not with..." His tongue teases mine with a skill that curls my toes inside my boots. I cling to his shoulders, my fingers digging into the firm muscle beneath his shirt, desperate to anchor myself against the tide of sensation threatening to sweep me away.

He pulls me closer until there is no space left between us. I moan at the contact. He tears his mouth from mine to trail a line of hot, open-mouthed kisses along my jaw and down my neck. My head falls back, giving him better access. A husky groan escapes me when he finds a particularly sensitive spot above my collarbone.

"Rosalia," he murmurs, his voice rough. "I need you."

The final bursts of fireworks cast us in flashes of crimson and gold. Everything else fades away—the crowds below, the concierge, my worries about moving too fast. There is only Sebastian, his heartbeat thundering against my palm, his breath warm against my skin.

He brushes my hair back, his fingers lingering at the nape of my neck. "Tell me to stop if this isn't what you want."

But stopping is the furthest thing from my mind. The cold April night has disappeared, replaced by the heat blooming between us. I answer him not with words, but by pulling him closer, surrendering to the current that's been drawing us together since that first day in my shop.

As his lips find mine again with a newfound urgency, one coherent thought remains: this night is far from over.

And I don't want it to be.

ChapterTwenty-Seven

Rosalia

Sebastian helps me stand from the couch on the balcony. I wrap my hands around his neck, pulling him to me for more of his kisses. In breathless disorientation, I find myself being swept inside the suite. My rational mind whispers we should slow down, but my body has stopped listening to reason. His lips never leave mine until the back of my legs hit something soft.

He lowers me onto the plush cushions of a couch and settles his weight on top of me. We stare at each other, our chests heaving, his eyes dark and wordless with anticipation. His usual composed demeanor has vanished, replaced by something primal and urgent. Then his mouth crashes down on mine once more, and I surrender to the flames.

His hand slides up my thigh, his touch leaving a trail of goosebumps in its wake. I shift, and his touch skims the lace edge of my panties, teasing, testing, drawing a sharp gasp from my lips. He pauses, his gaze locking with mine, silently seeking permission.

"Please," I beg, my hips lifting, seeking more of his touch.

With a low groan, he hooks the delicate fabric and slowly, torturously, drags my panties down my legs. His hands tremble slightly, betraying his thinning control. Cool air dances over my overheated skin, making me shiver. But his warm kisses quickly replace the chill as he traces them up my inner thigh.

Each press of his lips is a brand, a promise, igniting the fire that burns deep in my core. I squirm beneath him, my hands tangling in his hair, torn between the urge to pull him closer and the need to savor every second of this sweet torture.

When he finally reaches the apex of my thighs, I'm trembling with anticipation. He pauses, his breath teasing my sensitive skin, before dragging his tongue along my heated flesh in one long, slow lick.

"Oh," I gasp, my head falling against the cushions as pleasure sparks through me like electricity.

Sebastian hums against me, the vibration resonating through my core. Then, he sets to work in earnest. Oh. My. Wow. He moves between slow, languid strokes and focused attention, responding to my every sound and movement, pushing me toward the edge.

Pressure builds inside me, and my hips rock against his mouth, seeking more friction, more stimulation. He slides a finger inside me, then another, curling them just so, hitting a spot that makes stars explode behind my eyelids.

"Don't stop," I plead, beyond caring how I sound. "Sebastian, please don't stop."

My gasps come in sharp, staccato bursts. My heart pounds a frantic rhythm against my ribcage. His free hand is splayed across my lower belly, holding me in place as he redoubles his efforts, driving me relentlessly toward the edge.

I shout his name as a tidal wave of pleasure crashes over me, pulling me under, stealing the air from my lungs and the strength from my limbs. He guides me through it, his touch becoming tender but never stopping until the last wave of bliss has faded. I lay boneless and spent, my pulse hammering so loud that the sound seems to echo in the large room.

He crawls up my body, his eyes wild with need, pressing his hardness against me. "I want you," he growls. "I want you so much I can't think straight."

I reach for his belt, my fingers fumbling with the buckle in my eagerness, when a knock at the door freezes us both mid-motion. "Who?" I ask.

His fully dilated eyes meet mine. "I think our drinks have arrived. I'd suggest we pretend we aren't here...but given how loud you were moments ago, I don't think she'll buy it." He grins, and it holds satisfaction and simmering desire.

Heat explodes from my neck to my ears. "Was I really that loud?"

"And it's incredibly sexy." He places a light kiss on my knee. "Which means you'll have to answer the door."

"Why?" The crash from my orgasm must have left my mind foggy, because I have no idea what he's talking about.

He stands, and the answer becomes *very* apparent. The outline of his erection makes me want to reach for him, but nervousness skids along the edge of satiated passion. And not only because of his size. Would it be wise to keep going—to go all the way?

My body screams yes, but sleeping with him while my deal with Thorne still hovers between us is reckless. And unfair to Sebastian.

He sits next to me, kissing my neck. I straighten. "I—I'll answer it." I nearly sprint from him in my indecision, opening the door.

Jenny steps inside, asking where to set the drinks. I tell her the kitchen table is fine, hoping my panties aren't lying somewhere out in the open. After artfully arranging the glasses and napkins, Jenny returns to the living room.

"Thank you, Jenny. That's all we'll need from you tonight," Sebastian says from the couch. He pulls a wallet from his pocket and removes some money. Looking at me with a mix of apology and embarrassment, he asks, "Could you give her the tip?"

I look at the throw pillow placed strategically on his lap and pull my lips between my teeth to keep from giggling. He mouths, "Not funny."

"It is a little," I whisper back, taking the folded cash in his hand. Glancing down, I cough. There must be at least ten one-hundred-dollar bills.

I walk to Jenny, the cash heavy in my hand. She probably feels the same way about money, counting every dollar like I do. We have that in common, and probably many more things. More than I have with the man who handed over this fortune without blinking—the same man I was just kissing, who I'm supposed to be keeping at arm's length because of a deal I made to keep my tiny bookstore open. A deal I had to make out of desperation because my reality isn't thousand-dollar tips. It's shoestring budgets, overdue notices, and a dream I might have to let die because I'm beginning to care too much for this man.

I swallow, and my throat clicks, suddenly dry. I need to think this through. But if we're alone again and he kisses me and touches me, reasonable thought will be impossible.

Jenny thanks him and wishes us a pleasant evening. I stare at the closing door, peeling back my cravings and concerns in quick succession. I *so* want to stay and discover if Sebastian is as loud as me when he comes. But I should figure out my mess with Thorne first.

The clinking of ice cubes pulls my attention from my conflicting desires to Sebastian. He has walked to the table and downed his drink in one large swallow. Returning the glass to the table, he faces me. "With the fireworks crowd, I think it'd be faster for me to walk than drive you home," he says.

Is he kicking me out? My chest feels like it's caving in on itself. I know I'd been talking myself into not staying, but my disappointment is heavy.

"You want me to leave?" I ask, rooted to the spot near the living room entrance.

"Want? No." His voice is rough as sandpaper. "What I want is to carry you into that bedroom and not come out until morning. But what I need to do—" He takes a measured step toward me. "I see your hesitation. The last thing I want to be is your morning regret."

"But what about you? I, um…"

He grins crookedly. "Came."

My cheeks flush with warmth. "Um, yes." Doesn't he expect reciprocation?

As if hearing my unspoken question, he says, "You don't owe me a damn thing, Rosalia." Heat returns to his eyes. "And believe me, jus touching and tasting you was more than a fair trade."

The intensity in his gaze scorches through me, his words unraveling what little resolve I've gathered. My agreement with his brother suddenly feels distant, overshadowed by the man standing before me, all broad shoulders and intent eyes that promise all my desires.

My chest rises and falls with quickened breath. The room shrinks around us, the space between our bodies charged with unspoken possibility. Tomorrow looms with complications and betrayals, but tonight pulses with a different kind of promise. My hands reach for him without my permission. "I should…"

"Get home." It sounds like it hurt him to say this. His fingertips brush mine, and he sucks in a sharp breath at even this minimal contact. "If we don't leave right now, I'm not sure I'll have the strength to do the right thing. See if you feel the same in the morning."

I nod. "You don't need to walk me home."

"We've already been over this. Yes, I do. I'll get my jacket, and we'll leave."

He disappears into the bedroom to retrieve his jacket, and with his touch and kisses still searing my skin, I'm tempted to follow him. But the rational voice in my head warns me to slow down, to untangle myself from Thorne's web before diving headfirst into something with Sebastian.

He emerges a moment later, slipping on his jacket. "Ready?" he asks.

I nod, not trusting myself to speak. He holds the door open for me and I step into the hallway. Standing beside him, waiting for the elevator, gravity shifts, my body fighting its pull to him. Each passing second stretches longer than the last. His presence radiates a warmth that calls to something deep within me. My fingertips tingle with the urge to close the small distance between us.

The soft ping of the arriving elevator interrupts my thoughts but doesn't diminish their intensity. Does he feel this invisible current drawing us toward an inevitable collision, or is it only me?

Sebastian places a hand on the small of my back, guiding me inside. The brief contact sends a jolt of desire through me. I catch his gaze in the mirrored walls. His eyes are dark and intense.

"Rosalia," he murmurs, my name a caress on his lips.

"Yes?" I ask. If he's changed his mind and invites me back to his room, I'll go, and I'll worry about tomorrow, tomorrow.

He steps closer, his body nearly touching mine. His hand lifts to my face, thumb brushing my lower lip. For a breathless moment, I think he's going to kiss me. Instead, he closes his eyes and takes a deliberate step back. He opens his mouth, but then shakes his head slightly. "Never mind. Let's get you home."

The elevator reaches the lobby, and I step out into the bustling space. Guests mill about, chatting and laughing, their faces illuminated by the soft glow of the chandeliers. The world around me is dreamlike, hazy, and distant.

Sebastian's fingers lace through mine. The simple gesture fills me with a sense of comfort and belonging. Together, we navigate through the crowded lobby until we're out in the crisp night air.

We begin the short walk to my apartment and my mind races with the implications of the evening. I can't keep straddling the line between my arrangement with Thorne and my growing feelings for Sebastian. Something has to give.

But for now, I push those thoughts aside and focus on the man beside me. His large hand fits perfectly in mine, and his presence makes me feel safe and cherished. With a contented sigh, I lean into his side, relishing his solid warmth.

We reach my apartment building all too soon. He walks me to the top of my alley stairs, and I turn to face him, my heart in my throat. "Thank you for today," I say softly.

Sebastian tucks a strand of hair behind my ear, his fingers lingering on my cheek. "It was my pleasure. And my torture," he adds with a rueful smile that doesn't quite hide the heat still simmering in his eyes. "I'll dream about you tonight and pick you up in the afternoon for our hike."

Come inside, I almost whisper, but keep the words on my tongue. Instead, I melt into his touch, savoring the warmth of him.

He moves back too soon. "Goodnight, Rosalia."

"Goodnight, Sebastian." I unlock and open my door, sensing his gaze on my back like a physical caress. It takes every ounce of my willpower not to run to him and lose myself in his arms once more.

The door closes, and I lean against it, shutting my eyes. The memory of his touch, his taste, and his scent is still so vivid and visceral that it's branded on me. Yet, I know he made the right decision.

I slide the chain into the top lock before stepping into my living room, pacing along the couch. Putting on the brakes was smart. It might be wise to put space between us, to give myself time to clear my head and get my emotions under control.

My phone lies heavy in my purse. I should cancel our plans for tomorrow. I could tell him something came up at the shop.

Sinking onto the couch, I place my head in my hands. Even the thought of canceling makes my chest ache.

In the end, I climb into bed, hugging my pillow, trying to quiet my nerves that hum with uncertainty. Tomorrow, I'll decide: take a step back and cancel the hike, or take a leap of faith and embrace our connection, trusting that together, we'll overcome any obstacle.

ChapterTwenty-Eight

Sebastian

The parking area at Red River Gorge is busy with other hikers preparing for the trails. I get out of my truck and drag my fingers along the smooth metal on my way to the passenger's side, the vehicle almost too hot to touch. The spring heat is a stark contrast to yesterday during Thunder Over Louisville, when we'd walked along the Ohio River and Rosalia had tucked herself into my side for warmth.

I reach Rosalia's side as she's climbing out. "I was coming over to help you."

Her smile warms me like the sun. She's holding onto the window and door frame. I offer her my arm. Taking it, she jumps the rest of the way down. "This truck is a monster," she laughs.

Using all my willpower, I let her go once her feet are firmly on the ground. Before closing her door, I grab my backpack and tease, "And one I can drive."

Driving myself instead of having Tom bring the Bentley had been the right call. This truck belongs on rugged terrain like this, not sitting in my garage between trips to check on the horses and pick up supplies.

"I'll never doubt you again."

I look away from her words. She's joking, but I want them to be true. If she truly trusts me, I'll take care of her. She'd never have to doubt me. The irony isn't lost on me that I'm lying to her even as I crave her trust.

Turning back to Rosalia, I grin. She's checking me out. Her gaze moves from my legs to my torso and then to my face. When her eyes meet mine, I quirk a brow. Her cheeks flush a cute shade of pink. "You look so different out of your suit," she tells me.

"You look different too." I take in the enticing sliver of stomach between her cropped shirt and leggings, recalling how fantastic her ass had looked when I'd picked her up from her apartment and helped her into my truck.

She runs her fingers over her lips. It's her tell I'm now familiar with. It means she's thinking about kissing. She drops her hand and eyes my backpack, frowning. "What's wrong?" I ask.

"Your bag reminded me I'd packed us a lunch and left everything in my fridge. Caprese sandwiches and a strawberry salad, the ultimate picnic combination."

I pat my stomach. "That does sound delicious."

"I know you have a work thing after this, but when you drop me off, I'll run up and get you some of the food."

I nod. "There's no rush. I'm just swinging by the warehouse to make sure the company's balloon is ready for tomorrow's races."

"Did you change your mind? Will you be riding in Blackstone's balloon?"

I give an inward shudder. "No." Pointing to the trail, I ask, "Ready?"

"Yes." She starts toward the packed earth trail that winds between towering sandstone walls. The air is cooler here in the gorge, carrying the green scent of new growth and the mineral smell of damp rock. Redbud trees dot the landscape with brilliant purple blooms, and there's the distant sound of water trickling over stone.

"How did your meeting go this morning?" she asks.

"Fine. It was just a quick update with a taster from my Tennessee distillery. He was in town for the fireworks."

"Is that job what the title sounds like? This person gets to drink for a living?"

I chuckle. "Basically, yes."

"Hmm, why wasn't that job ever mentioned during my high school career day?" she jokes.

I grin, something I do a lot around her. "Because you didn't go to school in Kentucky."

"Fair enough," she says, stepping around a larger boulder. "So, what's your title? Bourbon baron?"

I chuckle. "That does have a nice ring, but no, master distiller."

"What kind of degree do you get in college to become a master distiller? Did you have to major in drinking and minor in frat parties?" she teases.

I laugh, shaking my head. "Not quite. Chemistry, actually. With a lot of hands-on experience at the distillery."

"Ah, so you were a nerd." She bumps my shoulder playfully. "A nerd who knows his way around a bottle."

"Guilty." I hold up my hands in mock surrender. "I love the science behind crafting bourbon. And I've been working at the distillery since I was twelve, working my way from the bottom to the top of our company."

"So did my brother and sister, with our father observing us the entire time. He even told us what to study in college." I pause, then add, "Well, he tried to. Lillianna had a huge fight with our dad over his choice for her, but Mom stepped in and convinced him to let her study education instead."

I don't want to talk about Thorne and his bid for my job and the wedge it drove between us. Instead, I tell her, "My father and I don't agree on much, but if a kid of mine wanted to join the family business, I'd also have them work their way up from entry-level positions."

"You want children?" Rosalia asks.

I glance over my shoulder, where we'd recently passed a family with toddlers. "I'm not against it. But having kids isn't my deal breaker."

"What is?" she asks.

"Trust."

If I have my own family, I don't want it to look like my childhood. More than bourbon would hold us together. I wouldn't pit my kids against each other. And I'd marry a woman who wants to grow old with me, who loves me more than my last name and power.

"That is the most important," Rosalia agrees. "Along with laughter. I think trust and laughter are needed for love to last."

My good mood dips a little, knowing we'll never have trust. That unhappy thought walks with me until we step through a narrow tunnel carved by centuries of water through red sandstone, our footsteps echoing off the walls. The air is cool and damp here, thick with the earthy scent of moss. When we emerge back into the open sky, the contrast is striking. Warm April sunshine greets us again, alongside the sweet fragrance of wild dogwood blossoms.

I look at Rosalia and my heart expands. Her face is tipped toward the warm sun, a slight smile on her lips as she basks in the tranquility of the moment.

"I miss this," she sighs, sounding wistful. She runs her fingers over a nearby blooming bush. "Being out in nature, surrounded by all this beauty."

She gestures toward the layered sandstone cliffs rising around us, their red and gold faces catching the afternoon light. A pair of hikers with climbing gear passes us on their way to the rock faces, nodding in greeting.

Her serenity strikes me. "You didn't hike much back in Michigan?"

She turns to me. "Hike? No, more like leisurely strolls. Michigan's pretty flat, at least where I'm from. Nothing like these hills."

"No wonder you were excited to come out here." I gesture to the trail ahead, a hint of a challenge in my voice. "Ready to tackle the hard part?"

She grins, her gaze glinting with determination. "Bring it on."

I eye her tennis shoes, then offer my hand. "Those won't have good traction. You might slip."

"Thanks." Her palm slides against mine and warmth spreads through me. Ignoring how much I enjoy the simple touch, I focus on the trail. "Where did you like hiking, sorry, walking, in Michigan?"

"I lived near an international wildlife refuge along the Detroit River. I'd walk there and other local trails at least once a week. And if I had a free day or two, I'd hop in my car and explore a new place. If I had more time, I'd head up north."

"Alone?" I picture her in another sexy athletic outfit, walking in one of Michigan's many forests.

"Not always. My mom would go sometimes. Or my ex. Though he wasn't big into outdoor exercising. He liked the gym." She looks away and mutters, "Probably because the egotistical jerk liked to look at himself in the many mirrored walls."

I raise an eyebrow. "Sounds like there's a story there."

She shakes her head, her lips twisting into a wry smile. "Oh, you know. Boy meets girl; boy confesses his love to her, and at least two other women..."

I give her hand a gentle squeeze, understanding that hurt all too well. "His loss."

Her gaze softens. "What about you? Besides hiking and horses, what do you do on your days off?" she asks.

I go with the subject change, though I don't have much to offer. "Days off? What's that?"

She giggles. "You've been going out with me, so you must take time off."

"Before you, I hadn't in a long time. Hell, besides our outings, I can't recall the last time I'd ridden or explored a new trail. Probably not since my sister was home," I tell her.

I could convince myself that I'm making time for her because I want to win the bet, but that would be a lie. The truth is, I genuinely want to be with her. It's unsettling how quickly she has become a priority. I, the notorious workaholic, am rearranging my schedule because I need to see her smile and hear her laugh.

"What about you?" I ask. "How does it feel to take Friday off instead of your usual Monday?"

She glances at the trail ahead of us. "Honestly, I can't tell much difference since I stay local. But as much as I love the city, it feels great to get out in nature." She takes a deep breath, as if to emphasize her point. "But I am really excited for Monday and Fest-a-Ville. It's so close to my bookstore, so it'll bring crowds my way. I've already sold out of the VIP seats for the local chef Q&A and book signings. And I'm certain the talented musicians coming to my store in the late afternoon and evening will bring people inside."

"Sounds like you've got it all figured out," I say, impressed by her business savvy.

The trail narrows as it begins its switchback climb up the ridge, hemmed in by towering walls of weathered sandstone. Moss clings to the shaded crevices, and small wildflowers peek out from between the rocks.

I grip her hand tightly as we navigate the uneven stone steps worn smooth by countless hikers. "Watch your step here."

Her fingers warm against mine. I love how natural it feels, this simple connection between us.

We're quiet, but it's comfortable. I'm enjoying the rustling leaves and occasional birdsong. Rosalia seems lost in thought, glancing occasionally at the canopy of trees above us.

"Do you miss her?" she asks suddenly.

"Miss who?" The question seems to have materialized from thin air.

"Your sister," she clarifies. "You mentioned riding with her earlier. And you must talk about books, if you're sending them to her. Are you two close?"

Her question catches me off guard. We'd talked about Lillianna weeks ago at Novel Idea. I didn't expect Rosalia to remember the conversation, let alone where my sister's currently living.

The trail curves around a large boulder, revealing red and gold sandstone cliffs through the trees. Rosalia pauses, her attention drawn to the scenery. Her foot catches on an exposed root as she steps forward.

She slips, jolting my hand that's holding hers. My heart slams against my ribs as panic shoots through me.

"Ow, Sebastian," she gasps.

Oh, shit. I loosen my hold, my face heating. "Sorry, I—are you okay?" I ask, pulling her closer to the center of the trail, needing her away from any potential drops.

"From tripping? Yes. But I think my fingers are broken," she teases.

I manage a weak smile, still rattled.

Before I can apologize again, she asks, "When is Lillianna returning from Thailand?"

"It'll be a while. At least a year. She's moved on to Cambodia to teach. Besides English, she speaks French and Spanish. She'll spend a year or two at a school before moving on."

"That's so cool. What an adventure!" Rosalia gushes. "She didn't want to work for the family business? Or is it a guy's-only club?"

"Kind of. My father wanted her to run marketing and public relations. He said she'd be the 'face' of the company. She refused, so I got stuck with that job."

Rosalia grins. "Good thing you have such a pretty face for it."

I laugh. "I've been called a lot of things. Pretty isn't one of them."

"Well, I'm saying it, and it's true."

I shake my head, smiling. "Anyway, since he retired and I took over, I'm changing things. Last year, the stillman and mashman I hired were women."

Rosalia snorts and it's the cutest damn sound. "Did you hire them to prove a point: the two titles with a man in the name are women?"

I laugh. "No. They are the best in the field. And I guess I should call them distillers and mash operators. Anyway, the point is that I want the best working for me; female, male, and non-binary don't fit into the hiring equation, only skill. I've tried to get Lillianna to come back now that Dad's retired, but so far, no luck." The trail widens, and I slow my steps until we are side by side, but I don't let go of Rosalia's hand. "She loves the vagabond life and has never been interested in the family business. Although I'm not ready to give up. I miss her, and she'd be an asset."

"What would've happened if you also hadn't been interested in taking over?"

"My brother would be living his best life." I frown, unhappy that Thorne has snaked into our conversation.

"He wanted to be master..." She snaps her fingers. "Um, master bourbon man."

I chuckle. "Master distiller. Yes."

She nods, continuing to the steep trail that will take us to the top. I'm not sure if the mention of Thorne has dried up our conversation or if she's focused on the hike, but I wish she'd keep talking. Her steady chatter keeps my mind off our final destination. The sandstone arch is only around sixty-five feet from the ground, but the height still makes my limbs tingle and my pulse race.

We reach the top all too soon. Natural Bridge stretches before us, a graceful arch of ancient sandstone spanning the gap between cliff faces. My stomach tightens as I take in other visitors scattered along the bridge. To my left, a family is taking photos near the edge. Past them, a couple of rock climbers are casually pointing out routes on the distant cliffs far below. The view opens up to reveal the rolling hills of the Daniel Boone National Forest stretching endlessly toward the horizon, painted in the fresh greens of early spring, but all I can focus on is the dizzying drop.

I point to the center. "Want to sit and rest?"

Shaking her head, she moves to the edge, toward the drop. My stomach dives while she merrily removes her phone from a side pocket and snaps pictures.

My feet are glued to the rock, but I reach toward her. "Rosalia, could you not do that?" I hate that my voice holds a slight quiver.

She looks at me, her cell poised in front of her. "Do what?"

A cold sweat breaks out as I move toward her, keeping to the center of the bridge, refusing to look over the sides and ignoring the way my legs tingle. "Please, don't go so close to the edge."

She tilts her head, her brow furrowing. "Are you afraid of heights?"

"I'm not a fan of them."

"Oh…" Her eyes widen as understanding dawns. "Is that why you were facing away from the window elevator at the Galt?" She pauses, then adds more softly, "And why you won't ride in Blackstone's balloon?"

I drag my sweaty palms down the thighs of my cargo pants. "Guilty."

"I had no idea." Her gaze sweeps the area around us. "And here I dragged you up to—oh wow, look at that hawk!" She points and shuffles back.

Panic shoots through me as I surge forward, wrapping my arms around her. "Be careful," I gasp.

"I will be," she promises, melting into me and making the sixty-five-foot heart-attack-inducing bridge worth it. "Look here." She wiggles her phone. "Smile."

I do, and she takes a quick photo. After sliding her phone into her pocket, she rubs my forearm that's wrapped around her. "Why did you agree to this hike?"

"Because you'd mentioned revisiting your favorite childhood hike was on your bucket list. I wanted to make it happen," I say against her ear.

"I'm glad I did it with you. To make this memory with you," she murmurs.

I'm in so much damn trouble. This woman and her sweet words have the ability to obliterate my resolve and rules. She made me hope for a future I'd thought was impossible during and after my divorce.

She's quiet for a moment, still within the circle of my arms, both of us looking out at the horizon. Then she asks softly, "Have you always been afraid of heights?"

I tense slightly, not expecting the question, but her warmth against me makes it easier to answer. "No. It started when I was eight."

"What happened?"

I hesitate, rarely sharing this story with anyone. "My father took Thorne and me to one of the rickhouses where we age the bourbon. Lillianna was sick, so she'd skipped. Anyway, there were six floors with these narrow walkways between the barrels. We were on the top floor. My brother was running ahead, showing off as usual. The railings back then weren't up to today's safety codes."

Rosalia shifts slightly to look at my face, her eyes encouraging me to continue.

"He slipped and fell through a gap. Somehow caught himself on the edge." Even now, my heart races remembering it. "His fingers were losing their grip. I ran and grabbed his wrist just as he lost his grip."

"Oh my god," she whispers.

"I was holding him with everything I had, but I wasn't strong enough to pull him up. He was slipping and I couldn't save him." The terrified look in my brother's eyes, my straining muscles to the point of tearing, and the dizzying drop below have never left me. I fucking hate that feeling of absolute helplessness. "Dad finally reached us and pulled him to safety, but ever since then..."

"Heights trigger that memory," she finishes for me.

"It's not rational. I know that. But my body doesn't seem to care about logic."

Rosalia turns fully in my arms, her expression soft. "Yet you came up here anyway. For me."

"For you," I repeat.

"Do you want to leave?" she asks.

"Whenever you're ready."

Neither of us moves. Contentment sinks into me. Despite the fear that had gripped me moments ago, her presence calms my nerves and fills me with peace. I let go of all that might go wrong with us and allow myself to bask in the warmth of her touch and the sweetness of her scent.

Reluctantly, I loosen my hold and step back to look at her. "Thank you," I tell her, my voice barely above a whisper.

Her warm brown eyes search mine. "For what?"

"For being here with me. For making this memory." I cup her cheek, running a thumb along her soft lips.

Her breath catches in her throat, and her eyes flutter close for a heartbeat. When she opens them again, they shimmer with emotion. "I'm exactly where I want to be," she murmurs.

I take her hand in mine, and we turn away from the edge of the bridge. We make our way down the trail, our fingers intertwined.

We stay like that for a few more minutes, neither of us wanting to break the spell. Eventually, though, the afternoon heat and other hikers remind us we should head back.

Reluctantly, I loosen my hold and step back. "Ready to head down?"

She nods, but something in her expression shifts as we turn away from the bridge. And the closer we get to my truck, the quieter and more distant she becomes.

I touch her elbow. "Is everything okay?"

She startles. "Yeah, I just..." Her gaze searches my face. "There's something I need to tell you."

My heart stumbles. Could this be it? Is she going to admit her deal with Thorne?

"What is it?" I ask, trying to keep my voice neutral.

A bird calls to another nearby, and Rosalia looks in the direction, twisting her fingers together in front of her. "I haven't been entirely honest with you," she begins, her voice trembling slightly. "The truth is, I..."

She falters, her gaze dropping to the ground. I stand motionless, my entire body tense. Just say it, I silently urge her.

But she shakes her head, a rueful laugh escaping her. "You know what? It's nothing. Forget I said anything."

She quickens her pace, moving ahead of me on the trail. I stare after her, disappointment and frustration warring in my chest. She'd been so close. So damn close to telling me.

But what would I say if she had? That I made a bet to help her? She doesn't need to know I had to play games to protect her. What matters is that it's working.

I jog the few steps to catch up with her, falling into step beside her. "Rosalia," I say, infusing sincerity and understanding into my voice. "If there's something you need to tell me, I'm listening. Always."

There's a flicker of guilt in her eyes, but she shakes her head. "Really, it's nothing."

I bite back a sigh, my jaw tight. "Okay."

It isn't fair to push her, not when I have my secrets, my own stupid fucking bet with Thorne. I have to believe we can fix the mess my brother has started because, despite everything, despite the secrets and the lies, I'm falling for Rosalia. Deeper and harder every day.

And when the truth finally comes out? I can only hope that what we had will be strong enough to weather the storm the three of us have created.

Chapter Twenty-Nine

Rosalia

Sebastian pulls his truck into the alley behind Novel Idea. My gaze travels the path of the metal stairs to my apartment. A sudden emptiness fills me. Our afternoon has passed much too quickly.

"Do you have time to come inside and eat? Or should I grab your food to go?" I blurt, my questions spilling from me in a single breath.

"I'm not in a hurry," he says, switching off the engine.

I smile. "Okay. Then let's eat."

The driver-side handle clicks and Sebastian is out of the truck and around to my side, opening the door in a few seconds. He offers his hand, helping me out. I don't let go right away, reluctant to break the contact and lose the comfort of his touch.

We walk slowly across the narrow alley, gravel crunching beneath our feet. The late afternoon sun filters through the buildings, casting long shadows that seem to wrap around us like a private cocoon. Sebastian's thumb traces gentle circles across my knuckles, and I match his unhurried pace, both of us seemingly reluctant to end this perfect day.

"I still can't believe we saw that hawk circling right over the bridge," I say as we reach the base of the metal stairs.

"Almost like it was showing off for us," he agrees, smiling and popping that sexy dimple.

"The whole day felt like that," I admit softly. "Just... perfect."

His fingers brush a strand of hair from my face, his expression warm. "It really was."

My breath catches at his touch. We linger here, neither of us moving toward my apartment. Then voices drift into our quiet cocoon, followed by a group of tourists turning down the alley, their animated chatter growing louder as they approach.

"We should probably..." I point toward the stairs.

"Yeah," he agrees. His thumb traces one more gentle circle across my knuckles before he lets go.

We climb the metal stairs together, his hand finding the small of my back, both of us stealing glances over our shoulders as the group passes below. They wave and we return the gesture.

But my giddiness drops to the welcome mat when I push open the door. My apartment is small and modest, a far cry from the luxurious estate where Sebastian lives. And my place is a mess. Yesterday evening, I'd shucked out of my skirt and blouse as soon as I'd stepped inside. Both are lying in my foyer, which is nothing more than a tiny square of linoleum that's as dated and worn as the rest of the space. What is he thinking?

I shouldn't care, but do. Turning and holding the knob, I press against the mostly closed door. Focusing on the collar of his T-shirt, I say, "Um, it has been a busy week, my shoebox apartment is a mess."

"Rosalia, all I care about is…" He tips my chin so I'm looking at him. "Are those sandwiches you made."

His words carry a playful edge, drawing out my laughter. A genuine warmth flickers deeper beneath his expression, radiating through me like sunshine breaking through clouds. His touch against my skin feels intoxicating. His fingertips linger at my jawline, their presence startling and familiar.

We stand separated by mere inches, yet it feels like the distance contains entire worlds of what-ifs. My body instinctively sways toward him like a compass finding north, even as my mind catalogs all the reasons to maintain our fragile boundary.

I swallow hard, needing to rein in my runaway emotions. I'm getting ahead of myself. We're here for food, nothing more.

"Typical man," I joke, twisting around and pushing open the door.

I swoop inside, picking up my discarded clothes. Sprinting to the bathroom, I shove them in the hamper before returning to the small living room. I glance at the kitchen. At least the counter is only littered with a few books and a bowl from this morning's cereal.

Sebastian stands by the door, looking around. My apartment should be a badge of my independence. It is, after all, entirely mine. However, the cheap, light blue couch and faux wood TV stand scream that I haven't figured out adulting.

Next to Sebastian's effortless polish and premium hiking gear that probably cost more than all my furniture, my DIY attempts at home decor look childish. Did I really think my dollar store frames of family pictures and my amateur photography were cozy? The only piece of real art—and that's debatable—is a too-small painting of the Kentucky sunset I'd created with Paige at one of those wine and art classes.

And how had I thought my refurbished wooden crate coffee table was cute? Honestly, the slender bookshelf my dad made to fit between the wall and the window is the singular nicest piece of furniture in the room.

Sebastian's gaze finds its way to me. I'm caught between embarrassment and shame for being embarrassed, all my words abandon me and I just stare at him.

"Are we waiting for someone or something? A ghost, maybe?" He jokes, stepping closer, making an old floorboard squeak. His scent of vanilla and oak with hints of spice envelops me. "I hope it didn't eat the food you made for us. I'm starving."

The playful note in his voice relaxes me. On our way back to his truck, he'd mentioned his dislike of snakes. I grin and widen my eyes. "No, not a ghost. My pet cobra."

He freezes like an ice sculpture. I bite back a laugh. "I'm kidding. I don't have one. Yet."

His shudder makes me grin. Nodding toward the bookshelf, he asks, "Do you mind if I look?"

I lift my hand, palm up, in a go-ahead gesture. "Are these your parents?" He points at a heavy frame doubling as a bookend.

"Yeah, my dad drove in when I graduated from college. That was taken right after the ceremony," I reply, moving to stand next to him.

"You have a beautiful smile," he says quietly, setting the photo back on the shelf. The space between us seems to shrink, the heat of his body seeping into my side.

He turns, his pupils dilating slightly. The playfulness vanishes from his face, replaced by something hungry and focused. He reaches up, grazing his fingers along the sensitive skin of my neck, leaving a trail of goosebumps in their wake. The brief contact leaves an invisible imprint, spreading heat from that single point of contact down my spine. "Sebastian..."

His hand traces the contour of my jaw. My eyes flutter closed and I surrender to his touch, my lips parting on a sigh.

Then my stomach rumbles.

He steps back, breaking the spell. "We should probably eat," he says, the words catching in his throat, rough-edged and strained.

I nod, not trusting myself to speak. We move to the kitchen, but space and distraction do nothing to quiet the drumming of my pulse. I busy myself pulling out plates and silverware, acutely conscious of his every movement as he takes a seat at the counter. After pulling the sandwiches and salads from the fridge and setting them on the counter, I come around and sit next to him.

We twist in our seats to face each other. Our knees touch, sending a ripple of awareness through my body. I press my thighs together, needing to alleviate the growing ache.

He glances around and says thoughtfully, "Your place looks loved, lived in."

Well, humiliation certainly helps kill lust. "Is that your nice way of saying my place looks tired and worn?"

"Not at all. I see your personality everywhere. From the novels," he points at the bookshelf in the living room and to the romance paperback next to the sink. I'd read it while eating my cereal this morning. "To the cozy throw on the couch. I can see you cuddled under it, flipping through a novel or watching TV on a rainy day." His brows pull together and he stands. Walking to the couch, he stops at the throw. "Did you knit this?"

"My mom did," I tell him.

"That's...wow." His reply has no derision. He touches the afghan, and I swear I see sadness in his eyes. "She must have spent hours working on this."

"God, yes. First and nearly last knitting adventure. Mom spent months on it. I'd find her still up at 2 a.m., cursing under her breath and unraveling whole sections. Like Penelope from *The Odyssey*, except Mom was both creating and destroying her own work. It was a labor of love." I tilt my head from side to side. "Or maybe stubborn determination not to be defeated by yarn."

"And you were in her mind the whole time she was making it. At least a little."

That makes me snort. "I'm *always* on her mind. You know that term, helicopter parent? That's her."

He laughs, but like his eyes, it holds sadness. "What's the name for the polar opposite?" I almost say neglect, but thankfully I kept my mouth shut. "Because that's my parents," he finishes.

What response could possibly acknowledge such vulnerability? In the end, I don't have to because he lets go of the blanket and returns to his kitchen stool and to the original thread of our conversation. "I like it here. It is a home, not a house."

"And what's your place?" I ask.

"They're all houses."

"All?" I motion for him to pick a sandwich. "How many do you have?"

"Three. A condo in Tokyo. The house you were at in Bardstown. Another in Aspen."

"Why Tokyo and Aspen?"

"Blackstone Bourbon has a collaboration partnership with a Japanese whiskey company. Since I travel there often, it made sense to have my own place. As for Aspen, I like to ski and hike. Not that I get there very much."

My family saved spare change in a jar for a year to afford a weekend ski trip a few hours from our house. What was it like to buy a home just in case I might feel like skiing? Yet none of it seems to bring him happiness. An ache fills my chest for him.

He huffs out a laugh. "Don't make that sad face. It's a choice. I enjoy my job." He takes a bite of his sandwich and moans, "Damn, that's good."

"Thanks," I reply, but I'm more interested in his life than the food I've made. "Do you like being married to your career?" I ask. Direct and personal, I know, but he learned during our first dinner date that I go places most people politely avoid.

"It's worked out better than my actual marriage did." He clears his throat. "That sounded bitter. I apologize. Let's talk about something else, anything else."

That suits me fine. The jealousy coils in my stomach surprises me with its intensity.

"Let's talk about food." I push the salad bowl toward him, then stand. "Would you like something to drink? I have tea, water, and pop."

His lip twitches. "You mean coke?"

"Sorry, I only have root beer and an off-brand lemon pop."

"Both are coke."

I laugh. "You Southerners are odd."

"Says the woman who calls coke, pop," he jokes. "And point me toward the root beer. You don't have to serve me."

"You're in my humble home. It's my pleasure to serve you."

His eyes twinkle with mischief as a suggestive grin spreads across his face. "Is that so?"

Laughter bursts from me. I adore this playful, sexy side of him. "Lunch, Sebastian. It's my pleasure to serve you *lunch*."

After retrieving two bottles from the fridge, there's little talk as we devour the food. I'm famished from the hike, but as my stomach fills, the fact that we're alone sneaks up on me again.

Not because I'm the slightest bit nervous around him. No, because as one hunger is taken care of, another, more primal appetite awakens. This craving throbs through me, settling between my thighs, making sitting still impossible.

I leap to my feet. "Do you want more food?"

He shakes his head, rubbing his flat stomach. "No. Everything was great, but I'm stuffed."

Grabbing our plates, I take them to the sink and begin washing. Sebastian comes up next to me. "Let me help. I'll dry."

I hand him a faded dish towel and watch as the head of Blackstone Bourbon, a man who probably hasn't ever washed a dish, carefully dries a plate. His sleeves are pushed up, revealing tanned forearms, and there's a slight furrow of concentration between his brows that makes me smile.

Here he is in my tiny kitchen, treating my thrift store plate like it's fine china. It's what draws me to him. I love how he makes everything in my world feel valuable simply by the care he shows it.

I hand him another plate, and our fingers brush as he takes it. The brief contact sends a little shiver through me, every nerve ending suddenly alive to his presence. The kitchen seems to shrink around us until all I can process is him beside me. Even the warm dishwater sliding over my hands and the gentle clink of dishes takes on new intensity, like an intimate soundtrack to our closeness

"I think you missed your calling," I tease, handing him another wet plate.

He raises an eyebrow. "As a professional dish dryer?"

"You are very dedicated to the task."

"I'm dedicated to doing things right." His eyes meet mine, and the intensity in them makes me forget about the dish in my hand. "Whatever I do." He steps closer, close enough that the heat radiating from his body calls to me. His hand rises slowly, thumb grazing my bottom lip with a touch that lingers far longer than necessary. "You had a bit of sauce, just there," he murmurs, his voice dropping to a whisper, but his thumb doesn't move away. Instead, it traces along my lip, his gaze fixed, as if he's memorizing every detail.

I lick the corner of my mouth. "Did I get it all?" I ask, holding his eyes.

His gaze drops to my lips and he sways forward, but then seems to catch himself. "Yeah, you're good," he says roughly, turning back to the sink.

I exhale unsteadily. My hands ache to run over his broad shoulders, to feel his strength shudder beneath my touch. The thought of his stubble scraping against my sensitive skin as his mouth explores mine makes me shiver. Biting my lip against a moan, I wonder how long we can keep up this dance before the tension snaps.

I force myself to focus on something safer. "Tell me the truth. Is this your first time ever drying a dish?"

He laughs. "I'd rather not answer that question."

"Why?" I bump his hip.

"Because you might want to choke me with the gold spoon Daniel's convinced was lodged in my mouth during my birth."

I shake my head, smiling. "I bet there are diamonds on that spoon too."

"Have you been talking to Daniel? He might have mentioned those as well." A softer smile replaces his grin. "I'm thrilled my first time is with you."

He leans in, brushing his lips along my jawline. I arch my neck, giving him more access, and practically moan, "I'll make sure it's a memorable experience then."

His touch glides across my skin as playfully as his innuendo. As his mouth moves to my ear, desire spreads through me like wildfire.

He makes his way to my mouth and a soft sigh escapes me when our lips meet. The kiss tastes of root beer and longing. His tongue traces my lower lip and I open for him. Our tongues meet in a passionate rhythm.

Gripping my hips, he sets me on the counter. Water from the sink soaks through my leggings. I don't care, all that matters is bringing him closer. I wrap my legs around his waist, my swollen need aligning with his erection. He doesn't grind into me, only continues to kiss me slowly and thoroughly.

I rock against him. "Sebastian, please."

He breaks our kiss and looks into my eyes. "Tell me what you want."

The raw hunger in his gaze burns away the last of my hesitation. I slide my hands into his pockets, grabbing his firm butt. "You. In my bedroom."

I'm about to cross a line to give myself fully to a man I'm certain I can't keep. But right now, with his hands on my body and his eyes filled with undisguised desire, I can't bring myself to care. All that matters is the heat between us, the promise of pleasure and connection.

His lips trail fire down my neck. My breath comes in short gasps, anticipation mingling with something darker. Thorne's smug face flashes in my mind like an unwelcome intruder, but I forcefully shove it aside. Tonight is about Sebastian and me, nothing else.

I squeeze my eyes shut. I want this, want him, with an intensity that scares me. The weight of my secret presses against my chest, an invisible barrier between us.

Sebastian must sense my hesitation because he pulls back, his eyes searching my face. "Rosalia? Is everything okay? Should we stop?"

Forcing myself to smile and focus on his perfect touch, I run my fingers through his hair. "Yeah, I just... I want this to be right. You and me." Without our lies killing everything we touch. The words are poison I can't spit out. Not now, not when it could shatter this fragile moment of magic.

He cups my cheek. "It is right. You and me, together. That's all that matters. But if you're not sure about this..."

I swallow hard, my doubts rising like specters in the face of his tender concern. Am I sure? Can I really let myself have this, knowing I might have to betray him?

But my yearning outweighs my fear, and I pull him closer. "I'm sure," I whisper, hoping he can't hear the quaver in my voice. "I want this. I want you."

He captures my lips in a kiss that sears me to my soul. I cling to him, pouring all my longing and unspoken apologies into the slide of my mouth against his.

I'll find a way to cut the strings Thorne has attached to me, a way to be worthy of the trust and affection shining in Sebastian's eyes. But for now, I'm surrendering to the heat of his touch and the promise of a future where secrets no longer stand between us.

Chapter Thirty

Rosalia

Sebastian kisses me deeply, and I wrap my legs around his waist. My small apartment, which is usually a sanctuary of books, soft throws, and quiet solitude, now pulses with a different kind of energy. This modest space that has sheltered me through so many lonely nights is suddenly alive with desire. The dishes we washed gleam on the drying rack, forgotten witnesses to this transformation of my private haven.

I've dreamed of this moment, of continuing where we left off in his hotel room. In truth, these thoughts have occupied my mind much longer than just last night, even before our first date. But lately, the hunger for him consumes my every thought.

His lips brush against my ear, a cascade of sensation travels from the spot. "Do you have any idea," Sebastian whispers, each word scraping low in his throat, "how much I've been thinking about this? About you?"

He slams his mouth against mine, pinning me to the counter. His hands grip my waist, fingers pressing deeper with each second. I barely recognize this man. Gone is the careful, measured Sebastian. His chest rises and falls in shallow, uneven bursts.

"Wrap your legs tighter," he orders, the bass in his command rippling through my belly.

I comply immediately, clinging to him as he carries me from the kitchen. My nails claw at his shirt, desperate to feel skin. "You're wearing too many clothes," I stutter, each syllable rushed and broken. We careen into the hallway wall, neither willing to separate long enough to navigate properly.

He laughs, and the sound dissolves into a groan. "Patience, darling." But his pupils have nearly swallowed the brown of his irises. "I plan on savoring all of you." His fingertips brand my thighs, pressing deep into my muscles.

"I don't want patience," I gasp. My fingers slip and fumble at his belt. "I can't—I need—"

"Tell me," he demands, forehead pressing against mine. His stare burns through me, the room tilting as my balance falters. "Tell me what you want, Rosalia. I need to hear you say it."

My heart hammers so hard my ribs ache. "I want you. All of you. Please." The plea escapes before I can stop it.

He pins me against the door frame, molding his perfect body flat against mine. He presses his palms flat beside my head and stares at me. His chest heaves and sweat beads at his temples. "Your wish," the words are barely controlled, a tremor running through them, "is my command."

He swings me around and we tumble onto the bed, limbs tangled. Between desperate kisses, fabric tears and falls away—my shirt, his belt, barriers disappearing as fast as our restraint. His precise touches grow wild, erratic. Every trace of his careful technique dissolves into something rawer, hungrier.

"Sebastian," I whisper, digging my fingers into his bare shoulders when his hand slides between my thighs, running along the lace edges of my panties.

He stops. "Keep going?"

I can only nod; words are impossible. My fingers tremble against his skin as I reach for him. "Don't—don't stop," I stammer, the breathy sound foreign to my ears.

He groans my name, sliding his hand inside my panties. My body jerks upward, needing more of his large and talented hands.

I touch him through his open slacks, his forehead dropping to my shoulder, rhythm stuttering. "Jesus Christ, Rosalia, I can't—" His mouth crashes back to mine, all teeth and tongue and ragged breaths.

"I need to feel all of you," I gasp through our kisses.

His pupils are blown wide, his jaw clenched, and his movements sharp and desperate. "I'm going to unravel you," he growls, the vibration against my collarbone raising goosebumps across my skin. "Piece by goddamn piece," he promises.

Between my thighs, he moves with purpose, one hand removing my leggings while the other caresses me, drawing a cry from my throat that echoes off the walls. My fingers twist in his hair, yanking hard.

"Please," I gasp, the sound barely human. "Sebastian, please—"

Moving down my body, he pulls my panties and leggings to my knees. He positions himself at my core, and coherent thought is impossible. His mouth devours, licking and sucking until stars explode behind my eyes. I pant his name like a prayer, mindless with ecstasy. Rational thought surrenders to pure sensation as he drives me higher and higher with his mouth and tongue until I snap, my orgasm exploding through me.

I bow off the bed, pulling at his hair. He doesn't let me come down until the pleasure is too much, and I twist away, letting him go.

He kisses my upper thigh. "Condoms? Or do you want to stop?"

"Umm, I'm not sure…" Do I have any? I'd gone on a handful of dead-end dates since moving here. None had led to sex.

Sebastian begins pulling up my leggings, his movements gentle but decisive.

What the hell?

"Okay," he says.

Wait, what? "What are you doing?"

"I'm stopping. You said you aren't sure." His eyes hold mine, steady and serious despite the flush on his cheeks and the rapid rise and fall of his chest.

My heart softens like butter left out in the warm sun. This man, capable of such intensity moments ago, now backs away at my slightest hesitation. I sit up and cradle his face, kissing him and tasting desire on his tongue. "I definitely don't want to stop. I meant I'm not sure if I have condoms."

"Oh. Okay." He nuzzles into my neck. "But know, I'm happy to explore your body all night with my hands and mouth."

"And I, yours. But I'd rather do more. Let me look to see what I have while you remove those." I push on his pants and pull them off his hips.

I twist around, yanking open the top drawer on my nightstand, and ransack the contents, tossing charger cords, books, and other clutter onto the floor. Nothing. No. No. Desperation crawls through me. There has to be one somewhere in all this stuff.

Behind me, the whisper of fabric against skin teases at my concentration. The mattress dips, and then his lips press against my spine, each vertebra receiving attention that sends shivers radiating outward. My search slows, then falters completely.

"Any luck?" he murmurs, his breath hot against my skin.

With effort, I drag my focus back to the task. I slam the now empty drawer shut and attack the one below. More books, boxes, and useless crap. Wait! A strip of individually wrapped square packages peeks from between the pages of an old paperback. I yank the makeshift bookmark from the drawer with a triumphant cry. "Bingo!" I shout.

He laughs against my back. "Found your prize."

"You." I turn, grabbing his shoulders and shoving him backward onto the bed. "Are my prize."

His smile starts sweet, then transforms—lips curling at the corners, teeth flashing in a way that makes my stomach clench. "And you are the sweetest treat. Like cotton candy that melts on my tongue."

I straddle him, impatient again, tearing at the condom wrapper with my teeth. My hands shake with renewed urgency. I grasp his erection and stroke him from base to head. His eyes slam shut, head pressing back into the pillow, every muscle in his neck standing out in sharp relief. The way his hips rock with my strokes is hypnotic.

I can't wait any longer. Releasing him, I rip open the condom packet and roll it down his thick, long length. The careful tenderness of moments ago evaporates like morning dew under a brutal sun. We're back to urgent need, primal and raw.

He surges upward, rolling on top of me, but he doesn't push inside. Instead, he glides along me, pressing into my clit, his kisses turning rough again, teeth scraping my lower lip.

"Sebastian, please," I hiss, spreading my legs and lifting my hips in invitation. He rocks into me, filling me in a way that's sin and heaven. His thrusts are shallow, each one slightly deeper than the last, giving me time to adjust and promising pleasure.

The restraint in his movements betrays his struggle for control. "How do you feel this good?" he asks, as he bites then kisses my shoulder.

He shifts onto his elbows, eyes finding mine. The raw vulnerability there catches me off guard. "Are you okay?" he whispers.

I nod, but I'm not sure if that's true. This is too good, too intense and consuming.

Fighting against my rising tide of panic, I wrap my legs around him and urge him deeper. When he's all the way inside me, he grinds against my clit. I gasp, sparks shooting through my belly, and the embers of my earlier orgasm flare unexpectedly.

"Rosalia, you're perfect. I'm damn near losing my mind."

My pulse thunders in my ears. Every nerve ending blazes alive. I kiss him hard, our teeth clicking together in my haste. "Then let go," I urge him.

"Not until you come again."

"That's impossible. You'll be trying all night and have nothing for your effort, so focus on yourself."

"Are you kidding? Nothing for my effort?" He drags his tongue along my neck, teeth scraping the sensitive spot below my ear. "Getting to be in this body all night long is all the reason I need."

He rolls onto his back, taking me with him. His hands lock onto my hips like iron bands, lifting me up until we're nearly separate, then driving me back down onto him, impaling every one of my swollen nerves, making me whimper.

I take over, setting a pace that borders on frantic. He explores my body, palms rough against my skin. His thumbs press into my clit, and a shock of sensation steals my breath as the possibility of another orgasm materializes out of nowhere.

My thighs begin to tremble, my muscles protesting the pace. Each downward thrust sends shockwaves through my core. The coiling within me intensifies, a pressure building that feels almost painful in its intensity.

With his other hand, he cups my breast, fingers pinching and rolling the soft flesh, eliciting a symphony of sensations that reverberate throughout me. As he tugs sharply at my nipple, a flash of rapture shoots through me, and unintelligible sounds spill from my lips as he urges me closer to the edge of release. "I—I was wrong," I pant, words slurring together. "I'm going to come. I'm so close."

In one swift motion, he sits up, taking my breast into his hot mouth, teeth grazing sensitive skin. I gasp and my body convulses as pure, blinding ecstasy consumes me. My world dissolves into a rush of sensation, consciousness narrowing to a single point before exploding outward. A shiver runs from my core to my fingertips, leaving me dizzy. Everything else fades away. There's only the pounding of my heart and the intense euphoria drowning me in waves.

"Kiss me," he demands, his words hot and broken against my mouth.

His thrusts turn harder and sharper, prolonging my pleasure. I clutch his sweat-slicked back, urging him to come undone. His body stiffens, and a second later, he growls out my name as his climax chases mine.

We lie there breathing hard, our hearts gradually slowing as the intensity fades into something softer. I roll onto my side and nestle into his arms. Our bodies are slick with sweat and lovemaking. In the hazy glow of the early evening sun, his skin shimmers like burnished gold. I can't resist trailing my fingers along the ridges and planes of his chest, memorizing them like a map. A fleeting worry crosses my mind. This moment is precious and fragile.

He hums contentedly, pulling me closer and pressing a kiss to the top of my head. "That was incredible," he murmurs. "You're incredible."

My chest tightens with something deeper than physical satisfaction. I close my eyes, breathing in the heady mix of sex and Sebastian. But even as I sink into this brief sanctuary, the first tendrils of unease curl around my heart. The very things that make this moment so perfect—the depth of my feelings for him, the soul-deep connection—are also what make it so dangerous. Secrets have a weight all their own.

He traces patterns on my bare skin, leaving goosebumps in their wake. I'd love to surrender to his touch, let go of everything except the sensation of his fingers against my body, but the nagging voice in my head grows louder. Sebastian presses a kiss to my forehead and murmurs, "What's going on in that beautiful mind of yours?"

I force a smile and shake my head. "Nothing, just... thinking how perfect this is. Being here with you."

His light brown eyes search mine, seeing too much. "You know you can tell me anything, right? I'm here for you, Rosalia, whenever you need me."

If only I could speak the truth without losing him. Without losing myself.

If only past choices could be erased as easily as footprints in sand. Life doesn't work that way. And I dare not imagine a future where I'm worthy of what he offers.

Tears burn behind my eyes, but I blink them away. I kiss him. "Tonight, let's be here, in this moment. No past, no future. Just us. Can you do that for me?"

His eyes hold mine for a long moment before he nods, pulling me closer. "For you, anything."

I lay my head on his chest, listening to the steady thrum of his heartbeat. In the gathering shadows of this last Friday in April, I allow myself this stolen happiness, this brief respite from reality. But next Saturday's derby party looms like an approaching storm.

And the weight of Sebastian's arm around me, the gentle rise and fall of his chest beneath my cheek, makes the choice unbearable. Each kiss, each tender touch from this man reveals a goodness I never expected to find. How can I possibly hurt him now?

Tomorrow will demand decisions. But tonight, wrapped in Sebastian's warmth, I'll treasure this perfect slice of happiness and pray for strength to face the impossible choice waiting for me eight days from now.

Chapter Thirty-One

Sebastian

The bright, whimsical melody of the ukulele lulls me between the realms of wake and sleep. The music is coming from nearby, but in my drowsy state, I can't quite discern if the musician is inside or outside. All I know is that Rosalia and I are on our tropical honeymoon. Her soft body, warm and fragrant, is blissfully pressing all along me.

I kiss the back of her neck, bury my nose in her silken hair, and consider asking the talented ukulele player to leave. Especially when Rosalia, still half-asleep, wiggles her hips, grinds her ass against my growing arousal. A low hum of approval escapes her throat, and heat blooms across my chest, spreading outward until even my fingertips tingle with anticipation.

"Crap, I'm going to be late," she mutters, her words piercing through my haze.

She moves away from me, and I hold tight. "The luau can wait."

Giggling and twisting around so we face each other, she says, "That sounds even better than a field of balloons."

The mention of balloons tugs me fully awake. The honeymoon suite dissolves, replaced by the cream walls and sheer lavender curtains on the wall opposite the bed. I blink, taking in the sight of Rosalia beside me, her hair tousled and her face soft with sleep. Glancing at my left hand resting on her hip, I see there isn't a ring on my finger.

It was a dream. Given our secrets, I should be relieved, but instead, disappointment settles in my chest.

She smiles, placing a palm on my chest. "Good morning," she murmurs, her voice laced with dreams.

"Morning," I reply, shifting onto an elbow, locating the ukulele—Rosalia's phone.

She rolls over and turns it off. "It's my alarm."

Laughing, I sit up and rub the stubble on my cheeks. "Tropical music as your morning alarm? That's an interesting choice."

She grins over her shoulder while reaching for a crimson robe hanging from the bed's metal headboard. "I thought waking up to a vacation song would be a nice way to start each day, but it's backfiring. The letdown each morning I open my eyes and do not find myself in a tropical destination is a major bummer."

I chuckle, but it turns to a curse when I glance at my phone on the nightstand and see the time. "No chance I'll make it home to change and still make my morning meeting." I pick up my cell. "I'll call Hanna and have her reschedule."

"You could get ready here. Have Tom bring you a change of clothes," Rosalia suggests, wrapping the robe around her and standing.

I blow out a breath. That would help with my packed schedule, but in all honesty, the bigger draw of this plan is having more time with her. "Are you sure?"

"Yup. Get in the shower. While you're in there, I'll wait for Tom and get your clothes from him."

"Don't worry about that. I've pulled too many all-nighters at work. I have spares in all my vehicles. Though the ones in my truck have been there a while. Hopefully, they still fit. And I'll have to go commando."

She takes in my bare chest, the thin sheet covering my bottom half. When she returns to my face, her eyes are fully dilated. Desire surges through me, shutting off my brain.

"Or…" I scoot to the other side of the bed, where she stands. The movement has the sheet falling away from me. Her gaze devours my naked body, and rational thought abandons me completely. Shifting, I sit with my feet on the ground and her between my legs. I slip a hand inside her robe, cupping her breast. "We could be late."

She gasps and takes half a step toward me. Standing, I lean in for a kiss. Just before I reach her lips, she stumbles back, placing a hand over her mouth. "I have morning breath."

"If that bothers you, I can kiss other places." I push aside the thin cotton of her robe and flick her peaked nipple with my tongue.

"Okay," she rasps.

Her phone cries from the nightstand, and her moan turns into a groan. "That's probably Dad or Paige. I have to answer."

Looking at the ID, she swipes and says, "Hi, Paige. What's up?"

She doesn't tie her robe closed, and I take that as an invitation. I sit back on the bed's edge and pull her between my legs, planting a kiss on her stomach.

Running a hand through my hair, she grips the longer strands on top, saying into the phone, "We can meet—" I shift to her hip and bite lightly. "M-meet in a…could you just text me where to meet?"

I smile against her warm skin. "No. No, I'm fine. Just, um, distracted." Happy to be her distraction, I run my tongue slowly from her hip, closer and closer to the apex of her thighs. She inhales sharply, then steps out of my reach, and mouths, "Get your clothes."

I push out my bottom lip, making her laugh. Then I stand. I really do need to get moving. I pull on last night's clothes and grab my keys before heading down to the truck for my spare outfit.

"Nothing. Just saw something funny out the window," I hear her say as I leave the bedroom.

Walking through her apartment and down the alley stairs, my heart swells with emotions I dare not name. They're all terrifying to acknowledge. I shouldn't feel this way about someone I can't fully trust. Reaching the gravel of her alley, I turn to the delivery door of the bookstore and sigh.

There'd been a moment last night where I thought she'd tell me about her deal with Thorne. I'd seen it in her eyes. The same when we were hiking. But she'd turned away, holding onto her secrets. Did he have her sign an NDA as well? Probably.

Fucking Thorne and his deals and wagers. He loves to gamble, and one day he's going to lose everything. Although today it feels like I'll be the loser. His wager hangs over everything between Rosalia and me, ready to destroy what we're building. In my mind's eye, I can see her face crumple if the truth comes out. I can hear the venom in her voice as she cries, "I trusted you."

Reaching my truck, I lean against the driver's side door. The honorable choice would be to drive away now, putting distance between us to make it easier for her to take the files from me. Let her save all she has worked for. But then I remember my employees and what would happen to them if my brother were to take over. It will hurt her to believe she's giving up her store and programs, but once this is over, I'll make sure she wants for nothing. Ever.

I grab my clothes and rush back up the stairs to her apartment. Opening the door, my gaze lands on the towel I'd tossed on the counter after we started kissing. I'd give anything to go back in time. Not to change things, because I'm a selfish bastard. I want to relive every moment.

"Rosalia," I call from the hallway to let her know I'm back.

"I'm in the shower. There's a new toothbrush on the counter for you."

I walk into the bathroom, thanking her. Right after washing and brushing my teeth, the rings on the shower curtain rattle as she pulls the material back. In the mirror's reflection, Rosalia stands naked, rivulets cascading down her curves. "Join me?" she asks.

The steam curls around us, carrying her intoxicating scent of summer fruits and warm skin. Turning, I suck in the humid air, hoping to steady my breathing, but every inhale draws me deeper under her spell. I ache to touch her, to lose myself in her warmth. But I hold back. This isn't physical craving alone. Rosalia has become my refuge, my solace. Stepping into that shower with her would be surrendering to something deeper than desire.

"I am having trouble reaching a certain spot. Could you help me?" She bites her lip, looking at me through long lashes lined with moisture.

I yearn to reach out, but hold back. This isn't just physical anymore. She's becoming someone I can't afford to lose, and that terrifies me more than any secret I'm keeping. "Rosalia, I..." I start, but the words catch in my throat. "Aren't you in a hurry?"

"My dad called right after I hung up with Paige. He's running a little behind."

Water from the shower hits her shoulder and neck, creating an enticing trail between her breasts. I can't look away. Her hand slides up her wet stomach and cups herself, sighing, "But you have your breakfast meeting..."

"I'm the boss. They can wait for me." I shuck out of my clothes and step into the shower, pressing her against the wall and kissing her until she's writhing against me.

When we pull apart, I pick up a bar of soap. She hands me a loofah. "I'd rather use my hands," I say.

I turn her around, and she rests her palms against the tiled wall. Goosebumps rise on her skin, and her quickening pants tell me she's as turned on as I am. Working up a lather, I slide my soapy hand along her shoulders, arms, then waist. Bringing them to her front, I cup her breasts. She presses back, her ass rubbing against my rock-hard dick.

Heat rushes through my body and I grind against her slick skin. All my blood and need rush south. Gliding a hand down her stomach and between her legs, I press my fingers against her clit. She moans my name. I love the sound on her needy lips.

She slides my cock between her thighs, wrapping her hand around the head. She's slippery and warm from the shower and her desire. In a single thrust, I'd be inside her.

She bends as if reading my mind, placing her hands on the opposite wall. Over her shoulder, she looks into my eyes and begs, "Please."

The condoms are in the bedroom, but I can't leave her. I come closer, like a magnet to metal, pulled by a force both invisible and undeniable. There's plenty to do with her beautiful body that doesn't have to end with me inside her.

She rises on her toes, gliding her heat along my length, and my need takes over. I reach around, palming her breast with one hand while the other slides down her stomach, returning between her legs. She rocks against my palm, pleading, "Yes, like that."

The motion has her perfect ass rubbing against my dick. Her quiet pants become loud moans. I lick the shell of her ear, murmuring, "Are you close?"

"Yes," she whimpers. "So close."

She twists her neck and kisses me with wild, desperate lips, her body stiffening. She sucks in a sharp breath and I press my hand in hard, giving her more friction. My name becomes her chant. I move my fingers in a circular motion, and the cries of her orgasm drive me to the edge of control.

Twisting in my arms, she slides down my body and takes me into her mouth. "Rosalia," I groan between clenched teeth, gripping her damp locks and forcing myself not to thrust down her throat.

Looking up at me, she skates her lips along my length until only the head of my dick remains between her full lips. Then her gaze locks with mine, and the unbridled lust in her eyes damn near makes me come.

She runs her tongue along the bottom of my length before sucking, taking me deeper and deeper. My knees lock, and I slam my palms against the slick shower wall. This is going to be over way too soon, but I'm powerless against the ecstasy.

I shudder, my muscles tighten, and my pulse races. Her hands grip my thighs as she finds the perfect rhythm, pushing me closer to the edge.

"You need to stop. I'm going to come," I groan, on the brink of losing control.

I make to step away, but she holds me tighter, taking me so deep that my pleasure explodes through me and down her throat. "Fuck, Rosalia," I gasp, nearly blacking out from the force of my orgasm.

She doesn't stop until I'm completely spent. Then she stands and I wrap her in my arms, kissing her neck. "You're absolutely incredible."

Her hot breath caresses my ear as she purrs, "You bring out a side of me I didn't know existed. I can't get enough of you."

"Christ, the way you touch me," I rasp. "You're intoxicating."

I capture her lips in a searing kiss. My hands roam her curves possessively, mapping every inch of her silky skin. My hand moves down her body with deliberate slowness, teasing and stroking her. "I never want to stop discovering new ways to drive you wild."

"Don't tempt me." She runs her hands up my chest. "But my dad will be here in about half an hour. And he has a key to my place…"

I sigh, turning toward the showerhead. "Naked is not how I want to meet your father."

Closing my eyes, I tip my chin into the spray. What the hell am I saying? She might have referred to herself as my girlfriend when she'd been grinding on my lap during the fireworks, but in the light of day, I doubt she sees me as her boyfriend.

Less than ten minutes later, we're out of the shower, dressed, and collecting our things to leave. "I'll walk you to your truck," she tells me, her cute ponytail swinging in front of me. "There's a bagel and coffee place around the corner. I have time to pick up something for my dad and me."

I follow her, mentally running through my packed schedule for the day. From the breakfast meeting I'm already late for, to the quarterly projections I need to review and calls with international partners that will likely run into the evening, my mind is a tangle of obligations and deadlines.

But then I'm distracted by the way the morning light catches in Rosalia's damp hair, and everything else falls away. A sudden, almost painful ache hits me. I'm going to miss her. Not eventually, but immediately, the moment I walk away.

"Wait," I say.

She turns, hand on the doorknob. Her gaze meets mine with that inquisitive look I'm coming to know well. The slight narrowing of her gaze, the tiny furrow between her brows that appears when she's intrigued.

"Have dinner with me on Monday," I tell her, stepping closer. Not a question, almost a plea. "I don't want to wait until the party to see you."

Her lips curve into a slow smile. "Monday? Don't you have a busy week? Isn't derby time like the Super Bowl for distilleries?"

I laugh. "It is, but I'll make time. Hell, I'd suggest Sunday, but I'll be tied up with Oaks Day events." I'm barely able to keep from begging, but manage to hold on to a little self-respect.

She steps toward me, closing the distance between us. "I'd like that," she says softly. "Monday sounds perfect."

Unable to help myself, I kiss her, slow and deep. Her arms wrap around my neck, and for a moment, I let myself imagine a world where there are no wagers, no secrets, no Thorne between us. Just this. Her warmth, her smile, the way she makes everything else fade away.

When we break apart, I inhale her citrus scent coming off her warm skin, needing to take a piece of this moment with me.

Reluctantly, I step back, and she turns toward the door again. That's when I notice the mark on her neck, right at the slope of her shoulder. It looks like I enjoyed the noises she made when I nibbled on the spot a little too much.

"Um, you might want to wear your hair down," I tell her.

"Why?" she asks, opening the door.

"I accidentally gave you a hickey." I kiss the spot. Her body stiffens, and I look up—right into a man's eyes, the same color as Rosalia's. Only this set has deep crow's feet.

The cozy bubble of intimacy that had enveloped me bursts, and my body tenses, preparing for a confrontation. I see surprise on Mr. Manchester's face, then his lips press into a thin line. In that look, I know the weight of my past; the reputation that precedes me isn't doing me any favors with Rosalia's father.

My hand twitches at my side, instinctively wanting to reach for her to show a united front. But I hold back, unsure if such a gesture would be welcome at this charged moment. I step from behind Rosalia, determined to face whatever judgment or disapproval her father throws at me.

I offer my hand. "Mr. Manchester, I'm Sebastian Blackstone. It's nice to meet you."

Her father looks at my hand for a beat too long. Then, he shakes it, saying in a flat tone, "Paul. Paul Manchester."

"You're early," Rosalia says to her dad.

"Traffic was better than expected. Are you joining us?" he asks me. His clipped tone makes it clear I'm not welcome.

"No. I have a breakfast meeting this morning," I reply.

The relief in the other man's eyes would be funny if he weren't someone important to Rosalia. Where did her dad's dislike for me come from? From the media or something else?

She claps her hands. "Okay, well, we better get moving."

"I'll talk to you later," I tell her, unsure if kissing her goodbye under her father's disapproving gaze is a good idea. She nods without meeting my eyes, so I turn to her father. "Again, it was nice meeting you, Mr. Manchester."

Stepping into the hallway, I walk down the stairs, pausing at the bottom, and look up at her closed door. I hate that her father sees me as someone unworthy of his daughter. I hate it more because he's right. As long as I'm trapped in Thorne's wager, I am that man. I need to escape our bet to untangle myself from this fucking web. There has to be a loophole or a way to negotiate. It won't be easy, but I'm determined to do whatever it takes to free myself from my past mistakes.

Because for the first time in a long time, I have a reason to fight, a chance at something real.

Chapter Thirty-Two

Rosalia

I tap the button on my phone's screen and the video stops recording. Tucking it into my jacket pocket, I keep my gaze trained on the sky, which is shifting from dark to light blue and filling with colorful hot-air balloons preparing for the race.

"I've missed this. All the derby fun," Noah tells his sister, and Paige nods.

"Do you not get to visit often?" I ask. Despite having only met this morning, conversation flows easily between us.

"Not as much as I'd like," he replies. I've learned Noah works in Cleveland as a software engineer. His gaze finds mine. "Though, given a reason, I'd visit more. An hour and a half isn't that far..."

My cheeks heat, and I tip my face toward the sky. I recognize the invitation, and on paper, he's a suitable match for me. He's handsome, successful, and grounded—a sweet, charming engineer who isn't infamous by birthright. And Paige is his sister, which is a hell of a lot better than having Thorne as a brother-in-law.

Yet Noah's gentle flirtation barely registers against what I feel for Sebastian. Even thinking his name sends a rush through me that no practical considerations can dampen.

He consumes me completely. It's not just the way he sets my nerve endings ablaze with every touch, but the quiet connections between us. Last night in his arms, lost in his gaze this morning, I'm certain no other man could compare.

Not that I can tell Noah my interest lies elsewhere, not with Dad watching me with his eagle gaze. During the ride over, he didn't mention Sebastian, but I'm certain his silence on the matter won't last. He's biding his time, sorting through his thoughts. That's his way.

Paige curses. "I forgot my thermos of coffee in the trunk."

"I'll get it," I offer, wanting to create a little distance between Noah and me.

Dad steps beside me. "I'll go with you."

Damn. Looks like he's sorted his thoughts, and my time has run out. Starting toward the car, I scramble for a topic that doesn't involve Sebastian. "Have—"

"Dating a Blackstone isn't a good idea."

I turn to look at him. "Excuse me?"

"You heard me." His tone is uncharacteristically firm, and his jaw is set in a way that looks at odds with his normally relaxed face.

"Why do you dislike them so much?" I'm truly surprised. My dad gets along with everyone.

"It goes back a long way. Louis Blackstone and I grew up in the same county." He kicks a pebble across the parking lot.

"Sebastian's father?" I ask.

Dad nods. "He was always causing trouble, but his daddy's money got him out of everything." His lip twists in revulsion. "Especially with women. The worst kind of trouble."

"But that's Sebastian's father. Not him," I counter.

"Who do you think raised him?" He must notice my bewilderment because his tone softens. "Listen, it's not like we're talking about ancient history. Louis hasn't changed. He has two kids who aren't from his wife."

"Again, Dad, that's not Seb—"

"What about Thorne Blackstone? He was dating Melissa Wright recently. Do you remember Mr. Wright from the bank? His daughter." I nodded. Dad's lip curls in disgust. "Well, let's just say, like father, like son."

I frown. "That doesn't mean Sebastian is the same.".

"His marriage ended before the ink dried," he counters. "Surrounded by the same kinds of rumors."

I stop and wait for my dad to do the same. Sebastian had a very good reason for leaving his wife. But telling my father that the marriage ended because he'd caught his wife with his brother wouldn't raise his opinion of the Blackstone family. "He can't help what's said about him. And you're never one to view rumors as gospel."

Dad has the decency to look ashamed. "I know it's wrong. But you're my daughter, and I don't like the idea of you getting mixed up with one of Louis's sons."

"I'm dating, not marrying Sebastian. We aren't serious," I reason.

"Last time we talked, he was a friend," he drawls. "Yet, your grandma tells me and anyone who'll listen that you went on a date with him to his family's fancy gala. And this morning…" He gives me a disapproving-dad look. "Very early in the morning, I might add, at your house."

My cheeks heat. I rub my thumb over the hickey, now concealed by the hair I let down. "I, um…" What could I say? Definitely not what we'd been doing.

"Like I said before, it's not a good idea to date the man who owns the building you're renting."

I freeze. "Why?"

"What if things go south between you two?" Dad lowers his voice. "I've seen what happens when someone crosses Louis Blackstone. He's vindictive. If Sebastian's cut from the same cloth and you upset him…" He hesitates. "Let's just say, he could make sure you never get another loan or even a simple checking account in all of Kentucky."

The thought chills me, yet a giggle bubbles up inside me and escapes when we reach Paige's car. "And here I thought Mom was the winner of creating worst-case scenarios."

"This is different."

"How?"

"Because it's me." He grins, but it fades. "And because I know the Blackstones."

"You know Louis and a little about Thorne. But not Sebastian." I pop the trunk and spot Paige's bright pink thermos.

"That's fair," Dad concedes. Grabbing the coffee and locking the car, I can't shake his words.

Do I really know Sebastian? We'd grown close over the past few weeks, but his family's reputation is hard to ignore. What if there is more to him than I've seen? What if he is like his father and brother?

We head back to the field. "But bear with your old man," he says. "And your mother. I know she tends to fret. A lot. It all comes from a place of love. Mine too. I worry about you. Sebastian Blackstone has the power to hurt more than your heart. Especially with what's happening with your lease."

I force a smile, hoping to disguise my anxiety. "None of that matters. I have an appointment with the SBA on Tuesday morning. Things will be cleared up."

I hope. Kinda.

If I take that route, I'll have to find a new store, which will require downtime and the extra cost of moving.

My stomach drops as a darker possibility emerges. What if the SBA does help me tomorrow, and I no longer have to help Thorne? He says I can walk away at any time, but what about the NDA?

When I signed it, his logic seemed sound. "I have no reason to tell Sebastian," he'd said dismissively. "That would give him time to change what's in the portfolio."

But now I see the dangerous loophole. The NDA only silences me, not him. If I walk away from our deal, nothing would prevent Thorne from telling Sebastian everything out of spite. Sebastian would believe I betrayed him, and I'd be legally bound from defending myself.

The trap feels complete, closing in from all sides, no matter which way I turn.

My dad taps my shoulder. His face tells me he's been talking while I've been spiraling.

"Sorry, did you say something?" I ask.

He nods. "Do you want me to manage your store while you're at the SBA meeting?"

"Won't you be at work?"

"I can let them know I'll be late."

My eyes blur slightly, and I blink hard. Even when he thinks I'm making terrible decisions, even when he's scared for me, he's still here. "I appreciate the offer, but I've already put up a sign saying I'll be closed until noon and cancelled the morning coffee hours. But thank you for always being willing to step in when I need you."

We start walking back across the field toward Noah and Paige, my dad's steady presence beside me grounding my scattered thoughts. As we approach the group, my gaze catches sight of the Blackstone Bourbon balloon, its distinctive logo bringing Sebastian back to mind.

Not the rumors or his family name, but the man who quieted my anxieties with gentle reassurances. The man who ignored his fear of heights for my happiness, who had my bike fixed because he'd noticed my distress. The careful way he held me last night as if I were something precious. Those moments reveal more truth than whispered rumors ever could.

The lease problem and Thorne's deal are all tangled together, and I'm not sure how it will work out. Maybe Sebastian is exactly who I think he is. Maybe he isn't.

But all these worries are built on 'what ifs' and other people's opinions. What I've actually experienced with him—that's real.

As another balloon rises against the brightening sky, a tentative resolution settles over me. I can't control what others think of Sebastian or me. I can't undo my mistakes with the lease or predict how tomorrow's meeting will go. But I can trust what I've seen with my eyes and felt with my heart. From now on, I'll try to listen to my voice above the chorus of well-meaning advice.

I smile, joining my little group with a lighter heart. Dad's hand finds my shoulder and I lean into his touch, grateful for his concern even as I silently choose my own path. I'll face whatever comes next as I have everything else: one step at a time, learning as I go, and trusting myself enough to rise above the fears that would keep me grounded.

Chapter Thirty-Three

Rosalia

The sun glints off the polished brass of the Blackstone Bourbon sign as the Bentley drives through the gates of the distillery. Now that my stress levels are much lower than they were the first time I was here for the gala, I'm able to appreciate the property's beauty, from the oak trees lining the road like proud sentinels to the rickhouses scattered in the distance. My gaze settles on the red brick buildings with their crisp black trim.

My phone rings from the small clutch resting on my lap. I pull it out, and a quiet happiness fills me at the sight of Sebastian's number flashing on the screen. "Hi, traffic was nonexistent, so we're a little early," I tell him. "Tom's driving past the main parking lot."

Background conversation and grinding machine gears filter through the phone. "Damn. I'm running a little behind. Would you like to wait in the car or come inside?"

There's a hint of frustration I haven't heard from him before. Is it the stress of running such a large operation or something else? Does he regret making plans with me?

"Go inside," I reply immediately. Seeing him in his element at work is too good to pass up.

"Okay, I'll have Tom escort you inside. And again, I apologize."

"It's fine. See you in a few."

We park next to a building with a brass sign that reads "Distillery." A minute later, Tom opens my door and offers his arm. "Mr. Blackstone would like me to accompany you."

I'm relieved. The two-story distillery is spacious enough to get lost in, and I have no desire to wander around in my crimson cocktail dress and three-inch heels searching for Sebastian.

We step onto a massive porch that should be at odds with a working distillery, but instead oozes southern charm. Tom pulls open the black metal door, steps aside, and waits for me to enter first. Undertones of caramel, vanilla, and oats greet me. The scent reminds me of summer mornings at my grandparents', eating oatmeal in their sunny kitchen, and helping them with the crosswords. There's even a slight fruity undertone in the air, like the berries added to the breakfast treat.

A large banner hangs across the entrance hall: "Blackstone Bourbon—Official Sponsor of the Kentucky Derby." Beneath it sits an ornate countdown clock: "Derby Day: Five Days!"

My stomach twists into a painful knot. The ticking of that countdown clock seems to follow me as we walk deeper into the distillery, each second eroding what little time I have left.

I take a deep breath and lock those thoughts away in a mental vault. Not now. I'll deal with it tomorrow. Today is about Sebastian, about us, about this rare chance to see him in his element. I plaster on a smile and focus on the people bustling around in jeans and polos with the Blackstone logo. Not that it helps much. I swear the clank of machines pauses, and whispered conversations follow in our wake. My gratitude for Sebastian asking Tom to escort me deepens.

We move past six massive, gleaming, polished copper—well, things. They resemble the Tin Man's oil can from *The Wizard of Oz*.

"What are those?" I ask Tom.

"Stills. They distill mash into bourbon."

"What's mash?"

"You're about to see." We arrive at a grated staircase. "Watch your step, Ms. Manchester—"

"Rosalia. Please, call me Rosalia," I remind him.

As we make our way up, a cereal-like scent that reminds me of cooked corn or warm bread grows stronger with every step. When we reach the top, Tom gestures with his free hand to rows of circular tubs. "This is mash."

The walkway has six massive cylindrical tubs on each side. Half are made of stainless steel; the others are wood. All but two are filled with yellow stuff. Some are thick like potatoes, others more like soup; all are at different stages of bubbling.

At the very end of the platform stands a man in a Blackstone polo talking to Sebastian. He isn't wearing his suit jacket, and his sleeves are rolled up, exposing enticing forearms. Strong, veiny arms are my weakness. Add in how well his butt and thighs fill out his slacks, and I'm craving more than dinner.

Both men turn at our approach. Sebastian's gaze locks on mine, and I catch the unmistakable heat that flares in his eyes. He clearly approves of the dress he surprised me with, and that look sends warmth pooling low in my belly.

He says something to the other man, who nods before leaving. When he passes us, the guy murmurs a greeting but keeps his gaze averted. Sebastian glances at the clipboard hanging next to a mash tub, makes a note, then walks over to me. "Sorry for the delay." He kisses my cheek before turning to Tom. "We should be ready to head out to dinner in about fifteen minutes."

"I'll call the restaurant to let them know you'll be a little late," Tom tells Sebastian.

"Thank you."

After Tom leaves, I say, "I've heard The Gilded Fork is strict about late arrivals. Will we lose our table?"

"It'll be there whenever we arrive," he replies with complete confidence. His gaze roams over me. "You are a fantasy come true in that dress."

I can't hold back my smile. "You're just saying that because you picked it out," I tease.

The day after we made plans for tonight's dinner, Hanna arrived at Novel Idea with a garment bag, two boxes, and a note from Sebastian that nearly melted my heart. He'd heard the stress in my voice about what to wear and wanted to help, so he got me a complete outfit down to the shoes and lingerie.

And I love it. I feel so damn sexy with how the sheath style hugs all my curves like a second skin. Even better? The way Sebastian can't seem to look away. I twist to give him a view of the back that drops to the curve of my spine.

He moves closer, his fingertips tracing along my backbone. In the near distance, metal clangs against metal, followed by an indistinguishable shout. Sebastian drops his hand and offers me his arm. "It's you who makes the dress stunning, not the other way around." He clicks his tongue. "Still, I miscalculated..."

I look at him. "Oh? How so?"

"Dinner is no longer what I want *spread* before me." The promise of pleasure in his eyes and voice sends a spark through me.

I really, *really* like it when the cool and collected Sebastian Blackstone is turned on. Witnessing his reserve slipping is a tantalizing treat.

Leading me down the stairs, he says, "I need to swing by my office to grab my jacket and a few files. It's a short walk from this building. Would you like to come with me or head to the car?"

"I'll go with you." Heat tingles through me, settling between my legs. I hope the office has a door and a lock.

As we navigate the distillery, we're interrupted by several people who need him. He greets each employee by name, and I'm struck by the loyalty and respect he inspires. Even now, as he jokes with one of them, I can see the easy camaraderie between them.

Near the exit, a young worker approaches with what sounds like a production issue. Sebastian listens intently, asking clarifying questions rather than dismissing the concern.

"The temperature rose two degrees in the new experimental batch?" His brow furrows. "Good catch, Elijah. That could have affected the entire fermentation process. Let's adjust the climate controls and document the variation. This is exactly why we monitor so closely."

The relief on his employee's face is immediate. Instead of panic at bringing bad news, there's pride in having his observation valued.

Further down the walkway, Sebastian pauses to check a clipboard of numbers, then calls over to a woman monitoring a mash tub. "Maria, these yields are exceptional. Whatever adjustments you made to the process are working beautifully."

The woman beams. "I just implemented those efficiency improvements you suggested last month, Mr. Blackstone. The team thought you were crazy at first, investing in that new cooling system when the old one worked fine, but you were right, the better temperature control means less waste."

"And better conditions for the team," he adds. "The reduced humidity makes for a more comfortable work environment, doesn't it?"

Maria nods enthusiastically. "Night and day difference. Productivity's up across all shifts."

I can't help but think about Thorne's assertion about Sebastian's "dangerous leadership" and "visionary ideas that will destroy everything." All I see is careful planning, prudent improvements that benefit both production and workers. These don't seem like the actions of someone running a family business into the ground.

Reaching the exit, Sebastian opens the door for me. The sun is beginning to set, casting a golden glow across the rolling hills and lush green grass. A gentle breeze rustles through a nearby cherry blossom tree, tickling my senses with a light and delicate floral aroma.

He tucks me into his side during the short walk, using a keycard to enter the administrative building. Inside is eerily quiet. My heels click on the gray wood flooring, echoing around us.

We pass an empty front receptionist desk. "Where is everyone?" I ask.

"The office staff usually goes home between five and six. When demand is high, those in the distillery have to work longer hours, but not usually office staff," Sebastian explains, turning us down another hallway, then opening a door.

He flicks a switch that illuminates the desk lamp crafted from a Blackstone Bourbon bottle. I had anticipated opulence, velvet curtains, and a large, intricately designed oak desk. Instead, there is a humble, yet well-made, black workspace positioned in front of a window that nearly spans the entire wall. On the opposite side, a bookshelf is mostly filled with bourbons; some appear to be antique. Drawers line the lower shelves, with one slightly ajar, revealing overstuffed files.

The sitting area is also simple, featuring overstuffed leather couches, sleek leather accent chairs, and a round, black granite table. The sole touch of opulence is an antique grandfather clock in the corner.

"Give me two minutes," he says, walking to a built-in cabinet.

The antique bottles lining the shelves near Sebastian catch my attention, amber liquid glinting in the soft light. The sight sends a pang of guilt and longing through my chest, a bittersweet reminder of the deal made with Thorne. Even if finding a way out is possible, I've still deceived Sebastian.

With a shake of my head, I push aside thoughts of that and the impossible choices looming on the horizon. The quiet of his office wraps around us like a cocoon. His capable hands move across a stack of papers, and I remember how they teased my skin. The lamplight catches the strong line of his shoulders, and desire uncurls in my belly. My fingers find the side zipper of my dress, my pulse quickening at what I'm about to do.

With trembling hands, I slowly unzip myself, letting the rich material pool at my feet. It's too pretty to leave on the floor, so I drape it carefully over the chair. The cool air of the office whispers against my skin, and I shiver, fighting the urge to cover myself.

I straighten my shoulders and face him, my red heels clicking on the wood floor. The sound draws his attention. He freezes and his gaze locks onto mine.

"Ready to cash in on that raincheck?" I ask.

His expression shifts from surprise to pure, unadulterated hunger. Heat floods my chest and spreads like watercolor on wet paper, bleeding into every extremity. "Yes," he rasps.

"Do you like the bra and panties you got me as much as the dress?" I twirl in my sky-high red heels, the crimson lace of my lingerie catching the lamplight. The delicate fabric hugs me like the melody of a perfect song, all sheer panels and intricate floral patterns that leave little to the imagination.

His eyes darken. "More. Especially with those shoes." His voice is rough as gravel. "Please, keep on the heels." And then he's crossing the room, his mouth crashing down on mine. I surrender to the wildfire that roars through my veins.

I kiss him back with equal force, my impatient fingers fumbling with the buttons on his vest. I need to feel his skin, need to touch him, and each button seems to take forever. He walks me backward as I work at his shirt, and when I finally slide the last button free and press my palms against the warm, firm expanse of his chest, the back of my thighs meet his desk.

He rocks against me, and pleasure shoots straight through my core.

"Please," I breathe against his mouth.

My hands tremble with anticipation as I fumble with his zipper. I wrap my hand around his erection, and he groans low and rough against my throat.

"You're going to be the death of me," he rasps.

I let go of him, needing to press my body against him. Nothing but a scrap of lace stands between us and what we both want.

"Condom. Do you have one?" he asks.

"In my purse." I get the square package.

He holds up a hand. "Stop."

My body instinctively listens.

He stalks closer. "I'll do that." Hooking the scrap of lace with his fingers, he drops to his knees. I smile as he slides them over the red heels, leaving the shoes on.

His hands falter as they slide up my calves, his touch reverent, yet hungry. His breath deepens, chest rising and falling more rapidly. The man who commanded a room full of employees with cool confidence now looks at me with dark, heat-filled eyes that can't seem to focus on anything but where his hands meet my skin.

"Rosalia," he whispers, like I'm his favorite dessert. "Sit." His fingers press more firmly into my flesh, possessive and wanting. His usually perfectly knotted tie now hangs askew, his usually immaculate hair disheveled where I've run my fingers through it. A flush spreads across his cheekbones, and the controlled executive facade melts away, revealing raw desire. Seeing this man—so controlled, so composed—completely undone by me sends a heady rush of pleasure through my veins.

I settle where he wants me, and I'm rewarded with kisses up my legs. Every touch makes me ache for more. By the time he reaches where I need him, I'm already breathless. I savor the rasp of his short beard against my inner thighs. It's a delicious contrast to his soft lips. Then his mouth is on me. There is no teasing, only hunger that demands satiation.

Digging my hands into his thick hair, I scrape my nails along his scalp, desperate to hold onto him to stay grounded as my rising pleasure threatens to break me apart. He moans, gripping my hips, pressing me into his face as if he can't get enough. And that's what shatters me.

Euphoria suffuses me even as a faint whisper of doubt threads through my ecstasy, warning me that this perfect, shining moment is as fragile as a soap bubble. I shove the unwelcome thought away with all my other ones and fall fully into Sebastian's touch.

I cry out as bliss races down my spine. Shock waves of ecstasy roll through me. Sebastian stands, pulling me up and to the edge of the desk. He tugs down his slacks, enough to free his erection. Rolling on the condom, he pushes inside me. I gasp at the intense sensation of him filling me, prolonging my orgasm.

He stills. "Are you okay?"

"Y—yes," I pant, wrapping a leg around him. "Don't stop, Sebastian." His name is a plea and a prayer on my lips. Burying my face in his neck, I breathe him in, memorizing the scent of his skin and the feel of his body against mine.

I rock, meeting each of his thrusts. His movements grow urgent. "You feel so good," he growls.

An impossible pressure builds at the base of my spine. "H—how? I—I can't come again. It's too much," I pant.

"You can. You will." His demand has my muscles clenching around him, and a deep guttural groan escapes him. His thumb circles my clit, and I freeze like I've been electrocuted as another orgasm engulfs me.

He slams into me, heightening my pleasure. Something heavy crashes to the floor, but Sebastian doesn't stop or even slow. He keeps moving inside me until his body stiffens, and his erratic breaths whisper my name.

My orgasm has left me boneless and I collapse onto the desk, Sebastian following me. I trace my fingers over his back as our heartbeats gradually return to normal. We lie entangled in the afterglow, and for these precious moments, the world outside doesn't exist.

"I needed this more than I realized," he admits quietly, his voice soft against my hair. "This week has been... intense."

His vulnerability reminds me of all the stress he's under—stress that I'm about to make infinitely worse. The weight of what I might do crashes back down, shattering our perfect bubble.

Sebastian pushes up from the desk and tosses the condom in the trash before tucking himself back into his slacks. I haven't even removed his shirt. He only has to button it back up, put on his vest and jacket, and he'll be ready to go.

I giggle. "You're basically ready for dinner, and here I'm in nothing but heels," I tease, trying to shake off my growing melancholy.

"You're dressed spectacularly as my perfect appetizer." He grins, helping me stand, resting his forehead against mine, his breathing still uneven. "I'm not usually like this," he admits, letting out a soft laugh. "I pride myself on control in all things. I'm all measured responses and careful planning. But with you...with you, I lose every bit of that control. It's never been like this for me."

I trace a finger along his jawline, savoring this rare glimpse of vulnerability. "I like seeing you this way. Not always perfectly composed."

"Only with you," he murmurs, the words sending a flutter through my chest. "Only ever with you." The wonder in his voice cuts me.

Avoiding his eyes, I busy myself retrieving my scattered clothes while he rights the fallen lamp. The dress slides over my body as my reluctant gaze drifts back to the shelf of bourbon bottles.

The grandfather clock in the corner chimes softly, another unwelcome reminder that this moment is fleeting. By this time Saturday, derby hats will be donned, mint juleps poured, and I'll have to choose between Sebastian and my bookstore.

He presses a tender kiss to my forehead. "I don't know what I did to deserve you," he murmurs. "But I swear, I'll do everything in my power to make you happy, to be the man you deserve."

I meet his gaze. His eyes are soft with affection and sated desire. A pang of longing hits me that is so sharp it steals my breath. It's not merely my livelihood on the line anymore, but my heart as well. Somehow, amidst all the secrets and lies, I've begun to fall for this man—his strength, his vulnerability, his unwavering passion. The thought of losing him, of walking away from what we've built together, cuts deep.

The weight of my impossible choice crushes down on me. Five days to decide: destroy the man I'm falling in love with, or watch everything I've built crumble.

I keep telling myself I could move locations, start fresh somewhere else, but that's a comforting lie. Deep down, I know Novel Idea only exists because of the community, the relationships, and the roots I've worked so hard to establish over the past two years. I press my hand to my chest, feeling like I might actually break apart from the inside out.

Chapter Thirty-Four

Sebastian

I open the heavy oak door of the limestone cellar. Cool air and the rich, caramel aroma of American oak barrels greets me. Following the sounds of footsteps and conversation, I find Thorne standing a little too close to our event marketing coordinator, Heather. There's also a half-empty glass already in my brother's hand, though it's barely past twelve.

"Good afternoon, Mr. Blackstone," Heather says to me, taking a step away from my brother. "I have the notes on all the tasting profiles for the Director's Cut marketing materials, just as Thorne requested."

"That's Mr. Blackstone," my brother corrects her sharply, shooting her a warning look. The momentary flash of hurt in her eyes suggests that my brother has been doing more than tasting bourbon with her.

Heather's cheeks flush as she avoids my gaze. "Of course. I apologize, Mr. Blackstone."

Thorne sets down his glass with a little more force than necessary and taps a barrel with a proprietary smile. "This one's perfect. Rich mahogany notes with just the right amount of vanilla and spice." He turns to me with barely concealed challenge in his eyes. "Don't you think so, master distiller?"

The words are on the tip of my tongue to remind him that barrel selection is my domain, not his. But I swallow them back. I came here to ask him to drop the bet, and starting with a territorial pissing match won't help my cause. I force my features into something resembling neutrality.

"I'd need to taste it myself before weighing in," I say diplomatically, though the effort costs me. Thorne's eyebrow lifts slightly, clearly surprised by my restraint. He knows me too well.

"This barrel's perfect for the Blackstone's Rose," he continues, pressing his advantage. The name hits me like a sucker punch.

I shove my hands in the pockets of my slacks. "Interesting name choice." Of course he'd choose a name that evokes my Rosalia.

My brother smirks. "It's a play on Run for the Roses. Clever, huh?" I can see he's lying, but I only nod.

"Should fetch a pretty price at the derby party auction," he continues, turning to Heather. "Make sure the label emphasizes the limited quantity. Only two hundred bottles from this barrel."

"Yes, sir," Heather nods, making notes on her tablet.

"If you're finished," I say, "I'd like to speak with my brother. Alone."

"Okay," she says, a little too cheerfully as she backs toward the door. "I'll be in my office if you need anything else."

"You should have asked *me* if I was done with her," he seethes.

Christ, I've bruised his fragile ego. That's not the best way to start a conversation where I want something from him. "You're right. I'm sorry." I swallow the distaste of apologizing to my brother.

It seems to work. His stiff posture loosens and he bends, retrieving a Whiskey Thief and placing the sampling tube inside the barrel in question. I backtrack to a shelf holding Glencairn glasses, grabbing one. He fills his and then mine. After sealing the barrel, we look at each other over our glasses.

Thorne performs a proper tasting. He holds the glass up to the light, examining the amber color and how it clings to the sides. Then he inhales the fragrance, takes a small sip, and lets the flavor sit on his tongue before swallowing. He seems to consider the lingering notes that remain after the bourbon is gone.

"Let me guess, you want out of the bet," he says.

He always could read me too well.

I take a sip from my glass. The liquid slides across my palate, velvety and complex. There's a subtle smokiness that leaves me wanting another taste. Thorne may be a bastard, but he knows his bourbon.

"This isn't fair to Rosalia," I tell him.

"What are you talking about? Unless she magically finds someone willing to give her a massive loan, I'm her only option. I'm practically her fucking fairy godfather."

I grunt and almost smile. "Aren't fairies supposed to be benevolent?"

"Not this one," Thorne says with a dry chuckle, swirling his drink. "Don't you remember, I always preferred the darker magical beings in my stories?"

A spark of what we used to have stabs my heart. Those nights as kids, we'd fight over shows. One of us wanted action, the other horror. We'd usually end up watching both, along with another that our sister had picked.

The memories hurt but I don't push them away, hoping the connection will help with my case. As if sensing my ploy, his features harden. "And you can't back out. You've read the fine print, right?"

"Yeah, you automatically win. Or we could end the bet." I sip my bourbon. It warms my throat but does little to calm me. "No winner, no loser. Neither of us leaves the distillery."

"No winner or loser, huh?" he scoffs. "Says the man who'll still be master distiller."

"I don't get it. You're great at acquisitions. Why do you want my job?" None of what I've said is bullshit. I can't understand my brother's motivation.

Thorne's chin juts in that stubborn way of his, which means he's digging in his heels. "This is the main family distillery. The largest. I am the oldest son. *I* should be running it, not you."

"That was Dad's choice, not mine." I hate giving our father any credit. He might not know us as his children, but he understands our business value. "And I've come here appealing to you as my brother. I like Rosalia, but your machinations are a noose around our relationship."

His brows raise. "Oh, you two are in a relationship?"

I swirl the bourbon in my glass, staring at it. "Hell, I don't know. But I like her. A lot," I tell him honestly.

He finishes his drink and sets the glass on the nearby rick. "You're looking at this from the wrong angle. This bet is a gift for you." He sounds like he believes what he's saying.

I eye my older brother. He's always had a way of finding loopholes, of turning any situation to his advantage. "In what twisted way is this a good thing?"

"This is the ultimate litmus test, a perfect opportunity to see if she's with you, for you," he remarks. The words hang in the air between many rows of barrels.

I fall silent. A test of Rosalia's devotion. Is that what this is? I can't deny I'd love ironclad reassurance of her feelings, but the knot in my stomach tells me this is wrong. "No," I say, at last, meeting Thorne's gaze. "Forcing her hand like this...backing her into a corner, is cruel."

"But if she doesn't take your precious portfolio, you know she really cares about you."

"Giving up the store she loves is too steep a price." That store isn't merely a business to her. It's her legacy, something she built from nothing. The way her face lights up when she walks customers through the shelves, sharing stories old and new. Taking that away would crush her.

Thorne rolls his eyes. "If I lose, we both know that's not happening. With your white-knight complex, you'll renew her lease or give her the damn building."

I would, and she deserves more for the hell they're forcing onto her. I try again. "She doesn't know anything about this wager between us."

"Again, *good*," he shoots back. "You say she's better than your ex-wife. Better than me. Let her prove it."

All remnants of my goodwill vanish, replaced by bitter hostility. "Don't bring Tiffany into this," I warn.

Thorne slams his palm on top of the barrel. "She's the reason for the bet. The reason you hate me."

"No. You're the reason I hate you. You knew my marriage was struggling, and how did you choose to have your brother's back? By trying to get my wife on hers!"

"We were drunk," he shrugs. "She came on to me. And it's not like we slept together."

My blood boils. He always has an excuse at the ready. "That's only because I walked in the fucking living room of our *parents' house* before it happened."

"That proves none of it was planned. And that we weren't sober." He jerks his head to the side. "Seriously, it was a fucking New Year's party…"

I crash into his personal space, the tension damn near suffocating as if the room can barely contain the weight of my anger. "You knew we'd fought before the party. You used it to your advantage."

"No, I didn't. But it does explain why she was so drunk, begging for attention. I know first-hand how you cut off people you supposedly love when upset."

"Well, it's a good thing she had you to comfort her," I snarl. How dare the fucker claim it's my fault. Classic Thorne, twisting everything around.

The muscles in my brother's jaw twitch. "Why do you place all the blame on me?" he grits out.

"Why can't you take any of it?" And that's what bothers me. Tiffany probably holds more fault. I don't doubt that she came on to Thorne. Like our dad, she seemed to like watching us fight. However, the way my brother refuses to acknowledge his part makes forgiveness impossible.

"I'm sorry for what it's done to us."

I jerk my head back. "That's not the same as *being* sorry."

"Nothing will ever be enough for you," he sighs, his voice heavy with resignation. "If I drop the bet, will you forgive me?"

"I could pretend."

He shakes his head. "So fucking stubborn. And too damn honest."

I already know the answer, but ask one final time. "Will you drop the bet?"

His shoulders hunch slightly, his posture reverting to that teenage slouch I haven't seen in years. For a fleeting moment, I catch a glimpse of the old Thorne, the brother who once confided in me. But just as quickly, the moment passes, replaced by a remote stranger.

"No," he answers.

Even though his reply isn't a surprise, my chest squeezes as if caught in a vice. There has to be another way. My gaze darts, desperately seeking an honest way out. But the harsh reality settles in. There isn't one.

Screw this. I'll cheat. Risk the consequences and tell her. She'll have to pretend not to know, and then when Thorne's long gone, she can have the fucking building.

"Fine. Fuck you very much." I drain my drink. The amber liquid burns down my throat. I slam the glass onto the worn wooden ledge. "Doesn't matter. I'll win. And like how you think this shit show is good for me, I believe you leaving is good for you."

"Oh, how so?" A faint sneer curls Thorne's lips.

"A fresh start, away from Dad's poison will free you."

"And what, you don't need the same? To escape Dad?"

"He doesn't get to me like he does to you. You've taken his 'life lessons' to heart, warping them even further."

"You always were the golden boy," my brother sneers. "The perfect son, the one who could do no wrong."

"It's not like that, and you know it," I say softly, holding his gaze. "I never wanted to be perfect. I just wanted to be your brother."

"Oh, that's rich. Saint Sebastian, you think you're superior to me. But you know what? I'm done living in your shadow. This bet, this distillery, is my chance to prove to everyone, including you, that I'm just as good as you are. And I'm not going to let you take that away from me." He glances at his empty glass, and I can see it in his eyes—he wants a refill. But he turns, leaving me alone in the cellar.

I stare at the empty glasses on the ledge, my reflection distorted in the curved surface. The silence presses against me, a stark contrast to my inner chaos. Pacing the room, my footfalls echo on the hardwood floor. The thought of losing Rosalia is a knife twisting in my gut. She's shown me a world beyond the cold, empty existence I'd resigned myself to after my disastrous marriage to Tiffany.

But the price of keeping her is steep.

Cheating, manipulating the situation, is a line I'd sworn I wouldn't cross. After witnessing my father's lies and our mother's bitterness tear our family apart, I vowed to be different.

"What choice do I have?" I mutter to the empty cellar.

Chapter Thirty-Five

Rosalia

The words on my laptop blurred before me. I reread the email, but the outcome doesn't change: "Due to the high volume of submissions, the Small Business Administration has a longer than usual turnaround time for reviewing applications."

I can't expect an answer from the SBA for at least another month, leaving me adrift when my lease ends. I'm sunk because below that email is the denial for the grant I applied for. Without those two and no banks returning my calls, I'm dead in the water.

My lungs forget their rhythm, stuttering between breaths as if the very mechanics of living require conscious effort. The walls of my future are slowly closing in, leaving no path forward and nowhere to turn.

Another email appears on the left sidebar. My mom's name is in bold on the address line, and it is a virtual hug. I glance around the bookstore. No one seems to need help, so I click on the message.

Subject: Surprise!

From: M.Manchester1289@gmail.com

To: NovelIdeaKY@NovelIdea.com

Hi Honey!

You seemed so down about your store last time we talked, and it broke my heart, but I have fantastic news for you! I updated your resume and sent it to a few of the schools looking for librarians. Three of them in Ann Arbor would love to interview you AND are willing to do it virtually. I've attached information about each of the schools. They're waiting for your reply to set up a time. Call me when you get a chance so we can talk about the schools and maybe practice your interviews.

Love,

Mom

I slam my laptop shut. "Are you freaking kidding me?"

"What's wrong?"

I nearly topple off my stool, my heart jumping to hide in my throat. Paige and Noah stand at my counter, each wearing concerned expressions. "I'm having the worst week ever. And it's only Tuesday." My voice cracks, choking on the weight of my bookstore's future.

I'm pouring my heart and soul into my shop and programs, but for what? I'm not sure I can do what Thorne expects of me. Finding a glimmer of hope amidst the gathering darkness isn't possible.

Paige comes around the counter and hugs me. The lump in my throat dissolves into a sob. "Let's step into the alley. You can tell me what's going on," she says.

I shake my head, looking to the ceiling so my tears won't fall. "I can't. My customers."

"Noah can keep an eye on things," Paige suggests.

"Yeah, I'll be fine. Go ahead," he replies quickly, shooing us away.

Despite my crappy mood, I nearly smile. Noah's tone says he'll do anything to create distance between himself and my breakdown.

I let Paige maneuver me to the store's alley because a sobbing shop owner probably isn't a good business look. The rough brick wall scrapes against my back as I slump against it. The sensation grounds me. The distant sounds of traffic and pedestrian chatter drift between the buildings, a reminder of the world carrying on despite my personal struggles.

"I take it the SBA meeting didn't go well," Paige says.

My head drops between my slumped shoulders. "No, it didn't. I'm told, given their limited resources and funding, they have to prioritize and help the business with the greatest need and impact on the state." I frown. "I guess books and reading aren't important."

"What about—"

"Please don't mention the grants. Or my attempt at crowdfunding."

Paige tilts her head. "You tried crowdfunding?"

I look at my hands. "I don't want to talk about it." Granted, I had no idea how to run one, but the amount I've made from it is too embarrassing to tell even my friend.

"Oh," she mutters. "Okay. Well, damn."

I've run out of all my other options except one.

Hurting Sebastian.

I swallow hard and look away. "Did I tell you, a few days ago, I tracked down that real estate developer who renovated the old factory buildings on River Street?"

Paige shakes her head.

"I begged him to consider letting me take a corner space with deferred payments for the first six months. He laughed and said he's already got three corporate clients bidding on every square foot."

I press my palms against my eyes, but it doesn't stop the tears. "Then I went full desperate and called my two friends from Michigan last night."

"The sisters whose family owns the Hayek Department Stores?" she asks.

"Yes, Abigail and Evelyn. They've always said they'd back me if I needed it. Turns out their retail division is fighting for survival right now with all the mall closures. The family is liquidating locations and pulling back all investments to shore up their core business."

I tug roughly on my ponytail. "Evelyn was devastated to tell me. Their lenders have put restrictions on any new investments as part of their refinancing. The timing couldn't be worse.

"God, that's awful," Paige whispers, her eyes filled with concern.

My voice breaks. "Both Abigail and Evelyn offered their personal money, but I can't take it. Evelyn is expecting her first child, and she works for her family's business, so she's caught in that retail apocalypse. And Abigail is opening her second flower shop and planning her wedding."

I refuse to drag them down with me when they've got their own families and dreams to protect. I'd rather lose everything than be the reason my pregnant friend has to cut corners or Abigail has to abandon her expansion.

Swiping away my tears, I look at Paige. "I even humiliated myself at the bank this morning. Went in person to the loan officer who helped me with my initial startup loan, since he wouldn't return any of my calls. I brought five years of projections, customer testimonials, everything. But he wouldn't even look me in the eye." I laugh bitterly. "Just slid a business card across the desk for a company that specializes in 'retail liquidation services' and suggested I call them before my inventory depreciates further."

The silence stretches between us as the reality sinks in. Each denial strips away another layer of possibility until the brutal truth becomes clear: all my scrambling for loans and new locations is just delaying the inevitable choice. Keep my store by betraying Sebastian, or lose everything to protect him. The comfortable middle path I've been desperately searching for is vanishing with every rejection.

"Everything I'm losing keeps flashing through my mind like a cruel slideshow," I sob. "Not merely books and shelves, but everything they represent. The weekly storytime where that shy little girl finally found her voice. The teen book club that gave those awkward high schoolers somewhere to belong on Friday nights."

"Rosalia…" Paige opens her arms and I fall into them, crying harder.

"All these lives touched, all these connections made, will vanish because I couldn't find a way to keep the lights on. And all my plans for expanding our community outreach, like the adult literacy program I've been developing and the author series for local writers, will never even get off the ground."

Thorne's bargain hangs over me like a guillotine blade: betray Sebastian or lose everything. The savage calculation of it claws at my insides. I found the one person who has made me feel like myself again for the first time in years, and his brother has turned him into either my destruction or my salvation. What kind of choice is that?

I suck in deep breaths through my mouth and let them out through my nose. I count to twenty, then leash in most of my wild emotions. I step away from Paige, wiping my knuckles along my eyelids, I ask, "Do I have raccoon tracks and boogers?"

Paige reaches behind her, sets a box of tissues on her lap, and removes one. "When did you get those?" I choke-laugh.

"Noah handed them to me from under your counter before we headed back here." She wipes my cheeks and under my bottom lashes. "Your eyes are a little red, but no sad snot."

I steady myself. "Thanks for letting me get that out. I feel better."

"What are you going to do?"

Everything within me droops. I grip the railing and force myself to stand straight. "I'm going inside to see if my customers need any help. Then, after closing, I'm going to have another good cry while I decide my last option—Thorne's deal." I push open the back door and step inside the storage room.

Paige follows, her footsteps quick behind me.

"Hey," she says, catching my arm gently before we reach the main floor. Her voice drops lower, more serious than I've heard it in weeks. "I could take out a loan to help—"

"No," I shake my head violently.

Before she can argue, Noah appears around a bookshelf and nearly runs us over in his hurry. His eyes are wide, his skin paler than usual. "Is everything okay?" Paige asks.

He looks at me. "So, after the balloon race, when I asked you out to dinner—"

"Oh, did you now?" Paige's tone is full of amusement.

Ignoring her, Noah continues, "And you told me you'd just started seeing someone..."

I nod.

"Is it, by chance, Sebastian Blackstone?"

My heart skips. "Yes. Why are you asking?"

His eyes manage to widen further. "*He's* the man you're dating." He swivels to Paige. "And why didn't you mention it?"

She shrugs and laughs. "Why would I? It's not like you told me your plans to ask out my bestie."

"Well, it wasn't my plan when I drove here for a visit. But, look at her." He points in my direction. "She's hot. And fun to talk with. And—"

"And lives in Kentucky," Paige retorts.

"I visit."

"Not often."

"I would—"

"Hi, um," I interrupt, moving around the arguing siblings. "Could we get back on topic? What has you asking about Sebastian?" I ask Noah.

Noah points toward the direction of the counter. "He's here, asking for you."

Sebastian is *here*. Why? He should be at his distillery. We aren't supposed to see each other until the derby party. Shame burns through me. How can I look him in the eye knowing what I'm considering?

I inhale deeply and press my palms flat against my thighs to keep them steady. "Thanks. I'd better see what he needs."

Noah nods. "Right. Um, we should probably get going then. I need to swing by my parents' house before I get on the road."

Paige's lips twitch. "Are you afraid of the big, bad Mr. Blackstone?"

"Absolutely," he says without hesitation.

I almost smile at their antics. "I'll walk you out," I say.

Paige hugs me. "Don't worry about it. Talk to your man or whatever Sebastian is to you. And call me if you need anything, okay?"

I manage a grateful smile. "Thanks, Paige. And have a safe trip, Noah."

Wiping my face one last time, I step from behind the shelves with them. The words die in my throat as I catch sight of Sebastian standing near the counter, his tall frame silhouetted against the late afternoon sun streaming through the front windows.

His eyes lock with mine, then flick to Noah beside me. Something dark and possessive flashes across his face. It's the unmistakable jealousy at seeing another man by my side. His wanting me as his might have thrilled me an hour ago, but now it's a noose of guilt wrapping around me.

He stalks toward us, then slows and his brow furrows. "Are you okay?" he asks.

The concern in his question guts me. This is the man I'll have to betray to have my dream. How can I even consider using what we have against him?

ChapterThirty-Six

Sebastian

"Give me a second," Rosalia tells me.

She walks past with Paige and some guy who looks like an adult Draco to the bookstore's front door. She doesn't have employees, so who is this asshole? I grind my molars to keep my demands for answers inside. Rosalia isn't Tiffany. I refuse to spiral, well, not spiral any further, until I have answers.

Before exiting, the man glances over his shoulder at me. My glare is ice, and he flinches. Good.

"What's wrong?" I ask when she returns.

"Long day," she replies, looking everywhere but at me.

Does her avoidance have something to do with the man who'd left with Paige? "Who's the guy? Did you hire him?" I try for casual, but it still comes out jealous.

"Why are you here?" she asks.

I'm trying not to push my baggage on her, my knee-jerk reaction that she's cheating. Which is ridiculous, she isn't even mine. Fuck. Why the hell won't she answer my question?

"I wanted to see you. But it seems I've come at a bad time. Busy with your friends," I couldn't keep the acid from dripping on that last word.

She frowns. "Paige is my friend. The guy is her brother, Noah. He was helping me out so I could talk to his sister."

Oh. Shit. I'm an asshole. "I apologize."

She nods, but something about it seems defeated. I look closer. And it's not merely that her eyes and cheeks are red and splotchy like she's been crying, but her usually vibrant energy is diminished. The other man vanishes from my mind, overshadowed by concern. "Will you tell me what's wrong?"

Her gaze finds mine, and it's raw and desperate. "Please," I say softly.

She scans the bookstore. Only two customers are browsing the shelves, both appear absorbed in their selections. She pulls out a small sign: "Back in 5 minutes" and puts it on the counter.

"Come with me." She slides her hand with mine, holding tight.

Her fingers are warm in mine as she leads me through the store to a doorway at the back of the bookstore. We enter a small storage room lined with boxes of novels and bookish supplies.

The moment the door closes behind us, she turns to me, presses against me, and her lips find mine with urgency. I'm caught off guard, but recover quickly, my hands moving to her waist. She tastes like coffee and cinnamon, and the soft whimper she makes when I pull her closer awakens a hunger I've been denying since I was last inside her. Desire floods through me until even my fingertips ache with wanting her.

"What—"

"Don't talk," she whispers against my mouth. "I just need…"

And I understand. We all have moments when we need to forget, to feel something else, to escape. And right now, she needs me.

For the first time in days, the constant carousel of worst-case scenarios in my head goes quiet. My thoughts narrow to her skin beneath my palms, her breath catching when I touch her, the weight of her body against mine. The anxiety that's been my constant companion fades to background noise, replaced with something baser.

Her hands press against my chest, backing me into a shelving unit loaded with inventory. A few tote bags with the Novel Idea logo slip from their hook as she moves against me, and I willingly allow her smaller body to pin me against the metal scaffolding. The cold edges of the shelves dig into my back, a sharp contrast to the heat of her mouth on mine. Her fingers tangle in my hair as she rises on tiptoe, each touch, each breath between us building on the one before, becoming hungrier, more desperate. The brush of her fingertips tracing my collarbone sends fire coursing through me. When my lips find the sensitive spot below her ear, she gasps, her body pressing harder against mine, and I groan against her neck.

"Sebastian," she breathes, and I swear my name has never sounded better.

We're both breathing hard. Her eyes are half-closed, lips parted, cheeks flushed. She takes my hand and deliberately places it under the hem of her blouse, guiding me to the soft skin of her lower back. Her eyes hold mine as she reaches for my belt, her intentions unmistakable.

A loud crash from behind me shatters the moment. I spin us both so she's behind me, shielded from the door. My heart hammers as I brace for someone walking in. But when I look, it's just a box that's fallen from the overhead shelf, the cardboard split at one corner.

"Books," I say, relieved but still breathing hard.

"Damn books," she mutters, peering around me. "Always demanding attention."

Romance novels lie scattered across the floor around our feet, which is fitting for the moment they've interrupted. "I shouldn't have. I'm sorry." Rosalia says from behind me.

I silence her with another kiss. "Don't apologize. Not for this."

She smiles against my lips. Her fingers trail down my chest, and she hooks one finger in my belt loop, tugging slightly before releasing it.

"If we continue..." Her voice drops to a whisper, the words catching in her throat as she swallows.

"You're calling the shots," I tell her.

"Not like this," she whispers. "Not with customers waiting and..." She gestures at the fallen books with a small laugh. "Not surrounded by fictional couples who'd judge our technique."

I press my forehead against hers. "They'd be jealous."

She leans against me once more, her head resting on my chest. I hold her, her heartbeat gradually slowing against mine.

"Do you want to talk about what upset you?" I ask softly. "Or was that enough distraction?"

She sighs, her breath warm against my neck. "My mom's latest stunt is really too much," she grumbles. In a voice tight with frustration, she tells me about the job hunting her mother is doing for her.

I shouldn't feel this selfishly glad about her unwillingness to even consider the jobs, but the thought of her disappearing to Michigan twists something sharp inside me. I want her here, in my arms.

Shit. I'm doing exactly what her helicopter mother's doing. I'm worse. At least she's being honest about trying to control Rosalia's life. I'm manipulating her life from the shadows, deciding what's best for her without giving her a choice.

And that's exactly why I need to tell her. She deserves to know what she's up against and to make her own decision about her shop and us.

"Rosalia, there's something important I need to tell you about."

The store phone rings shrilly, the sound penetrating even through the storage room door. The tension leaves her shoulders as she pulls away, which is strange.

"I have to get that," she says, smoothing her shirt. "That could be a supplier I've been waiting to hear from."

"Okay," I say.

She touches my face gently, and I swear that a flash of what might be guilt crosses her features. Then she's slipping out of the storage room.

I take a moment to collect myself, adjusting my clothes and trying to cool the heat still coursing through my veins. By the time I leave, she's already at the counter, phone pressed to her ear.

"What do you mean by 'unable to process'? The payment cleared from my account last week." She listens intently, her brows furrowing deeper. "You can't be serious. That order has to arrive by Thursday for the event."

She grabs a pen and jots something down. "Give me your supervisor's direct line. No, I need to speak with them today." She hangs up and looks at me, distress evident on her face.

"What happened?" I ask.

"This distributor is claiming they never received payment for my derby weekend shipment, despite the money already being taken from my account. If I don't sort this out immediately, I won't have books for my biggest sales weekend of the year."

I take in how her shoulders are tense, and how the stress lines around her eyes have deepened in the few minutes since the call. My confession about the bet can wait.

"Do what you need to do," I tell her, though relief floods through me and I despise myself for it.

She sighs, tugging at her ponytail. "I swear, it's always something. First, my mother's email, now this distributor mess."

"Can I help with anything?" I offer, more than willing to push aside my inner turmoil.

The tight lines around her eyes relax slightly, and a genuine smile replaces her grimace. "Thanks, but this will require some rather assertive phone calls and possibly contacting my bank. Not that they'll call me back," she mutters.

"Why wouldn't they?"

She shrugs. "No idea. But they and others haven't been helpful lately."

I swear to God, if this is Thorne's doing, I will kill him. No, I'll make him wish he were dead.

Her thumb brushes lightly over my knuckles, pulling me from my very, very dark thoughts. "I appreciate you listening about my mom. It helped to vent." She dips her chin and looks at me through her lashes. "The distraction in the storage room also helped."

I grin. "Anytime."

She comes from around the counter and hugs me. How in the world does she always smell so damn amazing? My phone vibrates in my jacket pocket. I pull it out and see five missed calls from Hanna and three from my office manager. "I'd better head back to the distillery."

Stepping back, she runs her hands through her hair, exhaling shakily. "Yeah, and I need to find out about my missing funds. But let me walk you to the door."

Halfway to the exit, she says, "Cheer me up one last time before you leave."

I take her hand, tugging her playfully in the direction of the storage room. "Fine," I groan with exaggeration.

She laughs and looks around at the busier aisles since I first arrived. "I wish," she sighs. "How about you say something sexy and swoony like one of my book boyfriends?"

"What's a book boyfriend?" I scoff, though I'm still grinning like a fool.

"You know, the men in romance books."

"Damn, that's a high bar."

"True. But I'm confident you can reach it."

"Thanks for your belief in me. Having a huge crush on a sexy bookworm probably helps," I flirt. And the delighted blush on her pretty cheeks makes my day.

At the door, I kiss her lightly on the lips. Someone in the store wolf-whistles, making us laugh. Rosalia looks to where it came from and shakes her head. "You are incorrigible, Mrs. Abernathy."

I wave bye to them both. Once outside, my earlier worries resurface. The light, playful atmosphere between us had temporarily pushed aside my concerns about the bet with Thorne, but now they're back. I had my chance to come clean and I let it slip away. My relief at the interruption sickens me, but the fear of losing her entirely terrifies me more.

The spring air does little to calm my plummeting thoughts. The Bentley pulls up next to me, but before Tom gets out, I open my door and slide inside. Sinking into the leather seat, I can't shake the feeling that my silence is a ticking time bomb.

Tom pulls away from the curb. I drift back to Rosalia in that storage room, to the desperation in her kiss and the way she clung to me like I was an anchor in a storm. She turned to me for comfort.

I'll find another moment to tell her about the bet before it's too late.

But even as I think it, I know it's bullshit. The bet ends in less than twenty-four hours. I've run out of chances. I've placed my bet on secrets and silence. Tomorrow I'll learn if I've gambled away everything that matters.

Chapter Thirty-Seven

Rosalia

Derby Day. The culmination of everything Louisville holds dear. Surveying the Mansion, I struggle to comprehend the existence of a place even more exclusive than Millionaires Row. And here I stand in a vintage scarlet dress worth more than a month of my bookstore's rent, contemplating an act that goes against everything I believe in.

I run a hand from the flat of my stomach down to the waist of the dress where it bells out around me, then reach up, running my fingers along the brim of my

Derby hat, though it doesn't need adjusting. My heart aches at what I'm about to lose.

Across the room, I spot Sebastian. He looks handsome in black slacks, a light brown tweed vest, and a blue and white striped shirt. His red leather portfolio is tucked under his arm, the Blackstone emblem embossed in gold on its surface. Inside are the company's supposed plans that he'll reveal to shareholders today.

"Just take it," says a man behind me, his bourbon breath reaching me seconds after he speaks.

I gasp and jerk forward on my stilettos. Whirling around, I shuffle back to face Thorne. He invades my personal space, and a wicked grin spreads across his face like a villain's.

Masking my distress, I retort, "If you're so worried about Sebastian's plans for the company, why don't you take it yourself? He'll set it down eventually."

"I can't be caught near it. You see that guy?" He points to a short man with massive shoulders and a neck as wide as a Greek pillar. "He's security. My brother's paranoid. He knows some of the board members want him removed. If I'm caught with that portfolio, I'll never get the support I need."

Sebastian sits on one of the camel-colored leather sofas, still holding his portfolio as he talks with an older gentleman in a seersucker suit sporting white wingtips with horses painted on them.

I face Thorne, my lips part, but no words emerge. I think of my bookstore, of the children who come for story hour, of the book clubs that have formed lifelong friendships, of my father's house that's been in his family for generations. All of it hanging by a thread.

But then I hear Sebastian laugh. I look over, taking in the way his eyes crinkle at the corners, and I know I can't do this to him. "I... I can't," I whisper. "I'll find another way to save what matters."

Surprise flashes in his eyes. "Your lease ends at the end of the month. There's nothing you can do in such a short amount of time."

"I can't do it," I repeat.

Thorne takes a heavy swallow of his drink. Looking at me over the crystal rim, he asks, "Why not?"

"I'm falling for him." The admission scares and thrills me in equal measure.

Thorne lets out a low, mean chuckle. "Rosalia, darling, Sebastian's not quite the prince charming you believe him to be."

The hostility coating him like sweat makes the need to escape nearly visceral. I turn away, frantically scanning the room for Sebastian. I need to find him, to warn him about his brother's plans for a corporate takeover.

"Where are you going?" Thorne calls after me, but I'm already moving through the crowd, my heart hammering against my ribs.

I push through groups of derby elite, ignoring their annoyed glances. A flash of blue and white striped fabric catches my eye. Sebastian is moving through the crowd. He disappears behind an ornate divider. I follow him into the private alcove.

He's standing by a tall window, his back to me, staring out at the track below with the red leather portfolio in his hands. At the sound of my approach, he turns, his eyes widening before his face transforms—warmth mingled with unmistakable determination. I recognize that look immediately; it's the face of someone who's made a difficult decision. I'm probably wearing the same expression

"Rosalia," he says.

"Sebastian, I—"

He crosses the alcove with purposeful strides, holding the portfolio out to me. "Take it."

I stare between his face and the leather folder. My hands lock at my sides. "What? Why are you giving this to me?"

There's movement behind me, and then, "What are you doing?" Thorne demands.

"I told you, I can't do it," I repeat, backing away from both of them.

At the same time, Sebastian says, "I won't do it."

I twist around to face him. The words "won't" and "can't" echo in my ears as I struggle to understand what's happening between the three of us. "Won't do what?" I ask.

Sebastian stands frozen, his mouth opening and closing without sound. He looks utterly lost. Then he swallows hard, and that determined set to his jaw returns, "This has gone too far. I can't keep pretending anymore." His words are stilted, as if each one costs him something precious.

Thorne stares at Sebastian with the portfolio outstretched toward me. His smug demeanor falters for a brief moment. Then he lets out a strained laugh. "So you both were willing to give up everything?"

He knocks back the rest of his drink and sets the glass aside. Reaching inside his sage suit jacket with an unsteady hand, he pulls out two folded sheets of paper. "Perhaps you should know what started all of this before you consider him your hero." Handing them to me, his shoulders tense as his expression hardens back to its usual arrogance, though uncertainty lingers in his eyes.

"Thorne, why?" Sebastian's face drains of color, and he seems too stunned to move.

"The truth will set you free and all that bullshit," Thorne replies.

"Rosalia, please give that to me," Sebastian pleads, reaching toward the papers in my hand.

I turn slightly from him and unfold the document, the paper crinkling beneath my unsteady grip. "Bourbon Bet" blazes across the top in bold typeface, followed by the names Sebastian Blackstone and Thorne Blackstone.

The dim lighting makes the words difficult to read at first. I squint, scanning past intricate legal clauses, catching phrases that blur and then sharpen: "subject of interest," "romantic involvement," "acquisition of property," finally landing on the section "Terms and Conditions."

Three sentences in, my back hits the wood-paneled wall.

"..wager on whether S. Blackstone can seduce R. Manchester into developing genuine feelings, causing her to voluntarily refuse to steal the portfolio, resulting in..."

A cold flush spreads from my chest outward, prickling across my skin beneath the vintage scarlet dress that suddenly feels like a costume I've been tricked into wearing.

"The deal was never the portfolio. It was a bet. And the bet was me." The words scratch my throat.

The truth hits me like a fist to the heart. This was never about Thorne needing my help or Sebastian being incompetent. This was about a bet. A bet with me as the unwitting participant. All this time, I thought I was caught between two bad choices, but I was actually the entertainment.

"Dad's house," I gasp. What have I done? A stab of panic shoots through me before the numbness takes over.

I look at Thorne, whose triumphant smile falters. The muted sounds of The Mansion filter into our secluded spot. The laughter, glasses clinking, and polite conversation are a world away.

My watery gaze drifts to the framed photograph of last year's derby winner, its glossy surface reflecting my face, flushed with humiliation, and my eyes gaunt with betrayal. The truth empties me from the inside, leaving nothing but the echo of my foolishness.

"How could you?" I choke, shoving the pages at Sebastian. My knuckles brush against the tweed of his vest, and I let go of the papers.

He clutches the contract reflexively, his body rigid. Thorne stares at us like he's witnessing a train wreck, his triumphant smile fading.

"You both have rotten souls and empty hearts," I say, walking away as fast as my stupid heels will allow.

This seems to unlock Sebastian, and he bellows, "What the fuck, Thorne?"

I'm halfway to the exit when violent sounds erupt behind me—a sickening thud of fist meeting flesh, followed by the crash of a body slamming against the wood-paneled wall. Crystal shatters. A table overturns. The refined murmurs of Derby Day elite turn into gasps.

"You ruined everything!" Sebastian's voice cracks with anguish and rage.

Another crash, heavier this time, like two bodies grappling and falling into furniture. Through my tears, I glimpse security rushing toward the alcove. Let them kill each other, for all I care.

A concierge opens the main door for me, his professional mask slipping enough to reveal his shock at whatever chaos is unfolding behind me, then he puts it back in place. Rows of sleek golf carts are lined up outside, each poised with a driver ready to chauffeur the elite to their destinations with a mere nod. Retrieving my cell from my clutch, I hesitate, torn between calling my dad or Paige.

"Please take me to the farthest parking lot," I tell the nearest golf cart driver.

My father's cautionary words about the Blackstone family echo in my mind. Dad would never say "I told you so," but I'd hear it anyway.

I call Paige. When the call connects, I choke out, "Will you please come and get me?"

"What's wrong?" she asks, her voice high with concern.

"Everything."

"Did you take the portfolio?"

"No, but I should have. I'm such an idiot." I shake my head. "Wait, you're probably busy with Derby Day. I'll get an Uber."

"I'm heading to my car. Give me your location."

"Fine." I'm too beat down to put up a fight, and I ping her my location.

"You're less than ten minutes from me. I'll be there in a few," she says before hanging up.

I step from the cart as another one screeches to a stop behind me. "Rosalia, wait!" Sebastian shouts, turning my limbs to reluctant marble.

If my world wasn't falling apart, I might have laughed, picturing his cart behind mine in what must have looked like an odd chase. Hell, I should laugh. It seems my life is one big joke to the Blackstones.

I whirl to face Sebastian. His previously immaculate hair is wild and damp with sweat, his striped shirt torn at the collar with a button missing, a red mark blooming across his cheekbone that will surely darken into a bruise. Blood stains his knuckles and the cuff of his sleeve.

I don't care. "You've won. Go back to your party and celebrate," I shout.

"If I lose you, I've lost," he says, stepping toward me.

He's not allowed to say things like that, not after he'd torn my heart to shreds. I move back. "You never had me. You don't own me like a piece from your favorite chessboard."

"I never wanted to own you. I was trying to protect you."

"Protect me," I scream. "My heart's bleeding because of you."

He flinches as if I've slapped him. "I fucked up. I let Thorne get in my head, and I'll never forgive myself. But what I feel for you is genuine—that was never part of the game."

"The guilt has been eating me alive, and I was... I was a stupid game to you two." My voice cracks. I can barely breathe. "I've been scrambling, trying to find another way, knowing deep down I couldn't go through with it. And you knew. You *knew*!" I cry. "You played me. I'm nothing but a toy to you and Thorne."

"No, Rosalia. No! I swear, the bet wasn't my idea," Sebastian pleads, then shakes his head sharply. "No. That's... I can't even do this right." He steps closer. "It doesn't matter whose idea it was. I said yes. I participated. I kept it from you even after I knew how I felt about you. Those were my choices and my failures. I won't insult you by pretending otherwise."

"And that's supposed to make all this better? You could have told your brother no! You could have told me!"

He holds out his hands as if in supplication. "I tried."

"Not that hard. Thorne walked into my bookstore two months ago. Or here's a wild idea, your damn company could have stuck to the verbal agreement of renewing my lease." The tears I'd managed to hold in thus far fall. "Instead, you dated me. Slept with me. Made me—"

"And you did the same. You aren't innocent." His eyes search mine, not with anger but with a profound sadness that makes my chest tighten. "How was I to know if you were or weren't doing all the same things to lower my defenses, making it easier to steal from me?"

The truth of his words hits me like a physical blow. A semi roars past us, and the rush of wind nearly knocks my hat off. I watch the truck until it stops at a red light.

Sebastian's right. I'm not innocent. My desperation to keep Novel Idea has led me here. But I can't help hating him for pushing me onto this path.

I face him. "We were doomed from the start."

Paige's car pulls up next to us. I open the passenger door. The pain in my heart is leaking everywhere.

"Wait!" Sebastian pleads. "Rosalia, don't go. I know I fucked this up completely, but what I feel for you—it's real. It's the only real thing in this whole mess. Please... let me fix this."

I should leave, but I turn to him. "How can any of this be real? Like you said, we aren't innocent. We've never had trust or truth."

"We can now." He comes closer. The desperation in his eyes nearly breaks me. "Let me make it up to you. I'll buy you a building for your bookstore."

I still. He's offering me everything I want. Yet, I can't accept. I shake my head. "You can't buy my forgiveness. I'm not for sale."

Getting inside Paige's car, I refuse to look at Sebastian as we drive away.

Chapter Thirty-Eight

Rosalia

I shuffle into my living room in a pair of ancient sweatpants and an equally old Wayne State T-shirt, my heart heavy and my body like lead. Each step requires more energy than I can muster. The usually cozy apartment mocks me with its familiar comfort, especially since I'll be forced to leave when the lease on it and my bookstore expires. I sink onto the couch opposite Paige, who handed me a Moscow Mule.

"What happened?" she asks.

The words are stuck in my throat. Saying it out loud will make it real, undeniable. I swallow past the massive lump in my throat, forcing myself to speak despite the pain. I tell her about the bet between Sebastian and Thorne.

"Those assholes!" Paige nearly shouts.

"And am I any better? I had my own deal with Thorne."

"That he strong-armed you into." She runs a finger around the rim of her drink. "The two of them probably orchestrated the whole damn thing so they could have their sick little competition.

"I'm such an idiot," I sigh,

"How so?" she asks.

"Didn't you warn me that Sebastian might know?"

"Yes, but not that he's a fuck face who was betting on you." She sets her cup down with such force that liquid sloshes over the rim. "Those entitled bastards. Playing with your life, your business, like it's nothing more than entertainment for the rich." She reaches over and squeezes my hand. "I'm so sorry, Rose. You deserve better than to be a pawn in their twisted game."

"I'm so stupid. I fell for it, fell for him, and now I'll lose everything. I told Thorne I wouldn't steal the portfolio because I was falling for his brother." I take a sip of my drink, the ginger beer fizzing on my tongue. Despite the weight in my chest, I mentally calculate how much I could get if I sold the rare books that I'd left in Michigan. Not enough to save the store, probably, but enough to keep making a few more payments on the loan so Dad's house is safe until I find a job—or three. "In a mere two weeks, my lease expires, and unless I agree to Sebastian buying me, I'm out of options to save my store."

Paige's jaw drops. "Did he Pretty Woman you? Is that what he was saying when I picked you up?"

I laugh, the sound harsh in the quiet room. "Kinda. He offered to buy me a building. As if my forgiveness and compliance are for sale," I scoff. "I'd rather lose my shop than be bought."

I close my eyes, and I'm back on Natural Bridge, the warm breeze lifting my hair as Sebastian calls to me from the center of the sandstone arch. Now I wonder if his vulnerability that day was nothing more than calculation. Had the Sebastian who held me on that bridge, traced my lips with his thumb, and looked at me with such tenderness been real? My traitorous heart aches remembering the safety of his arms, how right we had been together.

"Does this mean you're giving up?" Paige asks.

The memory of the hike fades, but another takes its place. The day I first unlocked the bookstore. The smell of stories waiting to be shared, the sunlight streaming through dusty windows, and the first customer who told me the shop felt like home. That place has been a sanctuary for so many, not just for me. The thought of all those readers without their haven sends a current of protectiveness through me.

"I tried," I say quietly. "The day I found out the lease wasn't being renewed, I called every damn bank in the state. None of them called me back. Not a single one."

"I'd be willing to bet it was those fucking Blackstone brothers."

"Please, no more bets," I joke weakly. "Remember that GoFundMe page, I told you about? It got a few hundred dollars from some regulars." I shrug. "It was embarrassing."

Paige shakes her head. "You did that alone, in panic mode, with no real strategy. I could help."

"It doesn't matter. People don't care enough about my little bookstore to save it."

"That's not true. You've created something special here. All those programs, the safe space you've built. People care, you just need to remind them."

My fingers drum against the couch cushion as I consider what she said. "How?"

Paige claps, bouncing in her seat. "Let's try crowdfunding again, but this time, with the whole community behind you. Noah can help set up a proper campaign. He's done them before and is great at them. And I know Anna from romance book club would help. Hell, the whole group would join."

A glimmer of hope fills me. "Isn't Anna a marketing specialist?" The initial numbness of shock gives way to a tiny flicker of possibility.

"Yes! And you have a whole community of people who believe in what you're doing. They'd rally for you if you just asked."

A little spark ignites into a flame. I tap my chin. "There's this guy who's always at the horror book club and stays to chat. He's some kind of online specialist. I'll give him a call."

For the first time since leaving the derby party, my mind is clearing. Though the traitorous part of me still clings to Sebastian's laugh and wants to curl up with a blanket and pretend none of this happened.

"You know," I say, sounding and feeling steadier, "maybe this is the push I needed to stop being anyone's charity case. I'll fight this with people who believe in what I'm doing, unlike my cruel fairy godfathers."

Paige pumps her fist. "Exactly, fuck the Blackstone boys!"

I can't help but grin, even if my stupid heart weeps at the loss of Sebastian. Paige's eyes light up. "Let's do crowdfunding and in-person stuff. We could organize an emergency 'Save Our Bookstore' community fundraiser! Get local authors, musicians, and loyal customers involved. Transform it into an all-night read-a-thon."

"I'll have my mom send me my rare books from my personal collection to auction off. And there's no sense holding on to that signed first edition of *Outlander* Sebastian gave me."

The memory hits like a punch. His barely contained excitement when he gave it to me, how he watched my face and said he wanted to be part of every story I loved. God, I actually believed him.

"Wait. That man got you a signed Gabaldon book, and it was a fuck-ing-first-edition-*Outlander*."

Paige's face is so conflicted, I laugh. "Are you okay?"

She's silent for about twenty more seconds, then says, "Sorry. I had to remember all this shit he's put you through so I can stay mad." She shakes her head and mutters, "Signed, first edition."

I grin. "And I've been holding on to my French first edition, 'The Little Prince', for a rainy day. Well, it's pouring now." The ideas are flowing fast, my business mind kicking into gear.

"Exactly!" She exclaims. "We could have a special book club or extra perks for top donors. And we'll livestream parts of the event for people who can't attend in person but still want to contribute."

Standing to retrieve my cell, I focus on the gratitude that cuts through my heartache. Though I've lost Sebastian, my friends' support is a glimmer of love shining through the darkness. And that's what I'll concentrate on: the steps I can take forward, refusing to dwell on what has shattered me.

"This will work," I say with near confidence.

Paige nods. "Because this time, you're not doing it alone."

Chapter Thirty-Nine

Sebastian

The red leather portfolio sits on my desk, right next to the lamp Rosalia and I broke. It is a silent reminder of my mistakes. It's funny how something so ordinary can represent what I've carelessly shattered.

My grip slips as I lift my coffee, sending drops across the polished desk. The dark liquid pools against the portfolio's edge. I stare at it, making no move to clean it up. It's been three days since the derby party and every time I close my eyes, I see

Rosalia. The pain I've caused her, the trust I've shattered, loops endlessly through my mind.

I reach for my phone as the compulsion to apologize hits me again. But as my thumb hovers over our message thread, I set my cell face down. There's nothing left to say that she would want to hear.

A knock at the door rips me from my self-loathing. "Come in," I say, my attention fixed on the broken lamp.

"My legal assistant said you needed me," Daniel says from the doorway.

I nod, gesturing for him to sit. The movement sends a sharp pain through my tense shoulders. I've spent too much time hunched over work that I barely focus on. I can't undo what I've done, but I can help Rosalia.

"Donate to her fundraiser. From my personal account. But make it anonymous." I don't need to tell Daniel who *she* is. He knows.

"How much?"

"Whatever she needs to meet her goal."

"That would be zero dollars."

My pen clatters to the desk. "What? Already? It's been three days."

He shrugs. "I checked this morning. More than the amount has been given." Daniel shifts in his seat. "There's something else you should know..."

I keep my face placid, but my pulse picks up. "What?"

"Thorne sent some papers to my office this morning. About Rosalia's bookstore lease."

Every muscle in my body tenses. Whatever game my brother is playing, I'm not in the mood. Technically, everyone forfeited—I was going to give her the portfolio, but she wasn't going to take the files. And Thorne went against his rule and showed her the bet. But knowing him, he'll still try to claim victory.

"What now?" I lean back in my chair, steeling myself.

Daniel holds my gaze for a long moment, then his face breaks into an unexpected smile. "He renewed her lease. Indefinitely." He hands me a sheet of paper.

I stare at him, certain I've misheard. "He did what?"

"Fixed rate, automatic renewal, no termination clause except with her explicit consent. It's ironclad. I reviewed it myself." He taps the paperwork. "Seems Thorne might have a soul hidden in that shriveled heart."

My brother renewed her lease indefinitely. The man I thought I knew wouldn't have done something so... decent.

"Anyway, even without that unexpected turn, Rosalia would have been okay. Yes, this saves her from having to find a new place, but she now has the money to do so. Her fundraising efforts are going really well. I checked this morning."

"Why are you keeping tabs on her?" I snap.

Daniel snorts. "Settle down, Jealousy Jones. The woman I'm dating, Anna, works in marketing. You met her at the gala. She's been helping. Along with a specialist in online services. Oh, and Rosalia's friend, Paige..." My asshole friend and lawyer smirks, "and her brother Noah."

A pang of jealousy shoots through me at the mention of the brother, but I force it down. I have no right, not after what I've done. "Fine, then give the money to one of her programs. Do the one for adult literacy. That was next on her list."

"How much?" he asks.

"Enough to cover the whole thing. And do it anonymously." I instruct.

"Why?"

"I want to take stress off her shoulders, but I don't want her to think I'm trying to buy her forgiveness," I explain. "This isn't about getting her back. It's about supporting something important regardless of whether she ever speaks to me again."

Daniel studies me. "You're not going to try to win her back?"

I rub the ache in my chest, that constant reminder of her absence. The pain is physical, like something vital has been torn out. I haven't eaten a proper meal since that night, and coffee and bourbon are poor substitutes. "I miss her, but given everything we had was built on lies, we won't work."

"And you're going to make sure of that, are you?" he asks sarcastically.

"What the fuck does that mean?" I shout, startling us both. The burst of emotion is unlike me. Running a hand down my tie, I take a deep breath. "I'm sorry. That was uncalled for. I shouldn't have let Thorne talk me into that damn bet, but I did, and once it started, there was no way to stop it."

"Bullshit. You're a smart man. You could have found a way out of it. But you didn't want to."

I flatten my hands on the desk so they don't curl into fists. "You know I tried."

"Barely. And like I said, you're smart, you could have found a way." Daniel settles back, his expression softening. "But you couldn't resist testing her, could you?"

"What are you talking about?" Although a small part of me whispers, I know what he's going to say.

"You create arbitrary tests for people, expecting them to pass without even knowing they're being tested. It's unfair. And it's holding you back."

I want to argue, but can't seem to find a defense.

"Take our friendship," Daniel continues. "Ever since your divorce, I feel like I'm constantly on trial, having to prove my loyalty to you. It's exhausting." He rests his elbows on the table. "I've known you for more than a decade. I know what this is about. You want to see if we just want to use you. And that's understandable, but you're pushing people who care about you away. The bet was your excuse, your test, this time. You wanted a guarantee she wouldn't hurt you."

"Is it so wrong that I want proof she saw me and not the Blackstone name?" I ask, my voice softer, defeated.

"Well, you got it." Daniel holds my gaze, unflinching. "And because of it, you lost her."

I look away. Maybe he's right. Maybe I've been setting up scenarios where I test people, but everyone has failed. Even Rosalia.

With the little bit of fight left in me, I say, "Why did she have to accept his deal? We weren't strangers. She and I were friends. I'd visited her store often."

"We've been over this," Daniel sighs. "Thorne was offering to save her livelihood. Are you honestly telling me you wouldn't screw over an acquaintance to save Blackstone Bourbon?"

"That's different."

His brows shoot up. "Why? Because your distillery is massive and your dream job holds a higher value than hers? She sells more than books; Rosalia's built a community. People depend on her bookshop. It's a safe haven, a refuge."

I pinch the bridge of my nose, letting my vision blur. In that darkness, fragments of Rosalia solidify. She kneels to help a shy kid find the perfect dragon book, her hand lingering on the cover as she shares something about the author. Or how she always remembers everyone's names, their children's ages, what they'd read last.

Regret winds tightly behind my sternum, like a spring coiling, ready to snap. I measured importance in balance sheets and workforce numbers. By every metric I valued, my work simply mattered more.

I dismissed her work as quaint. Decorative. Less than.

"Shit," I whisper, the truth punching me.

The distillery is my dream, but it is just that—*my* dream. I never once considered how her store stitched together the frayed edges of our city. Never saw how she built something I couldn't blueprint or replicate, something that existed in the space between people.

"And she's not the only person you were testing," Daniel says, forcing open my eyes and pulling me from my thoughts. "You're testing Thorne."

I bristle. "What test could I possibly want from him? There's no trust left between us."

"Maybe you hoped he'd see what he's become and change, stop being such an asshole." He scoots to the edge of his chair. "Look, you have over thirty years of history with him. Things only went to shit in the last decade. I didn't know you before college, but I've heard the stories—you two were inseparable. Even after everything, I'm sure you miss him."

A hollow laugh escapes me. "If that's the case, he failed me miserably. Again."

"No arguing there."

I drum my fingers against the desk, considering my brother and all he's done and also what he might have done. "I think Thorne was blocking her loan applications around town."

Daniel's eyes widen. "What makes you say that?"

"I had lunch with Marcus from First Kentucky yesterday. I'd mentioned Rosalia. And, not only did he know her name, which is unusual for a small business owner he's never worked with, but he got twitchy and muttered something about how he'd heard she was a poor investment."

"That's not just petty. It's illegal," Daniel sits up straighter. "Interfering with someone's business like that."

"And that surprises you?" I scoff. "This bet was extortion, you and I know it."

"True," he nods. "And knowing Thorne, he probably made sure the banks understood the consequences of helping her, just like he did with you."

Unable to sit, I move to the window. My reflection startles me. The dark circles under my eyes, the stubble I haven't bothered to shave. I barely recognize myself. Three days feel like three years, and I wonder if this hollow feeling is permanent.

I refocus on the Kentucky skyline that usually calms me, but today it offers no solace. "None of that matters now. I've made such a mess of everything." My words come out clipped, tinged with frustration.

"Maybe, but it's not too late to clean it up," Daniel says from behind me. "Not to play your therapist—"

I snort. "I thought it was your side hustle. How did I get so lucky? I get a friend, lawyer, and therapist all in one smart-ass package."

Daniel laughs. "Well, at least you admit to me being your friend."

I shake my head, surprised that I'm amused. "Don't let it go to your head. The bar's pretty low these days."

"Low bar, high standards. You're more complicated than you let on." He clears his throat. "Now back to playing your therapist. In the years we've known each other, I've seen your dad wear different hats—father, businessman... He's undeniably brilliant in the boardroom, but he's a bit of an asshole."

"A bit?" I snort. Daniel isn't telling me anything I don't know.

"Alright," he concedes. "I was being generous because he's your old man. Anyway, I get the need to build a wall around him. To keep *him* at arm's length, but you do it to anyone who has the potential to hurt you. Hell, that's probably why you married Tiffany."

"Oh, do tell me your full diagnosis of me, Dr. Daniel."

Just like in college, he ignores my snark, he continues. "Tiffany's a perfect match socially. Beautiful, from the right family, but way too much like your father—all scheming and narcissism. Someone you could never truly love."

I bristle, a defensive retort on the tip of my tongue. But even as I open my mouth to argue, doubts stop me. Could he be right? I turn from the window. "Exactly how many psychology classes did you take at university?"

"My minor was in psychology."

I rub my face. "Christ. Maybe you should have made it your major."

Daniel chuckles. "I think that's my cue to leave to do some lawyerly stuff." He stands and heads toward the door. "I'll make your anonymous donation to Rosalia's fundraiser."

"Thank you."

The door clicks shut behind Daniel, but his words remain. Each one chips away at the walls I've so carefully constructed. I return my attention to the sprawling vista outside my window. I can't change the past, but I can damn well fight for a better future.

Which means I need to make things right with Rosalia. But how? How can I prove to her that I'm willing to change to be the man she deserves? The thought of baring my soul, of letting her see the vulnerable parts of myself, terrifies me. Yet, it also fills me with a strange sense of hope.

I open the bottom drawer and pull out an old framed photo of my family from years ago. Thorne and I stood shoulder to shoulder before everything fell apart. There's unfinished business that keeps casting shadows over everything in my life, including what happened with Rosalia.

Before I can move forward, I need to deal with the past. I pick up my phone and dial my brother's number. He answers on the fourth ring.

"Sebastian?" His voice is weary.

"We need to talk," I say, keeping my voice even. "There are things that need to be said. Face to face."

A pause stretches between us that feels heavy with years of resentment and recent betrayal. "Where?"

"My place." After our fight at The Mansion made headlines in every local paper, the last thing either of us needs is another public spectacle. "Tomorrow morning. Ten o'clock." That'd give me some time to prepare what I need to say.

Another pause. I can almost hear him weighing his options, calculating risks and advantages like he always does.

"Fine," he finally says. "Ten o'clock."

I end the call without another word. The wall clock ticks, each second a reminder of time wasted on anger and mistrust. Tomorrow I'll confront my brother, unravel the knots between us. Only then can I stand before Rosalia with nothing held back—no games, no tests, no armor. Just a man asking for one more chance.

ChapterForty

Rosalia

I lock the door of my bookstore and flip the sign to "Closed." The street outside is mostly empty, with only a few people braving the rain. I prepare a mug of ginger and turmeric tea and carry it to the checkout counter. The warmth and aroma comfort me. Settling onto a stool and opening my laptop, a surge of hope ripples through me.

Refusing to let Sebastian's betrayal and Thorne's cruelty rob my dreams, I've thrown myself into work, planning events and brainstorming ideas for the future.

Saving my Novel Idea has become my singular focus, which is what I need to avoid dwelling on my heartache.

I glance at my phone's bank notification and vindication flares in my chest. A week of intense fundraisers has paid off—literally. Author readings and book signings haven't just brought literature lovers through my doors; they've brought financial salvation. I've got enough money to buy a vacant storefront down the street. It's not as nice as this place, but at least the move will be easier. The bookshop will truly be mine now, bought not rented, with enough left over to start dreaming bigger.

Clicking open my spreadsheet, I take in the numbers that once seemed impossible to reach. I've proven to myself these past weeks that I can solve my problems without anyone else's rescue. The Blackstone brothers' machinations forced me to discover a resilience I didn't know I had. If only I'd understood my own capabilities before they entered my life, perhaps my heart wouldn't be quite so battered now.

And that's the most infuriating thing: since I walked away from Sebastian, I miss him more, not less. It's a constant internal fight not to call him. I've deleted and restored his number three times now. The memory of his laugh when I'd recommended that ridiculous mystery novel haunts me, along with the way his eyes had crinkled at the corners when he smiled, a genuine smile, not the practiced one he used in business meetings.

Was any of it real? It felt so genuine. But was each shared moment calculated, part of a strategy to win a bet I hadn't even known existed?

"Focus on what's important," I mutter, turning my attention back to my laptop.

A sharp rap on the locked door jolts me so hard that tea sloshes from my cup onto the counter. I should be used to it by now. Most nights, bar revelers on Whiskey Row mistake Novel Idea for some literary-themed bar.

But the person isn't a stranger. It's Sebastian's lawyer, Daniel, who waves at me with the hand not holding an umbrella. With the other, he's pointing for me to unlock the door.

I consider hiding under the counter. But given that we've made eye contact, I'd look like a weirdo.

Sighing, I walk to the door and twist the lock. A quiet clunk reverberates through the store. Pulling on the knob, the pleasant, earthy scent of petrichor fills my lungs. I ask over the rain, "Can I help you?"

"I apologize. I didn't realize your store would be closed," he says.

"The weather will keep customers away, so I decided to close early and get caught up on paperwork." I'd also hosted a children's event earlier today that was immensely successful, but the strain of being on my feet all day had drained me.

Lightning flashes across the sky, followed by the angry bark of thunder. "Come inside," I tell him, stepping aside to let him enter.

The damp squeak of Daniel's shoes on the hardwood floor echoes through the quiet store as he follows me. Instead of returning to the counter, I stop at the small reading nook and motion for him to sit. I take the chair across from him, settling into the sage velvet cushion. "How can I help you?"

"I have some documents that need your immediate attention," Daniel says, pulling out his briefcase.

"I should have hidden under the counter," I mutter.

Daniel frowns. "That's not very nice."

During normal circumstances, I'd find his pout amusing, but he'd been the bearer of very bad news the last time he came to my bookstore bearing documents, and I told him as much.

"Fine, that's fair," he concedes. "But I bring good news this time."

After the months I've had, I'm all for good news and nod for him to continue.

He reaches into his briefcase and pulls out an envelope. "This came across my desk this morning."

I take it cautiously, as if it might bite. Inside are two documents on Blackstone company letterhead. One is a lease renewal, and the other is a lease-purchase agreement—for this building. Thorne Blackstone's signature is on both.

"I don't understand," I say, reading through the terms. "Why?"

Daniel shrugs. "Honestly? I'm not sure. Thorne didn't explain his reasoning to me. Change of heart?"

"You have to have a heart first," I retort dryly. "There has to be a catch." I flip through the pages again, searching for the loophole I must be missing.

"I've gone through it line by line. It's clean." Daniel leans forward. "Sometimes people surprise you. Even Thorne."

I set the document down, unsure how to process this unexpected lifeline from the last person I'd expect to throw one. The possibility feels too fragile, like it might vanish if I acknowledge it.

"This building..." I whisper, unable to finish.

This building I've come to love, the worn brick exterior and the morning light streaming through tall windows, could actually be mine. Not just the business, but the space itself.

"Are you okay?" Daniel asks.

"Wow, um, yes." I nod. "I just need to wrap my brain around it. I had it set that I have to move. Remodel a new place. Leave one that I love. And now I don't..."

Daniel clears his throat, shifting in his seat. "Do you still have an open spot for this upcoming Tuesday?" he asks.

The subject change snaps me back to business mode. "Yes." I don't ask how he knows my schedule. He's dating Anne, who's been a huge help in saving my bookstore.

He names the "it" author of the year.. "Would she work to fill the empty slot?"

I cough out a choked gasp. "How—" My eyes narrow, and I repeat, "How? Why would she come here?"

His gaze darts away.

"Daniel..." I warn.

"I'm not supposed to tell you..."

"Is Sebastian behind this?" Damn, it hurts even to say his name, but the suspicion that's been forming needs answers. "Is the massive anonymous donation from him too?"

Daniel's silence is answer enough.

My heart stutters in my chest, and I hate that he still affects me like this." Merely talking about him shouldn't have this effect on me anymore. He's not good for me.

Why does that feel like a lie?

"Why is he doing all this anonymously?" I ask, though I think I know.

Part of me wants to be furious that Sebastian is inserting himself into my life after everything that happened. But another part—the traitorous part that still misses him—is touched that he's supporting me without expecting credit or thanks.

Or is this some angle he's working?

Daniel holds up his fingers, counting off the reasons. "One, he's afraid you won't accept if you know it's from him, and he truly believes in your programs. Two, he doesn't want you to think he's trying to buy your forgiveness."

I raise an eyebrow. "He's not?"

"Did you miss the part about him not wanting you to know?" He asks gently.

I'm torn in two directions. There's a softness and ache for the man I'd been falling for, but also a heavy dose of unease. I'd learned the hard way that accepting help from the Blackstones comes at a steep price.

As if reading my thoughts, Daniel says, "He's not some evil villain twirling his mustache."

I let out a laugh, shaking my head. "He doesn't even have a mustache."

Daniel grins, holding a hand palm up. "See, that proves he's not an evil villain."

"Yeah, just your typical arrogant rich jerk," I grouse, my tone lacking true venom.

"I get that what he agreed to was dumb, but the bet wasn't his idea. He was manipulated into agreeing." He rests his elbows on his knees and interlaces his fingers. "Sebastian isn't a bad guy."

"Says the guy who merrily wrote up the bet contract."

Daniel scowls. "There was nothing merry about that shit." His expression softens. "Look, I agree that the bet was a terrible idea, but he was manipulated into agreeing."

I blink. Sebastian? "I find that hard to believe. He's a shrewd businessman who seems highly intelligent, not someone who's easily manipulated."

"I agree. He isn't, but Thorne knows him. Knows his weakness."

"Which is?" I ask.

"You."

"Me," I point at myself and scoff. "He runs Blackstone Bourbon. If he cared about me so much, he could have renewed my lease. Instead, he sat back and let it happen."

"Sebastian has a lot of responsibilities within the company, but property management isn't one of them," Daniel explains. "He wasn't involved in the lease decisions."

I raise an eyebrow. "He's the head of the company."

"Yes, but Blackstone is bigger than most people realize." Daniel pauses, clearly weighing how much to share. "Look, I shouldn't be the one telling you all the details. There's a lot about what happened between Sebastian and Thorne that should come from him."

"Yet you're here to defend him?" I cross my arms.

"I'm here because I think you deserve to know that things weren't as simple as they might have seemed. The bet was... complicated. And yes, what Sebastian did was wrong, but there were factors you don't know about."

My gaze falls to my lap. Part of me wants to hear everything now, but another part knows Daniel is right. If I'm going to listen to the full story, it should come from Sebastian.

"Thorne and Sebastian have a complex relationship," Daniel continues. "Family businesses can bring out the worst in people, especially with their father's influence looming over everything."

"You're being vague," I huff.

"Intentionally," he admits. "This isn't my story to tell. All I can say is that Sebastian had reasons for what he did, and they weren't as selfish as you might think."

"You know, I had initially refused Thorne's help. Then suddenly, no bank would give me a loan or even return my calls." I pause. "It's all connected, isn't it? He orchestrated everything from the beginning."

"I don't know for certain, but I suspect you're right," he admits.

I stand up, pacing between the bookshelves. The rain outside intensifies, mirroring the storm inside me. "He didn't just threaten my lease. He blocked my loans, cornered me into accepting his help, all to teach Sebastian some lesson?" My voice rises with each word, anger burning through my veins.

"Thorne's... complicated," Daniel offers weakly.

"Complicated is a fancy word for manipulative," I snap. The lease documents on the table now appear in a different light. Not salvation, but another chess move in a game between brothers.

I stand abruptly and run my hand along a shelf of nearby books, needing their comfort. "And Sebastian passively let it happen."

"That's not entirely—"

"He didn't stop it. He didn't talk to me," I sigh. The anger that flared so brightly dims, replaced by something more complicated. Despite everything, I miss him. My heart still wants him.

"He couldn't talk about it. Like you, he signed an NDA." Daniel stands and moves to my side. "He's been trying to make things right from the very beginning."

"What do you mean?"

"Talk to him. Let him tell you everything." He turns, goes to his briefcase, and zips it shut. "About the author for Tuesday, she'll be here regardless of what you decide about Sebastian. I've already confirmed with her, and she's excited about the event. Your 'anonymous donor' made sure of that."

I shake my head in disbelief. "So he didn't merely secure her, but made it ironclad?"

"He wanted to ensure you had the help you needed, no strings attached." Daniel shrugs, a smile playing at his lips. "Like I said, supporting what matters to you."

The rain drums against the windows, filling the silence as I consider all he's said. My fingers absently trace the spine of a nearby book. I glance at it and laugh softly. It's the romance novel I recommended to Sebastian months ago.

"I should hate him," I whisper, more to myself than to Daniel.

"But you don't."

No, I don't. That's the most maddening part of all. Despite the betrayal, despite the hurt, there's a stubborn corner of my heart that still believes in what we shared. That still misses him.

I return to my seat and pick up the lease documents. "Tell Thorne I'll review these with my lawyer before signing anything."

Daniel nods. Walking toward the door, he hesitates before exiting. "Sebastian has never been the villain of this story, Rosalia. He was someone who made a mistake."

After he leaves, I'm alone with the rain and my thoughts. The shop creaks and settles around me, filled with ghosts of what was and whispers of what could be. Each book is a repository of other people's second chances, other people's forgiveness.

I run my fingers over the lease agreement, thinking about second chances and whether some betrayals can be forgiven. Could it be like water, eroding what was solid, or might it, given enough time, carve something unexpected and beautiful from the wreckage?

The memory of Sebastian from around the first time we met surfaces. He'd said, "Some stories don't end where you expect them to." This is very true of us. But is ours over?

I'm not ready to forgive. Not yet. But for the first time since walking away, I'm ready to listen.

And that's the first page of whatever comes next.

ChapterForty-One

Sebastian

A gentle breeze drifts through the open windows of my master sitting room, carrying the scent of bluegrass and the distant sound of horses moving through the west pasture. I drum my fingers on the arm of my favorite chair, matching its rhythm, staring at the non-interaction agreement I'd had Daniel draft after our conversation the other night. It lies open on the coffee table, untouched since I set it there.

My jaw aches from Thorne's fist from our fight last week, but also from clenching it. Anger has been my constant companion. Some of it was directed at my brother for his endless manipulations, and the rest at myself for my damned pride and paranoia. But the strongest emotion is regret.

All I see on repeat is the way the light died in Rosalia's eyes when she saw the contract. The disgust that replaced her warmth.

My gaze drifts back to the open windows. The horses move freely through the pasture, unburdened by the complications that seem to define every human relationship in my life.

Shifting, I scan the legal document that outlines how Thorne and I can work in the same building without crossing paths: separate meeting schedules, different reporting structures, and communication through designated liaisons only. It's extreme, but necessary. We need something to stop this toxic cycle we've been trapped in for years.

I check my watch. My brother should be here any minute. Will he show up? I'm surprised he agreed to meet so readily. The old Thorne would have made excuses, deflected responsibility, or simply not shown up.

I grab my phone. Again. And not to call my brother. The compulsion to atone and win back Rosalia is constant. The screen unlocks to her contact information, her name blurring as I stare at it. How many times have I done this since she walked away from me, heels clicking against the pavement, each step widening the chasm between us?

Daniel's accusation won't leave me alone. "You set up these arbitrary tests for people, expecting them to pass without even knowing they're being tested." Is he right? Have I been sabotaging every relationship, waiting for people to fail tests they don't know they're taking?

Leaning back in my armchair, I look up at the ceiling like the answers will be hiding among the crown molding. Instead, unrest crawls over me like ants, making it impossible to focus. The agreement's clauses blur together, all of them meaningless compared to what I've thrown away.

The silence of the house presses in around me, and I stand, moving to the open window where a large couch sits beneath it. On it, Twain lies curled up asleep. Maybe I'll take him for a walk after Thorne leaves, or visit the horses. At least animals don't judge you for your mistakes, don't look at you with eyes that say you've shattered their world.

There's a knock at my door and my housekeeper steps through. "Mr. Thorne Blackstone is here, sir," she says, professionally neutral despite knowing the strained history between us.

"Thank you, Alex. Send him in."

My brother walks in, and my slouched shoulders snap back. My fingers stop their restless tapping, curling slightly at my sides. The exhaustion that's been weighing me down evaporates in an instant, replaced by the wary readiness that's become a reflex whenever we're in the same room.

Even with his fading black eye, he carries himself with that infuriating Blackstone confidence that makes me want to punch him again. Sure, it had been so satisfying at the moment, watching him stumble against those portraits of derby winners, but it was meaningless. It hasn't changed anything. He's still here and Rosalia is still gone.

Alex closes the door behind her with a soft click. I move from the window seat to one of the armchairs flanking the coffee table and gesture to the seat opposite. "Sit down. We need to talk."

Thorne takes the seat, his expression unreadable. "I figured this was coming."

"Things can't continue like this. Neither of us won that stupid bet, so we're stuck with each other, but I refuse to let that destroy Blackstone Distilleries."

"I agree," he says.

I'm surprised by his quick acquiescence, but don't pause to dissect the meaning. "I've been thinking about solutions. I had Daniel draft this non-interaction agreement." I push the papers toward him.

He glances at the document, then looks out the window. The casual dismissal makes my chest tighten, heat flooding through me.

"You know what? I'm done pretending this is only about business. We both know it isn't." My voice rises. "Whatever connected us as brothers is gone. The blood we share means nothing anymore. You're like a fucking black hole, sucking the joy out of my life at every turn."

I exhale deeply, needing to regain control. "I can't blame you for the lies I told Rosalia. That's on me. But I blame you for setting this whole thing in motion. For blocking her loans at every bank in town." I point at him. "There's no proof, but I know you did it. And that's low, even for you."

His gaze flickers to me, the paper, and back out the fucking window. I slam my palm against the coffee table, making the papers jump.

"Look at me." When he does, I say, "But the company doesn't deserve to suffer because we can't get our shit together. So I'm telling you, we have to find a way to make this work, or one of us walks away entirely."

Thorne continues to watch me. The hard line of his jaw softens. His shoulders drop an inch, as if the indifference he wears like armor is cracking at the edges.

He taps his knuckles lightly against his knee before saying, "I am."

I halt, my practice lecture derailing.. "You are what?"

"I've decided to transfer to our Quebec location. I can handle our acquisitions just as effectively from there. I'm leaving at the end of the month," Thorne says. "I'm heading to the airport after this to finalize arrangements. I had our legal team start the paperwork yesterday." The words don't compute, like he's switched to a foreign language. I blink several times, my hand frozen mid-air. "What? Why? I've read the contract a thousand times. There's no clear winner."

"The bet isn't why I'm leaving." He sighs. "Well, inadvertently it is."

Yet I find myself asking. "How so?"

"I saw the way Rosalia looks at you. It was the same way you watched her, like a person in love. I didn't think that shit existed."

"It does. I love her."

He nods like this doesn't surprise him. "And she must love you. Because why else would she not go through with it?"

The ground shifts beneath me. I stare at my brother. "What did you say?"

"At the party, she told me she wouldn't do it." His usual condescension is absent, replaced by what sounds almost like genuine appreciation. "She said she couldn't hurt you, no matter what it cost her."

My chest cracks open like a dam breaking. Even when cornered, even when I'd given her every reason to protect herself at my expense, she chose loyalty. To me. While I was busy testing her, she was busy protecting me.

"She wasn't going to go through with it?" It's what he said, but I have to ask to make sure I heard him correctly.

Thorne slides his hands into his pockets. "No."

The pain in my heart intensifies. I'm a damn fool.

I should be elated that she passed my, what had Daniel called them? Ah, yes, my trust tests. She's repeatedly proven her heart, yet I've been too jaded to see. My blindness has cost me the woman I love.

"Sebastian? Are you listening?" Thorne asks.

I blink, refocusing. "Yes. No. I just..." I need to see her.

"Rosalia opened my eyes. Granted, it took me a few to see what she taught me. And I panicked when it happened," my brother admits. "Without thinking things through, I voided the bet."

Technically, when she refused to go through with their deal, he'd lost, but I'd rather bring up another issue that bothers me more. "Why were you carrying around that contract? Did you plan on showing it to her to ensure things didn't work out between her and me?" I spit, all my anger returning.

He shakes his head. "That was an unlucky happenstance. I'd knocked over a pile of papers on my way out the door. I saw the contract and shoved it in my pocket without really thinking."

My fucking brother plows through my life like an uncaring tornado. Adrenaline rushes through me and my hands curl into fists.

And suddenly, irrationally, I need Thorne to suffer, to feel even a fraction of the pain I've experienced since Rosalia left me. I spring from my chair and stalk toward him, violence dripping from me.

He doesn't move. His arms remain relaxed at his side, as if accepting whatever comes his way. When I'm within a punch away, he says, "I'm sorry."

I still. I've waited almost two years to hear those words, to see the regret in his eyes. My hands drop, and my fists uncurl. "Why now?"

"Because she saw right through me. And now I see myself clearly," Thorne's voice roughens. "Her actions called me out in a way no one ever has. Not you, not Father." He glances down at his hands, which tremble slightly before he clenches them into fists.

I look at him, searching for traces of the boy who once knew all my secrets, who defended me against the world. Regret is there, but is it enough?

"I'm not sure I can forgive you," I tell him honestly.

Forgiveness feels like a bridge too far, a promise I'm not ready to make. But there's a sliver of possibility, like someday, we might find our way back to each other.

His gaze meets mine. "That's fair. At this point, I just want to be able to look at myself in the mirror without being drunk."

He stands and moves toward the door. "Anyway, it's past time I leave and find my way. I want to work for our family, but not with my family. I'm tired of living under your shadow. And Dad's."

Before leaving my sitting room, I call out, "Wait."

My brother pauses, turning to face me with a wary expression.

"I may never forgive you for the things you've done. Especially regarding Rosalia, but I understand where you're coming from, and I sincerely hope this move helps you."

Thorne nods before walking out the door, leaving me in the silence of my sitting room. In the quiet, I can't help but see the similarities in our situations. My brother has let jealousy and pride poison us. I'd let my fears and doubts sabotage my relationship with Rosalia.

If my brother has the courage to apologize, seek forgiveness, and start over, then I, too, can take the steps needed to mend things. I have to go to her and set things right before it's too late.

Pulse racing like a clock running out of time, I dash to my bedroom to change out of my lounge clothes. I need to see Rosalia. I'm done holding back.

"Mr. Blackstone," Alex says from behind me, "you have a visitor."

I shake my head. "Not now, I'm—"

My mouth snaps shut. There, standing just outside my master suite, is Rosalia.

ChapterForty-Two

Sebastian

Rosalia is at my house. Standing in my sitting room. Time hiccups, leaving me momentarily suspended between heartbeats. I lean against the nearby wall.

"How…"

"I borrowed Paige's car," she answers my unasked question.

I take her in after a weeklong absence. Her presence fills the room, stealing the air from my lungs in the best possible way.

"I was leaving—"

"Should I go?" she asks.

I want to kiss the downward curve of her lips and spend the rest of my life making sure she smiles more than she frowns. "I was leaving to go to your place." After spending the last couple of weeks scowling, the sensation of a smile spreading on my face feels odd.

"You were?" She bends to scratch behind Twain's ears. The dog's tail thumps against the hardwood floor in pure contentment.

"Yes, I'd needed to meet with Thorne first to work through some things. I wanted to have them figured out so I could come to you as a better man." My voice catches slightly on the last words, and I clear my throat. "To show you I was serious about making changes."

She straightens, meeting my eyes with an intensity that pins me in place. "That's why I'm here. We need to talk."

I motion toward the window. "Would you like to sit?"

She settles onto the cushions, and the light streaming through the window catches the highlights in her hair. I sit beside her, careful to leave some space between us. After everything that's happened, I don't want to presume she wants me near her.

"I love you." The words tumble out before I can stop them. Her eyes widen, but I keep going. "I should've led with that at the derby party. But I couldn't see past my fear until I had space from Thorne's games." I take her hand, relieved when she doesn't pull away. "I should have told you the truth from the beginning."

"Sebastian—"

"I'm sorry, I... I need to get this all out. May I finish first?"

She nods slowly and I lean forward, letting go of her hand and resting my elbows on my knees. "I wanted to make some grand gesture to prove how sorry I am. But I realized that's not what matters. What matters is honesty. So here it is: I'm sorry for not trusting you. I'm sorry for being part of that bet. Most of all, I'm sorry for not being brave enough to be honest with you."

She's quiet for a long moment, her fingers tracing patterns on the cushion between us. "I wasn't honest with you either. I made that deal with Thorne. I let him manipulate me into getting close to you."

"Yes, but let's state the facts," I say gently. "He didn't leave you much choice. And if I'd spoken up sooner about what was happening, you could have had more opt—"

"I know you couldn't have, at least not without huge consequences. We both signed NDAs," she tells me.

Shock ripples through me. "How did you know?"

"About your NDA? Daniel came to see me."

I shake my head with a slight smile. "Of course my nosy therapist did."

Her lips purse to one side. "Isn't he a lawyer?"

Laughing, I wave a hand. "He has many talents. What did he tell you?"

"That he suspects Thorne was blocking my loans at every bank in town. That he manipulated both of us from the beginning." Her eyes meet mine. "About your anonymous donation to my adult literary program."

Shit. "Daniel talks too much. I wasn't trying to buy your forgiveness."

"At first, I was angry." She laughs lightly. "Then Daniel reminded me you gave the money anonymously."

"Not that it worked with his damn big mouth," I complain.

I'm not truly mad. I'd have gone to Rosalia and begged her to talk, but I suspected Daniel's visit helped me.

"He was vague about a lot of things, said I needed to talk to you." She studies me. "And I've been thinking over the bet and timing. Did you try to stop it from the beginning?"

"I tried, but I made things worse." I look down, uncomfortable. "When this started, I had no idea about your lease until Thorne mentioned he'd bought the hotel next door. So I asked him to leave you alone."

"Why is that bad?"

"Because I need to work on my poker face. He saw I was interested in you and used that to get to me. I'm sorry."

She rests a hand on my arm, and the ache in my chest loosens. "How so?" she asks.

"He refused. And then…" I sigh. "He threatened that if I didn't agree to the bet, he would make sure you never opened another bookstore in Kentucky. Said he'd blacklist you with every bank and property owner from Louisville to Lexington."

She sucks in a quick breath through clenched teeth. "So you agreed to protect me."

I hesitate. I'd love to be the hero in her story, but complete honesty is the only way forward. "Partly, yes. I didn't want to see your business destroyed. But…" Taking a fortifying breath, I hold her gaze. "My brother knows exactly how to manipulate me. He played on my deepest insecurity."

She takes my hand and squeezes gently. I take it as a silent encouragement to go on.

"The truth is, part of me wanted to know if I could trust you. This is going to sound like 'poor little rich boy,' but people see the Blackstone name and see opportunity, not me. When Thorne suggested this 'test' of character…" I shake my head, ashamed. "A part of me thought maybe he was right. Maybe I needed to be sure."

She cocks her head. "And what did you risk? What would have happened if you had lost? Daniel never specified."

I rub the back of my neck. "If you'd taken that portfolio, I would have had to step down as master distiller—the position Thorne always thought should be his. And sell my controlling shares to him at half their value."

She pulls back slightly. "That's… a lot to gamble."

"Yeah, that's why Thorne's the gambler. He sees angles and advantages and loves the thrill of the risk. Meanwhile, I couldn't think straight with his threats hanging over you, and the possibility of being free of him."

"What do you mean?"

"If I'd won, Thorne had to leave our flagship distillery here in Kentucky. He also had to sign over ownership of your building to you. Free and clear."

Her expression softens. She's looking at me like some kind of hero. "You did that for me?"

"Did you hear the other part that drove me—him leaving?"

"Given your past with him, I can't blame you." Her grip tightens on mine, punctuating her point. "I don't blame you."

I look at our joined hands. "You know, Thorne and I weren't always like this. As kids, we were actually close. We'd spend entire summers together, racing horses through the fields, exploring every corner of the estate. When our parents threw their endless business parties, we'd sneak off, finding our own adventures."

"That does sound amazing."

I grin, pulling up another memory I'd forgotten. "As a kid, Lillianna was scared of thunderstorms, so Thorne would make up these elaborate stories to distract her. He was good at that, looking out for people he cared about." My smile fades. "But everything changed when we hit our teens and Dad saw us as assets to his bourbon empire. He started pitting us against each other, treating every accomplishment like a competition. We were his business, and it became a battleground."

Rosalia's fingers tighten around mine, a silent reassurance. "It sounds like you lost your brother long before you lost your wife."

Her insight catches me off guard, the simple truth of it striking deep. I nod slowly. "I think you're right. By the time Tiffany came between us, we were already strangers wearing the same last name."

My words emerge barely louder than my heartbeat. "But you showed me something different. You chose integrity over self-interest, even knowing it would cost you everything you'd worked for. When Thorne told me what you'd done at the derby party, how you'd refused to take the portfolio even after everything—" The words snag in my throat. "I've never been more ashamed of my part in this, or more certain of how I feel about you. I meant what I said, Rosalia. I love you. Everything else, the company, the money, all of it means nothing compared to that."

"I've spent the last few weeks thinking about trust. About how hard it is to give, how easily it breaks," she tells me, and the steel in her words gives way to something raw and unguarded. "The strange thing is, even with all the secrets between us, I was happy with you. We both were."

Does that mean this is all in the past? Or does she mean there's hope for a future together? "Tell me what you mean. Please." I sound desperate, but don't care.

A small smile plays at her lips. "If we could find that much joy with walls between us, imagine how much better it will be now that everything's out in the open."

Hope burns in me. "Do you mean..."

"I love you too, Sebastian." Her confession seeps into the cracks of my fractured confidence, reclaiming territories I'd surrendered to doubt. "Despite everything, despite the mess we made, I love you. And I'm tired of letting fear keep us apart."

Something inside me loosens, a tightness I've carried for months finally releasing. I'm overwhelmed by the simple relief of hearing those words from her. I take a deep breath, letting the reality of this moment, of her here, with me, choosing to try again, sink in.

"I'm not saying it will be easy." She moves closer, and I shift her so she can crawl onto my lap. "We both made mistakes. We both have trust issues to work through. But I want to try. I want us to try."

I cup her cheek. "That's all I'm asking for. A chance to rebuild, to do better this time."

"No more tests," she says firmly. "No more secrets."

"No more tests," I agree. "No more secrets."

Her lips curve into a smile that warms me from the inside out. "So what happens now?"

In answer, I lean forward, stopping just short of her lips. "Can I kiss you?"

She closes the final distance between us. We are gentle at first, a question and an answer all at once. Her hands slide up my arms to my shoulders, drawing me closer. I can't help but deepen the kiss. The careful control we've been maintaining dissolves into pure need.

The moment she straddle me, fire races through my veins. Every small movement of her hips sends shockwaves through me. I adjust to give her what she needs, my control hanging by a thread. The urge to claim her completely threatens to overwhelm me.

We kiss until we're both breathless, until the need for air finally forces us apart.

When we finally break apart, I rest my forehead against hers. "I've missed you so much."

"Same. I've been so busy this week, and even with the amazing success, at night in the quiet, everything felt empty, soulless," she whispers. "Like a book with half the pages torn out."

I laugh softly at her literary reference. Not to be outdone, I say, "For me, it was like bourbon that's lost its spirit. All the right elements, but nothing worth bottling."

She pulls back, a teasing glint in her eye. "Did you just compare me to liquor?"

"The highest compliment from a Blackstone," I counter, grinning like a fool.

Her laughter fills the room. She looks around and says. "So this is where the infamous Sebastian Blackstone lives. All I've seen is his impressive…" Her smile turns playfully wicked. "Barn."

I chuckle. "Would you like a tour?"

She bites her lower lip, her cheeks flushing as she looks at me through her lashes. "I'd like to see your bedroom."

Heat rushes through me. "We don't have to rush—"

She covers my mouth. "Sebastian. I miss you. I want you. I love you. Let's not waste another second apart."

I couldn't agree more. Standing, I offer her my hand and walk toward the door to my bedroom.

Pushing open the door, she turns, looking behind her. "Well, that's convenient."

"Indeed." I turn and, in one fluid movement, scoop her up, earning a surprised laugh as I lay her on the dark green duvet. She raises onto her elbows and glances around my room. With a playful glint in her eye, she asks, "Did you read the Harry Potter books?"

"Of course."

Her amusement bubbles into a laugh. "And were you team Slytherin?"

A hearty belly laugh erupts from me. After the divorce, I remodeled the bedroom, removing sterile colors and the minimalist design Tiffany had preferred. And, okay, I might have gone overboard with the forest green accents alongside a dark oak bed, bookshelves, and flooring. I was going for cozy. But with the curtains closed, the room is so dim it totally gives off a fancy-dungeon vibe.

I drop onto my side on the bed next, resting on an elbow. "Nope. Despite what this room says, I'm Ravenclaw."

Her smile turns serious. She runs her fingers over my mouth, along my eyebrows, and then through my hair. "I've missed you."

Cupping the side of her face, I kiss her softly, savoring, waiting for her to invite me in. She does, and a surge of longing pulses through me. The taste of her lips and the scent of her skin flood my senses. With anyone else, I would calculate my next move, maintain perfect control. But with Rosalia, I surrender to pure feeling, and the relief of it is staggering.

She presses my shoulder, and I roll onto my back, holding her hips, bringing her on top of me. I dig my hands into her hips, needing her as close as possible.

Rising slightly, she pulls her dress over her head in one quick movement, revealing red lace underneath, then lowers herself back down to straddle me like a goddess. I suck in a sharp breath. This woman steals my breath.

I cup her breasts, then run my hands down her sides to the lace edges of her panties. "My favorite fucking color," I murmur.

My fingertips memorize the texture of the lace against her soft skin. Her name escapes me on a whisper.

I've seen her like this before, felt the weight of her above me, but tonight my chest tightens with something more than desire. The word "love" pulses between us, changing everything. It's like seeing her for the first time all over again, but deeper, with every barrier between us finally fallen.

"Your turn," she says, tugging on the hem of my T-shirt.

I sit, pulling the back of my shirt over my head, and tossing it aside. I kiss her until she rocks against me again. I wrap her in my arms, falling back against the covers—finally, finally home.

Rosalia slides down me, her fingertips grazing the inside of my legs. Every touch feels like a promise that this is real, that we're really here together.

Reaching my waist, she tugs down my lounge pants, tracing her tongue along my length. My eyelids flutter closed. The heat, pressure, and perfect rhythm make my head spin. I barely manage not to thrust into her throat, my muscles lock with the effort. "Fuck—Rose—" the rest of my words fail me.

I tangle my fingers in the silky strands of her hair, gently guiding her movements, but also seeking a connection, a tangible reminder that this is real, that she's with me. I can't take my eyes off her. Need to see her. Need her to see me.

Before I come undone, I urge her up. When our bodies align, I look into her eyes. "I need to be as close as possible to you."

We've danced this dance before, but never with everything laid bare between us. The words "I love you" echo in my mind with each pulse, each gasp, breaking something loose inside me.

She nods, her gaze mirroring my yearning. We undress each other, savoring each revealed inch. I ache to taste her, but she rolls, pulling me on top of her in a rush of heat, kisses, and hungry touches.

"You're everything. Everything I've ever wanted," I breathe the words into the curve of her neck.

Her soft sigh mixes with my moan. We move together like we were made for this, our bodies finding a perfect rhythm. The heat between us builds slowly, each movement drawing us deeper into territory both natural and completely transformed. Passion builds until it's almost too much, until every nerve ending is alive with sensation.

With a shift of my hips, she cries out my name as she comes apart, and I follow her over the edge.

We collapse together, breathless and shaking. For a long moment, we simply hold each other, letting our racing hearts slow, letting the world settle back into focus around us. I brush damp strands of hair from her flushed face, taking in every detail of this moment.

When I look into her eyes, I see my future.

"That was…," I search for the right words to describe the indescribable.

"Incredible," she finishes, tracing patterns on my chest. "I've never felt this connected to someone."

"When I'm with you, it's like I've finally found my way home." I trace the curve of her shoulder. "And the funny thing is, I never knew I was lost until I met you."

She shifts off my chest, looking into my eyes. "I love you, Sebastian. You have all of my heart, and I promise to always protect yours."

A surge of contentment fills me. "And I swear to do the same for yours. You are my forever," I vow.

With her head on my chest, our breathing falls into sync. I imagine tomorrow, next week, next year. Our story won't be perfect—real love never is—but it will be ours, messy and beautiful and true. And that's better than perfect could ever be.

Epilogue

Rosalia

I lie with my eyes closed on a cushion as soft as a cloud, the ocean breeze warm against my skin. The sun and waves from the Indian Ocean lull me to sleep. My phone rings from somewhere in the honeymoon suite. It's probably my mom. Since returning briefly to Michigan to open my second bookstore, The Next Chapter, we've become closer, shedding our old dissatisfying relationship to work as a team to make the shop a success.

That's probably the reason for the call. Mom is working on an outreach literacy program with the old school systems she left to work full-time at the new bookstore. Everything is in the final stages. Before I can answer or even leave my comfy lounger, Sebastian calls my name.

I peek open an eye. The turquoise water surrounding Seychelles ripples like a jewel in the distance from our mountain villa. "Want me to wash the sand out of your hair?" he asks, his voice promising more than a shampoo.

That gets me up and moving. Palm fronds sway gently in the balmy breeze.

I walk past the shimmering infinity pool, my bare feet padding softly on the sun-warmed flagstones. Lush tropical foliage and bright flowers border the path. The tart sweetness of hibiscus, the creamy richness of plumeria, and an ethereal essence of paradise greet me.

Anticipation quickens my steps as I round a corner to the outdoor shower. It is an oasis of privacy, surrounded by a living wall of dense, glossy leaves. Sunlight filters through a latticed wooden roof, dappling the sand-colored tiles underfoot.

My husband is waiting for me, his tanned, muscular form silhouetted against the green. Steam curls invitingly from the rainfall showerhead. I smile, slip off my robe, step into the shower, and join him under the warm, cascading water.

"You've got a slight sunburn." He kisses my shoulder. There's the snap of a bottle opening. Seconds later, his strong fingers are massaging and washing my hair.

"That feels amazing," I moan, leaning my back against his front.

"The sounds you make are amazing." He slides his soapy hand along my shoulders, arms, and then waist.

His hands slide around and he cups my breasts. My head falls onto his chest, and a moan escapes from me.

Gliding a hand down my stomach and between my legs, he presses his fingers against my clit. I gasp his name, as addicted to his touch as I was the first time we were together. Maybe even more, because there's love mixing with our lust.

I bend, placing my hands on the opposite wall. Over my shoulder, I look into his eyes. "Please," I beg.

He sinks inside me with a groan, kissing the back of my neck. "My wife," he whispers reverently. "I love how you feel." He moves, and I meet him thrust for thrust."

"Please. That's perfect." That perfect pressure builds along my spine.

"Are you close?" he asks.

"Yes. Don't stop," I pant, reaching the peak of my pleasure.

"Not yet, my love. I need to see your beautiful face when you come apart."

Wanting the same, I turn. My breasts press against his hard chest, and there is so much love in his eyes. It matches what's in my heart.

His lips are gentle against mine, but his quick breaths tell me his desire is barely held in check. "I love you," he whispers.

"Forever and always," I reply, deepening the kiss. "Let me show you how I feel with my body."

He lifts me, and I wrap my legs around him as he sinks back inside me. His perfect thrusts have me on the precipice of pleasure within minutes. I begin to shake as everything in me coils tight.

"You're so close. I can feel it," he groans, shifting his hips in the way I love, throwing me into bliss that has me shouting his name.

He tenses against me, pressing in closer. His grip tightens as he finds his release. I hold him tight as he comes apart, murmuring my name like a prayer.

I revel in the way he loses himself in me. My husband hides nothing from me—from his pleasure to pain. It is a priceless gift.

We stay wrapped in our sated embrace until our heartbeats return to normal. Then he finishes washing me with thorough, gentle movements. I do the same for him. After, he shuts off the shower and carries me to the bedroom, laying me on the soft duvet.

Settling beside me, he asks, "Do you want to go to Mahé for dinner?"

I yawn. "Could we order in?"

We'd risen with the sun for a day of island-hopping on an eco-tourism trip to the remote island of Aldabra Atoll. We saw the famed giant tortoises on the beach before snorkeling along the largest raised coral atoll. It had been life-changing and beautiful, but I'm exhausted.

"I love that idea," Sebastian says. "Do you want Caris again?"

My mouth waters. "Yes, please." I could eat the famous Seychelles dish every day for dinner. It's that good.

Before he can reach for the villa's phone, my cell rings from inside my bedside nightstand. "That's probably my mom." I slide off the bed to retrieve my phone. "I think she called earlier, but my handsome husband distracted me."

I scuttle and half-slide to the nightstand, probably looking like one of the coconut crabs that nearly gave me a heart attack on our hike. Nothing with pincers should be that big. Snatching up my phone, I see it's not my mom, but my sister-in-law.

My heart swells. My life has changed for the better since Lillianna convinced Sebastian and me to buy the hotel next to Novel Idea and combine the two. I answer, and we talk while Sebastian places our dinner order. We hang up from our calls almost at the same time. I point toward the deck, more specifically, the infinity pool.

He grins. "After all the time in the ocean today, you want to spend more time in the water?"

"Yup," I pop the "p" and stand, moving around the bed and pulling him up. The other villas' distance and dense foliage mean bathing suits aren't necessary.

The waves crashing against the shore are loud as we slide into the refreshing water of the pool. We swim to the edge that overlooks the rocky landscape and ocean, now painted in the soft colors of sunset.

"Was it your mom who called?" Sebastian asks, draping his arms along the glass edge of the infinity pool.

I shake my head. Every cell in my body dances with joy. "Your sister. She called to let me know that our marketing during the Louisville Book Festival was a huge success. We're booked solid for next year's event."

Sometime before leaving for the Quebec Blackstone distillery, Thorne had bought the boutique hotel next to my bookstore and gifted it to me. My first reaction had been to refuse, but around the same time, Lillianna had returned for a surprise visit. We'd hit it off, and she convinced me not only to keep the hotel but to combine it with my bookstore. Together, we opened a book-themed hotel, which we named Beds, Books, and Bourbon, shortened to 3Bs.

"That's great," he replies.

The dip in his tone makes me poke his ribs. "Why do you always sound surprised that Lillianna and I are a great team?" I ask.

"You making a success of 3Bs isn't what shocks me. You have a great head for business and are fantastic with people.

That is a priceless stroke of good fortune. Paige would always be my best friend, but I consider Lillianna my sister from another mother. Heck, there might even be a place in my heart for Thorne as a brother.

Maybe.

He'd come to Louisville for the 3B's grand opening last year and again to my and Sebastian's wedding. Things between the three of us are still awkward as a dance with tangled feet—each step forward is met with a stumble and a wince. Yet, there's hope. I hadn't known him before the bet disaster, but I can see the change, like he's settling into his skin.

I let go of the pool's edge and move behind Sebastian. He lowers himself into the water until only his head and the tops of his shoulders remain above the surface. I rest my head in the crook of his shoulder, aligning my front with his back.

I close my eyes, listening to Sebastian's steady breaths, and swear I hear the final whisper of our past deceptions fade into the gentle ocean breeze. Over the last three years, we've built trust and honesty between us by embracing the promise of a future built on transparency, forgiveness, and unwavering devotion. And from the ashes of betrayal and deceit has risen a love stronger and more resilient than I'd ever imagined.

"I love you," he says with a tenderness that always melts my heart.

I wrap my arms around him, squeezing tight. "Forever."

The End

Bonus Story

Want more of the Hayek sisters? - Rosalia's Michigan friends

Sign up for my newsletter and receive a free novella featuring Abigail's story. When family heirlooms go missing and trust becomes a luxury she can't afford, Abigail must navigate a world where everyone has secrets—including the mysterious antique dealer who offers to help. Join our community for exclusive content and be the first to know about new releases. Your free novella is waiting!

Sign up on my website: DKMARIE.COM

A LAKE HOUSE LOVE NOVELETTE
STILETTOS
& Seashells
DK MARIE

Reviews

Dear Reader,

Whether you're a returning or new, thank you. It is wonderful to write, but a dream to share my stories with you!

When I started this journey, I feared I'd never finish my first story. After I did, I was afraid I couldn't write another one. Now, I'm on my third series – writing the second book of Blackstone Billionaire series.

If you're not ready to let go of Rosalia and Sebastian , talk to others about them—by suggesting their story to others, leaving a review on Goodreads, or whatever book site you love.

These sites are great for discussing books. Not only will it let you chat about stories you love, but they help me out immensely. Even a simple sentence would mean the world to me and will keep this story minds and hearts of other romance readers.

Also by DK Marie

Lake House Love

- **Making Waves**- She's navigating the stormy waters of divorce. He's a single dad unwilling to sail into the uncertain winds of love. Neither of them expects the currents of desire to run this deep...

- **Smooth Sailing** – She's rebuilding her life one project at a time. He's the business partner who makes her want to break every rule she's made about mixing work with pleasure.

- **Stormy Waters** - CEden can save any child's life, but she's never learned to heal her own heart. When she meets the one man who sees through her perfect facade, she'll have to choose between the safety of control and the terrifying beauty of letting someone in.

-

Opposites Attract

- Fairy Tale Lies- Perfect Daughter. Perfect Heiress. Perfect Lie.

- Love Songs- She's chasing rock stardom. He's counting down the days until he can escape it. But what happens when the music between them becomes impossible to ignore?"

- Taste of Passion- She's a spoiled socialite. He's her grumpy soon-to-be brother-in-law. Planning their siblings' wedding should be torture—so why does their sparring feel like foreplay?

- Colors of the Heart- He's a young widower who's learned that love means losing everything. She's an artist who's built her life around avoiding messy complications. But some connections are too powerful to resist—even when they terrify you.

All titles available at DKMARIE.COM

About the author

DK Marie is an Amazon #1 bestselling author of eight published works—seven romance novels and one poetry collection. Her stories focus on unexpected connections and second chances, blending heart, heat, and humor with relatable characters that readers love. When she's not writing, she enjoys photography, motorcycle rides, and reading with coffee or bourbon, sharing her home with her husband of 20+ years, two kids, and a judgmental cat who supervises her writing process.

Thank you!

There are countless people who deserve my gratitude. First and foremost, my family, who have supported me through this journey, even when they don't quite understand my need to disappear into fictional worlds for days, weeks, and months at a time. They also gently pull me back to reality when needed, and though I may grumble in the moment, I'm deeply grateful for that balance. I love you all.

To my writer friends—I would be completely lost without your wisdom, encouragement, and late-night conversations. You keep me grounded and inspired. Shanna, thank you especially for being with me from the very beginning (actually, before the beginning). You are living proof that the best happily-ever-afters happen in real life too, and I treasure our friendship beyond words.

I'm also incredibly grateful to my talented editors, Dani G. and Jessica B. Thank you for your keen eyes and thoughtful guidance in helping this book reach its full potential.

A special shout-out goes to my cover designer, Avery Kingston, whose artistic vision never fails to amaze me. Thank you for creating covers that are both beautiful and perfectly capture the spirit of each story.

Finally, to you, my readers—without you, these stories would remain nothing more than private musings. Thank you for allowing me to share these worlds with you and for making this dream possible.

www.ingramcontent.com/pod-product-compliance
Lightning Source LLC
Chambersburg PA
CBHW020239010826
48973CB00006B/1581